"TH...
THEIR OWN NEWS FOOTAGE?"

"Sounds like it's been on the news in Israel for a while now. The Israelis are reacting to it. Street fighting has started."

"Just as was meant to happen," McCarter said. "That's cold-blooded. They contrive the murder of those civilians just to stir up the population. Not that the Palestinians weren't doing their share of slaughter."

"Somebody wants a war and doesn't care what sacrifices the public has to make to get the ball rolling," Katzenelenbogen said. "So far it looks like the plan is working."

"We have to screw up those plans," Delahunt said, and strode out of the room, even more anxious to stamp an identification on one of the mystery attack helicopters.

Maybe it would point the finger at whoever was behind this horror.

DON PENDLETON'S

STONY

AMERICA'S ULTRA-COVERT INTELLIGENCE AGENCY

MAN®

PRELUDE
TO WAR

A GOLD EAGLE BOOK FROM

WORLDWIDE®

TORONTO • NEW YORK • LONDON
AMSTERDAM • PARIS • SYDNEY • HAMBURG
STOCKHOLM • ATHENS • TOKYO • MILAN
MADRID • WARSAW • BUDAPEST • AUCKLAND

First edition June 2002

ISBN 0-373-61943-X

PRELUDE TO WAR

Special thanks and acknowledgment to
Tim Somheil for his contribution to this work.

Printed in U.S.A.

PRELUDE
TO WAR

CHAPTER ONE

Village of Khodr, West Bank

"Prelude to peace?"

The words were bold and white on the little black-and-white television, sitting on a table made from plywood on a stack of cinder blocks.

Hisham Fahd made a harsh sound in his throat and spewed saliva at the screen, where it obscured the image of the Boeing 777. Displaying the Star of David, the jet ascended powerfully into the skies from a takeoff at the airport in Tel Aviv. On board was the Israeli prime minister, embarking on a trip to the United States of America for what could be a historic meeting, the Camp David Economics and Peace Summit.

The scene changed, showing another airport, another aircraft. This time it was hours-old video of an Airbus taxiing for takeoff in Damascus. Fahd shook his head when he saw it, awash in bitterness.

The betrayal of the Syrians, that was what stung the hardest. Fahd had come to expect the worst of the Palestinians, his own people, over the years. They cowed to the Israelis, compromised with them, surrendering ever more of their sanctified land and sacred honor. Syria, in the old days, had always stood up to the Israelis, putting the fear of God into them. But now this—flying off to meet with the Israelis and the Palestinians to negotiate in the land that some of his people called the Great Satan, the United States of America.

Fahd's son, a boy of eleven, was sitting on the floor scooping his lunch from a bowl, looking up when the voice-over of the newscaster began again.

"The summit is the brainchild of the U.S. President, who hopes to merge further peace talks aimed at broad-based disarmament with long-term economic agreements. The President hopes economic ties between these nations will provide added incentive to maintain his proposed peace initiative."

Suddenly he was there, the American President, on the screen. It was video of his plea for peace at a press conference a few days ago. "This is just the start of a long-term undertaking that will eventually grow, I hope, to include other nations of the Middle East, creating an intertwined economic community that will enable all parties to prosper and compete economically while slowing the flood of violence that has become, sadly, a hallmark of Middle Eastern relationships."

Fahd wished the President of the U.S. were here right now and he would spit into his face personally. There was no single human being on the planet that he hated more. He was the figurehead of the great interferer, the United States, which had come into this land, *his* land, time and again to manipulate the Arabs for profit. The British had been bad enough. It was the beginning of American involvement in Palestine that signaled, in Fahd's mind, the beginning of the troubles. That was May of 1942.

Fahd knew his history, and he saw this date as most important. May 1942 was when the New York Zionist conference developed, without the input of Palestinians, a policy allowing unrestricted immigration of the Jews into Palestine. That was when Britain, more concerned with its own war efforts, succumbed to U.S. pressure and looked the other way as the American government exerted increasing influence in the region. Eventually, it took one of the hated U.S. presidents, Truman, to drive the illegal formation of the State of Israel in 1948, again without regard for the rights of the Palestinians, evicting them from their homes by the thousands. But that was simply the inevitable result.

The real mistake, the true cause of all the misery that was to come for decades afterward, was the involvement of the U.S. in the first place. U.S. manipulation in the Middle East had never faltered. In 1990 and 1991, the Americans put their armies in Saudi Arabia and slaughtered Iraqi Arabs in uncounted numbers.

It was the same to this day. Without soldiers, this time, but just as surely, the U.S. was using the gullibility of the new Syrian leadership and the war weariness of the Palestinians to force them to surrender more of their God-given ascendancy of this land to the nation of the Jews.

Fahd got the idea for naming his militia when he heard about a Greek freedom-fighting group called Revolutionary Organization 17 November, named after an infamous date in Greek history. Fahd like the idea. It kept the past, and the cause, alive. He therefore named his freedom militia May of '42.

Not that the group, just five or six men from the village of Khodr, had done much fighting. Mostly they met and talked and vented their anger, and went with the teenagers to throw rocks at the Israeli police when the street fighting came along.

That might change soon. As of two days ago, May of '42 was an armed militia.

Fahd's son was furrowing his brow as he sought to understand the political machinations at work. The boy knew his father cared about this deeply, and was especially angry with the Syrians, whom he had professed to like in the past. But the boy did not understand. He saw peace with Israel as a good thing, like many children of his generation. Despite Fahd's insistent education of his son, the insidious propaganda of the West worked to dominate the opinions of Arab children, and the propaganda was winning. Each generation was more docile than the previous.

Fahd knew his son would see the day when Arabs were assimilated and their culture neutered, and worst of all, he might not even know enough to mourn when it happened.

As he was wrestling to control his urge to backhand th boy for his suicidal naiveté, his son looked abruptly at th ceiling and said, "Helicopters."

Then Fahd heard them, too.

The Russian-built warbird led a collection of aircraft com ing out of the west, steering a single-file formation into a angled descent that brought it to the west end of the smal village. The helicopters leveled out just above rock throwing range over the rooftops, the rumble of the engine and the pounding of the rotor blades summoning the peopl of Khodr into the streets.

It was an ungainly formation of mismatched aircraft. Th largest member of the squadron was a Sikorsky heavy-lift commercial cargo craft, thirty years old if a day. Behind it came a pair of midsized EADS C-295 military transport helicopters. At the front and the rear were the lethal ladies.

The one in front was a Russian Mil Mi-24 Hind, the attack helicopter first fielded by the Soviet Union in the early 1980s. Its design purpose was to attack armored vehicles, and to that end it had antitank guided missiles set on its stubby wings.

At the rear of the formation was the meanest bitch in the brood, the AH-64. The Apache was one of the world's most lethal airborne weapons systems, powered with twin 1,900-horsepower GE gas turbine engines providing a cruising airspeed of 145 miles per hour. She tucked away seventy-six folding-fin rockets, ideal for taking out soft-skinned targets.

Lightly armored vehicles. Human beings. Also useful for this purpose was the 30 mm automatic gun, for which the Apache carried 1,200 rounds. But like the Mi-24, one of her primary responsibilities was disposing of more heavily armored vehicles, and for that task she carried sixteen Hellfire missiles. Laser guided, they could take out a tank a mile and a half away.

Hovering one hundred meters above the fast-flying formation, like a sparrow harassing a migrating flock of vultures and eagles, was a Bell 206B JetRanger III, a commercial helicopter.

CRANING HIS NECK at the sky, not even noticing the crowds of his neighbors gathering around him, Fahd felt his blood run cold. The pounding tumult of the aircraft became deafening when the configuration passed directly over the street where he stood, and Fahd knew that what he was watching was a display of force. He recognized the gunships for what they were, and even if he hadn't known them the wing-mounted weapons would have made their purpose obvious.

The other helicopters didn't pose a threat that was as apparent, but Fahd knew men and machines were inside the swollen bellies of the C-295 military transports, waiting to be deposited on the sandy soil and engage the enemy.

Every one of the helicopters, those Russian or U.S. in origin, military or commercial, was painted dark blue. Most telling was the Star of David insignia plastered hugely in the most obvious place on every aircraft—usually the broad underside of the belly.

Fahd had been told an attack on Khodr was coming, and soon. His May of '42 militia was thankfully prepared for it. In fact, there were weapons enough for more than half the men of the village.

His son shouted—with exhilaration—as the noise crescendoed. Fahd was snapped out of his reverie of dread.

"Find your mother and sisters," he ordered the boy. "Get them into the hiding place."

The boy looked at him strangely, and only then did it begin to dawn on the child that there was something amiss. His trust in the world was slow to lose its conviction. This innocence touched Fahd in a little-used corner of his heart, but he didn't have time to dwell on it. "That's right, son," he said more compassionately. "It is time to hide. It is the time I always told you might come. Do what I say and gather the women."

"I want to stay with you," the boy protested simply.

"You cannot stay with me. I need you to protect your mother and sisters. The women need a man to see them through this. You have to be a grown-up today. You have to be the man until I get back."

"Where are you going?"

Fahd didn't want to answer that. If his intuition was right, where he was going before this day was finished wasn't an earthly destination.

IN THE PLANNING STAGES, the helicopter pilots had called the dramatic swoop over the village a beauty pass, but its intent had been to inspire terror instead of admiration. Beauty pass finished, the spectators still craning their necks, the helicopters rose in a long arc that took them back to two hundred meters and without a word of radio command they separated into two distinct formations. The Bell JetRanger rose straight up to 350 meters and monitored the proceedings.

With their rotor tips threatening to touch, the pair of gunships came side by side and winged ahead over the rocky ground, then slowed and banked into a 360-degree turn, moving into a hover as they again faced the village. They were a pair of floating mechanical death's-heads, regarding the people without pity.

The second aircraft formation consisted of the transport choppers, which spread out and turned deliberately, circling the village clockwise and coming to ground at a point less than a thousand yards from the first house on the western end of the village. Even before the landing skids of the transport choppers touched the dry earth, rear end facing the village, the loading-bay doors were swinging down, the soldiers debarking. They were followed by a topless military-style jeep from each chopper, sporting a .50-caliber deck-mounted machine gun. As the two jeeps pulled away, the transport choppers became airborne again, heading toward Israel.

The thirty soldiers assembled and stood together in a single line, an arm's width apart and facing the village, in silent formation.

The Sikorsky cargo helicopter touched down and opened its bay doors. A pair of men stepped to the ground and efficiently withdrew and placed a pair of steel ramps, a crossbar holding them in position. Then, at a signal from somewhere, a flat-topped vehicle rolled down the ramp and slowly powered away from the helicopter. A twin vehicle followed.

The Sikorsky pilot had an ear trained to the headphones as he waited for the okay from the crew. If there were signs of response from the town, and there wouldn't be this early in the game, the radio alert would come to him from the observer in the JetRanger, at which point the pilot was prepared to go into a quick ascent.

No signal came. Everything was moving along as expected. The copilot was making the thumbs-down sign to tell the pilot that the cargo was now on the ground. Seconds later a thumbs-up told him the crew was back aboard and the doors were closed. The pilot brought the cargo chopper gently off the ground, like an elegant whale becoming improbably airborne, and took her into the western sky.

The cargo wouldn't be retrieved. This job was over.

On the ground the flat-topped vehicles drew up side by side and paused. After their on-board operating systems shuttled through a test of software and a sensor functionality analysis—ultrasonic sonar, active laser, millimeter wave radar and multiple stereoscopic video pickups—the hydrostatic four-wheel-drive train moved the vehicles forward at a walking pace.

They were no bigger than the jeeps, which were waiting with their drivers behind the formation of soldiers, but these vehicles had no windows or doors. And there was no human driver on board.

THE OUTDOOR MOBILITY Platforms, hybrids of technology developed by Robotic Systems Technology, were augmented with vehicle navigation software and sensors that would have allowed the units to navigate unaided through the semiarid, rocky environment they now found themselves in. They used a combination of global positioning satellite information feeds to follow their course and sensor input to map the terrain, choose the least-obstructed path and circumnavigate obstructions.

Many of those decision-making functions wouldn't be required for this operation. The OMPs were provided beforehand with a detailed topographic surveillance of the village and surrounding landscape, digitized for its analysis. Forty-one hours earlier, when the information was downloaded into it, another computer and its operators determined the most optimal course for the OMPs to follow. Like the prototypical grunt, each OMP had a brain but wouldn't be required to think with it. They simply had to obey orders: march into the war zone and kill.

Unlike the grunt, there was no fear, no prebattle jitters, no hesitancy. Only the heartless efficiency of the nonliving machine.

THE SIGNAL to commence was the lack of a signal. The pilots of the twin gunships had been waiting for a one-syllable radio transmission that would have dictated a delay and, not getting one, knew that the deployment was proceeding as planned. The gunships advanced; the attack commenced.

With a steady thrum the Apache moved with effortless vigor from her hovering stance, accelerating to just twenty miles per hour and again descending to low altitude over the dirt road that meandered through the rocks into the village, passing over the main street as the population scattered for cover—mostly men, but there were boys and even a few women still on the streets. The M-230 chain gun burped fire, sending down a lethal torrent of 30 mm rounds. The panicking mass of people was packed together, stampeding into narrow side streets and front doors. It was impossible for the rounds to miss. The crowd absorbed the fire, and people blew apart. The ground was left streaked with red.

Confusion and terror were amplified tenfold. Until the moment that the gun fired, there had been a possibility in the minds of the villagers that this was some sort of harassment or exercise. It had been hopeless optimism. This wasn't harassment.

This was murder.

The Apache didn't waste rounds. Twenty or thirty dead and wounded was a sufficient tally for a first pass. The gunship pulled up and banked over the village, returning to its starting point.

Behind it the Soviet attack helicopter, the Mi-24 Hind, was flying on an identical course over the village main street, moving no faster than a man could run, and unleashing a barrage of 12.7 mm machine-gun fire. The gunner found it was no great effort to cut down more men and one fear-paralyzed woman in a head-to-toe black robe.

A man rushed back into the street toward a fallen, blood-soaked old man, who was raising his hands to the sky. The rounds from the Mi-24 homed in on them at the moment their hands came together. They knew death was imminent and gazed fearlessly, together, at the gunship. An eighth of a second later they were torn to pieces by 12.7 mm rounds, fired by a gunner who had trained himself to not see the faces of his victims.

Then the Russian gunship spun to the right, circled back and staged itself again at its starting point.

The Apache was on the move. These attack sequences were perfectly choreographed and timed. As the Mi-24 Hind arrived at its starting point, the Apache was launching its Hellfire missiles. The targets had been identified and plotted during the attack planning stages, and the laser guidance system was almost wasted electronic effort. The mosque took two precise hits in rapid succession and collapsed. The women and children seeking cover there were buried before they knew what was happening.

The Apache pilot heard a small metallic click near his foot and made his first evasive maneuver, throwing the gunship on her side with a sudden whine and pulling her low over the rooftops before coming to a halt.

"Are we taking fire?" he asked into his radio.

"Affirmative," said the voice from the JetRanger observational helicopter. "Man with a rifle."

The pilot tilted the gunship forward at a shallow angle so he could look down her nose as he rose back above the streets, searching for movement, and spotted the man with the AK-47 at once. A quick burst of three 30 mm rounds exploded one after another on the fleeing heels of the man, who made it into a nearby building, then the last round burst on the roof of the building and reduced it to rubble.

Something behind the smoke and dust cloud.

"That's one lucky SOB," the gunner said.

"Please be sure you get that man," said the voice from the JetRanger.

For the first time since the operation started, the voice of the operation commander came over the radio.

"Soldier One here. Are you marked, Bird Two?"

"Unknown."

"Exterminate the witness."

"No shit," the Apache pilot muttered under his breath.

The Apache hovered with her nose aimed at a low building. It was the logical place for the gunner to have run for cover. Probably, the pilot thought.

This problem with the aircraft markings was the weakest link in the entire operation, he was thinking, and he was going to be pissed off if tracking this one man took him out of the action.

There was a burst of movement and the AK shooter flew out the window in a wild dive that sent him crumpling in the street. This wasn't a man of action. The fall was heavy and awkward and had to have dazed him, keeping him down for a few lingering seconds while he fought to regain his equilibrium. His equilibrium never did come back. At that moment the Apache's chain gun triggered enough rounds to shred a station wagon. The man and his Kalashnikov were chewed to pieces.

"Bird Two here. The witness is exterminated," the pilot radioed.

"All right, Bird Two, let us take a look at you," said the observer helicopter pilot.

The Apache pilot grimly pulled the warbird into a near vertical ascent that took him to a thousand feet, then sat there as the tiny Bell 206B moved in close, circling the gunship slowly while the human and non-human observers examined her skin.

A pair of articulated photographic lenses, mounted independently on X-Y servo-adjusters, used infrared distance measurements performed at a rate of hundreds a second to evaluate the distance, develop a mean focus, then keep the focus adjusted. Photogrammetric plotting instruments made use of the digital stereo photography to paint a picture of the precise contours of the gunship, whose dimensions were already recorded, literally down to the thickness of the paint. A quick comparison would show if any of the thick layer of dark blue temporary exterior coating had been chipped off.

"Why doesn't he stick his finger up my asshole and feel around for lumps while he's at it," the pilot muttered, then regretted it. For all he knew, the commander linked to Bird One was listening in on every word. And the pilot was getting paid too well to risk angering the boss.

The Bell JetRanger pulled away as it sank twenty feet below, allowing the passenger and the stereo lenses to see up under the front end of the Apache. That was where the AK rounds had impacted.

"Bird One here. You're okay, Bird Two."

"Then let us get back to our fucking job, asshole," the pilot muttered. But he radioed simply, "Affirmative." He pulled the Apache into a descent that would take it back to the slaughter.

THE Mi-24 MOVED in low and slow, a cat ready to pounce on prey, and it paused on the outskirts of the town with the skids brushing the tops of the few scrubby trees. The pilot radioed, "Bird Three here. I'm ready for another maneuver."

"Understood. Hang on, Three."

Above him, at one thousand feet, the Bell was performing its examination of the Apache, but when it was done it tipped down to take a look at the situation in the town.

"Bird One here," came the radio voice. "You have full cooperation from these good people. Proceed."

The Mi-24 pilot brought the deadly lady to life with a burst of power that took her from a standstill to high speeds in just seconds. It sailed over the rooftops like a rock out of a sling, and suddenly flew into the open over the ruined, smoky clearing where the mosque had been. The people had already begun to gather around, trying to shift the collapsed wreckage in a frantic attempt to get to their buried loved ones.

That was anticipated.

They had indeed heard the approaching gunship. And they had started to run. And—as had also been predicted—they hadn't run far enough when the gunship unleashed its guided missiles. The rounds were designed for cracking open tanks. They slammed into the terrified crowds in a sudden, merciless onslaught. Without pause the gunship ascended from the horror it had created. The detritus of the blasts had not even stopped falling.

FAHD FELT like a panicking puppet, flying on his strings from one side of the stage to another. After frantically digging up the plastic bag containing his new, precious FAL, he had raced about the end of the town trying to get a fix on the helicopters. He chased the Apache to the mosque, only to arrive a few heartbeats after the blast that leveled the building. Ignoring the screams of the trapped, he chased the aircraft through the streets, trying desperately to get a good shot at it. He didn't even know if the rounds from the FAL could do any damage to the chopper, but, by all the dead and dying, he was going to try.

Darting from alley to alley, he tried to determine the gunship's purpose—then realized it was chasing another gunner. Fahd wasn't the only man to risk his own life to defend his people. Fahd arrived only just in time to recognize the man. It was Qaissi, a man of strong conviction and a member of the May of '42 militia. Qaissi suddenly flew into pieces in the street. The butchery performed by the chain gun was horrific.

By the time Fahd recovered from the shock, the Apache had risen well out of his range.

Then he heard the engines of the second gunship, operating at a higher frequency, as if it were racing in for a high-speed attack. Why would that be necessary?

At the same moment it occurred to him there had to be some sort of ambush involved, he began running after the aircraft. Maybe he could reach it before it reached its victims.

That was foolish. A joke to even hope for it. When he heard the next series of explosions Fahd pictured in his mind the new disaster at the mosque site, and the sound of the Russian-manufactured gunship was already receding.

The reality of the fresh carnage was worse than what he had imagined, but his mind was already in cleanup mode. It was time to start helping to save the survivors and bury the dead and express their outrage to the world.

Fahd and his neighbors somehow never dreamed that the battle was only beginning.

Until they heard the sounds of a new barrage.

CHAPTER TWO

The ancient truck screeched to a stop, and the driver barely afforded a passing glance to the smoking ruin that had been the mosque.

"The Israelis are attacking!"

It seemed to be a profoundly stupid thing to say.

"I mean the ground forces!" the man added, perplexed at the lack of response. Fahd pushed to the front of the somber crowds.

"What about the attack helicopters?"

"They've landed, in the west, behind the enemy soldiers."

"One of our people hit one of them with gunfire," Fahd said. "The gunships are too valuable to risk. They'll subdue us with ground forces before sending the helicopters at us again. We have to fight them. This is the assault we knew would come."

"Who are they?" an old man asked. "Why are they killing us?"

Another stupid question. "Israelis, who else?" Fahd snapped. "They are killing us because we are Palestinians."

"What Israelis have so much hatred for us when they know the peace is coming?"

"There will never be peace! It is all lies and politics," Fahd said bitterly. "If there is one point upon which we agree with these enemies, it is that peace between Israelis and Arabs cannot happen. Even if the U.S. tries to force a solution on us, it will not last. We are oil and water.''

Most of the crowded men nodded and voiced their agreement with these words.

''We were told this conflict would come and it has come,'' Fahd pressed on. ''We have armed ourselves for it, and now it is time to make the fight.''

''We're not soldiers.''

It was the old man raising his voice again. The old ones, Fahd thought, should know better than to say things like that. Fahd stood erect in front of the him. The old man was bent with a frailty of the bones, and, staring into Fahd's chest, he rolled his eyes up.

Hisham Fahd was a tall, narrow figure with a powerful, stony face and piercing eyes. With the presence of a natural commander, a fierce confidence in his beliefs minor and major, and a wily mind, Fahd was looked upon as one of the leaders in the village. They all knew too that he had fought Israelis before as leader of his militia. It was natural that he be the one to assume command here and now.

''All Palestinians are soldiers whether they are strong or weak,'' Fahd said in a loud, clear voice, nodding just slightly in the direction of the old man, although it was clear he was speaking to the entire gathering. ''We have been oppressed for too long. We have lived with the shame of our ancestors' weakness. They lost our holy land and we must redeem it. At the very least, we must protect our women and our children so that some day they will have the courage to take the stand we do not.''

When he spoke to the men of the town just days ago, Fahd had said much the same words and had failed to have much of an impact. He spoke then of the shame of the Palestinians for allowing themselves to be herded into pens by the Israelis, and how that shame perpetuated each day they allowed Israelis to go on living on Palestinian land. He had spoke of the imminence of an Israeli attack on this very village. This was the warning the stranger had given him.

"Why would they attack this place first?" another of the old men had asked him.

"Because they know we have been fighting for the return of our land."

"So have the people in a hundred other places. It is hard to believe your handful of men in the May of '42 army stands out above the rest on the list of Israel's enemies."

"We're close to Israeli-occupied territory in the West Bank," Fahd said. "My informant has said these will be private soldiers, with secret state sanctioning but not official. They will want a way to get at us, make their attack, and get out without being seen by others outside this village. The Israelis will be required to make a military response, but they can do nothing if the lawbreakers are gone before they get here."

"Your informant told you this?" the old man asked. "A man you do not know? Why would you believe this and why should we believe it?"

"He had more to offer than just words, friends," Fahd had said grimly.

That was when Fahd had revealed the weapons cache provided by his informant. Enough to arm most of the adult males in the Khodr.

Now, in the aftermath of the attack he had prophesied, Fahd announced, "We have weapons to defend ourselves. We have the men. But do we have the courage?"

It was a slap in the face to each and every one of them.

"I will go arm myself to fight off the Israelis," Fahd continued. "If they have come to kill my wife and my son, they will have to kill me first! If I must fight and die alone, I will fight and die alone."

Fahd turned and marched away from the crowd.

But the crowd followed him.

Tel Aviv, Israel

THE WIDE-ASPECT video display showed the entire village in high resolution, picked up by the camera array mounted on the underside of the hovering Bell 206B JetRanger. The bouncing and wavering of the helicopter was digitally removed to create a near motionless image of the village, so sharp that the heads of the townsfolk could be seen moving along the streets.

The man watching the screen was stroking his chin between his finger and thumb. He pulled his lower lip away and let it snap back with a liquid pop, then his mouth hardened into a grimace of satisfaction. The operation was proceeding as expected. He had known it would because the planning had been meticulous. Several brainstorming sessions had gone into developing and assessing the eventualities of every scenario.

Still, it was gratifying that no deviations occurred. It satisfied a nagging doubt he had been experiencing. There had been doubts that his vast array of skills and intelligence couldn't be applied to this new undertaking.

Now he was assured.

The Palestinians were reacting as he had known they would.

Lambs to the slaughter.

Touching the button on the second laptop, this one controlling his communications, he spoke aloud, his words broadcasting to every operator and soldier on the system.

"Khodr is responding as expected," he announced. He just couldn't help sounding smug.

A few of the men of the village were being left at the east side of the town, stationed there to keep an eye on the attacking army, as the rest moved through the streets, each just a single dark shape floating between the buildings. They were headed toward the big black spot in the center of the screen.

The man announced into his communications system, "The good citizens of Khodr are converging on the weapons store."

Khodr, West Bank

THE BURNED-OUT HOUSE was a symbol of some kind, although Fahd had never heard the explanation articulated.

When the man of the house heard his son had been shot dead by Israelis, who accused him of attacking them with a flaming gas can, the man had become mad with grief and a lifetime of helpless rage against the Israelis. Using the same device as his son, a flaming container of gasoline, he burned down himself and the house.

It was in the black, charred ruin of the tiny building that Fahd and the other villagers had hidden the crates of weapons from their unknown benefactor. They pulled the crates from the ruin, raising billows of grimy black dust, and opened them on the street.

Tel Aviv, Israel

THE MAN WATCHING the images on the screen turned to the third laptop on the hand-sculpted stainless-steel desk. This screen's display was an identical image of the town, but overlaid with a white grid. Twice tapping the black smudge on the screen in the middle of the town, the image zoomed digitally onto the smudge.

The crates were now clearly discernible. The man counted the crates. All there. Then he counted the men. Forty of them, plus three remaining on the east side of the town keeping an eye on the attackers, exactly equaling the forty-three fighters their planning and reconnaissance had told them to expect.

He laughed.

Slouching in his chair, he idly withdrew a bottle of raspberry tea from the mound of ice in the small cooler at his feet, twisting off the top and sucking down a third of it in a single swallow. Icy cold and delicious.

Life was full of pleasures great and simple.

As he was enjoying the drink, he kept his eyes on the digital countdown in the corner of all the screens and watched for the red warning display that would come up if any problem or abnormality was noticed, in the field or by his team of operators, who were ranged around the large dining-room table of his home, down the hall from his home office. He heard very little in the way of conversation out there. None was needed.

It took the townsmen eight minutes and forty-seven seconds to assemble at the east edge of the village, while the plans had estimated more than ten. The man at the desk grinned and said to himself, "Uh-oh, major malfunction!"

His team would probably be capable of handling that deviation, he thought with a smile.

Better yet, the team would just ignore it and attack at the time mark already decided upon.

Let those pieces of human shit sit there and wait for death to come rolling in.

Khodr, West Bank

"WHAT ARE they waiting for?"

"Who knows?" Fahd wished he had a better answer.

The soldiers stood in formation, a single razor-straight line, with about two yards separating each man at the shoulder. A jeep now sat at either end of the line, engine running, with one soldier at the wheel and another stationed behind the .50-caliber machine gun in the rear. From what Fahd could observe at this distance, every man among them was dressed and armed identically, wearing desert camouflage devoid of insignia of rank or allegiance, heavy black footgear, and a rounded desert camou helmet. A black bar protruded from the base of each helmet and circled the wearer's chin, while bug-eyed goggles covered every soldier's eyes. Fahd squinted. Was that a flat cable running out of the helmets at the ears and disappearing behind his back? It had to be some sort of headphone for battlefield communications. Probably a microphone in that curved piece at the chin.

The jeeps weren't new, with one showing the shallow crater of a collision on its front right fender. The only unusual attribute was the paint job, which was the same deep blue as the aircraft. The same stark white Star of David was emblazoned big enough on the hood for a point to reach each side.

The same paint job decorated the two other vehicles, which now sat unmoving, without visible windows or passenger compartments, in the no-man's-land between the Israelis and the Palestinian town.

What were those things? Fahd heard the distinctive puttering of their diesel engines.

"There's only thirty-four soldiers," someone said excitedly. "We outnumber them!"

Why was he fated to fight alongside the stupidest men created by God? "They could wipe us out with those machine guns alone," Fahd retorted savagely. "Who knows what kind of firepower they've got in those tank things."

The townsmen were taken aback by his tone of voice more than the words he spoke. Minutes ago he had been rallying them on to victory and now he spoke as if they were doomed to die.

"Are there men inside them?"

"I doubt it," Fahd said. "They are radio controlled or something, by whoever is up there." He nodded up at the observational helicopter sitting in the skies above them, like a patient vulture flying circles above a mortally wounded rabbit.

"So what do we do?"

Fahd considered that and spoke in a low voice that resonated among his men. "Just because those things aren't alive doesn't mean we can't kill them."

The diesel pop grew louder when the faceless vehicles rolled forward, unhurried, as if they had all the time in the world to reach their destination and perform their function.

Tel Aviv, Israel

FOR THE MAN at the stainless-steel desk the minutes had dragged on like an eternity and the thrill bubbled up inside him, like a child waiting in line to an amusement park. He was forced to stifle the urge to order the acceleration of the timetable. He'd get to ride the roller coaster soon enough.

Finally the countdown display reached the start time for the next phase, and the man flipped his comm laptop to a split screen, each half showing the primary remote command video feed on the pair of outdoor mobility platforms. The OMPs were fed the same time signal as all operators and field personnel, and were programmed to begin their approach without external commands.

The camera showed the rocky, scrubby ground stretching nearly level to Khodr, where the townsmen were gathered around the buildings bordering empty scrubland. They were gripping their weapons uncomfortably and watching as the robots approached, unsure what to make of them. Their agitation was growing. Somebody had to have given an order, or maybe the group nervousness reached a fever pitch, and the firing commenced.

When the man sitting at the stainless-steel desk saw the muzzle flashes like white pinpricks on the video displays, he leaned back on the cool leather of his custom-made chair and laughed out loud.

Khodr, West Bank

"STOP IT! You are wasting bullets!"

Fahd ran along the rear of the uneven lines of men as he shouted. All these men had learned to fire a weapon at some point in their lives, but only a few showed skill or judgment. Even the experts among them might as well be throwing their bullets in the trash for all the good it was doing them now.

But a kind of euphoria swept over the impromptu army of Khodr. Using the weapons was an empowering exercise, ramping up their confidence and adrenaline. Those with their weapons set on automatic rattled through their magazines in an eye blink. Those who hadn't known how to turn the settings to automatic were doing their best to catch up with their neighbors anyway.

Fahd didn't have to watch the approaching vehicles to know few if any bullets were actually reaching them, and if they did the rounds didn't have energy left to do more than dent the metal shielding or chip the blue paint. He resorted to shoving and kicking the men.

"What is wrong with you?" It was Zaqtan, a squat man who had been an old friend of Fahd's father. "If you are going to try and lead this defense, you better make up your mind what you want us to do."

"I never told you to fire," Fahd retorted angrily. "Look at those things—you think you can do any good from this distance? You men just flushed a thousand rounds into the latrine."

"So what *are* we supposed to do?" the stubby man demanded.

Fahd sensed the mood. These men were afraid, yet firing the guns had briefly given them a sense of conviction, which Fahd was now calling foolish. If he wanted to remain a positive influence on the outcome of the day's events, he needed to consolidate his position and project a high level of self-assurance. Generate some confidence, earn some allies.

"I know how to stop these things," Fahd said without a hint of doubt. "We have just minutes, so listen close. First we must assign two men to watch these troops for signs of movement into the city. The rest of us will go stop these— cars."

There was a sudden argument as men jostled for inclusion in one side or another. All at once Fahd was a well-loved leader and everyone wanted to stay with him. He shouted wordlessly and raised his hands, reducing the crowd to silence. "You and you, guard the front. Go!"

As the guards fled to their posts, Fahd chose one of the youngest men for special duty, then rushed to outline his plan. He prayed they would understand.

ZUHEIR SLIPPED into a east-end house and watched the pair of machines approach until they passed into the streets of the city. Zuheir had been a boy not many years ago, and he was tempted to think of the vehicles as big robot toys. After watching the slaughter at the mosque, he knew these things also had to have some lethal purpose.

The vehicles didn't act as if they were traveling together. Somehow Fahd had presumed as much and had ordered Zuheir to track one vehicle from a distance as his two armed units neutralized the other.

Watching the vehicle disappear around a corner, Zuheir exited the house and jogged to the wall, peering around it, half fearing the robot would have put on a burst of speed and given him the slip.

The houses and streets were strangely empty with all the women and children gathered in one place, all the men in another. Khodr felt abandoned.

The robot rolled down an alley and turned a sharp corner with an improbable twist, all four wheels moving independently. Zuheir hid at the next corner, then stepped out behind the thing.

As he looked at it from a closer perspective, he saw it had tractorlike tires and a diesel engine. Pretty mundane components for the self-aware technological cyborg unit he had been picturing in his head. Really it was just a car with a PC under the hood. Maybe Fahd could defeat these things.

If the vehicle saw him, it sure didn't care. It just kept rolling.

Rolling where?

A few minutes later, Zuheir felt fresh horror as the answer became clear. It was headed to what the townsfolk called the Bunker, an old concrete basement that was the foundation of long-gone building, now covered with a false floor. Months ago Fahd had insisted it be roofed for use as a retreat by the women and children.

How did that machine know where it was?

That didn't matter—he had to summon Fahd's army units. The young man bolted across the street. He never saw the eruption from the hidden battery of short-barrel, 12-gauge combat shotguns mounted under a lip of metal at the rear of the unmanned vehicle.

Tel Aviv, Israel

"HA! I GOT HIM!" shouted the man at the stainless-steel desk. The figure in the display from the A-OMP's rear video camera had dropped to the street.

It was a joke. Of course he got him. The battery of shot-guns rigged under the cowl produced a hail of buckshot over a 130-degree spread from the rear of the vehicle.

Still, he had been the one to design that gimmick, along with most of the unique offensive and defensive character-istics of this special pair of OMPs. He was proud of his achievement and was silently relieved that his first kill had been so easy. He simply moved the cursor and clicked the fire-battery button on the A-OMP command window. It was just like closing an unneeded application.

The shotgun-battery design hadn't been optimized. The unit could fire just once, but that was okay. The operational lifetime of this OMP pair was extremely short.

In fact, its time was almost up.

CHAPTER THREE

Somewhere over the Mediterranean

The gray Airbus Industries A-310 floated effortlessly at thirty-five thousand feet. The pilot appreciated the high level of sound insulation and ergonomically pleasing cabin features. Even the seat was comfortable after hours in the air. Civilian pilots, he reflected, had it easy.

He wouldn't want to fly commercial aircraft full-time, nevertheless. It was too comfortable, too automated. Not like real flying at all, compared to the harsh sports-car suspension and thrill-a-minute handling of, say, an F/A-18 Hornet.

Their Airbus A-310 was factory fresh. The newly molded resin parts were releasing thermoplastic fumes and giving him a headache. One of the light bulbs in the controls had burned out. Glitches had to be expected in a machine this complicated when it came right from the manufacturer. The cover story was that the pilot was delivering the aircraft for interior refitting in Saudi Arabia, after which it would be used by a U.S.-Bahrain oil firm for ferrying company executives globally.

The story would be tough to disprove, since there was no evidence on the aircraft of its true owners and operators. The only markings were factory-applied serial and ID numbers. No paperwork was on board. The software in every on-board system had been rewritten to erase incriminating or traceable information. If forced down and searched, nothing could tie the aircraft to its true proprietor. If it crashed, no evidence would tell investigators what its actual identity and mission were. Any compromise to its security integrity would result in the automatic disintegration of what little electronic evidence existed of the company that was listed as its owner, further foiling an investigation.

The pilot wasn't bothered by his lack of identity. His normal good nature made him impervious to such worries, and at the moment, he had bigger concerns—mainly, pumping every last mph out of the pair of Pratt & Whitney PW4000 engines. He had to get his passengers into Israeli airspace as fast as possible. He didn't understand why—not fully. It didn't matter. He understood the urgency, and that was enough.

The engines had been coaxed and pushed and driven hard all night since leaving Washington, D.C., exceeding their design specs as if they, too, recognized the need for speed. The Airbus was more than an hour ahead of schedule. Maybe that would be good enough.

It wasn't. The pilot got the radio transmission over the private satellite feed and intuited that it was bad news, patching it into the passenger cabin and handing the stick to the U.S. Air Force colonel who served as copilot. The pilot went to join his companions in the rear.

Five men in desert camouflage had been sorting packs of military gear, just to pass the time. The gear had already been checked and rechecked. Now they were staring at the wall-mounted TFT-LCD display, where a beautiful but matter-of-fact blond woman was describing a disaster-in-progress.

"The attack came within the last fifteen minutes, if our information is correct. We're relying solely on phone calls coming out of the town. Nobody official is on the scene yet, but it sounds just like the scenario we were anticipating—a Palestinian town attacked by a heavily armed unit of some kind. The callers have described attack helicopters firing rockets, lots of other air activity, and deployment of ground troops. The call came from a woman or several women in the town. Somehow they had a cellular phone. Any landline phone service to the town has been cut off.''

''Who and why?'' demanded one of the men, a six-footer with short blond hair and noticeable British accent. His eyes were blue, icy with anger, but his question was rhetorical. None of his people could answer it.

''We've got a sky eye coming online,'' the blonde said with a nod to someone off-screen. ''Here we go.''

Her face on the screen was replaced with a black-and-white satellite image.

''We're in luck. It's an NRO ten-see-em sat,'' the blonde stated. ''The President may have ordered it into position at the same time he was giving us our directives.''

Several U.S. National Reconnaissance Office satellites kept their eyes on hot spots around the globe. The Middle East was, naturally, high on the NRO's priority list. Satellite focus and positioning could be controlled from Earth to an astonishing degree, allowing it to home in on the surface with a grayscale resolution of 10 cm. There were probably no sharper eyes in orbit. Stony Man Farm didn't always have access to the best equipment belonging to other agencies. The clandestine organization had to wheedle and steal much of its access to satellite imagery. Getting a look this good was a stroke of luck.

Grayscale images started flashing on the screen at one frame per second, showing what looked like nothing more than a vast and empty stretch of desert with the single jagged line of a road stretching through the rectangular jumble of a town. The images were being snapped even as the satellite was focusing and zooming in on the tiny, unimportant

West Bank community of Khodr. They could see the dots of aircraft obscuring the ground focus, and the fact that those dots barely moved indicated they were not fixed-wing. More dots in a regular row in the sand might be people. Soldiers.

When the rectangle of the town filled the screen, the high-contrast imaging should have made distinct the geography of buildings and streets. Instead a pall of smoke obscured a quarter of it, coming out of a small square in the lower left quadrant.

"What was hit?" the Briton asked.

"We're seeing this for the first time, too, so your take is as good as mine," the blonde answered. "The caller mentioned the destruction of a mosque. It gets confused. She said the mosque was destroyed by missiles twice."

The Briton happened to glance into the eyes of one the other men. His companion had the look of a Hispanic, with grizzled black hair and a light brown. When his brown eyes met the cold green of the Briton's, understanding passed silently between them. They had, like the others, been witness to more evils than they cared to remember, sometimes individually but often together. They knew what the Palestinian woman meant when she reported that the mosque was destroyed twice. Once to bring down the building, once to slaughter those who came to rescue survivors of the first tragedy.

Not at all subdued by what he was seeing, the youngest man in the large cabin of the A310 was in a fury. "Why wasn't something done to stop this before it started?"

Another rhetorical question, but the younger man said nothing for a moment, as if awaiting an answer. In reality he was fighting to keep his fists from slamming into the bulkhead. "There are some cold-blooded sons of bitches in charge of the world these days," he said in a twang out of the American Southwest.

The tall, slim black man was staring at the screen. "Check it out." He tapped a spot on the screen partially obscured by smoke.

The Briton leaned in closer. The odd shape of humans seen from almost directly above, clustering at buildings, in the vicinity of the dark rectangular image of a vehicle.

"Can't make it out."

"The emblem on the hood—it's a Star of David," the black man said in a controlled but intense voice.

The Briton leaned closer.

The next frame advanced, and the spot where the rectangle had been became a white, bright circle.

"Bloody hell! It just blew!"

The smoke was minimal, and three frames later they could see the shapes of humans again. This time they were easier to identify, since most were flat on the ground.

"There's another one," said a barrel-chested figure, tapping the screen with almost casual slowness. He had the complexion of a fishing trawler captain, ruddy and weathered, and gray eyes that were locked on a small grouping of pixels under the haze. "There."

The Star of David was unmistakable on the hood of Vehicle Number Two, which turned a couple of corners over the next few seconds before bolting suddenly into the side of a building.

"Close-up on that vehicle, quick!" shouted the gray-eyed man.

The response was immediate. The image was zeroing in on the rectangular shape as fast as the space-based imaging would allow, and not a breath was exhaled in the cabin of the Airbus. Silently, with each passing frame, the town became half a town, then a quarter of the town, then just a handful of buildings—and again the curious images of human beings, now streaming out of the building where the vehicle hit, the distending arms and legs showing that they were running and clawing for freedom. None got more than a few steps.

This time, when the explosion came, the entire screen went white.

Khodr, West Bank

FAHD WAS PULLING men to their feet when the blast came, and he froze just long enough for the sound of the explosion to echo through the town and flee into the desert. A moment ago he had been ecstatic. His two units' combined attack on the robot had been successful, with enough automatic gunfire slamming into it to knock out its hidden sensors or electric eyes or whatever it was that let it see where it was going. Fahd's shouts urged his men to stay away from the seemingly dead unit. The twin blasts from shotguns hidden under the front and rear cowl had done no more than scar the buildings.

Fahd guessed a self-destruct was coming next and ordered a retreat from the disabled robot. They had been pulling back when the blast came, knocking them flat and killing the one man foolish or absentminded enough to have moved too far out into the open, where his body was shredded by flying shrapnel. The others were covered with bruises and scrapes from metal pieces. There were thousands and thousands of scraps of metal covering the street. An entire wall of a small, concrete house had been imbedded with shrapnel no larger than a coin.

Fahd briefly examined the obliterated ruins of the robot. It had been designed to fragment when it blew.

It could have been much worse. All the men realized that without Fahd's insightful warning, they would have been on top of the vehicle trying to pry it open when the explosion came. They all would have died, providing the Israeli attackers instant victory.

Then the second blast, identical in register, echoed through the alleys of the town and rushed over the rooftops like an ill wind. Fahd tried to conjecture the location of the explosion by the sound. He thought he knew where it would be.

No, there was no doubt. When he tried to imagine what target these well-informed murderers would choose, it was obvious.

Praying he was wrong, he ran to it.

The explosion was there. The blast struck the town's improvised Bunker, where the women and children had been huddled. The roof was collapsed into the hole, the inches-thick plywood burning intensely.

Any future the people of the Khodr may have had was gone with the families.

Fahd didn't have the will to react when two men plunged hysterically into the conflagration in an effort to rescue those who were already dead.

He simply watched the flames for a long time.

Most of the men were weeping when Fahd finally turned to them. He spoke in a soft voice that carried over the crackling of the fire. He was going into battle, he announced, to hunt down the murderers of his people. He would die this day avenging this atrocity—he would see to it. Living to see another day after this was unthinkable. He was fully prepared to march into the desert alone, a one-man army, but he would welcome the company of any and all who cared to fight with him.

When Fahd marched into the desert to meet the enemy and his own destiny, every surviving townsman marched behind him.

CHAPTER FOUR

Over the Mediterranean

His name was Thomas Jackson Hawkins, and he considered himself to be an ethical man. He had seen more human evil than most at his relatively young age. In his current role it was part of the job to be exposed to the world's worst-case scenarios in terms of human savagery. But if he never understood the rationale for slaughtering innocent people, at least he could comprehend why the perpetrators understood the rationale.

Drug dealing, for instance. He found it deplorable, but he understood why it happened.

Right now he was facing a different reality, and the worst aspect was he couldn't understand it.

"Approximately forty-three," Barbara Price intoned in a controlled voice.

Forty-three women and children had been in that building when it blew. It was the kind of information they didn't need to know and wouldn't help them perform their function, but T. J. Hawkins had demanded to be told.

Price wasn't speaking now, sitting silent in front of the video pickup six thousand miles away, in her command center below the farmlands of Virginia. The cabin of the Airbus was equally silent under the hush of the engines.

Hawkins made a fist and looked at it.

"If I don't hit something soon, my head's gonna blow up."

"We can be ready to off-load you guys in seventeen minutes," said the pilot, Jack Grimaldi. "You can slug somebody on the West Bank."

"I'd rather be air-dropped on the White House. Show the President how I'm feeling about his foreign policy."

"He made a political decision, T.J." The speaker was male, gruff, but without anger. The face of Hal Brognola appeared on the screen.

His expression was bland, but his eyes were looking with an air of authority through the two-way video feed into the tense eyes of the youngest warrior on the Phoenix Force commando team.

Brognola was a big man in every sense of the word, with several long decades of tenure with the Department of Justice. Despite the extra weight he was carrying just above the belt line these days, he was physically imposing, even on the screen. Although Justice wrote his paycheck, Brognola took orders directly from the Man.

Hawkins wasn't intimidated. "That's a poor excuse for allowing forty-three women and children to die in a fire."

Brognola nodded slightly. "Maybe."

News of the plot had reached the White House via a secure communiqué from the office of the U.S. ambassador to Israel. A paid messenger, just a boy, had walked into the Tel Aviv embassy and delivered the sealed envelope, labeled For The Ambassador's Eyes Only.

The explanation was brief. An attack was scheduled on an unnamed Palestinian village in the West Bank, near the border with Israeli-occupied territory. It would take place before the upcoming Camp David Economics and Peace Summit and was designed to keep the meetings from ever happening. The attackers would be agents of an unnamed Jewish terror group, eager to prevent the Palestinians from consolidating legitimate occupancy to what they considered to be Israeli holy land. The goal was to goad the Palestinians into more violence against the Israelis. Once new hostilities commenced, peace talks of the kind the U.S. President was sponsoring would be considered premature at best.

The President thought it was a hoax, designed to derail his peace plan before it started.

The Man needed a success here. The July 2000 peace talks, sponsored by the previous president, had failed and been forgotten in the flurry of violence that had raged for months throughout Israel and the occupied territories at the close of that year. Even if it hadn't resulted in a Middle Eastern peace, the effort reflected well on a president who was desperate to go down in history as something more than a dirty old man.

The current President wanted to duplicate those public-approval benefits. His peace plan was better. This time Israeli and PLO representatives would have real economic reasons for forging strong ties and better relations. The infrastructure the President was proposing would result in thousands of Palestinian jobs and the establishment of mutual-trade relationships virtually overnight. Even the legal red tape of establishing Israeli-Palestinian joint ventures would be addressed during the summit. The whole thing would be heavily financed by the U.S., and the goods the new companies produced would find a ready market in North America. Every country bordering Israel was being invited to be a part of the plan and share in the U.S. investments. Egypt had accepted. No surprise there, but Syria's announced intention to joint the new economic alliance came as a welcome surprise.

The key to the agreement's lasting benefits to the region was the involvement of fourteen firms based in the burgeoning Tel Aviv and Haifa technology corridor. These firms needed cheap labor for new factories, and Palestinians could provide it. The Palestinian leadership needed to provide lifetime jobs for their people, and any technology training would have long-term benefits.

The President had an ulterior motive. The Tel Aviv–Haifa technology corridor included some of the world's most prolific state-of-the-art weapons technology companies, selling mostly to the highest bidder. Increasingly that high bidder was China. Despite official Israeli condemnation, even North Korea had come up with enough cash to make shopping trips into Israel. The President's plan would call for these companies to turn their expertise to consumer electronics, home computer systems and manufacturing technology. Although the weapons-technology sector had generally opposed the summit, enough Israeli consumer electronics producers and commercial-industrial electronic component suppliers supported the summit to give it the potential for huge commercial success. Shared financial interests would steer all parties away from violent conflict resolutions.

The points the President would score, with Congress, the people of the U.S., everybody, were too numerous to count. If he pulled it off the way he hoped, he'd be in the running for a Nobel Peace Prize, which would be a major coup for a President.

When his ambassador to Israel received the threat to obstruct the summit before it even occurred, the President stampeded into denial mode.

Hal Brognola had met with the Man less than forty-five minutes later, by which time the President had spoken to the Israeli prime minister.

"The Israelis got the same message," the President said as Brognola finished reading the faxed copy of the handwritten note.

"How did they respond?" the big Fed asked.

"About how I did. They think it's some extremist Israeli's imagination getting the better of him. In a country like that, they have all kind of factions trying to manipulate events to their own agenda.''

Brognola didn't doubt it, but... ''What if it is true?''

''Can't be.''

''Why not?''

''The destruction of a Palestinian village? Think of what it would take,'' the President said.

''A single armed tank could accomplish it,'' Brognola retorted, keeping his tone level. ''A few well-placed explosive devices.''

''Read the note,'' the President responded irritably. ''He describes air support, ground troops, heavy weapons fire, radar jamming, all originating in Israel. Don't you think the Israelis would have intelligence on a group capable of mounting that kind of an attack?''

''Israel's intelligence is very good,'' Brognola admitted. ''I think they placed most of their resources to monitor their enemies, not their own people.''

''In that atmosphere? Come on, Hal, they've got potential threats coming at them from every direction, including inside. I'd bet they put the old KGB to shame when it comes to Big Brothering their citizenry.''

''What intelligence I have doesn't show—''

''The Israelis would know,'' the President stated firmly, leaning forward over his Oval Office desk and landing his hands on the flat surface with a slap.

Brognola and the President of the United States regarded each other without speaking for a long fifteen seconds. It wasn't the first time the man from Justice had faced contention across that historic desk. It wasn't even the first time since this particular man took over the Oval Office.

''Mr. President, why am I here?''

''I don't want to take any risks. I want to have your men on the scene, just in case.''

Brognola exhaled, wishing it wouldn't be unseemly to pop an antacid tablet in the middle of conversation with the Man. "Mr. President, you've got a timetable to consider. Your summit attendees are supposed to arrive tomorrow. If this attack comes, it will come in the next several hours."

"Yes?"

Brognola blinked. Surely the Man could comprehend the problem.

"My people are at the Farm now and ready to move, and I can have them in the air in less than five minutes," Brognola explained, patting the cell phone in his breast pocket. "But we're still talking about a flight halfway around the globe."

"You're my sole option, Hal. I can't put official military in the field in the West Bank, for God's sake."

"And if my men are too late?"

The Man's agitation peaked. "Hal, read my lips—you are my only choice."

"No, sir, that's not true. The Israelis should be pressured into responding to this threat themselves. The Palestinians need to be alerted to the danger."

The President closed his eyes momentarily, gripping the air in frustration as if there were an invisible softball in each hand. "I assure you there is no threat. Your SOG will be on hand only as a precautionary measure. What do we waste? Just some jet fuel and a couple of days of your people's time."

Before Brognola left the room he said calmly, "Mr. President, with all due respect, you can't have it both ways. The threat is either genuine and local defense initiatives must be employed, or it's a hoax and no reaction is called for. In this instance sending in my people is a half-assed response, in my opinion."

"Your opinion," the Man said, "wasn't requested."

Now, watching the Airbus cabin from his office thousands

of miles away, in a Virginia farmhouse, Brognola wasn't about to use the same line on Hawkins. The man had a right to his anger. The President had made a big mistake. A very poor gamble. The count of dead women and children showed how big an error it was.

"We have the word authorizing us to go in," Brognola said, sounding official. "The Man would like these hostilities quelled soonest, obviously."

"Obviously," Hawkins muttered. "He's got a PR campaign to stage."

"He's got a damned good plan for bringing about some sort of lasting peace where there isn't any," Brognola replied. "Don't make this personal, any of you. Keep it professional."

Hawkins narrowed his gaze and glared at the screen. Before he could speak, David McCarter, the British commando who served as leader of the Phoenix Force commando team, answered for him. "We always keep it professional, Hal."

"I didn't mean to imply otherwise. Barb." The big Fed's face vanished from the screen and Barbara Price was back.

As mission controller for Stony Man Farm's Sensitive Operations Group, she was the brains behind the nuts and bolts of this action. She had called in members of Phoenix Force the moment Hal Brognola phoned to say he was being summoned to the Oval Office, often a sign the Farm's help was going to be needed.

IN THE CABIN, Price's image disappeared midsentence and she stopped speaking. There was another voice coming over the speaker. It was Aaron Kurtzman, the genius behind the immense cybernetics intelligence-gathering systems housed underground at the Farm. He was attempting to bring satellites from various authorities under his command, without necessarily having permission to do so.

"Sorry to interrupt," he said. "You've got to see this."

The familiar National Reconnaissance Office satellite image reappeared, although Kurtzman had pulled back and retrained the image on the swathe of scrubland to the east of the village, where the frame-per-second animation showed a conflict under way between bunches of Palestinians and the well-disciplined Israeli attackers.

The Palestinians, against all odds, appeared to be winning.

The Israelis were pulling back. A moment later they began to run.

Somebody in the cabin of the Airbus said, "What the hell is going on?"

Khodr, West Bank

FAHD'S LAUGH was hyena-like. "They didn't expect this, brothers!" He tossed himself to the ground as another volley of automatic fire spit from the Uzis and bounced noisily around him. One of his men was too slow to react and caught a round in the thigh, grunting as he toppled.

The wounded were being left behind. Maybe somebody would rescue them eventually, but the army of Khodr was on a death march. It had no time for humane gestures. It would march and it would fight until it was dead.

Fahd spotted the man with the Uzi, at the point of the retreating column of helmeted soldiers, and triggered the AK-47 in a succession of bursts that finally caught the man in the chest. The white Star of David became tattered, and the soldier collapsed on his back with his hands out wide. Fahd stayed down. He was already learning how this bunch of well-equipped but gutless soldiers behaved. They would put down a hail of cover fire to recover the corpse, haul it into the nearby jeep and continue their retreat.

"Stay down," Fahd ordered. His men obeyed. When the

body recovery was complete, he gave a new command to attack. "Take down that jeep."

The men on the south end of the line of men strung across the scrubby wasteland had been trying to stop it for ten minutes, but their AK rounds bounced off the armored skin, and the tires were shielded with steel sheaths that so far hadn't been penetrated. The vehicle kept its distance, holding the villagers back with the long-range .50-caliber fire from the mounted machine guns, which had killed two of the townsmen.

Now the Khodr army advanced, making a leapfrog approach as if trained in the maneuver. The jeep crew acted disdainful, although they were expressionless behind the darkened eye shields of the helmets. They brought the jeep to a halt and watched the Palestinians approach. The driver touched his hand to the helmet at his ear, then nodded, shouting back to the gunner. The gunner nodded, then started firing on the Palestinians.

The thunder of machine-gun fire filled the open desert as if it were a closed room, and the townsmen went down again, seeking cover in the small dips and rises to the landscape. Using meager cover they began returning fire, trying for a shot over the tempered windshield to take down the machine gunner himself. The gunner wasn't cooperating, returning fire at the low shapes that hugged the ground. Missing his flat, still targets wasn't easy. The impact of the big rounds chopped at the figures and silenced the AK flashes, one after another.

Tel Aviv, Israel

THE MAN AT THE DESK counted the dead. The belly-mounted camera on the Bell JetRanger was switched to infrared. The firing guns were easily discernible. The cooling guns and thermal images of motionless body heat showed him clearly who was alive and who was dead.

He was slightly amused when he watched a red-hot chunk of someone's body get blasted a few feet away by the murderous impact of the .50-caliber gun. He smirked and touched the key on the radio to send a broadcast throughout the system.

"That's five casualties, Gun One. Give it up."

"Gun One here. We'll give it up."

West Bank

THE KHODR ARMY WAS being annihilated, and Hisham Fahd fretted over how he could get past the longer range of the machine gun. As he worked his way forward, the tables turned unexpectedly. The machine gun ceased firing with the sound of metal parts grinding together. The gunner fell into a crouch and began gesturing to the driver, who stepped on the gas and spun the jeep in a tight circle. It was an escape scramble.

"Fire at the jeep!" Fahd shouted. "Stop them quickly!"

Ten AK-47s rained a torrent of rounds at the fleeing jeep, but the gunner was protected by a steel panel bolted on the rear. The panel grew speckled with dents from the 7.62 mm rounds, like the surface of a puddle in a sudden rain shower. The body panel was penetrated and the vehicle lunged before stalling.

"We have them!" Fahd shouted.

The jeep crew had to have seen the writing on the wall, and their heads appeared briefly as they ejected themselves over the hood of the jeep, keeping it between them and the AK fire as they fled. The gunfire slackened, but rounds were still slamming into the rear of the jeep when the fire started. Orange flame leaped in arrow tongues from the rents in the steel, then the vehicle became a ball of fire. A heartbeat later, it exploded like a bomb, the shock wave slamming into the Khodr gunmen.

Fahd regained his feet and swore viciously. A moment ago he had the plan of appropriating the jeep, even if the machine gun was hopelessly jammed. There had to have been explosives in the vehicle—hand grenades or other incendiaries. It would have been a worthwhile prize.

The other jeep wasn't being brought into the battle since the Israelis were reserving it for hearse use. The bodies were piling up around the unmanned gun mount. No corpse was left behind yet. These Israelis had met with far more resistance than they had anticipated. They expected just a few guns among the Palestinians of Khodr and couldn't handle the full-scale army that was now breathing down their necks as they made a frantic escape.

The only factor confusing Fahd was the lack of air support. Five helicopters were employed at the outset of the battle, but now the gunships had pulled back and simply observed the rout while the transport vehicles were nowhere to be seen. The Bell commercial chopper stayed right above them, watching and affecting nothing.

Fahd didn't really care why the air support was absent. He only cared that they were succeeding. The men of Khodr would have their vengeance. Fahd couldn't ask for a more satisfying turn of events.

Tel Aviv, Israel

THE MAN AT THE DESK couldn't imagine a smoother-running operation. The complex logistics, the high degree of communications and computer technology being run together, should almost inevitably result in minor problems. So far the problems hadn't happened.

"Status report?" he called after touching the key that switched the communications system to internal. He was heard by every operator in the operations room. Each operator had responsibility for a specific sphere of hardware and-or human monitoring.

"Gun Two is optimal," reported the young man who was watching a screen of sensor readouts from the second jeep, piled with the bodies of the soldiers.

"Walkers are optimal," reported the woman whose displays included a small window for each of the soldiers who was still mobile. Each display reported the soldier's physical state: heart rate, respiration, body temperature and so on.

"Troop communications are optimal." This man had even more windows dominating his screen, each monitoring continual diagnostic profiles on the soldiers' secure radio communications systems.

"Air communications are optimal." The second half of the complicated routing system involved the aircraft. The satellite uplink and its backup were in the twin transport choppers, where they received signals from the gunships, the Bell 206B and the troops.

"Laydowns are ninety-five percent."

That was an irritation. "Explain," he demanded.

An older man in the next room monitoring the vital signs of the bodies in the hearse jeep had noticed a series of out-of-parameter readings and radioed the soldier on a private channel for an explanation. The soldier explained his shoulder armor had apparently failed. He had a gunshot wound, not life threatening, but he was in minor distress. The operator related the situation to the man at the main desk.

The man at the desk shook his head. Their testing indicated the armor itself offered the best ballistic protection available anywhere in the world. It was a new type of Ultrax fiber composite material, purchased from Verseidag-Indutex. It was state-of-the-art. The problem was in joining the material; the seams were the weak link. Tests with the armor overlapped at joints and seams indicated reduced soldier flexibility.

The man at the desk would put his mind to this issue when he got the chance. He'd come up with a better alternative.

It simply wouldn't do to have his soldiers getting wounded in the field.

"ETA?" he asked into the microphone.

"Sixteen-point-five minutes," replied one of his operators. "We're on schedule."

"Fine."

In sixteen minutes more innocent civilians were going to die. This time they would be Israelis. The man at the desk was relieved that the idea didn't disturb him. A warrior, he thought, settling back into the cool leather of the chair, had to be heartless.

CHAPTER FIVE

Shaalvim Settlement, West Bank

Israel was running out of room for Israelis, and began settling people in the disputed West Bank territory. This basic factor was behind long-simmering discontent in the region. The 2000 peace talks had addressed the issue without solving it, and the violence late that year had seen many of those settlers attacked and killed.

But Israelis continued to flow into the West Bank. By 2002, more than 230 Jewish settlements and civilian land-use sites were established there. These sites were home to approximately two hundred thousand Israeli settlers. The Palestinians continued to rankle over the annexation of the land they claimed.

The Israeli sites turned the long-barren real estate into suburban neighborhoods that would have been the envy of North Americans and Europeans alike. The level of protection these outposts received was impressive. Israel defended its own.

But this day, the defensive resources it had in place at Shaalvim Settlement would turn out to be woefully inadequate.

The uniformed officer, responding to a frantic phone call from a terrified housewife, rushed through the neighborhood in his patrol car, siren wailing, then spun his wheel as he stood on the brakes, skidding the car to a sideways halt that lifted a spray of gravel and dust.

There was an army coming out of the west, following the dirt road that led through the West Bank. At Shaalvim the dirt road became a paved highway used by daily commuters from the settlement into the Israeli city of Ramla.

The army was Palestinian, of course. But where had it come from? Why was it attacking? Why now? Why here?

The officer's head was spinning with these questions even as he was calling for assistance. It took a moment for his commanding officer to believe what he was telling him. Even in turbulent Israel, it was hard to believe an army would simply march out of the West Bank to attack the people without warning or provocation.

"Wait a second," the officer said, squinting above his head to see out the top of his windshield. "Several aircraft are arriving. Helicopters."

"What's that?" his CO demanded.

"Helicopters. Big ones. They're closing in from north and south. I think the ground troops are firing at them."

"It must be Israeli air forces responding."

"They sure aren't marked like Israel Defense Forces," the police officer returned. "In fact, they have no markings whatsoever."

THE STAR OF DAVID insignias were gone. They had been big and white, visible for miles against the dark blue paint of the hull of the transport choppers, impossible to miss or mistake. The choppers had disappeared after dropping off their men and vehicles, and now they were back, suddenly unmarked.

What could that possibly mean?

"They have to be different helicopters," one of the townsmen said.

"Why would they have two choppers to drop the troops

off and two different but nearly identical choppers to come and get them?'' Fahd asked.

Nobody had an answer.

"We have to stop them," urged Zaqtan, the friend of Fahd's father, even as the choppers hovered just a few hundred feet above the ground but more than a quarter mile away. "We can't let these despicable men just fly away unpunished."

The army of foot soldiers that had attacked the town had proved to be all flash and no substance. Their shiny visors, sleek helmets and trim camouflage outfits had given them only the appearance of a trained army, and faced with the unorganized but purposeful wrath of the townsmen, they fled in panic. Armed response clearly wasn't in the Israelis' plans, and now it was apparent the transport chopper hadn't planned on a pickup so soon. It was satisfying to see them running scared.

But the Israeli soldiers were fit, at least. The soldiers of the Khodr army weren't used to the exertion of running miles over scrubland. They had fallen back.

"They're going to make a run for the choppers through the settlement," Fahd said. "They're gambling we won't bring the fight into a Jewish neighborhood."

"They're wrong," someone said. It didn't matter who. They were all thinking it. They weren't going to let this conglomeration of Jew hovels, erected illegally on Palestinian land, stop them from meting out justice on the men who murdered their families. In fact, Fahd thought eagerly, it made a certain kind of ironic sense to engage the enemy here.

"Our feet must have wings!" he hissed.

To a man, their weary march turned into a sprint.

THE ISRAELI POLICEMAN absolutely couldn't come to a decision when he realized he was looking at two fighting forces. They men at the fore wore desert-camouflage gear and what might be motorcycle helmets. They had Uzis, but there were no markings signifying their allegiance. So who were they?

Their pursuers were Palestinians, many in traditional robes.

Which meant the camou soldiers had to be Israelis, right?

The foot soldiers escorted the jeep, laden with bodies, up the hill into the streets of the community. Not that the cop could have stopped them if he tried. He was all alone today, thanks to an unannounced exercise that had pulled away four other stationed officers.

The Palestinians were approaching at a run and the Israeli cop panicked, twisting the wheel and slamming the car into reverse. Gravel spit from the tires as a ragged volley of Kalashnikov fire sputtered behind him.

"Thank God I'm not in range yet," he muttered under his breath. "Thank God I'm not in range yet."

He did not know that for sure, but he hoped praying for it would make it so.

THE AIRBUS WAS SLOWED almost to a stall. Rafael Encizo was the last man to toss himself out the aircraft into the sudden chaos of rushing air and flying limbs. Stretching his arms and legs, he allowed his tumbling body to come to terms with its sudden descent. As he stabilized, he used the views of the West Bank from fifteen thousand feet to get his bearings. It was an odd sensation to be seeing this scenery from a higher-altitude perspective than the satellite image he had been watching minutes ago inside the aircraft.

They hadn't even had time to learn the name of the Israeli neighborhood that was now the ground zero. The name didn't matter. All Phoenix Force cared about was getting down there fast and putting a halt to the inevitable killing. They had watched on the satellite feed as the Israeli troops spread out, using apartment buildings and houses as cover while the Palestinian troops pushed aggressively into the settlement. The people living in those apartments and houses were caught in the middle. Phoenix Force watched figures running for cover, and saw some of them falling motionless before they reached it.

What exactly was going on down there? Nothing about this action rang true. Encizo didn't know what was wrong with this scenario, but there was something.

Let Stony Man figure it out.

He had a job to do.

He descended in a hurricane of wind to six thousand feet and yanked on the cord just moments after the other four ram-air parachutes sprang open below him. McCarter's rectangular canopy—at Fort Bragg MFF school they called it "square"—was veering to the east, to lead the team to a landing on outside the eastern edge of the settlement, where the short highway traversed the rocky, uninhabitable stretch of wasteland that separated it from the nearby boundary of Israel proper.

Slowing to a swift glide, Encizo could see where the Israeli soldiers had taken up refuge in a court that was shielded from a western attack by a low apartment building. Their enemies would have to cross an extra wide street to get at them, exposing themselves. The cover was a good choice, picked because it couldn't be approached under cover by the Palestinians unless they took the time to circle the town entirely and come in from the opposite direction.

Encizo gritted his teeth when he spotted a frantic scurrying of small figures outside a single-story building next door. It had to have been a school. A larger figure, which Encizo assumed was a teacher, was running back to grab the minuscule stick-figure of a girl who had pitched to the ground.

He could hear the gunfire now.

This, he thought, was going to be a bad one. He didn't know why for sure. Sort of a vibration in his bones. It made him feel slightly sick.

Then the situation got stranger.

What caught his attention was so anomalous he couldn't figure out what he was looking at for a moment. When he realized what he was seeing, he leaned into the steering cord on the ram-air, pulling it into a sudden bank that sent him veering away from the agreed-upon landing spot.

"PHOENIX ONE, this is Phoenix Two."

As David McCarter reached for the radio button on his helmet with a free hand, he twisted his head in an attempt to see the sky above him, where the staggered canopies should have showed the entire team in tight formation. The formation was coming in at just enough of an angle for him to make out three canopies trailing above and behind, with a fourth canopy heading away in the opposite direction, into the settlement.

The MC-5 ram-air canopy used for free-fall jumping operated like a wing. While round chutes offered more weight-carrying capability, they didn't have the maneuverability Encizo was using now to steer his own course.

"What are you up to, Phoenix Two?"

"This mess stinks worse than we thought, Phoenix One," Encizo radioed back. "The Israeli corpses are coming back to life."

"Say again?"

"They're playing mind games with the Palestinians," Encizo explained. "All the dead Israelis piled in the jeep weren't dead at all. Just playing possum. Now they're rising from the grave to join the fight. I'm going to get a better look."

"How close do you think you're going to get without getting shot down?"

"We'll see, Phoenix One. Too late to turn back now."

Indeed it was. McCarter swore at Encizo as he craned his neck for a better look at the rapidly shrinking rectangle of the canopy, then turned his attention to his own landing approach.

"Did you get that, Stony?" he asked into the chin-mounted microphone.

"Got it, Phoenix One," said the calm voice of Barbara Price. "We're keeping an eye on Phoenix Two."

Lot of good that'll be, McCarter thought. If Encizo went down, that was all Stony Base *could* do. Watch.

McCarter leaned into the twin steering lines as the rocky ground rushed underneath his feet, steering himself with a lean on the guide wires into a swooping, sudden stall at an altitude of under three feet. Then he plopped to the earth, running out the momentum, twisting hard to grab the lines and wad the ram-air into a ball. It took him precious seconds to remove himself from the quick releases and redundant buckles on the canopy harness. He cast the ball of material away like a used burger wrapper. The canopies were unmarked. No one would trace them back to the Farm.

"I'm down, Stony Base," he reported, shrugging off his second pack as the other three Phoenix Force warriors came in for running landings, one after another, within a few paces of his position.

"Rafe is right, Phoenix One," Price stated. "We're watching the situation at maximum resolution. Most or all of the bodies on that jeep are back on their feet and appear to be joining the fighting."

"We counted fourteen casualties going into that jeep," McCarter said, as if in protest.

"Not anymore. The jeep is empty."

"We thought those guys were getting their butts whupped," T. J. Hawkins said angrily as he methodically but hurriedly prepped himself from his own pack. "They were trying to psych us out."

"Not us. The Palestinians," growled Gary Manning, who to all appearances was taking his sweet time arming himself for battle. But he somehow finished the task a few seconds before Hawkins and stood ready. Calvin James was prepped before either of them.

McCarter scanned the three of them. It was an unsettling feeling to be the leader of a team that was short a man.

They set off in a trot, up a low, rocky rise and down again in the direction of Shaalvim Settlement.

On cars and on foot, civilians were emerging fearfully, running while they had the chance. Some of the cars raced along the highway with horns blaring, and others were starting and stopping to load up on those who were on foot. The sounds of staccato automatic rifle fire echoed from over the rooftops. When the quartet of commandos appeared, a general panic erupted, women screaming and stampeding off the highway and a slim knot of men gathering to defend their families. Unarmed men. The Phoenix Force warriors didn't have the time to ease their fears and had been urged to keep their identities secret as possible. They marched past the knots of civilians wordlessly.

The stream of refugees slowed to a trickle by the time they reached the outskirts of the neighborhood and began a swift, careful march into the battle.

"Stony Base here. The plot thickens," Price reported.

"Explain," McCarter said.

"The army in the jeeps have removed their Star of David emblems," she said. "They were there and now they're gone."

"Do they know they're being watched from above?"

"Unknown. I assume it was the Palestinians they wanted to fool."

"You saying they might not even be Israelis?" McCarter asked.

"Who knows what these jokers are up to?" Price said.

"They know we're here yet, Stony Base?"

"They don't act like it. Take that for what it's worth."

"Understood."

"Phoenix Two here," said the voice of Encizo, just as McCarter was about to ask for a status report from him. "You got my position, Stony Base?"

"Affirmative," Aaron Kurtzman replied.

"Phoenix One here. Tell me, Rafe."

"Phoenix One, I'm on the roof of a four-story apartment building at the rear of the Israelis' staging ground. I've got a bird's-eye view."

"Do they know you're there?"

Tel Aviv, Israel

THE MAN HAD PURCHASED the four-hundred-dollar desk plaque with his first big bonus. What he really liked about it was that, at first glance, it looked like any engraved plaque that might sit on any executive's desk. Wood, with a brass plate screwed in, engraved with his name. But the wood was hand-carved and polished, and the metal plate was actually pebbled gold. Engraved in the metal was his name: Kesher Nir.

The desk itself had been purchased when he got his first *really* big bonus, which came within a month of the market launch of Nir's first independently developed electronic targeting system. The response was huge, orders from all corners of the globe. Every Third World defense department wanted the capability of improving its missile accuracy, and a simple retrofit of the new IsAlliance Techsystems CPU and sensor array accomplished it.

The retrofit Nir developed was so easy it could be accomplished without special skills, and the component went in without extra programming. The results were increased accuracy and better engine burn, which gave it the added advantage of even longer flights.

At a profit of several thousand percent of manufacturing costs, the system netted IsAlliance Techsystems a small fortune, and they knew better than to forget to reward the brain behind it. General Director Mason also knew his new rising star was going to be heavily recruited by every other defense and computer firm in Israel, and beyond.

The bonus wasn't just extravagant—it was outright bribery. A loyalty buy. It worked, but not in the way the president had hoped. Eleven months later, as Nir's next big product hit the market and company profits skyrocketed, Nir calmly and efficiently took over.

It had been humiliating for General Director Mason—a company-wide meeting, Nir accepting his bonus and recognition award, then stopping by the podium to say a few words. Those words were straightforward and without anger. He was taking control of the company in twenty-four hours as the new general director or he was walking away from it forever.

The board flew into a rage, then thought the matter through and acceded. The old general director was out, severanced into decades of good living, and Kesher Nir was the man in charge.

The board put a number of accountants in place to monitor their new thirty-year-old general director. Just because he was a genius at electronics design didn't mean he would manage a corporation. But in fact a corporation generating extremely successful products was hard to manage poorly, and profits failed to drop.

IsAlliance Techsystems was on a hell of a roll, but Kesher Nir was already bored with it all. He had begun to search for other diversions.

A short tone caught his attention, and his eyes locked on a message that popped up on his display, then he stabbed a button on the keyboard to bring up the designated window. His prematurely snow-white hair was dangling in clumped strands on his forehead, itching his skin, and he pushed it away in irritation as he peered at his display.

"You seeing this?"

It was his second in command. The short woman in the doorway looked concerned and irate at the same time.

"Yes."

"Who is it?"

"That I do not know," he said as the five rectangular shapes drifted across the display.

"Somebody is on to us."

"Yes."

"What're we going to do about it?" She was a tight spring.

When Nir looked up he was peeved and it showed in his light blue eyes and tight, small mouth. She was always saying things like that, just for a little drama. Nir hated it. "You know what we're going to do about it. I'll start immediately."

"You going to pull Blinders on them? You know I think it is too early to use it."

"We don't have a choice, Sandra," Nir said calmly as he pulled up the control screen he wanted.

The actual Blinders unit was alongside the road just inside Israel proper, halfway between Ramla and the settlement. That was as close as Nir had been willing to risk putting the unit. It was one of his most valuable pieces.

The truck trailer had been stabilized on six concrete braces poured five feet into the earth to keep it absolutely stable. Accuracy was the main thing with a laser that had to hit a target miles away and smaller than a human head. The unit was already powered up and ready to operate, and at the start-up sequence an electric motor at the front of the trailer engaged to withdraw the thin nylon screen that hid the interior from eyes above.

As the screen withdrew, Nir watched the start-up diagnostics check the unit out and self-align on the U.S. National Reconnaissance Office satellite orbiting over Israel—the only spy sat with a good view of Shaalvim Settlement at the moment.

"You don't even know they are U.S.," Sandra protested.

"Whoever they are, they have U.S. support and access to NRO spy sats. That's how they zeroed in on us this quickly. Somebody is watching our operation and directly or indirectly giving intelligence to those men, whoever they are, wherever they come from."

"I suppose."

Nir activated the Blinder with the touch of a key, and the unit in a parking lot less than eleven miles away from the settlement of Shaalvim came silently to life. Automatically, the satellite began attempting to compensate for the distortion the laser created. When the operating system judged it was up against an unknown optical phenomena, it closed its lens to prevent damage. Only a manual override from the satellite operators would open it again.

An *okay* message told Nir the satellite was out of commission.

"What about radio?" Sandra asked.

"I'm on it."

Nir scanned radio frequencies in Shaalvim and almost immediately identified anomalous chatter on several frequencies that had to be some sort of secure RF comm-link. The encrypting couldn't be broken in real time, according to the application that analyzed it. Since he couldn't listen in, Nir would turn it off.

His four broadband antennaes, openly installed on four Shaalvim apartment buildings, would send a distributed radio signal that turned the radio frequency spectrum for miles around to murk.

"THEY EITHER DON'T KNOW I'm here or they don't care," Encizo replied. He was lying on the gravel roof, feeling the heat of the pebbles against his chest as he trained Fraser-Volpe M-25 binoculars on the courtyard below. The field glasses offered the stabilization freedom of plus-or-minus eight degrees, giving him a solid view of the activity. "Be prepared, my friends. These guys could be bad news. I'm seeing heavily wired headgear. They've got good communications. I'm seeing segmented face gear. Infrared, maybe. LED readouts, maybe proximity detection, who knows."

"Just great. So why don't they know they've got hostiles coming up their rear end?" McCarter demanded.

"More bad news. These guys have some high-end bang sticks. Stony Base, I'm going to feed you an image if I can get one."

"What for?" McCarter asked. "Don't tell me you can't ID a bunch of guns."

"I can't ID this bunch of guns, Phoenix One," Encizo snapped. "They are carrying some sort of a multifunctional battlefield rifle. I'm seeing grenade-launching capabilities built in, and who knows what else they can do. Hold on." Encizo swallowed the "Uh-oh."

"Uh-oh what?" McCarter demanded.

Below, one of the soldiers slid away a panel built into the rear of the now emptied morgue jeep, exposing an interior compartment momentarily, and Encizo thumbed up the digital zoom on his field glasses in a hurry. "Satellite uplink stowed out of sight in the rear of their vehicle," he announced. "They're communicating with home base somewhere."

There was a moment of radio silence, then McCarter spoke again. "Stony Base, how sure are you that these guys aren't Israeli government troops?"

"Who said we're sure at all?" Price replied.

"Who else would be humping in the desert with battle-field cybernetics and weapon designs so new we don't know about them? Is there anybody in the Middle East with hardware capabilities like that except the Israelis?"

"Not as far as we know," Price said. "But there's plenty of money to buy it."

"The Russians?" McCarter demanded. "The Tahitians? Who?"

"I'm telling you we don't know," Price responded, putting an edge on her calm voice. "We're working on it."

Encizo was scanning the courtyard as the conversation played in his ears, looking for anything that might translate into useful intelligence on these faceless players. Eight soldiers remained with the vehicles and adopted a casual attitude awaiting the arrival of Palestinian gunners. Well trained. Battle seasoned. These were the assessments Encizo was making from body language and offhand attention to their weaponry detail. No signs of rank and no more stars or other insignia of national origin. Kind of like the Phoenix Force commandos at that moment. Wouldn't it be a riot, Encizo thought, if this were some other clandestine U.S. team?

Yeah, hysterical.

"How fast are you working on it?" McCarter growled. "Because we'll be on top of them in about thirty seconds."

There was a sound that Encizo was sure indicated Price was taking a breath and about to speak. Then somebody else spoke over the radio, in the background, and it sure the hell wasn't Barbara Price.

"—eyes," he said. "I have no eyes."

Stony Man Farm, Virginia

THE YOUNG MAN'S VOICE was controlled but urgent, and carried so many inferences that Barbara Price took almost three seconds to come up with a response.

"What took you down, Akira?" she asked as she turned to look at the wide-screen LCD monitor wall-mounted in front of the Japanese man's workstation.

"Unknown. Some sort of distortion," responded the young cybernetics wizard. She could see that there was a mass of shapeless fluctuations appearing on the monitor, until it suddenly went black.

"We've got a failure?" Aaron Kurtzman demanded as his powerful hands spun the wheelchair around his desk, just in time to see the screen die.

"Not us, man!" Tokaido said, his voice rising in a tide of excitement as his hands flew over the keyboard fast and furious. Price thought he couldn't possibly be hitting the keys he meant to hit, yet diagnostics protocols were opening on the monitor. He jumped to his feet and leaned in, inches from the monitor. "It's not us, it's not the uplink, it's not the OS. We are still in control of the bird. Dammit, it's the eye itself. They're jamming it!"

"No way," put in Carmen Delahunt, a small, pretty, red-haired woman against a back wall, not daring to tear her eyes off her own workstation.

"Yes way!" Tokaido replied sharply. "They're zapping it with a damned laser or lighting up chromium dust in the atmosphere or something."

Kurtzman stared at the darkness that dominated Tokaido's display and began a rapid-fire dialog, as if with himself. "They'd have to know the sat was there, they'd have to know its trajectory down to the millimeter and they'd have to have a big laser that aimed very well."

"Yeah, *very* well," Tokaido snorted at what he considered to be a tremendous understatement.

"Irrelevant at the moment," Price said sharply. "Akira, I want you running every diagnostic you have. I don't care how right you think you are. If there is any chance of getting those eyes back soon, I want it done."

"Will do." Akira Tokaido wasn't one to argue with Barbara Price.

"Aaron," Price said to Kurtzman, "if that satellite is being blinded by a terrestrial source, we can't stop it at the moment." Her look asked for confirmation of this assumption.

"Correct."

"The other eye?"

"We'll have control in three minutes, twenty-three seconds," reported the redhead from the back.

"Why not sooner?"

"The NRO won't let go."

"Can you make them cooperate?"

"If I ask, they'll say no. Hal's the only one carrying enough weight to make the NRO listen. I've got system access, so maybe I can get control via the back door." Kurtzman's bear arms flicked over the wheels of the chair, and it zipped across the room with the speed of a radio-controlled toy, coming to a halt next at Delahunt's workstation with a tiny squeak and a six-inch black rubber skid mark. The woman surrendered the station to her boss, who began pounding in commands.

"Phoenix One," Price said tensely.

There was a moment of silence on the line. The moment stretched, and then across the room a man stood abruptly. He was a U.S. Navy major, an expert in digital communications, brought in for a stint with Stony Man to help the Farm in its continual electronics upgrading.

His eyes looked hollow.

"No ears," he said in a gloomy voice. "No ears."

CHAPTER SIX

Shaalvim Settlement, West Bank

McCarter realized with a shock that he was on his own. The Farm was off-line. At the moment he couldn't worry about how it had happened. He had bigger problems to contend with. Keeping his men alive and on mission was foremost. If it was the uplink that was down, then maybe he had communications capabilities with his team.

"Phoenix Two, talk to me," he said to the microphone mounted near his chin. "Phoenix Two."

He was talking to himself, and he turned to the others as they closed their ranks to allow for quiet conversation.

"We don't even know what building he's sitting on," Manning said.

McCarter shrugged. "I'm not worried about Rafe, mates. He's safe and sound up in his hidey-hole. We are the ones in trouble without support. Let's stay sharp, shall we?"

"We altering our purpose, Phoenix One?" James asked in an even tone, but the use of the radio designation made it clear James knew the seriousness of the question. It was one thing to send five experienced commandos into a battle in which they enjoyed the benefits of tremendous intelligence support, another to send them in blind. Especially when you started adding up the number of gunners on both sides.

"We aren't altering the plan," McCarter responded levelly. "We need to know who these blokes are and what bug exactly is up their arses. I want intelligence on them. What organization they represent, names of commanders, where they're based, numbers of actives, resources and backing. Everything."

"And maybe we can stop a few civilian murders before they happen," Hawkins added.

Gary Manning said, "A point worth considering—they know we're here. The radio jamming was meant for us."

"Why not the Palestinians?"

"They don't have communications equipment."

"Somebody must have spotted our descent," McCarter said. "They already had equipment in place to do it. Lord knows what else they've got in store for us. These appear to be expensively equipped bad men. Let's stay sharp, keep tight."

ARNOLD FOGELMAN DIDN'T like this kind of fighting, but he was being paid too well to be uncooperative. The package of incentives and benefits his employer built into the pay scale made every stage of the operation a bonus-earning undertaking for every man on the team. Big money. But big risk. The feints at the Palestinians and the subsequent fall-back cross-country to Shaalvim Settlement had been structured to avoid an Israeli response, but once they were in the settlement there would be plenty of screaming civilians with cell phones spreading the word.

An Israel Defense Forces response was inevitable and planned for, but Fogelman didn't have much faith in their ability to force the march southwest cross-country to the rendezvous point. They would have divested themselves of their military gear by then and would be fleeing in an ancient furniture delivery truck. Maybe they'd slip past or get waved through the Israeli army blockade that was also inevitable. Maybe not.

The weather was milder here, but all things considered he would have rather been at home in Arizona.

What he hated most was this sitting around doing nothing.

"Radios are off-line. We gotta switch to the phone system," his second in command reported. Fogelman and his second hadn't adopted military titles. They were simply Fogelman and Snell. It sounded like the name of an accounting firm. They were in reality mercenaries with a hard-earned global reputation for doing professional work.

This wasn't it. Nothing professional about sitting around with your thumb up your butt waiting for the right time to bugger out.

"Come in, Fogelman," he heard as he swapped out his headphone connection from the radio to the cellular system.

"Fogelman here."

"Them Ay-rabs is making a push to the center of town and they're using mostly the three main streets."

"Okay. Don't fire on them unless they start wandering off course."

"Can't I shoot just one or two?"

It was a joke and Fogelman didn't bother to respond. Radziewics knew his orders and wouldn't go against them. Radziewics wasn't anywhere near as stupid as he came across. The shooting was reserved for Snell's trio of sharpshooters, now taking up a position on the apartment building behind the school. They would have clear shots at the Palestinians.

This was the part Fogelman hated most. But he would go through with it. A deal was a deal. And getting full payment was contingent on a successful operation at the school.

He had felt sickened, like a sniper recruit on the way to his first kill, when he personally sent a burst of high-intensity fire at the teachers and students, forcing them back into the school.

As long as he didn't have to actually do any of them himself.

"Snell, your shooters?"

"Ready when you are," Snell replied without pulling away the field glasses that seemed to have been surgically attached to his eye sockets.

"It's not me who has to be ready, it's them Ay-rabs," Fogelman said, imitating Radziewics's pronunciation.

"Here they are."

Fogelman lifted his own glasses and spied the gunners from Khodr moving down into the cross street. This was no army. Just untrained, undisciplined, unkempt villagers. All they had on their side was guts full of motivation and more hardware than they could carry. What mattered was that they would go down in history as the men who started the great Israeli-Palestine war that cut the throat on the Mideast peace effort.

"The show is about to begin," Fogelman announced into the phone. He was sure Kesher Nir was hanging on his every communiqué.

"Cameras are rolling. We're going to make some history!" Nir enthused over the line.

Fogelman felt vaguely ill. Being a soldier had never caused him this kind of discomfort before now. But there was no way this could really be called soldiering. This was manipulation of the idiot masses.

He'd been feeling this way since the outset. Thinking about his paycheck helped at first, but not anymore. But he sure the hell wouldn't back out. "Hold your fire until I give the order," he said with his hand over the microphone.

"They won't fire until given the word." Snell was statue still, his eyes on the Palestinians. They were now braving the open ground and wondering, doubtless, where the runaway Israelis had gotten to.

If they only knew.

Fogelman felt as if he was going to puke, but the section of his brain dedicated to being a trained military strategist told him, as the Palestinians forayed as a group into the open street, that the time had come.

"Open fire," he said, thinking that, if indeed there was a hell, he'd never escape ending up there.

"WHAT ARE THEY standing around for?" Manning growled.

"It's some sort of a trap, but I'll be damned if I know what they're up to," McCarter said. "Any ideas?"

They didn't.

"So if they know we're here, how come they're not watching out for us?" Manning asked. "They've got no watch posted on this side."

"You got me," McCarter retorted.

"It's because they're fucking maniacs," Hawkins explained.

McCarter recognized the indications of a high-strung group of men. He was one of them. "Let's chill, mates. We're not going to do anybody any good by going in all surly."

Hawkins gave him a sidelong look, but never got to respond before the chaos started.

THERE WAS A BURST of white fire and the rear end of the school went up in a flash of flames, the conflagration engulfing the rear half of the building in seconds. Then came the distinctive retort of large-caliber sniper fire. McCarter traced it immediately to its source on a building just forty paces away and hidden from the view of their own hiding place. More shots told him there were two or three gunners up there. They weren't shooting at Phoenix Force.

So whom were they shooting at?

Then he figured it out.

"Holy Christ."

The others looked at him with question marks branded on their faces. No time to explain it. "Cal and Gary, cover us. T.J., you're with me."

Hawkins bolted to catch up with his commander, who led him in what had to be a suicide run into the open. They were exposed to shots from the command center and the snipers. The snipers were McCarter's goal, but what was the hurry? They raced across the scraggly grass of the courtyard and Hawkins got a glimpse of the Palestinians between the buildings, scurrying for cover from the sniper weapons tagging them over the top of the burning school.

The Palestinians realized they were trapped in the avenue and began returning fire frantically.

The teachers and students huddled inside the school were emerging from the front, driven out by the smoke into the middle of battle. The Palestinians assumed they were a human shield and began firing into the building. Within seconds the innocent victims were littering the streets.

The scene disappeared as the burning back end of the school came between them. Hawkins's mind wouldn't fully register what he had seen. It was too savage.

As he and McCarter arrived at the base of the three-story apartment building, the snipers finally took notice. One of them did a double take, and it was almost comical.

But Hawkins suddenly wasn't in a laughing mood.

The M-16 erupted in his hands like a live thing, sweeping across the belt line of the middle sniper as he tried to bring his sniper weapon into play for a hasty close-range shot. With a small movement he drilled another burst into the chest of a second sniper. The weapon paused there, firing a continuous full-auto barrage, rounds eating into the chest cavity long after the man was dead.

He wasn't dead enough as far as Hawkins was concerned.

McCarter's hand latched on to Hawkins's sleeve and pulled him away as shots slapped into the wall from the command center across the courtyard. Hawkins felt the sting of flying concrete chips.

"The third sniper?" he asked as they jogged around the outside perimeter of the courtyard. They were still in full view of the command center, but the gunners staged there were busy keeping their heads down as James and Manning pinned them under steady fire.

"I got him." McCarter said without further comment.

"We gotta stop that," Hawkins said, looking ahead to the fiery battle occurring in the streets.

But they were too late. The slaughter wound down before they arrived, and with the frontal assault gone the Palestinians were retreating the way they had come. Huddled bunches of figures hugged the buildings up and down the street, mostly too shocked to seek cover. Not everyone was dead. But enough of them were.

ENCIZO WATCHED the placement of the snipers without understanding their purpose. It was video cameras that intrigued him. There was a man in a second-story window setting up the camera on a tripod. This wasn't a Shaalvim citizen but one of the Israeli soldiers, in camouflage uniform and helmet. When he closed the window blinds, the room was obscured. There was just a gap in the blinds large enough for the lens.

Encizo assessed the terrain between himself and the cameraman, coming to his decision in a heartbeat. He had to do something, and with radio contact out he was essentially his own boss. They had come in for intelligence and Encizo had a feeling that cameraman-terrorist would have some to sell his life for. Once the decision was made, the Cuban-born commando didn't second-guess it. He took a running start and threw himself off the edge of the building.

The narrow street flashed sixty feet below, but Encizo didn't look. Looking couldn't accomplish anything constructive. He descended to the gravel-covered roof of the next building, a story lower, and went into a wild dance as his feet slipped on the loose gravel. He felt as if he were ice skating for the first time, but the skid helped deplete the force of the impact before he collapsed into a judo tumble. Still, his shoulder was aching by the time he was on his feet again. Across the roof he found a steel fire ladder that took him in a barely controlled plummet to a narrow, unpaved alley. He moved back, around the building. He could only guess what was the least dangerous route and bolted into the street just long enough to cover the distance to the apartment building with the cameraman, sliding through an entry door wedged open on a skull-sized rock.

The door was dirty glass in a steel frame and the daylight lit the vestibule, with two ground-level apartment doors and a set of concrete stairs. Encizo vaulted up the steps, making no noise loud enough to give himself away to the cameraman on the second floor. There was a burst of noise outside. Some sort of explosion, gunfire and shouting. The little Cuban had missed the arrival of the Palestinian mob by seconds, he thought, and then he saw the open door.

There was a young face looking out at him, smeared with dirt, eyes wide. Too young to tell if it was a boy or a girl. The child's hand was on the knob as if he or she had just been going to find out what all the commotion was about outside.

Then the door swung open fast, taking the knob out of the child's hand, and another wide-eyed figure appeared. The child's mother wore a mask of terror and a hiccup caught in her throat when she saw the man in her hall.

Her terror turned to caution. Maybe it was the un-

Palestinian-looking gear, or Encizo's reassuring nod with a finger to his lips. She stifled any further sound except a stuttering breath. She and the child withdrew into their flat and the door shut.

Encizo tried the door to the cameraman's flat, found it locked and forced it open with a quick shoulder thrust, surprised to find himself standing in the doorway unnoticed by the Israeli cameraman. The wall of noise coming from the street below had hidden the rending of the lock. Encizo caught glimpses of the chaos and forced himself to ignore it.

Bent close over the five-inch display on the digital video camera, the cameraman's lightweight body armor was riding well above his belt line. With a swinging jab Encizo buried his fingers into the exposed two inches of abdomen, a perfect shot to the kidneys. The cameraman dropped like a bag of rocks, hitting his head against the hard tile floor.

Damn. Encizo had picked the blow because it was debilitating without rendering the victim unconscious, and the guy went and knocked himself out. Then he realized the cameraman's eyes were still open, even if they were rolling back into his head, and he moaned and grabbed at his stomach. Encizo pulled his hands behind his back, securing them in plastic cuffs.

"I want names and addresses."

The man tried to look over his shoulder at Encizo. "You're American," he grated.

"Who's your boss? What kind of half-assed scheme are you guys trying to perpetrate here?"

There was blood on the tile under the man's mouth. "Nothing half-assed about it, American. This is a very full-assed operation." He chuckled painfully into the puddle of blood, then coughed up more of it.

"Whose operation is it?"

"You'll learn nothing from me."

"I don't have much time to try to convince you, so gentle persuasion is out of the question."

"You'll learn nothing. Do what you will. "

Over the spasms of coughing Encizo heard the buzz of headphones and found them on the windowsill, overlooking the conflagration and terror below. It was a cellular phone set. Whatever was jamming Phoenix Force's radios was apparently designed not affect the phones. He pressed one of the earpieces to his ear.

"Camera One, are you getting this? Report, please!"

Encizo glanced into the LCD display, which made the burning and the bodies look fake. Why would they be taping this horror? He contained the urge to tell the voice on the other end to go fuck himself, slipping the phone into a pocket of his shirt without turning it off. Maybe, just maybe, there would be something traceable Stony Man could jimmy out of the phone's electronics.

"Okay, buddy, time to talk," Encizo said, bending over the cameraman. "Why the video equipment?"

"We're proud of our work."

"I bet you are."

"We want the world to see what has happened here today," the man said, the corners of his mouth twitching into a sick smile. "Innocent Jewish women and children murdered by Palestinians. Gunned down in cold blood."

"That's not what happened here."

"That is what the world will see, American."

Encizo's anger was lost in his confusion. "But why? To what purpose?"

"War." The cameraman grinned weakly and lowered his face into the expanding puddle of blood. "We have the means to start and to win the war that will make the holy land ours again. We will purge God's land of the pestilence that is the Arab. When the people witness the latest and most hideous Palestinian atrocity, they will know peace is a pipe dream. They will flock to join *our* army, the army that will fight the Arab until the Arab is a memory in our land.''

Encizo shook his head stoically and leaned close as the cameraman closed his eyes, shuddering. "Listen to me, you sick piece of human trash, your great plan didn't count on me showing up. There's no way I'm gonna let your video tell your lies for you. I'll destroy it before that happens.''

The cameraman opened his eyes and made a tremendous effort to twist his body so he could look back—he wasn't looking at Encizo but past him, out the window. The cameraman grinned.

"Too late," he croaked.

Encizo felt the passage of a shadow and heard the curious buzzing at that instant. As he spun at the window, he was triggering the Heckler & Koch MP-5 submachine gun. The camera crashed to the floor and the window glass shattered, the blinds ripping open just in time for the Cuban commando to witness the thing that was outside.

It had a circular gray steel hull, a foot high and almost six feet across, with a flat top from which protruded a metal motor cowling. On top of the hull was a tripod of tubular steel mounts, sporting wiring, electronics and lenses. As the device hovered twenty feet from the ground it filled the room with the sound of the whirring blades inside the hull, and two of its lenses were articulating on servo motor mounts to stare into the second-story window at Rafael Encizo.

The Phoenix Force warrior didn't stop to think about it. He laid on the trigger and sent a hail of 9 mm rounds crashing into the flying thing. It responded with a whir of the hidden fan, but its response wasn't quick enough. A section of tubing and wiring flew apart and dangled uselessly as the device rose out of sight. Encizo pushed his head out the window just in time to see it hugging the building face before disappearing over the roof.

Gunshots from nearby forced him to withdraw in a hurry, but not before he spied two more of the hovering gray units suspended over the street in either direction.

They rocked and swayed gently in place, their unfeeling lenses observing with cold dispassion as down below the humans killed. And died.

CHAPTER SEVEN

"Did you see that thing?" James demanded as he fell against the cinder-block wall that was serving as their cover in their standoff with the nest of terrorists across the courtyard.

"I didn't get a look at it," Manning said. "Hold on."

The big Canadian stepped into the open and unleashed a half magazine of full-auto rounds that sent the gunners behind the wall of jeeps ducking for cover. The vehicles were battered and holed, tires deflated and windshields shattered, but so far they had protected their owners. Manning spotted what James had seen.

It was a car without space for passengers. The top was flat. It rode on four, big-tread mud tires. The one crucial difference from the Khodr robots was some sort of erect barrel protruding from the front end.

"What do you think?" James asked.

"Same robotic mobile platform we saw on the sat pics," Manning answered. "Hard to tell more than that. They must be buying them in six-packs."

"Heavily armored and definitely armed—I think I saw a grenade launcher stuck in the front end," James added. "A launcher with an adjustable base. "

"They knew the Palestinians wouldn't get close enough this time to let themselves get blown up by one of them,"

Manning commented. "They had to equip it for longer-distance killing."

As if in answer, they heard the crack of an explosion and a fresh eruption of distant gunfire. They both heard the voice of Rafael Encizo as the radio static abruptly died in their earpieces.

"Anybody out there?"

"Phoenix Three here," Manning responded.

"Shit!"

Even as Encizo spouted profanity, their ears were blasted with a roar of sound. Yanking away the headphones in a hurry, they heard the explosion from the far side of the building.

"Phoenix Two, speak to me." It was McCarter.

"Phoenix Two here. I got some sort of RC car here with a really big popgun on one end. It wants to play and I don't want to. I shot it and that just made it look at me funny."

"What's your location?" McCarter demanded.

"Across the main north-south street," Encizo replied. "I was in a second-story apartment. The Israelis spotted me and sent their toy after me. I gotta draw that thing away from the building, Phoenix One. There's civilians inside."

"Understood," McCarter said. "The street in front of you is clear at the moment, Rafe. Get there and head north, then let the thing see you when I tell you to. We'll be ready to put a stop to it."

ENCIZO HAD MUSCLED his way through the locked door of a rear apartment and crossed to a window, which he dragged open. He dangled from the ledge and dropped onto packed earth as hard as concrete, and as he rolled through the landing he could feel a throb of pain shoot into his legs. After what he'd been through it was funny that it had been the most painful fall of the day. Kind of funny, anyway. Jogging along the rear of the tenement he cut down an alley and glanced into the street, finding the flat-topped robot vehicle squatting under the window where he had been standing.

The first round had impacted the wall of the tenement just before radio contact was reestablished, and it had done no more than knock him off his feet. The thing could only fire at him from a sharp angle. A few more rounds, and the front wall would be wide open for rounds to insert themselves.

It wasted no time lobbing another 40 mm grenade at the flat. Whoever was controlling the robot had to know one of his own men was in that apartment, but it didn't seem to matter.

Encizo bolted from his cover as a shower of debris and dust fell into the street, wondering idly if robots had peripheral vision.

Dead lay everywhere. The gunfire and the burning he had glimpsed moments ago was now reduced to a field of corpses and smoking ruins. The reality hit him as he jogged through the macabre obstacle course: they were killed by their own people, set up to die as a tool for inspiring war, so more people could die. A vicious acceleration of butchery.

"Phoenix Two here," he said into the chin-mounted microphone. "I'm on my way."

"We see you, Rafe," said the voice of the Phoenix Force leader. "Keep coming, mate. That thing is still staring at the wall. We're in an alley forty feet up and on your right."

Encizo spotted Hawkins peering around the corner. After working with somebody close enough for long enough, you learned to recognize them even under headgear and battle cosmetics. You could even see it when their expressions went from a state of taut expectancy to sudden alarm, and when he saw it Encizo knew the robot had spotted him.

The little Cuban veered to the opposite side of the street and listened to the whining of the thing's engines as it powered after him, servo motors rotating the grenade launcher.

When he heard the servo motors stop, he veered in the other direction, simultaneous to the thump of the firing grenade. If he'd been standing still, his legs would have been blown out from under him.

He dived into the alley at the feet of Hawkins and McCarter. As he was getting to his feet, he was wondering how fast the robot could go. Pretty slow if it tried to maneuver among the bodies. He looked out quickly, and with stomach-churning realization saw that it was going over rather than around.

He had seconds to spare.

"It doesn't know you're here," he explained to McCarter in a rush. "I keep running, it comes after me and you tuck something up its ass."

"It'll tag you before it gets to us," McCarter replied.

"All I have to do is keep moving," Encizo said. "It won't fire without being able to lock on to a target."

"You know this based on your long-term experience with this technology?" McCarter demanded.

"The longest thirty seconds of my life," the Cuban said with a grin, then he bolted into the open again, jogging in a zigzag. He could hear the servo motor humming constantly as it tried to get a target lock, listened for the moment when he judged it was going by McCarter and Hawkins. When he heard the muffled twin bursts of explosives, he knew it wasn't the robot's grenade launcher and risked a glance back.

The thing was dead in the street, its wheels amputated, and it looked like some huge bull that had died without falling on its side. While smoke was seeping from its underside and sparks flew out of a popped seam in the metal, the top and turret were unscathed. Encizo was leery that the launcher might still be operational; maybe it was only stunned.

McCarter and Hawkins darted around the smoking machinery, and Encizo joined them against the cover of the nearest doorway.

"I knew it had a soft underbelly," Hawkins said morosely.

"Think it'll blow like the ones in Khodr?" Encizo asked.

The sound of the blast was magnified by the close-set buildings that walled in the street. Protected, they witnessed a blizzard of debris fill the street like a sudden storm.

"Yeah," Hawkins said dryly. "It'll probably blow."

"PHOENIX THREE HERE," Manning radioed. "Our boys are pulling out."

"Which ones?" McCarter asked. He, Encizo and Hawkins were backtracking through a city that looked postapocalyptic. The people who called this settlement home were in hiding or dead. There were no soldiers in sight.

"All of them," Manning answered over the radio. "The Israelis funneled off to the south end of the city. Must have transport staged there. They tried to bring their dead with them, but they didn't have time to gather them all. Guess they took more casualties than they were counting on."

"What about the Palestinians?" McCarter asked.

"We heard them whooping and shooting to the north and then saw a bunch of them marching away in the opposite direction of the Israelis. Guess they got tired of each other. Crap!"

The trio heard heavy thumps and broke into a run as McCarter shouted for Manning to come back on the line. As the big courtyard swung into view again, there were fresh fires breaking out in the stone nest that had served as the Israeli command center, as well as in pockmarks around the yard.

"These guys are cold," Manning said on the radio as he and James came into view a hundred yards ahead, greeting them with a wave. "They just blew their own dead via remote control."

"Guess they don't want them IDed, Phoenix Three," McCarter said as he and his two companions gathered around the nearest smoldering mass. Indeed, it had been a body. Now it was a flaming mass of gore. The burning smell was thick.

"Who are these guys?" Hawkins said, choking back the bile.

Encizo strolled a few paces until he could see again, in the distance, the face of the building in which he had taken out the man with the video camera. There was a hole from the robot's grenades, and a fresh tongue of flame was licking the bricks, sputtering out quickly. The cameraman had been destroyed, as well.

"They're really covering their trail," he said.

"Wouldn't you?" McCarter said.

They were all surprised when the voice of Barbara Price materialized in their headsets. "You with me, Phoenix?"

"Stony Base, nice of you to join us," McCarter said.

"No time for explanations. You need to extricate yourselves now. The Israeli army is ETA 4:30 minutes." She read off coordinates for a helicopter pickup several miles deeper into occupied territory.

"Aren't the Israelis going to have eyes all over the West Bank?" McCarter demanded, irritation in his voice. He didn't like being abandoned by his support in the middle of a hostile situation.

"Not immediately. Air support is still ten minutes away. Ground troops are going to take it slow. They believe they have an entire Palestinian army to contend with. We saw the Palestinians head out, but we aren't going to tell them that."

McCarter was already leading his team through the settlement. They couldn't count the bodies they saw, and while there were no living humans to be seen, the presence of the survivors, terrified and hiding, was tangible, like acrid smoke.

"Not much left here but fear," Hawkins said as they put Shaalvim Settlement behind them.

CHAPTER EIGHT

Tel Aviv, Israel

"What's happening?" Sandra Honig demanded, closing the office door behind her. Her brow was pulled low in worry, but her eyes were glimmering.

"History is happening," Kesher Nir said with a grimace, trying to stay calm, trying to keep from jumping to his feet and running around the room laughing. On all his television feeds the reports from Israel dominated the news, the anchors trying to stretch the few facts they had about the developing situation in the Middle East into an ongoing report. CNN's anchor wore his best mask of stern tragedy as he related the events of the afternoon.

"The attack came out of the middle of nowhere late in the Israeli morning, with an army of at least one hundred Palestinian soldiers descending on the Jewish West Bank settlement of Shaalvim firing automatic weapons," the anchor was saying. "The few Israeli police patrolling the settlement were driven off immediately when the attack started. By the time the Israeli military responded, the battle was over and the settlement—" he paused, just for a fraction of a second, but the effect was of somber and dramatic "—was decimated."

"Nice," Nir said as Honig stepped behind his chair, resting her hands on his shoulders, and he leaned his head back into the cushion between her heavy breasts, flipping to another station with a tap of a key. This time it was BBC.

"This should be good," Nir enthused.

It was good. Nobody could emphasize the drama of breaking news like British anchors, and this guy was putting his heart into it.

"This started out as a peaceful morning in the quiet residential West Bank settlement of Shaalvim. Before noontime it would transform into a day of unutterable horror for the families that call this place home."

"The file footage would have looked good there," Honig said. It was an accusation, but even as she made it she was standing behind his chair, pressing her soft front into the back of his head and neck.

"No," Nir said. "They'll have it soon enough."

The BBC anchor continued.

"The attack came without warning just about 11:00 a.m. local time. A band of Palestinian soldiers marched into the streets of Shaalvim and began shooting women and children indiscriminately. There are reports of explosives being used to burn out families in hiding. The death toll is unknown at this hour as Israeli military continue their search for bodies."

"Talk about why it happened, you stupid twit," Nir said, stabbing at the keyboard to switch to another global news feed.

A stern, pinched young anchorman declared,

"The attacks are almost certainly aimed at derailing peace talks scheduled to start just hours from now at Camp David in the United States. The Camp David

Economics and Peace Summit is scheduled to start just hours from now in the United States, where the American President will propose a peace plan based on forging sweeping economic ties between Israel, the Palestinians and other Arab nations. Insiders have described the plan as complicated and expensive to implement, but the plan is generating widespread optimism. With promised financial assistance from the United States, a new Middle East economic infrastructure would forge financial ties to reinforce the accompanying peace initiatives. Plan supporters are much less optimistic tonight.''

"Oh, yes," Nir said, nodding, eyes wide and glittering. "Very well said, my friend. He certainly brings the point home."

There was a quick electronic purr to announce an intercom transmission, and then a voice said quickly, "The Syrians are turning back."

"Show me!" Nir commanded.

The newscaster winked off and was replaced by a foggy, low-contrast image on the monitor, an overhead shot of a commercial jet hovering high over a daylit ocean. The image was just large enough and at just steep enough an angle to see the colors of the Syrian flag painted on the tail of the aircraft. The time display on the corner of the screen told Nir he was watching an image just fifty-five seconds old.

The jet leaned into a slow bank that took her in a miles-wide U-turn. Kesher Nir's jet was hovering miles above and behind the Syrians, taking digital video of the U-turn using a computer-targeted and steadied video system—what in the 1980s had been classified military spy satellite technology.

"It's graceful. It's beautiful," Nir said, enraptured by the image as he rewound it and replayed it on the hard drive recording all his media feeds.

"And symbolic," Honig said.

He turned and looked into her eyes. "Mostly symbolic," he agreed. Then he touched the intercom again and said, "Get that video clip to all the networks. I want to be seeing it live in five minutes."

"You got it," said the operator. It took the operator seconds to isolate the footage as a digital file, type in a one-sentence caption for the benefit of the networks and jettison the file into cyberspace.

Producers at every global and many national news networks knew the name attached to the video file when it arrived seconds later. They trusted that source. He never failed them. He didn't fail them now. The shot of the Syrian aircraft turning in midflight to return home was as eloquent an image as any of them could have asked for.

Nir didn't have to wait five minutes. He didn't even have to wait three.

On the screen was the face of the President of the United States, standing at the podium at a hastily assembled news conference.

"…asking the people of the Middle East, Muslim and Jew alike, to look past the atrocity of today and toward a future of peace. That peace will come only when all the peoples of the Middle East have agreed to work together to achieve mutual prosperity, and by seeing beyond the tragedy perpetrated today by extremist factions…."

At that moment the news network split the screen in two, bringing down the volume on the President in order to display for the world the image of the Syrian aircraft making its stratospheric U-turn.

It was up to the news anchor to point out the obvious. "And even as the American President makes a heartfelt appeal to those scheduled to be around the table tomorrow at Camp David, it appears that the Syrian representative is pulling out. Here you can see footage just a few minutes old of the aircraft that was transporting the Syrian delegation to the summit. But as you can see, it is turning around in midflight, somewhere over the Atlantic Ocean. We can only assume the delegation is heading back to Syria.''

Kesher Nir let out a long, deeply satisfied breath. ''They played it right on top of the President,'' he said.

''Good timing,'' Honig said.

''I couldn't have planned it better.''

''God is smiling on you.''

Nir grinned as he flipped the channels and found other stations interrupting the President with the stunning image of the Syrian jet turning around in midflight. God, he was thinking, had nothing to do with his successes here today.

''We're supposed to be in a technical analysis meeting,'' Honig reminded him gently.

Nir glanced at the small monitor time display. It was two minutes before the hour, and reluctantly he pulled himself away from the media circus he had orchestrated.

Stony Man Farm, Virginia

THE ROOM WAS FULL. Rarely were Stony Man Farm technical meetings lumped in with field strategy conferences, but this time the man in charge, Hal Brognola, had requested they be combined.

He wanted to know why the most technically advanced paramilitary operation on the planet had dropped the ball like a bunch of amateurs.

He took attendance at a glance as he strode into the War Room. The cybernetics staff, huddled together, was going over various technical documents, doing last-minute data analysis. Their head man was Aaron Kurtzman. There was also a tall black man with graying temples and the buttoned-down demeanor of an Ivy League college professor—the kind of guy you expected to find in his off-hours in a leather easy chair at the fireplace, reading Coleridge or Dante. Huntington "Hunt" Wethers had been a college professor, in fact, but his expertise was in computer systems, not literature. With Wethers was a vivacious, attractive redheaded woman, Carmen Delahunt, and hacker genius Akira Tokaido.

At the opposite end of the table was Barbara Price, in a denim shirt with decorative Western-style stitching, beautiful even with the grim look on her face. On one side of her was Yakov Katzenelenbogen, Stony Man's tactical adviser. After decades in the field, including years as leader of Phoenix Force, Katz had retired to his current role, for which his field experience made him eminently qualified. Sitting on the other side of Price was John "Cowboy" Kissinger, Stony Man's weapon smith, a man who could dismantle and rebuild almost any weapon system that could be placed in front of him.

On one side of the table sat the three members of Able Team. Carl "Ironman" Lyons lead the trio, a soldier so capable that some very tough people called him scary. Lyons wasn't a lighthearted human being. Some said he was morbid and moody, but they didn't say it to his face.

Rosario Blancanales was called "the Politician" for his ability to deal with, and manipulate, his fellow human beings. Brognola had always thought Pol would make a good senator or used-car salesman if he wasn't so notoriously ethical.

Hermann Schwarz was known as "Gadgets" for his technological brilliance. He would have excelled working for either Kissinger or for Kurtzman, but he wasn't exactly looking for that kind of sedate career.

Aside from the senior staff, several other individuals were

present, all of whom would have a bearing on the discussion.

"Striker?" Brognola asked as he lowered himself heavily into his chair.

Price shrugged.

There would have been a time when Hal Brognola would be mad as hell to learn that one of his operatives was out of touch. He still would be if it were anyone but Mack Bolan. Bolan, the man called the Executioner, once a vigilante with a taste for Mafia blood, had been hunted by Brognola. Then an uneasy alliance had formed. After working under the big Fed, Bolan chafed at the restrictions even as loose as those of Stony Man Farm, which he had helped establish. These days he was highly independent, returning to the fold only under his own terms. He might disappear for days and weeks at a time, location and status unknown—but when a request for assistance came from the Farm, he was unlikely to refuse.

The request couldn't exactly be made if they didn't even know where on the planet Bolan was, Brognola thought. "I guess we'll just have to manage without him," he said. He looked from Price to Kurtzman, and his gaze landed lastly on the communications officer, who fidgeted in his seat. "Well? What the hell happened in Israel?"

"Technology happened, Hal," Kurtzman replied, coming at once to the comm officer's rescue. "We got outclassed."

"That's not supposed to happen," Brognola said. "You know what kind of funds we channel into this place to make sure it doesn't?"

"Sometimes it is going to, regardless," Kurtzman said levelly, refusing to meet Brognola's anger with anger. "Unless you want to quadruple our research staff and put a few hundred ferrets into the field in all the global high-tech centers, we can and will fall behind the state-of-the-art. Not often. Not for long. But sometimes."

"All right," the big Fed growled as he popped an antacid. "So how'd we get out outclassed?"

Kurtzman touched a small device on the table in front of him, and a wall monitor came to life.

"Is this some kind of joke?" Brognola demanded, his voice rising to just under a roar.

"Not at all," Kurtzman answered easily.

"It's a flying saucer!" the big Fed said.

"It's a Sikorsky. A Cypher," Gadgets Schwarz informed him.

"You're right—at least we think so," Kurtzman agreed, not at all surprised that Schwarz recognized the equipment on the screen. "At the very least it's probably based on the Sikorsky design."

"Brief me on it," Brognola demanded.

"The Cypher was designed to be one of the first operational UAVs—Unmanned Aerial Vehicles," Schwarz explained. "It's just over two yards wide, so a lot of lift isn't needed, and the rotor system's lift is augmented by the ducting. The rotors are designed around a coaxial advancing blade concept, which gives them extra lift. With a fifty-horsepower motor, that thing will cruise at more than eighty knots. The prototypes I saw could exceed eight thousand feet and fly for three hours."

"This is military equipment?" Brognola asked.

"Not exclusively," Kurtzman said. "The military is investigating ways of using them for ground and marine surveillance, but there are potential civilian applications, too, such as search and rescue. Think what the DEA could do with them. Or forestry staff watching for fires in remote locations. They can also be used by civilian or military for relaying communications."

"Or blocking them," said the Navy communications officer.

"You telling me ET blocked our satellite feed?" Brognola asked.

"That's what we think," Kurtzman said. "We'll never know for sure, because we didn't have the kind of pattern-tracing equipment on the scene that would have pinpointed the radio block, but the simple fact that our aircraft continued to communicate with us without hindrance and the ground-based forces couldn't indicates there was interference staged between the satellite uplink on the aircraft."

"Our system doesn't take into account that possibility?" Brognola asked. "Battlefield communications jamming has been around forever."

"Not like this," Kurtzman said coolly.

"We're not equipped to go into a battlefield, Hal," Price said. "That's not what we're about. We don't fight wars. But a war is what we got ourselves into. Our opposition on that battlefield was expecting the Israeli army and was prepared to keep them at bay until they achieved their goals. We had only five people on the ground, no vehicles, and no air support to speak of. Phoenix performed admirably under the circumstances. But the circumstances sucked."

Price's gaze rested on Brognola, an expanse of table and a lot of silent people caught between them. Brognola had the distinct impression that, if he dared contradict her assessment of her team's performance, he'd go home a eunuch.

Brognola leaned back in his chair and put an antacid tablet and the unlit stub of a cigar into his mouth, nodding for the meeting to proceed. The tension dispersed like clearing smoke.

"What do you suggest we do to make our field signal more secure to this type of jamming?" Kurtzman asked the comm officer. "Can we get past this jamming electronically?"

"Sure, if we knew what it was precisely," the Navy man

answered. "And I could come up with various solutions that would probably work. But we would not know for sure until we're in the situation."

"An inconvenient time to realize we didn't get it right," Kurtzman said.

"There are better temporary solutions," the comm man said. "Simply landing a transceiver nearby to bypass the jamming would be a good answer. We make sure we have line-of-sight clearance to a portable local transceiver set up by our team. That sets up an umbrella of radio coverage underneath their UAV, assuming it's the source of the jamming signal. Phoenix Force has the equipment it needs. I'll have Mr. Hawkins rig them up for airdrops as needed."

"You expecting Phoenix to be in this kind of situation again before this is over?" Brognola asked.

"We don't know what to expect," Price said. "Can you lend a hand in that department?"

"I can't give you a thing," Brognola admitted with a long sigh, as if blowing out a lungful of smoke from the unlit cigar. "The President wants us to pull out all the stops."

"I don't have to remind you I'm uncomfortable doing the President's dirty little favors."

"You and me both, but this time his dirty little favor is directly tied to national security. Global security, in fact. I think you can see it's more than executive butt-covering now."

"What kind of official authorization do we have for acting inside Israel?"

"There are a very few top Israeli officials who know we're there. They approve of our presence, unofficially. But we're not going to get an assist from them if the going gets tough."

"That's not good. We can't even get a liaison with their investigative teams," Price complained.

"Why not?" Brognola asked.

"Nobody will risk it," said Yakov Katzenelenbogen. "Every arm of Israeli military and intelligence is on some sort of ultra-high-alert status. They'll be watching for trouble and not sure how to react to it when it shows up. If Phoenix gets caught trying to bring down—whoever it is—responsible for this mess, and any Israeli insider gets linked to us, there's a chance they can kiss their career goodbye."

"There's not entrenched support for these terrorists already?" Brognola asked.

"No. Not yet," Katzenelenbogen said. "The bottom line is, we can get a plane in and we can arrange to be left alone so long as we don't attract attention to ourselves. That's all the help we're getting."

Price was tapping her pen on the table. "All right, we need to get a better line on whoever is behind this, and that means we have to track down the source of the technology used in the attacks. That's not as easy as it sounds."

"Why not?" Hermann Schwarz asked. "They used some unique stuff. That technology doesn't develop in a vacuum."

"Assuming the user can be linked to the developer," Kurtzman replied. "There are many possibilities in Israel."

Price turned to Able Team. "What do you think about traveling to Israel, Pol?"

Rosario Blancanales raised his eyebrows. "Sure you have the right man for the job?"

"You look like somebody who could originate around the Mediterranean," Price said. "I can't afford to peel Rafe off Phoenix. I want them at full strength just in case they run into a bad situation."

"I'll need some help to pass as a local."

"I'll help you out there," Katzenelenbogen said with a grin. Katz was an Israeli himself, and had served as an Israeli intelligence chief during the Arab-Israeli wars, retiring as a colonel prior to joining Mack Bolan's Phoenix Force in its early days.

"You think you can turn that Latino into an Israeli?" Schwarz asked.

"I'm a quick study," Blancanales retorted.

"Good. We'll have you ready to insert under cover. Maybe you'll shake loose some meaningful intelligence," Price said, then added almost apologetically, "Frankly, I've got nothing else for Able to do at the moment."

"Then let us go with him as backup," Carl Lyons said without hesitation. "Even if he's undercover, Rosario will have to push hard to get the answers he needs as quick as we need them. He'll be at risk. He should have support."

"I'd prefer to have you here with us," Price said. "Even if I don't have anything for Able to do here now, that could change in an instant. In fact, we expect it to change. There's got to be a U.S. end to the organization behind all this."

"Why 'got to be'?" Lyons asked.

"Because much of the technology that we saw used in the Khodr-Shaalvim campaign was developed in the U.S.," Kurtzman stated. "The urban mobility platforms, the Sikorsky UAV. Rafe thinks he may even have seen the Israelis toting unusual guns that could be hybridized versions of the DoD OICW prototype. All these technologies have their beginning in the U.S. Once we have better leads, we'll need to send you out after them."

"Doesn't sound promising," Lyons retorted bluntly. "Just because the technology was sourced here doesn't mean there's much of a tie to this end. I don't like sending Rosario undercover without backup."

"Neither do I. But he can fend for himself," Price said decisively.

She turned to her tactical adviser. "Is there a chance we can get any kind of help from your contacts in Israeli intelligence circles, Katz?"

"I've been in on the phone with a few old friends," Katz said. "There's talk flying around over there, but I couldn't glean even a scrap of useful new intelligence. I'm convinced Mossad doesn't know any more than we do at the moment."

"What about Aman?" Price asked.

"If Israeli military intelligence knows more than Mossad, they're not letting on," Katz said.

"Could they be playing it close to the chest, planning to hog the credit for solving this?" Brognola asked. He, better than any of them, knew the realities of politics between departments of the same government that saw themselves as being in competition with one another for funding or simply prestige.

"Of course," Katz said.

"Can you put out feelers?" the big Fed suggested.

"I can, but I can't make promises."

"Understood."

"Tell me this," Brognola said, taking the conversation suddenly in a new direction and facing Kurtzman and his cybernetics team. "There were aircraft- and ground-based robotics on the field in Khodr and Shaalvim Settlement, operating without humans present. So they were remotely controlled or did they operate automatically? Either way they were transmitting back to home base. Why couldn't we trace those signals?"

"If we had equipment on the scene to make the trace, sure, we probably could have done it," Kurtzman said. "If their RF sending was as sophisticated as the rest of their systems, their signals could have been untraceable or simply too scrambled to pinpoint."

"Did the sat images pick up anything?"

"We were able to track the mercenaries and their surviving equipment moving away from Shaalvim to their pickup point," Wethers stated as he made adjustments to the controls at his seat, and the monitor took on the pixilated images of satellite photographs blown up to maximum size. Gray-and-white background of the scrubland was sprinkled with the dark dots of men and the dark squares of vehicles. The satellite images advanced at a frame-per-second rate, which greatly sped up the army's jittery forced march. Then more shapes blurred into the frame and coalesced into transport helicopters. The jeeps drove up cargo ramps and the soldier dots merged with the aircraft blur, then the pair of choppers sped out of the scene in just a few frames, vanishing.

"That's as far as we got."

"Why didn't we follow them?" Brognola asked.

"We tried," Kurtzman said with a frown, unable to disguise his dissatisfaction. "They bumped us off the sat."

"Who's 'they'?" Brognola asked. Not that it mattered now.

"NRO," Kurtzman said. "It was a National Reconnaissance Office satellite, but of course who knows what agency was specifically assigned to that time on the sat. I couldn't get control of the thing again, regardless."

"Could you have tracked them closer than the NRO?" Brognola asked.

"I could have followed them to their front door," Kurtzman said. "I could have given you the address on their mailbox and the number of pets in the backyard." He was clearly not bragging, simply pointing out a failed opportunity.

"You're telling me we have nothing," Brognola summed up after a pause, rubbing his forehead heavily. "Nothing to go on. Not a scrap of a lead to put Phoenix on."

"Well," Price said with a slight lift in her voice, "that's not exactly true."

Brognola's hand went back to the table, and he looked up curiously. "Tell me."

Kurtzman nodded to Wethers, who touched a few keys

on a nearby keyboard and brought another satellite image onto the screen. The grain was more apparent, and only when Wethers began cycling the image through a faster cycle of animation could Brognola make out movement among the pixels. He squinted. He frowned. He still couldn't figure out what he was looking at.

"The Palestinians," Kurtzman answered the question without being asked. "What you're seeing is the survivors making an escape into the West Bank. We count sixteen men."

"When?" Brognola demanded.

"Forty-three minutes after Phoenix and the Israeli terrorists pulled out of Shaalvim. Watch."

There were vehicles racing into the scene suddenly, and Brognola watched the tiny, light-gray dots move faster, meandering over the darker gray of the landscape. Then one of the dots halted, elongating slightly, as pinpoints of gun flashes appeared from the vehicles. The two vehicles looped and twisted as they separated the collection of Palestinians, herding them one at a time away from the protection of their fellows. Then would come the flashes of light.

"Is that what I think it is? A roundup and slaughter?"

"Yes, they're getting systematically murdered," Kurtzman stated. "These small SUVs or jeeps are breaking the group apart, running then down and shooting them."

Another tiny dot became elongated. Then another. Brognola felt sick. "There's some cold sons of bitches behind this business."

"They get ten of them before it's over," Kurtzman said, but thankfully, he gave Wethers a nod and the professor keyed off the video so they wouldn't have to watch all of it. "There was a standoff that lasted ten minutes, then the jeeps left in a big hurry and the Palestinians fled to a small village. Not long before Israeli military of some kind started showing up."

"Were the Palestinians taken into custody?"

"No," Kurtzman said. "They searched the village but didn't come away with prisoners. The villagers kept them hidden."

Brognola frowned. "Aaron, what satellite took this video?"

Out of the corner of his eye, Brognola saw Akira Tokaido break into a grin. Kurtzman looked at his fingers on the tabletop. "We managed to find our way inside a satellite system that doesn't necessarily belong to us."

Brognola considered that for a moment, then demanded in disbelief, "You hacked an Israeli spy sat?"

"It will motivate them to increase their security," Kurtzman said in a reasonable tone, sounding perfectly justified.

"Tell me they can't trace the hack," the big Fed pleaded.

"No way," Tokaido interjected. "We covered our tracks."

"You one hundred percent sure?"

Tokaido and Kurtzman exchanged glances. "Ninety-nine percent," Tokaido said.

"Ninety-eight," Kurtzman corrected.

Hal Brognola thumbed a few more antacid tablets into his palm and chomped down on them.

Israel

THE MEETING ROOM WAS on the fifteenth floor and commanded one of the most impressive views of the city of Tel Aviv that exorbitant lease rates could buy, but the window glass had been dimmed electrically to allow for viewing video of the first-phase operation. The flat screen that rose out of one end of the table showed an aerial video image of the Israeli West Bank settlement of Shaalvim. The image was digitally stabilized as it looked on the robotic Outdoor Mobility Platform crawling in the street below. There was a flash of movement, just a passing shadow, seconds before the thump that brought the OMP to a halt.

"We've studied the image and the system response to the assault. We've concluded that the commandos put a pair of high-explosive grenades directly underneath it," explained the engineer with OMP design responsibility, a man named Saranow. "At the time it happened we actually saw them do it by way of the right-hand video pickup, but it happened too fast for us to react."

The image switched to a close-up, street-level view of buildings rolling by an OMP video pickup. They saw the sudden appearance of the soldier, who tossed the explosives and vanished again in under a second. The camera abruptly ceased functioning and the image was gone.

"We shielded the underside of the Outdoor Mobility Platforms," Nir stated.

"We reduced that shielding on first-phase OMPs," Saranow reminded him. "First-phase devices were designed for a thorough self-destruct at the end of the phase. Shielding it would have added weight and reduced completion of the breakdown at end of phase."

Nir considered this, looking frankly into the engineer's eyes as if waiting for him to back down from this argument. Then Nir nodded. "Yes. I agreed to that shielding reduction. I recall signing off on the spec sheets. None of us counted on these people showing up." He tapped the screen, where the commando was now frozen in midstride on the video display. Then he nodded at the time-coded display at the bottom of the screen. "What continued to function?"

"CPU, redundant trigger, redundant power supply. All the hardened components mounted under the top deck of the unit. Farthest from the crush of the explosion."

"But spread out," Nir observed.

Saranow nodded vigorously, warming to the topic and pleased Nir was perceptive to the design subtleties. "Yeah.

Which is why we don't think the shielding on the underside was penetrated. The explosions forced the shielding into the bottom-level components catastrophically, but didn't allow shrapnel to penetrate, or else all interior components would have been junked instantly. You can see that top-level parts were still good as new. Functioning until we blew her. Kaboom." And it was at that moment that all the digital reads at the bottom of the screen showed an off-line state.

Kesher Nir backed the video and started it looping through its final two-minute segment, which showed the pursuit of the American commando down the street of the Israeli settlement. At the top of the screen the baseball-bat-sized turret was swinging back and forth vainly trying to secure a target on the commando.

Nir tapped the monitor. "He learned its weakness in seconds."

"The others didn't," Saranow argued. "Its score for the day was impressive."

"Those numbers do not impress me," Nir said. "Anything can be used to take out grouped civilians. This piece of equipment is supposed to serve as an adjunct to our urban soldiers in future phases, which means it has to be capable of taking out other soldiers. Trained men. It didn't."

Saranow shrugged and was silent, his way of avoiding actually admitting there was something wrong with his equipment.

"Put in new targeting code. You know how to write a routine to evaluate a target's behavior and make educated guesses as to its position at the time of impact?"

Saranow gave him a peevish look. "Of course I can write it, but there's no telling how accurate it'll be. You can't program battlefield instinct. That's what this guy's got that our machine's can't replicate."

Nir nodded. "But when it reads this kind of a situation, it can make the determination to use multiple rounds to cover the spectrum of potential targets. With the computer power to make targeting determinations, we won't need instinct. If we simultaneously target all the positions in which a man might be, it doesn't matter which position he actually chooses.'' Nir smiled. ''No matter where he is, no matter how good his instincts, he's still dead.''

CHAPTER NINE

Village of Dahamshah, West Bank

The afternoon in the West Bank was so pleasant and bright a photo could have been used for a vacation poster. The land around them was empty, a mild breeze coming up to brush away the heat of the sun. There were even some birds flitting from a small copse of ground-hugging shrubs. None of it dispelled the hard fact that, at that moment, Phoenix Force was at risk from so many eventualities that David McCarter was having trouble keeping them all straight. Nervous Palestinians with itchy trigger fingers. Israel Defense Forces on increased patrol of the region. Virtually anybody who stumbled across this heavily armed, highly illegal paramilitary outfit would have good reason to open fire and ask questions later.

The best possible outcome of this probe would be that Phoenix Force remained unseen except by those they were seeking. The worst possible result would put them in an Israeli prison. Or blasted out of existence by an Israeli air attack.

McCarter was increasingly worried about what would happen if he and his mates were taken into custody by the Israelis, and the longer they stayed around the more likely that became. They'd be branded spies, certainly. Refusing to disclose their affiliation would confuse the issue. The multinational makeup of the team would add fuel to the fire, but a U.S. link would be obvious, even if they admitted nothing. So where would it end?

Stony Man Farm would do what it could to get them free. Brognola would call in favors. Kurtzman and Price might find a way to conjure up a back story to appease the Israelis.

The worst-case scenario would be the exposure of the Farm itself. The Farm would cease to exist in short order. The scandal would be huge and would stretch back over how many presidential administrations?

Forget it. Nothing to gain by worrying about it. They'd have to simply not get caught.

Easier said than done as they were racing across the open, treeless land of the West Bank in a pair of unmarked Chenowyth Advanced Light Strike Vehicles without serial numbers or markings. The ALSV was the newer incarnation of the Light Strike Vehicle used by U.S. special units, such as the Rangers and Delta Force.

Chenowyths of one kind or another had been in use for more than thirty years, and in the Gulf War they had been the mode of transport for special forces units on clandestine strikes into the desert. The ALSV was designed with all-wheel drive and a powerful diesel engine, for high-speed agility on rough terrain. A primary weapons station on the rear possessed a 360-degree firing range, and came mounted with an M-2 .50-caliber machine gun or an MK19 automatic grenade launcher. The two units Phoenix Force had shipped in with them from the U.S. included one of each configuration.

"Phoenix One here," McCarter radioed as he studied the electronic topographic map mounted on the dash of the ALSV. The small blue icons showed the GPS positions of the Chenowyths and, appearing at the edge of the display, the orange jumble of squares was the village itself. Tiny windows beneath the map showed the distance in kilometers. "We're less than two klicks off, Stony Base."

"Stony One," Price asked, "have you placed the uplink?"

"Doing so now," McCarter responded as he slowed the vehicle and gestured ahead. Behind him Calvin James brought the second ALSV to an abrupt halt and Gary Manning hurried out the rear with an anodized metal case. He dropped into a crouch and duckwalked to the apex of the rising slope, where he found an indentation in the ground surrounded partially by shrubs. He deposited the case there. It would be tough to spot, even if someone happened to pass through the area prior to Phoenix Force's return.

It took Manning under a minute to open the case and withdraw the small satellite dish on its hinged base. The dish powered up automatically and adjusted itself with the hum of small servo drives, preconfigured to lock on to the correct signal. A green display told Manning when the uplink was locked on and he gave a thumbs-up as he jogged, still bent at the waist, back to the second Chenowyth.

The remote satellite uplink was a redundant system to the uplinks built into the vehicles. If the Chenowyths' uplinks were jammed, even if the vehicles were destroyed, there was a good chance the commandos' radios would still be capable of communicating with the Farm via the remote link. Probably overkill, McCarter had guessed, but after what happened in Shaalvim he wasn't taking chances.

Less than a minute after halting, McCarter had his ALSV moving again. The second Chenowyth, with James at the wheel and Encizo and Manning as passengers, would wait and watch.

Choosing to take the overland route instead of the dirt road, which wound directly into the West Bank village of Dahamshah, made for a bumpy ride, but had kept them unseen. They even managed to keep the dust cloud of their passing to a minimum by steering over the thickest of the vegetation. Now McCarter and Hawkins mounted the peak of an incline and the land fell away in a long slope to the village. There was no sign that their arrival was expected, judging by the attitude of the people moving about unhurriedly in the streets.

That changed almost at once. The Chenowyth couldn't be missed as it crawled like a quick-moving spider down the slope. Townsfolk began running in all directions, seeking cover.

"Lots of civilians," McCarter muttered into the radio. There was no response from Stony Man Farm or the other commandos. All knew the added risk of taking a fight into the realm of the civilian, where any stray bullet could mean the death of an innocent bystander. None of them wanted that kind of notch on their conscience.

McCarter wished there was another way to advance this investigation, but this was the one lead they had and there might be little time left to do it. Within an hour Israeli forces were expected to blanket the West Bank, closing roads and locking down every Palestinian town and village. Dahamshah was the only option Phoenix Force had. He had come up with a scheme that would, just maybe, separate the targets from the cover of the Dahamshah villagers. It depended on how good an actor McCarter was.

The ALSV powered aggressively over uneven terrain as it reached level ground and McCarter put the vehicle into low gear, forcing the big diesel engine into high, noisy revolutions when he steered it jerking and roaring into the streets of the small town, composed of tiny frame houses and packed dirt roads. There were faces in the windows, passing in blurs as McCarter made a dramatic show of swerving the big, bizarre vehicle drunkenly through the streets, sounding the piercing air horn. When he found the gravelly main road, he careened toward the center of town with a spray of flying rocks and a thrubbing of engines.

"Yee-ha!" Hawkins shouted in time with the honking horn.

"All right, Tex," McCarter said sourly. When the road widened into a small market that served as the central square of Dahamshah McCarter spun the wheel and skidded the Chenowyth into a one-eighty that brought it to a noisy halt, and suddenly the only sound was the burble of the diesel in idle.

The square showed signs of recent desertion, with goods still in their stalls and the litter lying where it had fallen. McCarter stood in the seat of the ALSV and spotted a gray head hidden behind a counter selling bagged vegetables and citrus fruits.

"Well, here we are," he said in a quiet voice into the radio.

"How are the locals taking it?" Price asked.

"They're in hiding. Nobody's showing him- or herself. Phoenix Four?"

From their lookout more than a mile outside the town, James responded, "Looks like a ghost town to us, Phoenix One."

McCarter felt like a bully. "I'm gonna look like a huge arsehole if our intelligence is wrong, Stony Base."

"Understood," Price replied, to which Kurtzman broke in and added, "It's our own intelligence, if that makes you feel any better."

"I guess so," McCarter said without conviction. "Uh-oh. I see something stirring in the bushes. We've got company coming."

The gang of locals emerged in a determined stride from a side street into the market square. Hawkins was wriggling like a pinned bug in the passenger seat and glanced over his shoulder worriedly at the big MK19 mounted behind them.

"You want I should—?"

"Don't even think about it," McCarter warned. He felt like enough of a schoolyard ruffian as it was. This was a risky and volatile position he had put them in, and the risk was to the civilians of the Palestinian town of Dahamshah. He wasn't going to spark the tinder by pointing heavy weapons in their direction.

"You with us, Katz?" McCarter radioed.

"I'm right here," said the familiar voice of Yakov Katzenelenbogen.

"Let 'em know where we stand," McCarter said. "I'm patching you through—now."

With the flip of a switch, Katzenelenbogen was on the public-address speaker rigged to the hood of the ALSV. He spoke for about fifteen seconds. The plan was to inform the people that they had evidence that the attackers of the Shaalvim Settlement were being hidden in the town. The entire town was going to bear the consequences if the killers weren't produced immediately.

The words brought the crowd, all men and older boys, to an uneasy halt, and when Katz's address finished they gathered in a hastily arranged town meeting that quickly rose to shouts and argument.

"They're discussing it," McCarter reported. "Wait. Here they come."

One of the old men in the crowd, his forehead bunched into a mass of wrinkles that was pulled low over his eyes distrusting. He spoke sharply.

"Get that?" McCarter asked.

"Yeah," Katz said. They had rigged up an omnidirectional microphone with the speaker just for this purpose.

"Let me guess, he wants to know who the hell we are."

"Yeah, and where the hell you get off accusing his town

of harboring killers,'' Katz replied through the radio channel. Then he spoke again through the speakers, and McCarter and Hawkins watched the old man sneer when he realized he was talking to someone who wasn't even on the scene. The old man began telling Katz what he thought of a man who didn't have the courage to face those he's making accusations against. Then the old man began explaining his opinion of the hired guns who had been assigned to do the dirty work.

Hawkins relaxed a little as the conversation lengthened. "This just might take a while," he muttered, and reclined slightly in his seat. McCarter tried to appear patient, as well.

That was precisely what the Palestinians wanted. The longer they distracted the soldiers, the better the chance their harbored killers would make good their escape.

If escape was the option chosen. After five minutes the old man seemed to be warming to his subject, as if he could talk like this for hours, and McCarter had heard nothing from the Farm or the second Chenowyth. The Phoenix Force leader spoke softly into his radio.

"Stony Base, nothing's happening?"

"Not a thing," Price replied. "Let's ramp up the pressure and see what happens, Yakov?"

Without breaking stride, Katz switched from Arabic to English. "How long until the search teams arrive, Corporal?" he asked loudly enough for half the village to hear it.

Who? Me? McCarter thought. He glanced at his watch and said aloud, "About fifteen minutes, sir."

Hawkins rubbed his nose and grinned behind his hand. "You're a pretty good actor, Corporal McCarter."

"Can it."

The exchange found its mark in the crowd. The old man understood what was said, although he tried to hide the telltale shift in his gaze, which went to a man in the crowd. There was a casual relay of a message through the gathered onlookers, and McCarter watched out of the corner of his eye as one of the teenage boys retreated from the rear of the crowd and was gone into one of the side streets.

"You got their attention, Stony Base," he radioed quietly.

But there was no guarantee that the Palestinians would respond as the Farm hoped. Maybe the threat of an Israeli search team would only send the killers into deeper hiding.

Luck was running with Phoenix Force, at least for the time being. Within minutes Price was back on the radio. "Stony One here. We have a vehicle leaving the village on the northeastern side. They're not following any road we have mapped."

"Phoenix Four here. We see them, Stony," James reported. "It's a pickup truck with an enclosed bed. They're going overland."

"Can you catch up?" Price asked.

"If I was jogging I could catch up. They're bouncing all over the place just trying to get over the landscape."

"Let them get well out into the open before you make yourselves known," Price reminded him.

"Wait, Stony Base, we have another vehicle. A car this time."

"We see it," Price said.

"Huh!" James said. "It's a Mercedes. A 280. About a 1975. Pretty it ain't."

"This one isn't going to get away from you, is it?" Price sounded worried.

"No way," James said.

"But it ups the odds against you," McCarter interjected.

Unlike military radio communications of the past, like the old push-to-talk, half-duplex military radio systems, the communications system Stony Man Farm put in the field with its teams was a full-duplex radio net allowing transmission and reception simultaneously. It operated more like a robust conference phone call than a traditional radio network. This meant McCarter could speak his mind when he needed to—even interrupt.

"Give them enough time," he told James. "Then T.J. and I will cut it short and drive like hell to catch up about the time you intercept the runners."

"We're equipped to handle this, Phoenix One," Manning said.

"We don't need you to handle those guys, Phoenix Three, we need you to interrogate them. You can't question corpses," McCarter stated tersely.

"Understood, Phoenix One," Manning said.

"Phoenix Four, alert me when you're moving out and keep me aware of your ETA," McCarter added.

"Understood."

The dialogue between Katz and the old Palestinian man rattled on as if the two were old sparring partners covering well-established arguments. The old man thought he was keeping these bad Israeli enforcers from discovering the escaping men of Khodr. Phoenix thought it was letting the killers from Khodr get into an indefensible position in the wasteland before moving in. McCarter silently hoped Phoenix Force really did have the upper hand.

What if the runners were dupes, meant to distract them while the real killers escaped in the opposite direction? McCarter heard Katz use the English words "United Nations" in the middle of a diatribe to the old man, and the old Palestinian's eyebrows shot up like exclamation points.

"I hope he doesn't piss the old guy off too bad. We still have to get out of this town without killing any of them or either of us," Hawkins said.

But the old man was in a fervor, pacing a small rectangle as he exhorted against Katz's comment, waving his hands and stomping one foot for emphasis.

"I could keep him going all day," Katz said on the radio channel.

"Not much longer now," Price said. "Stony Four?"

"We're letting the Mercedes put a solid three klicks between the town before we move, Stony."

"You're at 2.5 kilometers now, Phoenix Four," Price reported.

McCarter folded his arms on his chest, forcing himself to appear casual, but he was quite tense. His men were going into battle without him. He despised being in this position, but he couldn't let the Palestinians see him getting agitated. He scratched his jawline to further the appearance of nonchalance.

What, he wondered, if the Palestinians had reinforcements staged in vehicles, ready to follow after the runners if there were signs of trouble?

"They're at three klicks, Cal," Price said coolly.

"Affirmative, Stony Base," James reported without emotion. "We're moving out."

If they Palestinians figured out what they were up to, they might move in as a crowd and take out himself and Hawkins before their guns could cut down more than a handful of them. McCarter tried not to think about it.

JAMES DRAGGED the Chenowyth into gear and fed diesel to the engines, sending the vehicle into a sudden lunge. From their lookout point, just below the lip of the rise, they were catapulted over the top and the tires dug into the rocky earth with the nose pointed down the long slope. With gravity on their side and the suspension giving them control on terrain that would have bounced the best sports utility vehicle, they streaked down the side of the slope on an unerring course to the valley. Far ahead was the bouncing, humping dot of a pair of unfit cars fleeing across the valley, raising puffs of dust.

The ALSV ate the distance rapidly and the Phoenix Force trio rode it out in silence. Cuban commando Rafael Encizo nodded to the town, where a figure on a rooftop was being joined by another pair of men, all of the gesturing frantically.

"Phoenix Two here," Encizo radioed. "We're spotted."

"Understood," McCarter said. "We're moving out, Katz."

"Reinforcements coming," Encizo added on the radio succinctly. "They were ready for us, Stony."

"We see it, Phoenix Two," Price said in a voice without expression. "Them, I mean."

"Don't keep me out of the loop," McCarter insisted.

"We've got two more vehicles moving out from Dahamshah," Encizo responded. "Jeeps or some other all-terrains. Moving fast."

MCCARTER SLID down behind the wheel of the ALSV as Katzenelenbogen was quickly issuing some sort of excuse to the Palestinians. The suspicious but relaxed mood of the past few minutes was transformed abruptly to tense confusion. McCarter ignored them as he steered the Chenowyth in a tight circle that took him through the scattering men, who had been gradually tightening their circle around the vehicle. Their glances flitted rapidly between the ALSV and the old man, whose indecision stalled them.

"I told them we just heard the killers were in another town twenty kilometers away," Katzenelenbogen said into the radio. "Thought it might buy you a few minutes."

Hawkins twisted in his seat as McCarter accelerated through the main street. The Palestinians converged around the old man, and a runner came upon the group shouting. News traveled fast, Hawkins thought. They had left not a moment too soon.

"Phoenix Five here. That's a nice try, Katz, but the news

is reaching them about now, by the look of things," Hawkins radioed.

"Too late for them," McCarter declared through gritted teeth as the last small houses of the village fell away behind them and the ALSV roared onto the dirt road at highway speeds. McCarter steered into a broad right-hand turn that sent the Chenowyth sweeping in a broad curve, raising a quill of dust a hundred yards long.

"Phoenix Two here. We're getting more than we bargained for."

"Stony One here. Affirmative, Phoenix Two. You've got three tails now by our count."

"How fast are they moving?" McCarter demanded.

"They won't reach Phoenix Four's vehicle prior to them intercepting the runners," Price reported.

"We can't afford to engage the runners, Stony Base," McCarter radioed back. "We'll end up with corpses and no intelligence."

"Agreed," Price said.

"What's the plan, Phoenix One?" James asked.

McCarter had the Chenowyth's speed edging upward as he skirted the town and spotted the pursuing vehicles by their dust clouds.

"Let's make sandwiches, Phoenix Four."

The VW van, a tiny Peugeot and a larger Toyota struggled on the uneven terrain in pursuit of James's ALSV. McCarter knew what would happen if they reached the scene before Phoenix Force halted and disarmed the runners. There would be gunfire. Maybe the runners would survive it, and maybe not. It was a chance he couldn't take. They had to have the intelligence the runners could give them. They had to know more.

They more or less knew why. They had to know who.

The pursuers couldn't be allowed to prevent that questioning.

McCarter closed the distance, keeping the ALSV firmly buried in the dust cloud, then eased off the accelerator at a couple hundred yards, pacing them.

"I don't think they even see us," Hawkins shouted over the rush of wind and the diesel rumble.

"And you would know that how?"

"Beats me. Just a guess."

"Get ready to take them out when we're in range," McCarter said. "Put the rounds in front of them if you can."

Hawkins scrambled into the rear and dragged himself into a standing position behind the big grenade launcher mounted in the rear bed.

When a glance in the rearview mirror got McCarter a big thumbs up from the Texan, he stomped on the pedal.

"Go, Phoenix Four," McCarter radioed, and Manning held tight to the braces on the machine gun as James braked the ALSV hard and steered it into a controlled one-eighty, then spun the tires on the earth before the tread gripped and pulled it into sudden acceleration back the way they had come.

The trio of pursuing vehicles never slowed, but the VW van in the lead sprouted the upper torsos of four gunners with rifles. They were shaking their fists and rifles, shouting into the wind. As the distance closed, they pulled their weapons into firing positions, ready to unleash death on the intruders.

Then, to their shock, Phoenix Force struck first.

Manning, with the best view of the closing distance, called it. "Now," he said into the radio, and before the word was out of his mouth there was a puff of light from the McCarter-Hawkins Chenowyth. The grenade hit just in front of the VW van and an arm's length away from the right fender, throwing up a plume of earth and dust. Manning was already triggering the M-2, forcing a stream of

.50-caliber rounds into the ground in front of the VW van. The driver panicked and saved his life temporarily by taking the best possible evasive maneuver, steering abruptly away from the explosion and machine-gun rounds, pulling the lethal stream across the passenger window. He fought to control the van as it became a two-wheeler and veered wildly, shouting at the added shock of discovering that the man in the seat next to him was now a corpse.

The Peugeot never saw it coming. The machine-gun fire slammed into the engine block and windshield, killing the engine and the driver simultaneously and sending the little car in a sideways skid before it hit a dirt rise and rolled onto its side, coming to a halt on its roof.

It was the Toyota's turn, but the driver had seen it all happen and hit the brakes just hard enough to maintain control and find a way through the confusion, which meant away from the van and the Peugeot and into the freshly dug crater left by the grenade. He reacted fast, swerved just in time to avoid the giant car-stopping pothole and accelerated, giving the ALSV with the machine-gun a wide berth and racing to join the escaping runners from Khodr.

McCarter's Chenowyth flashed by James's, an arm's length of space between them, and they heard the Briton radioing simultaneously.

"We're after him. Disable the others."

"Understood," James replied as he brought the Chenowyth to the VW van, which had landed against all odds on its wheels. It wobbled, like a drunk getting his bearings, then the driver cranked the wheel and brought the little box around to face the ALSV. As James accelerated, the VW started up, and they ran at each other like knights at a joust. But the Phoenix Force horse was stronger, and their lance was a lot longer. When Manning started sweeping the M-2 in a broadside figure-eight, the Palestinians were still out range for their Kalashnikov rifles. They fired them anyway, while the driver tried to escape. The gunners' and driver's efforts were both wasted. The .50-caliber rounds punched hammer holes through the body of the van and slammed through its passengers, filling the interior with spraying blood and clouds of shredded seat stuffing. When the VW faltered and stopped, there was no sign of life inside.

By then James had the ALSV turning on the turtled Peugeot. The tires, still spinning in the open air, looked undamaged, and the driver and passenger were struggling to get themselves out the side windows. They couldn't be allowed to get the car righted and moving again.

"Let's disable it," James called over his shoulder.

"Understood." Manning flexed his arms and aimed the M-2 level, prepared to chew up the tires and undercarriage of the car until it was absolutely undriveable. As it was, he never fired a shot. With the crunch of aluminum the Peugeot's roof flattened, trapping the two escaping passengers at the waist. Both screamed and pounded on the car.

James turned the Chenowyth away without a backward glance.

McCARTER LINED them up on the rear bumper of the Toyota as they came to a flat depression that might have been a lake centuries ago. Now it was low, scrubby weeds that gave the automobile suspension less trouble than the rocky ground and the vehicle moved faster, as easily as cruising on an interstate. For a heartbeat the ALSV was being outdistanced. McCarter punched it to the floor, bringing the back end of the Toyota at them fast. "Bugger those bastards," he shouted over his shoulder.

Hawkins aimed and triggered fast, compensating instinctively for the motion of both vehicles, and watched the round explode just a few feet in front of the speeding car. A sandstorm of debris billowed up for an eye blink, then the Toyota was on top of it, swallowing the blast. The force was too far diminished to damage them, and Hawkins had placed the round right in the center, so the tires straddled the freshly drilled pit without going in. The Toyota emerged from the dust without damage, still moving fast.

"You'll have to do better than that," McCarter called.

"Count on it," Hawkins said as he adjusted his aim and triggered again, this time sending the round directly into the back of the car. It broke the back windshield as it slammed into the edge of the roof, then filled the interior with billowing fire. The Toyota was now a lifeless hulk of metal careening out of control. McCarter braked to let it get out of his way. He didn't really care where it ended up. The unwatched Toyota rolled to a stop on burning tires, which popped and settled. There was no more movement except the black, oily smoke.

Moments later James brought the second ALSV alongside McCarter's, and only about a quarter mile ahead was the pair of runner vehicles, struggling over the terrain. The killers from Khodr had nowhere left to run. There was no more help coming from Dahamshah, and they were smart enough to know they couldn't hope to fight against the long reach of the ALSVs. The cars halted and the runners emerged, hands in the air, bitterness written on their faces.

BY LATE AFTERNOON the news of massacres at Khodr and Shaalvim Settlement was spreading throughout Israel, the occupied territories, the Middle East, the world. The stories changed with the telling.

Reports on Israeli television called the attacks on the West Bank settlement "unprovoked," and "the result of the continued and baseless Palestinian animosity toward a peace-loving Israel."

"As an excuse for murdering innocent women and children, the killers claimed they were provoked when Israeli soldiers first attacked their nearby village of

Khodr. However, no Israeli military units were outside their scheduled sphere of operations, which spheres of operations did not include Khodr, and no military maneuvers took place within ten miles of the supposed attacks against the Palestinians. No evidence has been found of Israeli military presence in Khodr. Palestinian army officials have verified that no Israeli military operations took place in the West Bank vicinity of the Palestinian village.''

Palestinian news services, written outside Palestine and distributed worldwide, had a different take on the facts:

Khodr endured a direct attack by organized military forces wearing Star of David insignia. These forces included missile-armed military helicopters. These high-grade explosive rockets, designed for tank killing and use against heavily armored military targets, were launched at the town's small mosque, killing those who sought refuge there. Remote-controlled vehicles also entered the village, emblazoned with the Star of David a full meter and a half wide. The first such device self-destructed in a crowd, but fortunately the people had given it wide-enough berth so that only one man was killed. A second remote-controlled device, however, detonated at the hiding place used by women and children of the village, killing most instantly. Grief-stricken men of the village pursued the Israeli foot soldiers, who took cover in a school in one of the illegal Israeli West Bank settlements.

CHAPTER TEN

Stony Man Farm, Virginia

"As darkness falls in the Middle East, Palestinian officials have arrived at Shaalvim, the Israeli West Bank settlement, and in the village of Khodr, which you can see behind me. The Palestinians are demanding to be included in the investigations of events at both sites. We've been told by the Israeli investigators they have no intention of allowing Palestinian investigators into the Jewish settlement, and it appears they're being kept on the outside at the Palestinian village, as well. In the last hour a standoff has developed between Palestinian investigators and the Israelis who have cordoned off the village.

"The markings on the vehicles indicate that the Israeli investigators are from Israel Defense Forces. In Israel the Israel Defense Forces includes all Israeli military branches, which makes it difficult to pin down the affiliation of the investigative force. And the Israelis aren't yet talking.

"Frank Ford, the West Bank."

Barbara Price realized Carmen Delahunt was standing next to her, watching the newscast. Price hadn't even noticed her enter the room. She took the handful of sheets

Delahunt offered and flipped through them one after another, the frown lines on her forehead deepening. "Not a player in the bunch?"

She was looking at a stack of reports culled from Israeli and other global databases on suspected agitators and known terrorists in the West Bank. The Israelis kept good records on those they considered dangerous to the Jewish state. But none of the reports they'd pulled data from indicated that Phoenix Force's Palestinian prisoners were considered important or exceptionally prone to anti-Jewish violence. Not by Israeli standards of violence. While Hisham Fahd was reported to be the leader of a militia that called itself May of '42, it was just one of hundreds of tiny "freedom fighting" organizations among the population of the occupied territories. Israel considered them no more than social clubs. Few of these militias ever actually acted against Israel.

"Not one of them rates a priority. Strictly low-level or no-level freedom fighters," Delahunt said. "Some of the names had no files whatsoever. It looks like this group is what it claims to be—a bunch of regular Palestinian joes pushed too far."

"What's the chances that any of them is an undercover agitator for Hamas?" Price asked.

"Could be." Delahunt shrugged.

"This is the man in charge, as far as his authority went," Price said, tapping the printed photograph of the Palestinian named Fahd. "His story checks out?"

"All the way," said Aaron Kurtzman as he rolled into the Computer Room with Yakov Katzenelenbogen a step behind. "I've done the most comprehensive inspection I know how on this man. I've searched by name, fingerprints, digital facial analysis, everything. If Fahd's a big man among the Palestinians or anywhere else, he's done a superlative job of hiding himself away for years. All I found was his Israeli file. They say he's just a malcontent. One of the thousands they keep records on.''

"That is also how he came across to Phoenix,'' Price said. "Cal says he's blinded, with multiple wounds and nearly dead from exhaustion and blood loss. If he did have a terrorist career in the works I think it ended with this campaign.''

"Is questioning still going on?''

"Yes.'' Price nodded to the small video image coming in from the West Bank, where the eighth and last of the Palestinian runners was being questioned on camera about his involvement in the attack on Khodr and subsequent Shaalvim Settlement violence. "The story has been the same every time. A shipment of weapons is brought to Khodr by Arab strangers, along with dire warnings of imminent unprovoked Israeli atrocities against the people. A few days later the town is attacked without warning, wiping out the women and children using sophisticated air- and ground-based explosives delivery techniques. The men fight back, pursuing their attackers across West Bank no-man's-land to the settlement, where the tables are turned on them and they are nearly wiped out, but only after they've slaughtered Israeli women and children.''

"It sounds like somebody orchestrated the scenario from beginning to end. The men of Khodr were just game pieces,'' Kurtzman said. "It's unbelievably callous.''

Price nodded. "And it was done as part of a media campaign, which makes it more heartless. We know Rafe's cameraman wasn't the only video being shot at the battle. There may have been video pickups on the ground with the soldiers. We know the Cypher or a standard helicopter videotaped a feed that went to news organizations worldwide in the last couple of hours.''

Delahunt showed surprise. She hadn't heard that news. "The terrorists provided their own news footage?''

"Yes," Price said. "It's very graphic. I'm sure they will be showing it again—you know how news networks operate."

"We also know the attackers went out of their way to identify themselves as Israelis to the Khodr villagers," Katzenelenbogen added. Kurtzman handed him a stack of sheets, and he pulled out a pair of photographic prints. "This is from the recording off the satellite feed we were watching. Good thing we have it. I'd have trouble believing the claims of the Palestinians if we didn't have evidence."

Price took the prints from Katzenelenbogen. The Star of David symbol was tiny but unmistakable on the hood of one of the machine-gun-armed jeeps sitting outside the village.

"These designations were removed by the time the fighting reached Shaalvim," Price said, shaking her head slowly.

"Factor in the possum-playing Israeli soldiers—first they're dead and then they're not—and what do we end up with?" Kurtzman asked, looking at Price, then Delahunt, then Katzenelenbogen for an answer.

"You got me," Delahunt said. "Somebody's trying to manipulate somebody."

"We know the victims of manipulation are Palestinians," Katzenelenbogen said. "We can assume the people pulling the strings are probably Israeli."

"It's not their own people, certainly, with that kind of firepower and funding," Price said. "I've never heard of a Palestinian group with hardware like that."

"I've never heard of any terrorist group anywhere with that kind of technology," Katzenelenbogen added. "So where do we start looking?"

Price sighed. "I was hoping Phoenix's questioning would turn up a lead. So far…" She shrugged and flipped on the comm-link to David McCarter, who could be seen on the video conversing again with Hisham Fahd, the blinded leader of the Khodr survivors. It was night now in the Middle East, and McCarter and his team were working in near darkness to keep from attracting the Israeli patrols that had closed down roads throughout the West Bank. "Stony Base here, Phoenix One," Price said. "Tell me you've got something."

McCarter, to the surprise of Price and the others, wore a grin when he looked at the camera. "Stony Base," he said, "I've bloody well got something."

"Don't keep me in suspense."

"Our friend Fahd came up with it. Guess he's decided we might be decent blokes and now he wants to cooperate," McCarter explained. "Listen to this story. He says he saw a bunch of paint peel off one of the helicopters that was attacking his village. He says it came off in a big sheet, like peeling the wrapper off a piece of candy."

Delahunt looked baffled. "I don't get it."

"I do," Kurtzman said excitedly. "They had the hardware disguised. They used some sort of temporary paint or plastic coating."

Price blinked. "You saying they laminated an attack chopper?"

"Yeah, something like that," Kurtzman said. "Actually, it was probably applied as a highly viscous spray, designed to stay in place when it was applied since they couldn't risk it dripping into vital components before it set. After an hour the curing would have made it strong and durable enough to last for their mission, but not so tough that it couldn't be sliced and removed by hand when the mission was done."

"It must not be as tough as they thought, Bear," McCarter said on the link. "Not if a big chunk of it peeled off and gave our man Fahd an eyeful."

"An eyeful of something useful, I hope?" Price asked.

"Part of a serial number," McCarter said.

"Can't get more useful than that, unless it's the entire serial number," Price agreed.

McCarter rattled off the seven digits, and Delahunt jotted them down, then jumped up, heading off to start work on them. She paused, looking at the muted television screen on the wall. The others followed her gaze as she turned the volume up.

"Civilian street violence has come to be expected whenever tensions grow thick in this strife-torn part of the world. After today's events it was to be expected. But this time there's a twist to the story. We go live to Dwayne Manfred in Jerusalem."

"This is a turn of events we don't see often in Israel. A crowd of young people—Israeli young people—have taken to the streets, throwing rocks and taunting police, who have been gathered to keep the mob from marching into Palestinian sectors of the city. Police are using antiriot gear and tear gas in an attempt to control the crowds. We've seen all this before, but in the past it's been used almost exclusively against Palestinian rioters.

"As far as we know, there's been no use of the famous rubber bullets against the Israelis. Not yet. This crowd formed spontaneously, I'm told, and there seems to be no leader or clear objective here, although we can all imagine what the results would be if this angry crowd broke into what is, for all practical purposes, enemy territory.

"These angry crowds began forming almost immediately after the first Israeli broadcast of the videotape that has come to light from the attacks today at the Israeli West Bank settlement of Shaalvim.

"I am Dwayne Manfred, in Jerusalem."

"Thank you, Dwayne. This network came into possession of the Shaalvim video just ninety minutes ago. Apparently Israeli television got it almost three hours ago. We will run it again now, although I must warn you it may be considered disturbing."

"Oh, God," Delahunt said as the video played. Price had turned away from the screen.

Delahunt saw the fire. The smoke. The framed timbers of the building that she knew was the school. She was seeing what Encizo had seen from the camera view on the second story, across the street from the burning school in Shaalvim Settlement. She saw the women and children inside, their faces etched with horror. They were trapped in the blaze and they knew it. Over the rush of the flames and the rattle of gunfire, they were screaming as they burned.

The screen went blank. Delahunt had turned it off without even deciding to do so.

Katzenelenbogen hadn't seen it until now, either, and he was as pale as a ghost. A warrior from a thousand battles, he was sickened by what he saw and what he knew—the reason for the killing.

"Barb? You still with me?" It was McCarter, waiting on the line.

"David, the video from the settlement is in the hands of the media," Price said. "Have you seen it?"

"The terrorists provided their own news footage?"

"Sounds like its been on the news in Israel for a while now. The Israelis are reacting to it. Street fighting has started."

"Just as was meant to happen," McCarter said. "That's bloody cold. They contrive the murder of those civilians just to stir up the population. Not that the Palestinians weren't doing their share of slaughter."

"Somebody wants a war, and doesn't care what sacrifices the public has to make to get the ball rolling," Katzenelenbogen said. "So far it looks like the plan is working as intended."

"We have to screw up those plans," Delahunt said, and strode out of the room, even more anxious to stamp an identification on one of the mystery attack helicopters.

Maybe it would point the finger at whoever was behind this horror.

DELAHUNT LOST no time in calling up access to a database spider, Stony Man Farm's software for dynamically accessing multiple databases around the world. She plugged in the mystery serial number and let the spider loose, sending out its tendrils through the Farm T3 Internet connections.

When it came down to it, she didn't have all that much to work with. She knew the vehicle in question was a helicopter. The Palestinian had called it an attack helicopter, but just about any armed helicopter would qualify as such to an untrained eye. Delahunt broadened her search to include any VTOL aircraft that matched her numbers.

The spider began coming back with results almost immediately, and it turned out that Fahd had identified the aircraft accurately—it was a military gunship. The helicopter in question, if the numbers were accurate, was an AH-64, an Apache.

But the serial numbers, it turned out, were the manufacturer's identification number rather than a military designation. Why would an aircraft still have its original serial numbers, unless it was brand-new? This Apache wasn't new at all.

The AH-64 had started life as the Hughes helicopter entry in the U.S. Army Advanced Attack Helicopter program, a midseventies competition aimed at developing a new attack helicopter to be based in the field with ground troops, an outgrowth of combat lessons learned in Vietnam. The YAH-64 prototype beat out the Bell YAH-63 in the competition, and Hughes began producing the chopper in the early 1980s.

The Apache served the U.S. Army well in 1989 in Panama and had an important role as a tank killer during Operation Desert Storm. The advanced AH-64A served in Bosnia.

Trying to match the serial number with a specific aircraft was made more challenging by the convolutions of records resulting from corporate changes. Since the birth of the YAH-64, Hughes Helicopters was bought by McDonnell-Douglas. Then McDonnell-Douglas was bought by Boeing. The records for units made and shipped years or decades past were intact, but weren't exactly made easily available to any passing hacker. It took some effort to find the archives she needed. Once she did have a trace on the correct piece of equipment, she had to follow its trail after leaving the factory, which occurred in 1992.

If the U.S. Army was the only user of the AH-64, it would have been hard enough to track down a single aircraft among its more than eight hundred Apaches. But the gunship was also sold to Egypt, Israel, South Korea, the United Arab Emirates and various other militaries, all of whom would have resented Delahunt snooping in their equipment records. Had they known she was there. She felt a surge of elation when she suddenly came upon the service history for the very aircraft that was in question.

Not that it solved any of their problems.

HOURS LATER, when Carmen Delahunt presented the evidence to Price, Kurtzman and Katzenelenbogen, she announced, "If the serial number is legitimate, there's only one attack helicopter in the world it can be," she announced, setting a warm printout on the table in the War Room.

"Even with just a partial number you can narrow it down to a single piece of equipment?" Price asked.

"I cross-referenced the number every possible way. There are no possible matches," she said assuredly.

"And?" Kurztman asked.

"It's a Greek gunship."

The others stared at her.

"At least it was. Until thirteen months ago, when the Greeks decided they couldn't afford to maintain some of their older helicopters and sold her off to a new technology firm, Gold Aeronautic Electronic Systems. They're based just outside the city of Herzliyya."

"That's less than twenty miles from Tel Aviv," Katzenelenbogen said.

"Smells like bingo," Kurtzman said.

"How would a technology firm justify the purchase of a gunship?" Price asked.

"Gold Aeronautic specializes in making retrofit control subsystems for aircraft and has been branching off into military aircraft. That's what their paperwork said when they bought the Greek Apache."

"A white lie?" Katzenelenbogen asked.

"Well, no," Delahunt said. "I researched Gold Aeronautic and found that the firm did retrofit this particular AH-64 with their new control system and presented the system in prototype form to at least three military procurement boards. Including the Greeks they bought the aircraft from in the first place. The Gold system replaces some of the most expensive and troublesome components with newer, cheaper, more robust electronics. The components haven't actually been delivered yet, but I don't think the company could have faked its development this far."

"So what we need to know is this," Katzenelenbogen posed. "Are the employees of Gold Aeronautic using their AH-64 to bomb Palestinians on the weekends?"

"Good question," Delahunt agreed.

"Send in Pol?" Kurtzman asked Price.

"Rosario's still hours away," she said, glancing at her watch. "It's nearly dawn in the Middle East. I'm worried about what a new day is going to bring to Israel and the occupied territories. You remember how fast the violence escalated there a couple of years ago."

Kurtzman nodded as unbidden images flitted through his mind of the 2000 violence. Newspapers all over the world printed the photographs of a twelve-year-old Palestinian boy lying dead in his father's arms. He noticed Katzenelenbogen looking at the tabletop, deep in his own thoughts.

It was Katz's nation being battered by the forces of terror. Kurtzman knew that the fact that Israeli-Palestinian fighting had been going on for decades made it no less troubling. Having resided outside Israel for some time made the issues behind the conflict easier to consider objectively, but didn't make the violence and sorrow less piteous.

"Yes," Kurtzman said, almost under his breath. Then, louder, "It would be great if we can make our move preemptively. Who knows what today's got in store."

"How near is Phoenix to Gold Aeronautic?" Delahunt asked.

"They're rooming with Jack aboard the Airbus at a private airport in Tel Aviv," Price explained. "If I give them a wake-up call now, they can beat the morning rush hour."

"They'll stand out in the Chenowyths," Kurtzman observed half-seriously.

Price smiled. "The ALSVs are tucked away inside a couple of eighteen-wheelers. I've arranged for less obvious transportation."

"It's our only lead," Kurtzman added. "What's Pol going to do with himself."

"Maybe going into Gold Aeronautic will solve all our problems, but I doubt it," Price said grimly. "We still need more intelligence. I'm counting on our friend the Politician to scrounge some up."

Herzliyya, Israel

THE WOMAN in the plastic hair net jumped to her feet and strode across the office space on an intercept course with the intruder, talking in lightning-fast Hebrew.

"Speak English?" demanded the barrel-chested figure who had barged into the building well before office hours.

"You can't go in there," the woman said in English without missing a beat. "That's a clean-room environment. We're manufacturing highly sensitive electronic—"

The man she was trying to halt moved his hand only slightly, and when a handgun appeared in his grip it was like watching a cartoon character pulling a comically oversize mallet from behind his back.

The woman blinked. "All right," she said. "Go on in."

"Thanks." He waved the weapon at the keypad. "Mind punching in your pass code?"

"Look, asshole, I'm not going to stop you from going in but I'm sure not going to help you," the woman declared matter-of-factly.

"Fine." The big man shrugged, and somehow in the midst of the shrug the handgun fired at the locking mechanism point-blank, shattering it abruptly.

Ms. Hair net jumped and made a noise in her throat, backing away. She felt wetness on her face and touched a blood spot. A shard of flying detritus from the gun blast had ticked her face.

That was the last straw. The intruder was now ignoring her, going through the double doors into the factory, so she stomped to the corner desk to call the police.

GARY MANNING GRIPPED the handgun close to his face, pointed at the ceiling. That way everybody could see it. And everybody did. Work ceased in the small factory as the door crashed open and he stepped inside.

This wasn't like many factories he'd seen before. No greasy concrete floors and smell of stressed metal. The walls, ceiling and floor were all white and so brightly lit it made him squint. The workers were in white smocks, white operating-room slippers over their shoes, more hair nets, and masks over their mouths. The assembly line was tiny and square, moving jerkily among several expensive-looking pieces of equipment. Manning had seen bigger living rooms.

"Who's the foreman?"

The frozen workers looked at one another.

"I'm in charge of this production line, if that's what you're asking," squeaked a small man with glasses.

Manning thought he looked like a rodent. Something rat-like and greasy. A possum or maybe a weasel. "Take me to your helicopter."

Whatever the weasel was expecting him to say, it wasn't that. "You…you want to see our helicopter?"

"Yes."

"You do know it's not flyable."

"Just show it to me."

"Now wait a second—"

Manning didn't want to wait a second. He touched the muzzle of the Beretta handgun against the thin metal bridge between the thick lenses of the foreman's glasses.

"Okay, okay, okay, I'll show you the helicopter!"

They exited the rear of the factory into a less brightly lit vestibule. As the door closed behind them, a rush of wind came from the vents in the walls on one side and was sucked into the vents on the opposite wall. The door on the other side of the vestibule clicked open with a tiny glow of a green light.

They stepped onto a small landing and Manning found himself looking at a rocky, empty field. A hundred yards away was a wooden outbuilding that looked more like a barn than a hangar.

"Where the rest of it?"

"The rest of what?" asked the foreman.

"The rest of Gold Aeronautics."

"You just took the grand tour, buddy," the foreman said with irritation. "Design and management up front, manufacturing in the rear."

"That's all?" Manning said.

"What did you expect?" The foreman wasn't just confused; he was getting angry.

"That's all there is," Manning explained, speaking over the foreman's head.

The foreman was startled to see more gunmen showing up from around either side of the building. They weren't just toting handguns, either. Two had automatic rifles or machine guns of some kind. One of the men was black. Just as the foreman was assuming the group was American, another one of them began speaking in what was clearly a British or maybe Australian accent.

"Not a very big place to start a war from," said the Briton. "Let's see the gunship."

The foreman wasn't about to argue as the five figures encircled him loosely, and he dolefully marched across the rocky ground that served as their landing pad on the rare occasions they actually had the Apache in a functional state. He pulled the plastic shroud from the security control and punched his code into the keypad.

The lock's small display said Failed.

He punched in his numbers again.

Again it Failed.

"Stop jerking me around, buddy," said the barrel-chested man. The guy would have intimidated the foreman if he was standing there unarmed and in his boxers, let alone in vaguely military street clothes and waving the big handgun.

"The code must have been changed," the foreman

whined, and he stabbed out his number repeatedly. The display continued to read Failed.

"Who could have changed the code?"

"Just Stuart. Nobody else has access here."

"Who's Stuart?" Manning demanded.

"Stuart Gold. This is his company. He must have changed the code without telling me."

"Where is he?"

"I don't know," the foreman exclaimed. "It's early. He sometimes doesn't show up for work until nine, or not at all. He's the boss, so he does what he wants."

"Fresh oil," Hawkins announced, crouching and touching a black spot on the rocky ground.

"Let's check it out," McCarter said with a gesture toward the door.

"I told you," the foreman complained, and he never got any further, because Manning's lock pick triggered again and shattered the electronic panel. The bolt held until another two rounds finally cracked the lock frame, then Manning shouldered the door until the bolt wrenched out of the socket and the door slid up without resistance. Inside was the poised gunship, silent in the dim daylight coming into the windowless hangar.

"Well, there it is," the foreman said. "Happy now?"

"She's armed," Encizo said.

"Of course it's armed. We have to be able to test the systems we build for," the foreman protested. "But the rounds are all blanks."

"She's been flown recently," Hawkins added. He was something of a pilot himself, although he had yet to sit behind the controls of an Apache. "She fired her weapons recently."

"Absolutely not," the foreman snapped.

Hawkins grabbed him by the collar and pushed his face

against the barrels of the M-230 30 mm chain gun. "Smells fresh to me."

The foreman smelled it, too, and stopped squeaking, standing there bewildered when Hawkins released him. "She's been flying?"

"Who could have taken her up?" Hawkins asked.

"Nobody. I mean, nobody except Stuart. But Stuart wouldn't do it. She's not even airworthy at the moment. He was designing a new control subsystem and he had her systems dismantled—"

"Somebody was flying her. That means she must be airworthy, no matter what your friend Stuart told you," Hawkins said.

"Check it out." Rafael Encizo had a sliver of black plastic sheet between his fingertips, less than a millimeter thick.

"Looks like black plastic wrap," Hawkins said.

"Keeps your helicopter from going stale," Manning quipped.

"There's more scraps scattered around," Encizo observed, strolling to the wall where he nudged a small pile of scraps with his foot. "Somebody cleaned up most of it, but they didn't do a careful job."

"Didn't think there'd be anybody investigating right away," McCarter said.

He said to the foreman. "You going to try and tell us you've got legitimate uses for this kind of stuff?"

The foreman stared at the scraps without comprehension. "No. Of course not. We don't use any material like that."

"By the way," said McCarter, "we'll be needing Stuart's home address. We'd like to pay a call."

The foreman provided it, almost without thinking. He was confused and worried. He didn't know who the intruders were, but he was more worried about the implications of what they had discovered. Stuart—someone, anyway—had been flying the helicopter and shooting its weapons systems.

Who? Why? He knew it had to tie in to an attack on a Palestinian village in the West Bank, leading to a vicious retaliation against an Israeli West Bank settlement. The Palestinians claimed their village was destroyed by a sophisticated military force, including helicopter gunships. The foreman had laughed it off, along with everyone he knew, as Palestinian aggrandizement. He was trying to remember the news reports he had heard that morning on his way in to work. The corpse counting was continued. They had yet to unearth them all. Surely Stuart wouldn't bear some responsibility for *that*.

He was still worrying the thought when the gunmen departed the scene without warning, to the sounds of approaching police sirens.

CHAPTER ELEVEN

Herzliyya, Israel

"Gold Aeronautic Electronic Systems was started in 1995 by Stuart Gold, right here in Herzliyya," Kurtzman recited over the cell-phone speaker in the front seat of the rented Ford Excursion.

"Did he invent something in his garage?" McCarter asked.

"Yeah. In his dorm at college, anyway," Kurtzman said. "In 1994 he put together a new electronics and software package for a German firm making commercial aircraft. Didn't even prototype the thing, just patented the schematics and e-mailed them to the firm's engineering department. They saw the potential in the design and built the prototype on their own. It was such an improvement over their own control components they paid him more than four million U.S. to lease the design. He used the money to start Gold Aeronautic without even knowing what he was going to do with the company. He made more electronic parts and eventually brought manufacturing in-house. I guess he is some kind of a genius. Mostly it looks like he was the right techno-geek in the right place at the right time."

"I hate those kinds of guys," Hawkins said from the back seat.

"He's selling components globally, getting into military

aircraft in 1996. Since 2000 the company's biggest customer has been China," Kurtzman said.

"He's selling the Chinese parts for their military aircraft?" Encizo asked. He was at the wheel, steering them through the dawn-lit streets of the Israeli city.

"That's right."

"Him and half the other techie firms in Israel," Hawkins said. "It's no secret."

"Why do they do it?" Encizo demanded. "The Chinese aren't exactly the ones we want to be providing military advantages, are they?"

"You're taking a U.S.-centric view of the situation," Kurtzman said. "The Israelis don't see things the same way we do. Just because the Chinese are Communist doesn't necessarily mean they're the enemy. The State of Israel doesn't prohibit it. There's a healthy high-technology industry in Israel, in what's known as the Tel Aviv–Haifa technology corridor, and a lot of Red China's yuan helped finance its development."

"We shouldn't let them get away with it," Encizo said.

"What are we going to do? Pick a fight with Israel?" asked Manning with a grimace. "We need any Middle East friends we can get."

"So outside of selling technology to Commies, what's this guy's background like?" McCarter asked, eager to get the conversation back on a productive track.

"Not too exciting. He's kind of a playboy. Just turned thirty-one. Never been married, known to have lots of girlfriends and lots of parties. Got an Israeli pilot's license when he was twenty-six and a helicopter pilot's license when he was twenty-eight. Both despite the fact that he has a police record. Get this—seventeen arrests, all small-time marijuana possession charges, and only one conviction, and that one got him just a slap on the wrist."

"Money talks," Encizo growled.

"From what I am hearing so far, this doesn't sound like the kind of guy who would put together yesterday's operation," McCarter said.

"I agree. But he might have been a part of it," Kurtzman added. "Israeli intelligence thinks he's been hanging out with some vehement pro-Israel extremists in the last year and a half."

"Name some names," McCarter said.

"We've got Jonathan Bard and Saul Levi, both known to have ties to Kach and-or its offshoot Kahane Chai. Both groups have a single overriding goal to restore the biblical state of Israel. There's a woman named Sandra Honig, known to run with the militant subset of the Faithful, or the Gush Emunim. In college she had friends in the Ateret Cohanim, a Jewish student group. Gush Emunim and Ateret Cohanim are both dedicated to tearing down Islam's holiest mosque in Israel."

"What's Mossad's take on these groups?" McCarter asked. "Would they have the know-how and the funds for the operation we saw yesterday?"

"Not according to their intelligence files," Kurtzman said. "Keep in mind the Israelis don't really consider these groups to be extremists or terrorists at all. There's been little or no police or military response to these groups."

"Even since the resurgence in violence in 2000?" McCarter demanded.

"There's been a few high-profile arrests since 2000, but little substantive change in the underlying attitude. On another note, we've been trying to track down anyone in the Middle East capable of pulling off the West Bank attacks. Anybody with the access to military hardware and prototype technology and high-tech brains behind the operation, financing and soldiers."

"What'd you come up with?" McCarter asked.

"Nada. The only known entity that could have pulled it

off was the Israeli military, or somebody high-level within the military who assembled a cadre of nationalists to pull it off, covertly, under the brass's noses,'' Kurtzman explained. ''That's unlikely.''

''Especially factoring in our friend Stuart Gold,'' spoke up Gary Manning. ''He's not exactly military. Why would they use him?''

''That was our take,'' Kurtzman said. ''But it brings us back at square one. Our basic question is still—who is responsible?''

''We'll get back to you with an answer in just a few, if we're lucky,'' Encizo said. ''We're there.''

IF HERZLIYYA HAD a ritzy part of town, they were in it. In a nation where apartments were home to most of the citizenry and home sites were scarce and expensive, the houses in this neighborhood had a definite sprawling aura to the design, as if the owners were flaunting their wealth by spending extravagantly on square footage.

The Stuart Gold home was a plain, oblong box, wide and flat roofed, his two acres landscaped with cultivated palm trees and flowering desert plants. There were bars on the windows, and the front door was protected by a wrought-iron gate. The concrete driveway descended slightly from the street into a garage that was a half level belowground. The windows in the garage door revealed a gray BMW and, low down, a red sports car of some kind. It looked as if Stuart Gold was in this morning.

McCarter's last message to his team was a warning not to get complacent. ''This guy may come across like a rich party boy, but don't underestimate him.''

Encizo wasn't going to make that mistake. Now that they had linked him to the previous day's West Bank attacks, it was clear there was more to Stuart Gold than his reputation suggested. If nothing else, Gold might have some of his soldiers housed here.

Encizo wasn't the electronics whiz that his younger teammate, T. J. Hawkins, was, but he knew what to look for. And he found something entirely different.

The tiny rounded nub of silver protruding from the fieldstone fence surrounding the Stuart Gold grounds wasn't familiar. With a gesture he brought his partner, Manning, to a halt.

Encizo touched his radio. "Phoenix Two here," he said quietly. He was standing in the next yard and watched for signs that Gold's neighbors might storm out to evict their trespassers, but all was still.

"Go, Phoenix Two," said McCarter after a pause.

"We've got sensors of some kind. Be on the lookout for small metallic studs embedded in the rock wall."

"Understood."

"Stony Base, here, Phoenix Two," Price said, monitoring the probe. "What kind of sensors?"

"I couldn't say."

"Can you give me a look at that item?"

"Affirmative, Stony Base." Encizo flipped out the tiny LED screen mounted on the chin bar of his radio mike, lining up the tiny video pickup, snapping off a digital image.

"Got it," Price said. "Thanks, Phoenix Two. What do you think, Gary?"

Manning, the security expert, was bending low to peer at the small stud. "I can't tell what it is. The sensors are built into the wall and the power source is inside, probably hardwired to feed back whatever data it's picking up to a system in the house. They're not video, and they don't look like audio pickups. I don't know how they could be useful as thermal sensors, not on the outside of the wall. I'm guessing they're sensing weight. Pressure on the top of the wall. We'll set something off if we go over."

"What if we just jump over the top?" McCarter asked.

"That will avoid setting them off, if they are what I think they are," Manning said without conviction. "Avoid touching the wall in any way."

"How about providing us a lift up, Phoenix Four?" McCarter said.

James was stuck with the vehicle as a getaway driver. He wasn't happy about it, but they all sometimes had to sit out the action when circumstances called for it. "I'm here. Who do you want to send over first?"

"Rafe and Gary," McCarter said.

"In case there's dogs?" Manning asked.

"Yeah. I figure by the time they get around to T.J. and me, they'll have lost their appetite."

A rocky hillock behind the house descended out of sight, leaving just enough room for the twin bare-earth paths of an access road. They couldn't see the vehicle coming until reaching the corner where the wall turned to enclose the rear of the Gold grounds. As the big Excursion came to a halt, Encizo stepped onto the hood in a crouch, raising himself just enough to see over the top at the house. More of the same desert-themed landscaping and bare ground. A free-form swimming pool-hot tub was surrounded by a patio of beige ceramic bricks. There was a brick barbecue and bar covered by an awning, as well as beach chairs. One of the chairs was occupied.

"What do you see?" Manning asked in a hushed voice.

"Topless babe," Encizo said.

Manning appeared at Encizo's side as if he had levitated there and the front end of the Excursion sank a few inches on its front-end suspension.

"No shit!" Manning exclaimed, getting an eyeful.

The young lady was on one of the lounge chairs with her hands dangling over the sides. Puddles on the bricks and the sheen of her skin showed she'd just taken a dip in the pool. Her hair was blond and finger combed away from her face. Her skin was darker than her hair, demonstrating that she spent a lot of time in the sun, and the lime-colored triangle of her bikini bottoms contrasted against the earthy burnish of her skin.

"Wish I brought field glasses," Encizo said.

"Yeah."

"To see if she's asleep," Encizo added, shooting Manning a look.

"Oh. Well, if she's sleeping, she hasn't been for long. Too much water."

"Are you guys just up there for the view?" James whispered, getting impatient and sticking his head out of the driver's window.

"You should see the view," Manning answered.

He added to Encizo, "We can get to her before she knows we're here."

Encizo considered this, then nodded. "Yeah."

Without further discussion, Encizo shouldered his weapon, stepped onto the roof of the Excursion, and flung one leg over the top of the wall, pulling his other leg after him. He never touched the wall, hit the ground and rolled onto his feet, moving aside as Manning landed beside him.

Riding out the pain of the impact on the hard ground, Manning wanted to comment on how rich people should put out the cash for real lawn, but he didn't dare. The sound of their landings was worse than he had anticipated, and he locked his eyes on the building for signs of response. All was quiet. The woman on the lounge chair wasn't moving.

"Phoenix Two here," Encizo radioed in a whisper as he heard the engine of the Excursion move on in a near idle. "We're inside the grounds. Any sign of alert?"

"Phoenix One here. Everything's quiet."

Before he spoke again his eyes fell on more of the tiny chrome nubs stuck in the wall, and pointed them out to

Manning. The big Canadian frowned and shook his head. He was beginning to think he didn't know what those things were.

"There's a wrinkle on this end," Encizo added, and briefly explained the presence of the sunbather.

"She could be anybody," McCarter said. "We'll have to regard her as an innocent bystander until we learn otherwise. Can you get her detained before she raises a fuss?"

"Can't make you any guarantees."

"Stony Base here," Price said. "Give us a shot of her if you have the time and opportunity."

Moving in, Encizo realized the takedown would be easier than he'd anticipated, since the sunbather was wearing stereo headphones that kept her oblivious to them. When and Manning came to within a few paces of the rear of her chair they could hear the hum of British pop music. She had her MP3 player cranked.

The hot midmorning sun was cooperating with them in one respect, putting their shadows behind them as they made the approach. But it also glared on the rear windows of the house, turning them gold. Anybody could be standing there, aiming any kind of a weapon at them, and the Phoenix Force pair would never see it.

Manning's big hand, callused from years of woodcraft in his off-hours, engulfed the small face of the woman so only her gently closed eyes were visible, becoming huge, round and terrified.

Manning felt the scream against his palm. She tried to claw his hand away, fingernails sinking into the flesh and tendons of his hand before Encizo pulled her hands away and removed her headphones.

The big Canadian placed a finger to his lips. "I'm going to take my hand away," he said in a level tone. "You are not going to scream. Got it?"

She moved her head in what tried to be a nod.

"You're an American?" were her first bewildered words.

"Canadian," Manning said.

She gaped at him, then craned her head back to see the darker-skinned man holding her other wrist.

"Not me," Encizo said with a winning smile. "I'm from Cuba."

Her eyes moved between the two of them as if she couldn't believe what she was hearing, as if she thought she were the victim of some sort of tremendous practical joke. "What do you people want?"

"We'll explain it all to you later," Manning said. "For the time being, you're going to have to get put in a safe place. Sorry." He snapped the plastic handcuffs onto her wrists before he'd finished speaking, then moved on to her ankles, snapping a cuff on one, looping her wrists through before cuffing the other ankle. The young woman was bent at the waist and couldn't straighten.

"What are you going to do with me?" she asked, her terror growing again as her eyes glanced fearfully at the swimming pool.

"Nothing of the sort," Manning said in a hushed voice, then he hoisted her by the belly under one forearm and carried her to the bar next to the barbecue. Under the plank top was a pair of cabinets, virtually empty. Manning pushed aside half-empty bottles of vodka and removed the shelf with a one-handed yank. He uprighted the woman and inserted her into the open space, folding her limbs tightly to make her fit.

"How long will you leave me here?" she pleaded.

"Not long," Manning said. "Unless you make a lot of noise. Then I'll have to forget where I put you. Got it?"

She was nodding wide-eyed as he shut the cabinet doors.

"The civilian's secured," Encizo radioed.

"Affirmative, Phoenix Two," McCarter replied. "We just got inside. We're making an approach on the front."

"This seems too easy, doesn't it?" Manning asked as they made their way up a pair of brick steps to a landing outside a sliding glass door. Half the glass was shielded by wooden blinds, the other half revealing an empty kitchen.

Encizo nodded. "Yeah. Stay sharp, friend."

"You better believe it."

Tel Aviv, Israel

"WE'VE GOT a big problem," said the plump, mousy haired woman as Kesher Nir sat up in bed.

Nir swore silently. He had been lying in the semidarkness thinking that everything had gone as planned, with no comebacks. It had been too good to be true.

"What is it?"

"You mean 'Who is it,'" Sandra Honig said, pulling her robe tighter to close the open collar and the skin she had been showing off. "The answer is Stuart Gold, of course."

"Stuart? What's he done now?"

"He fucked up, Kesher. I don't know how exactly, but I'll bet he got stoned and careless last night. I told you from the beginning he was the weakest cog in the machine."

"I'm coming," Nir said, running his fingers through his snow-white hair as he rose from the bed in his long silk pajama pants and followed Honig out of the room to a small security monitoring station in the circular landing at the top of the stairs. There was a flashing display bathing the landing in scarlet, and Nir wondered how he had managed to not see the illumination shining under his door as he lay there foolish and blissful in the darkness.

The bank of monitors were fed signals from eleven security systems monitoring all the IsAlliance Techsystems facilities and the homes of all Nir's Soldiers of Solomon associates. It had been a contingency of partnership in the venture. None of the partners knew how extensive Nir's security systems were, or that they were slaved to the Nir monitoring system and were never turned off. It was one of the ways in which he guaranteed his own security—he could watch for signs of treachery.

"Somebody knows," Nir grunted hoarsely, shocked to see soldiers in the video monitors.

"Somebody found out," Honig corrected him.

"Who are they?" he demanded, watching a pair of Caucasian men cross the grounds and reach the front of Stuart Gold's house. They had short-barreled, room-broom weaponry, the type of urban assault hardware that was perfect for interior penetrations.

"Not Israeli, I don't think," she said. "Not Arab, either. Those guys are as white as cheap bread. But there's another pair out back." She touched a button on the desk, and two of the images changed perspectives to reveal a barrel-chested white man and a darker-skinned man, identically armed and camouflaged. Nir stared at the dark-skinned man. He might be an Arab. Maybe.

"Who do we have in the house with Stuart?"

"Three soldiers," Honig replied. "Our own. Not mercs."

"Why are we finding out about this before they are?"

"Because there was no alert at Stuart's end," Honig replied caustically. "As far anyone there knows, the security system is completely shut down. It was the BCs that picked them up."

Nir nodded. A BC, or ballistocardiac sensor, used motion-detector arrays to feed sound into an applications with a detection algorithm to identify the presence of heartbeats. It literally measured ambient noise and picked out the mechanical force of the human pulse. The science behind it had been identified at the U.S. Department of Energy's Y-12 facility in Oak Ridge, Tennessee, and was initially tested for use in airplanes, to detect stowaways, and in prisons, to count inmates sight unseen. Nir's application was his own design, and only Honig knew he had it.

"Who turned off the standard security?" Nir demanded, bringing up the status window for Gold's estate, as if he needed to prove to himself such a lapse had actually happened.

"Stuart's cheap meat of the month," Honig said. "He must have showed her how to shut it down. She got up early to sunbathe. As far as I know, Stuart's still sleeping."

"Our soldiers should be making rounds," Nir declared. "They're supposed to patrol around the clock."

"Yeah, well, Stuart's ship runs a little loose there, you know?" Honig snapped. "I buzzed them on silent. Whoever responded claimed he was awake when I called, but I don't believe him."

"We've got a merc team in the area?"

"You know we do," Honig replied. "Fogelman himself, and three of his men."

"Get them to Gold's house now," he said calmly.

"I called Fogelman already. They're on their way," Honig replied. "Their response time during our drills was excellent. They'll be at Gold's within two minutes."

"Let's use the time to figure out more about these people," Nir said determinedly, ignoring her insulting attitude. But he wasn't unaffected by it, and the internalized anger brewed in his stomach like indigestion from bad seafood. He'd bring it up later.

He took control of a bottom screen and broke it into quadrants, shuttling the independent displays through the nine camera feeds from the Gold home and reversing at top speed. The security feeds, audio, video, ballistocardiac and all other sensor inputs were written to hard disk in a seventy-two-hour loop. Nir could rewind through the video from the past several minutes without interrupting its continued recording. First he found the video of the two in the rear jumping over the wall, then the two coming over the wall in front.

The time display said seventy-five seconds elapsed between the time the first pair came in the back and the second out front. "They used a truck as a platform to go over the wall," he explained.

"I'll tell Fogelman to watch for more paramilitaries outside the grounds," Honig said, punching a single button on the desk phone. The speaker played them the ringing on the other end.

"Goddamn."

Honig looked at Nir, staring at a freeze-frame of one of the commandos. She recognized him, too.

"Those are the soldiers from Shaalvim."

"But how could that be?" Nir demanded quietly.

"I don't know how, but it is. They tracked us down."

Nir had been fretting about the appearance of the commando team at Shaalvim, wondering where his organization was leaking information. The appearance of the same team a second time... "This could indicate a major security breach in the organization," he surmised. It was difficult to admit.

"I thought that went without saying. And the security breach is named Stuart Gold."

"We'll need to do something about him. After we clean up this mess."

"You *know* what we need to do about him, Kesher. We might as well have Fogelman and his goons handle it while they're mopping up the commandos."

"On the contrary, the commandos should be spared," Nir said. "Just long enough to provide us with their pertinent details. We have to be sure that the hole is plugged when Stuart is."

Honig was mildly surprised at this response. It demonstrated a ruthlessness she hadn't expected. Nir and Gold were friends from years back, since their college days. Honig had known there might come a time when Gold would prove to be a liability, and she had always wondered how Nir would react when faced with it. She had expected some sort of protest or rationalization. The only reaction she hadn't expected from Kesher Nir was cold acceptance of the necessity to execute his old friend Stuart.

Honig had witnessed this calculating mercilessness for the first time the previous day, during the strikes at the Palestinian village of Khodr and then especially at Shaalvim. When she was prepared for him to show last-minute reluctance to go through with the procedures, there had been only a gleam of chilling enthusiasm.

The click of the phone line interrupted her disquiet. It was incoming from the mercenary leader.

"Fogelman, what's your ETA?"

"Twenty seconds. We see the house already."

"Listen, this is more serious than we thought. Looks like we've got a paramilitary outfit, heavily armed, and there's a minimum of five of them. We think it's the bunch you met up with at the settlement."

"Dammit!" Fogelman retorted, then covered the phone and issued succinct commands to his driver before coming back on the line. "You people told me you were security experts."

"Security-technology experts," Honig replied. "We've got some loose screws in the personnel department. That's why I want you to take care of Stuart Gold while you are there. Make him a nonproblem."

There was a pause while Fogelman digested this. He and his mercenaries were fond of Stuart. During the merc team's extended stay in Israel, Gold had treated them well, buying them playmates and liquor. "You want me to shoot Gold in cold blood?"

"I don't care what method you use," Honig replied. "Just get him out of the picture."

"You know, I'm awfully damned tired of murdering innocent people for you," Fogelman complained. "It's not the job I was hired to do."

Honig closed her eyes briefly. This same argument yet again. Finally convincing the mercenaries to go through with the Shaalvim Settlement procedure as planned had ended up costing them a half-million dollars U.S. "You're a killer," she said. "It's what you do."

"I'm a soldier," Fogelman answered, as he always did. "There's a difference between killing during a military operation and cold-blooded murder."

"Have one of your men take care of the job if you don't want to," Honig said. "Here's my offer—the man responsible for removing the Stuart Gold problem gets a bonus of ten grand, all for himself."

"All right. I'll let them know—after the house is secure," Fogelman replied with a sort of sigh. "I don't want them fighting to get at him first."

"I want to know who these commandos are. When the house is secure, contact me from the security room on the top floor, next to Stuart's bedroom, and we'll take care of the questioning there. That way Kesher and I can be in on it."

"What's their position now?"

She checked the camera numbers and read out the coordinates of the two pairs of commando teams.

"I'm going to keep the phone with me and the line open," Fogelman reported. "I'll need you to keep me updated on their positions. First, though, I have to take out the truck driver."

"Split up," Honig said. "Send a pair after the driver and another pair inside after the commandos."

"No, thanks," Fogelman shot back. "I've seen these

guys work. In fact, I want Snell and the rest of the teams brought in for backup.''

''You're overreacting,'' Honig responded. ''Your men are staged all over the city. By the time they reach you, this will be over.''

''I call the shots in combat,'' Fogelman said tersely. ''That's in the contract.''

''I'm calling him,'' Honig said. She rang the nearest of Fogelman's mercenaries and ordered them to the scene.

''We've spotted the truck,'' Fogelman said as she got back on the line. ''It's a big sports utility wagon. We'll decommission it, then get inside.''

The Gold house had no cameras outside the walls. Honig contented herself with watching the trespassers. The team coming in the front, two white guys, one young, one a little older and as grim as hell, made short work of using the security bars on a lower window as a ladder to get them to a second-story windows, where they used a decorative concrete ledge as the staging point for the next part of the ascension. This time the young one climbed up the shoulders of the older man. It was like watching a high-wire act. Honig's view, from a wall-mounted video pickup forty feet away, zoomed in close enough for her to see their alert but calm demeanor.

These guys were good.

There were electronic feeds in the conductive glass of the window. This part of the security system remained active even when Stuart's stupid slut turned off the doors. Honig would have said the leads were undetectable, but the young one simply dug into the concrete with some sort of stainless-steel tool, exposing one end of the electrical lead and clamping it with tiny alligator clips that penetrated the insulation. It completed the connection when a length of wire from the clip was affixed with adhesive tape to the far side of the glass. The system monitoring the window quivered when the young man scored a large portion of the glass with another tool and tapped it with his palm to break out an entrance more than three feet wide.

Her analytical mind was thinking this was an excellent test case scenario for the security equipment. The electrical variance tolerance levels were clearly too high. The small dip caused by the removal of the glass didn't exceed what its programming considered normal, and thus no alert sounded.

A minute later the young one had slithered inside and he hauled up the sour-faced one.

They were professionals, but that wouldn't save them from Fogelman. The American mercenary commander had been in an unbelievable number of combat situations. He had a worldwide reputation. It made him very expensive. Every man on his team was a killer, with plenty of hours spent in the trenches, and none had been with Fogelman for less than three years. He had assured Honig and Nir that they obeyed his orders without hesitation, regardless of the nature of the job. Working for him made them rich men, and being rich was what they wanted most.

"I wonder how these guys managed to get the upper hand on Fogelman yesterday. He claimed there was an army of them," Nir wondered aloud.

Honig was thinking about that, as well. Had Fogelman been overestimating their numbers in the settlement? Or was there a small army of them waiting in the sidelines at Gold's house right now?

"How good are our soldiers—the ones in the house with Stuart, Kesher?"

Nir considered that for a moment.

As easy as the two out front had it, the soldiers in the rear weren't challenged in the slightest. Stuart's piece of university ass might as well have welcomed them in. Honig didn't know the girl but despised her anyway. Cute little face, tight little boobs. Honig had hated every incarnation of that girl she had ever known.

Now Stuart's trashy little sex toy was tied up in the liquor cabinet on the patio. It occurred to Honig the girl just might be the one who served as the avenue for intelligence about the Soldiers of Solomon to reach the outside world.

Honig decided she would tell that pansy Fogelman to wheel the cabinet into the swimming pool before he and his men left. And she would tell them not to look inside before they did it.

The sight of a helpless young female with firm bare breasts just might reduce them to tears.

"PHOENIX FOUR HERE—come in, Phoenix One."

"Go, Cal."

James glanced in his rearview mirror. "I've got a tail."

"You're being followed?" McCarter asked.

"Yeah. But not for long. These guys are heavily armed and looking for a fight. Probably four of them. They're in a Toyota SUV. I'm gonna lead them on a wild-me chase away from the house, but there may be others in the vicinity. Be on the lookout. They know we're here."

"Get that, Team Two?" McCarter asked.

"Got it," Manning replied.

"Don't do anything foolish, Cal," McCarter said.

"Hell, I outweigh these guys by about a couple of tons." The black commando saw the vehicle grow suddenly larger in his rearview mirror. "I'll get back to you."

The Toyota Land Cruiser Colorado closed the distance at a quickening pace and veered to make a sweep around James, and he stomped the pedal to the floor. The rumble of the 6.8-liter Triton V-10 increased to a roar, and as the big SUV accelerated, the Toyota managed enough speed to bring itself alongside. A head and shoulders emerged from the front end, the man bracing himself on the door and bringing the butt end of an Ingram Model 10 close to his body for stability. It was a tiny box of a submachine gun and with the extendable metal stock out of the way, it was ideal for this kind of work. At the moment the Toyota and the big Ford matched speeds, the gunman triggered a burst of 9 mm rounds at the Excursion.

James knew the windows on his vehicle were supposed to be custom bulletproof glass, but he wasn't a hundred percent at ease with a hail of 9 mm rounds flying at his head. He hit the brakes, bringing the Ford into a brief squealing skid. As the Toyota SUV raced away, a light cloud of smoke drifted around the Ford and James smelled the acrid stench of overheated tire rubber.

He tromped on the accelerator again and sent the Excursion barreling ahead. The Land Cruiser started circling just prior to pulling out of the quiet neighborhood onto a busier road into a commercial district of the city.

James looked for cross traffic, decided he had a five-second window of opportunity and bore down on the Land Cruiser like a grizzly after a bobcat. There was shock on the faces of the driver and the gunner at his side, but somehow the driver managed to avoid getting mashed by moving fast and steering at a right angle away from the Excursion. James saw the move coming and steered hard left to stay on target as the Toyota drove off the road onto rocky ground, bouncing wildly. James barely felt the change as his wheels left the surface of the street and sped after the dodging Land Cruiser. It moved too quickly for the big Ford to close on it, but James did manage to bring his front end into its rear left corner one time, folding the body panel and wrenching off a hunk of molded plastic.

The Toyota twisted onto the asphalt and headed back into the neighborhood.

"You guys give up way too easy," James muttered as he went after them, taking a shortcut over a steep hump of earth at least thirty feet high, raising a cloud of dust as his wheels fought for purchase on the loose soil. When he started down the other side, the tires dug in hard and the Excursion made good use of its seven thousand pounds of mass. James saw the surface of the earth coming straight at him and he gripped the wheel hard as the front end crashed into it, then with a thud he was on asphalt again. The shortcut was well worth it. He homed in on the Land Cruiser while the two back-seat passengers shouted at the Toyota's driver.

This time the smaller SUV didn't have time to maneuver clear and the front end of the Excursion crushed into its rear with a crunch. The Land Cruiser jumped forward, and for a moment James watched a swarm of pebble-sized glass pieces hovering in the air like bees. Beyond the swarm the Land Cruiser twisted, somehow staying upright as it skidded off the pavement again. The driver steered into the skid, wrestling to regain control, and found himself careening toward the painted facade of a tiny power utility building.

James witnessed the driver accomplish a small miracle, bringing the vehicle's skid into an arc that skimmed the corner of the utility building. The Phoenix force commando could swear he saw no light between the passenger-side doors and the building.

Whoever was behind the wheel of the Land Cruiser was a skilled driver, but his quick work left James with a job undone. He was going to keep this foursome and their Ingrams away from his teammates at all costs.

The driver of the Toyota had other ideas. When the Excursion rumbled at him the Land Cruiser sprinted around the back of the utility building, and James had to spin the wheel hard to make the Excursion follow. Only then did he witness the Toyota squeezing between a chain-link fence enclosing an electrical transformer. There was a passage of just a couple of yards between the fence and a wall of packed earth that had been partially carved away when the utilities were installed. The Land Cruiser jolted as it scraped dirt off the wall, but it did manage pull itself out the opposite end of the narrow passage, then turned sharply onto the street.

There was no way the Excursion would make the same maneuver. It was a whale of a vehicle, twenty feet long. James had a fraction of a second to make a decision. He could slam on the brakes and still end up with his front end stuck in the passage. Or he could go through.

Well, he thought, it was just a rental.

He hit the gas and muscled through the small opening with the ten-cylinder, 6.8-liter powerhouse thrusting like a mad bull against the clanging, tooth-rattling impact with the chain-link fence. The crash went on and on like no car wreck James had ever been through. He fought to steer the vehicle away from the earth wall only to find himself doing battle with the rattling, screeching fence as if it were a living thing, the Excursion crushing support poles, wrestling with the flexing links and chewing the barbed wire atop the fence, finally wrestling over it as it collapsed.

James couldn't believe the vehicle would emerge in driveable condition, but when the fence disappeared from his windshield he powered ahead, feeling the tires bounce over it, and cautiously headed for the street. Then he heard the scraping sound and looked in the rearview mirror.

Half the fence was coming with him.

It had to have been a ten-foot section of ruined chain link, complete with support poles and loose strands of barbed wire. It had to have got hung up on the Ford's underside and was trailing the vehicle, throwing up sparks and screeching on the street surface.

As the Stuart Gold house came into view, the Land Cruiser was pulling away from the front gates with a pair of gunners being left behind. One was punching a code into the security system while the other watched up and down the street, an automatic rifle held at his side. The gunner spotted the Excursion just as James floored it, rushing at the pair and filling the Israeli morning with a metallic scream, like hundreds of steel fingernails dragging on concrete.

James steered to the edge of the asphalt and targeted the gunners. If he plowed into them, he'd take them out, no doubt, but the Excursion wasn't going ride out an impact with a stone wall as it did a chain link...

The Phoenix Force commando grimaced savagely as he drove up to highway speeds on the narrow neighborhood lane. The gunner's face mirrored his surprise, and he unleashed a steady torrent of machine-gun fire at the armored front end of the Excursion while his companion kept stabbing frantically at the keypad. By the time they got the idea James wasn't going to they were trapped. The gate wasn't opening, they didn't have time to jump clear. The maniac behind the wheel of the big Ford was going to kill himself and them together.

They never dreamed what was actually in store for them until the Excursion veered at the last possible second, skidding hard and swinging its back end at them. The mass of sparking, screaming metal slammed into their bodies and crushed them into the gate, chain link and loose and broken metal ends ripping into their clothing and flesh crushing organs and bones. Then the momentum carried the Ford and its mass of scrap metal away and the tattered, ragged bodies flopped out.

The decorative iron gates swung open silently.

One of the gunmen was still alive, moving his arms and legs slowly and without purpose. As James put the Excursion into reverse and sped back toward the bodies, a sudden strident beeping filled the huge interior and it took a half second to realize it was the Ford's reverse sensing system telling him he was about to hit an obstacle.

"Very handy," he said, placing the vehicle in park and

popping the rear end. He jogged to the rear and grabbed the nearest of the two men. His face had received a massive impact and his nose, cheekbones and eyes were crushed. His entire body had become one hematoma, every inch of uncut skin turning black before James's eyes as his bled beneath the skin from thousands of broken blood vessels. Somehow he was still alive and conscious. He made no sound when James searched him, pocketed his handgun and hoisted him into the rear of the Ford.

The second guy wasn't salvageable.

James jumped back behind the wheel. He still had a score to settle with a little blue Land Cruiser.

CHAPTER TWELVE

Calvin James radioed a quick report to the house, alerting his teammates to the imminent arrival of two more gunners.

"I'll stop them if I can," he concluded as he took a short-cut to the back of the house through a neighbor's lawn, mowing down a small stand of shrubbery that blocked his path. He made a hard left as he reached the end of the wall and stomped on the gas. The Toyota Land Cruiser was parked and the gunner with the Ingram was on the roof, about to make the leap into the yard, but he rose into firing position and triggered the submachine gun with cat-fast reflexes.

The guy was good, James thought, realizing the man was going for the front left tire of the Excursion—a weak point even on an armored vehicle. Even on run-flats, James would lose speed and agility without good air pressure. He yanked the wheel right and left to dodge the burst of 9 mm rounds but steered inexorably into the front end of the SUV. The driver was still at the wheel, and he extricated himself through the driver's-side window in an impressive move, using the roof-mounted luggage rack to flip himself out the window and onto the top like an acrobat. In the half second before the impact his feet touched the roof, as his companion with the Ingram went bodily over the wall. But the driver was a fraction too slow, and before he could bound over after him, the Excursion crashed into the Toyota. The front end flattened like a human nose crushed under the impact of a two-by-four, and the vehicle leaped backward with a grinding noise, the angle of its front tires steering it into the stone wall.

James allowed his body to fly into the air bag as it deployed and deflated, then pushed it out of his way and snatched the gearshift, backing the Ford away. He spotted the Toyota's driver, dazed but conscious, his upper body flopped on the ruined hood of the Land Cruiser, his lower body jammed between the SUV and the wall.

The Phoenix Force commando kept the Excursion in reverse and cranked the wheel, flooring the gas pedal and listening to the transmission protest. The vehicle bounced off the opposite side of the access road in a big circle, completed half the radius of its turn on the steep hillside with rocks and soil spilling from under its tires and emerged on the road as the gunner raised his torso, shocked. But he recognized that he was the target of the maniac in the Ford for the second time in the past ten seconds and now he couldn't flee. No gymnastics were going to get him out of the way this time. All he could do fumble the handgun out of his thigh holster, level it at the driver through the rear window, and squeeze the trigger over and over.

With the transmission whining like a turbine and .38 rounds cracking into the rear window, James heard the sudden beeps of the reverse sensing system. They grew more strident, then became a sort of wailing alert just before the rear end crushed into the Toyota's hood, pushing it into the wall.

Over all the noise, James heard the sickening crunch of the gunner's upper body slamming onto the hood as his lower body flattened to pulp.

"Phoenix Four here," James radioed in a hurry. "One of them got inside—be on the lookout."

He didn't get an answer.

GARY MANNING HEARD the tread on the stairs long before he saw the man, who was attempting to move silently. He signaled Rafael Encizo with a glance, and the little Cuban slipped into a niche behind a pair of stainless-steel refrigerators.

Manning didn't hide. Without laying eyes on the figure creeping down the steps, he knew the guy was nervous or an amateur or both. The big Canadian played on it. He opened one of the refrigerators and stuck his head in, as if searching for a snack. His handgun was pulled against his chest. He tucked his shortened submachine gun on the middle shelf of the fridge.

The newcomer came into the kitchen on the toes of his bare feet, and halted a few paces behind Manning. Well, that was smart at least, putting too much room between them for Manning to simply make a grab at his gun. Manning had assembled an arm full of packaged meats, sprouts and squeeze bottle of mustard, and he grinned easily when he saw the frowning Israeli. "Hey. Where's Stuart keep the bread?"

The man clearly wasn't Stuart Gold. He was late forties, his face twitching and his eyes unable to remain focused on a single point. He had the starved, bony body of a prisoner of war, his bare chest sunken and his flesh grayed as if through malnutrition. "How do you know about us, American?"

"About who?"

"The Soldiers of Solomon. Playing dumb will not save your skin. We know why you're here."

"I've never heard of the Soldiers of Solomon, buddy. I'm just a friend of Stuart's and I stopped by to have lunch. His girlfriend told me it was okay to come in."

Manning's performance was convincing enough to give the gunner serious second doubts. He shifted from foot to foot as if the floor were cold, his eyes scanning the kitchen as if the cabinets and appliances held evidence to confirm his suspicions. He shifted the suppressed Uzi from hand to hand. Manning wondered if he had taken too great a risk. This guy was more than nervous. He acted deranged, advertising his mental instability in the ebb and flow of his facial expressions.

But he came to a decision all at once and stepped back to the edge of the stairs, shouting up without looking away or moving the business end of the Uzi from Manning's chest. "Blum, get Stuart and tell him to get down here right away."

Reinforcements. That can't be good, Manning thought. Time to neutralize the nut.

"You stand right there until Stuart comes down," said the Twitcher. "We'll ask him if it's okay for you to be here."

"Can I put this stuff down?" Manning asked.

"No."

"Suit yourself," Manning said. He fired the 92-F and the gunner threw both arms up, the Uzi tumbling across the floor while a thin trail of blood splattered the cabinets. The gunner collapsed into a crouch and made a grab for the Uzi, only to stop in disbelief when he saw that his hand was shattered, limp, bloody and useless.

Manning had dropped the sandwich fixings and leveled the Beretta. The wounded man stared at the weapon as if seeing something supernatural and his scalp trembled, his facial muscles moving into constant spasms.

"I should have shot first," said the Twitcher.

"Now you know," Encizo replied, coming out from behind the refrigerator and snagging the Uzi with his foot without removing his two-handed grip on the MP-5 SD-3.

The Twitcher squeezed his eyes shut and opened them again, as if trying to wipe away the distortion that was Encizo from the lenses of his eyeballs.

"Time for answers, friend," Manning said.

"You get nothing from me. Nothing but my name, rank and serial number."

"We'll start there."

"Name is Berel Riskin," he said, then smiled through the onslaught of pain as it finally started reaching his brain from his hand. "Riskin. And we don't have ranks. We don't have ranks or serial numbers." Despite the pain he looked be amused by that.

"You might as well talk, Riskin. You've already given us the name of your organization," Manning said. "That's more than we knew a few minutes ago."

"The knowledge dies with you in this house," Riskin said.

"Too late for that," Encizo told him, touching the half-inch round lens mounted on the chin piece of his communications headset. "Say hello to the folks back home."

Riskin's face dropped and he shuddered, drooping looking at the floor as if shamed.

"Why not tell us what the Soldiers of Solomon are trying to accomplish," Manning demanded.

"Go to hell. To hell."

"You first."

Riskin was suddenly fearful, cowering like a frightened dog. Would this man actually gun him down in cold blood? Manning could see Riskin was about to make some sort of move when they heard footsteps on the stairs, descending quickly. Encizo moved faster than Riskin could get out a warning shout, the butt of the submachine gun cracking into his skull. Riskin toppled with his warning unspoken, but the sound of violence warned the newcomer anyway. He swept around the corner with his finger on the trigger of his Uzi. Manning beat him to the punch, snapping out a round from the 92-F that plowed into the gunner's sternum and sent him into a back bend while the Uzi coughed harshly through its suppresser and sent 9 mm slugs into the hand-textured ceiling. Manning stepped in fast and appropriated the Uzi, but he need not have bothered.

The single round had shattered the bones in the gunner's chest, and the fragments had cut the heart to pieces.

DAVID MCCARTER EMERGED into the hall facing one way, T. J. Hawkins the other. Their weapons went unfired. The hall was empty.

The house was built solidly, absorbing their small sounds of movement. They explored the top floor without finding a living soul, but discovered one of the large bedrooms at the end of the hall with three narrow, unmade beds.

Hawkins placed his hand just over the rumpled sheet and felt the radiating heat of its former occupant.

"They're been out of here a few minutes at most," he said quietly.

McCarter nodded, examining a thin communications laptop. An open window on the screen showed an instant messaging application. It had been forgotten by the occupants in their haste. McCarter scanned the most recent time-coded message:

intruders split up
2 coming back door
2 coming window top floor
Respond

"Somebody saw us getting inside," Hawkins said quietly.

"Both teams," McCarter agreed. "Remote video monitoring, probably buried in the stone with the other sensors."

"But they missed the final message," Hawkins pointed out. "They didn't respond to it. They don't know we came in this way."

McCarter nodded. "Yeah, I guess that's how it looks."

Hawkins got the point. He scrolled up the window of messages. It went back just six minutes. "They knew we were here about the time we went over the walls," he read. "'F. alerted, help coming.'"

"F. must be the guy in charge of Cal's Toyota," McCarter said.

They had received the alert from James just as they made it into the uninhabited top-floor bedroom of the Stuart Gold house. Phoenix Force had expertise, but McCarter wasn't surprised the team had been unable to get in undetected. The possibilities of electronic coverage were too numerous to avoid without the benefit of extensive preplanning, which had been impossible.

In fact, the interior might be rigged with motion detectors or video, tracking even now. Not that there was much he could do about it. They left the bedroom and reached the top of the stairs, hearing nothing.

Down, McCarter mouthed.

As if there was any other way to go.

Then came a shout from the first floor. "Blum, get Stuart and tell him to get down here right away."

McCarter and Hawkins heard a hissed conversation on the second floor, then a door opened and the words became audible. In Hebrew. McCarter didn't speak it and he knew Hawkins didn't, either.

But he could tell there was some point of contention, then one man emerged onto the stairs and tromped down them. McCarter peered down and caught sight of him holding an Uzi submachine gun.

The Phoenix Force leader led the descent at the moment the man disappeared, but found more closed doors. From downstairs they heard the retort of a suppressed handgun. The "silenced" cough was loud enough to hear distinctly one floor up. Even if it wasn't, the short chatter of Uzi fire filled the house. At the same moment the voice of Calvin James came through their earpieces, his tone urgent. McCarter heard James's words without comprehending them as the nearest door opened abruptly, and the black-haired, black-bearded man stared at them. His reaction time was nearly instant and his Uzi triggered before it came up from the floor. Hugging the wall, McCarter didn't have a shot and he stepped into the open to get clearance, but Hawkins was already triggering a burst from his subgun. Eight rapid-fire 9 mm shockers couldn't miss. The man died on his feet never quite getting the chattering Uzi into target acquisition.

Hawkins lashed at the door with his foot and it crashed into the far wall as McCarter rushed through it, sweeping the room. They found a single, haggard-looking man holding his palms toward them as if to protect himself from a punch. He was talking fast. Again it was in Hebrew, but McCarter had no trouble understanding that the man was begging for his life.

"You must be Stuart Gold," he said.

Gold switched to English. "Yes! I'm Gold! I'll tell you whatever you want to know. Just please don't shoot me."

"How many bodyguards in the house?" McCarter demanded.

"Three! Just three! Including him." He looked fearfully at the dead gunner in the door.

"Did you catch what Cal said?" Hawkins asked.

"No," McCarter said, but he had heard the urgency in James's voice. Compounding that concern was his worry about the exchange of gunfire on the first floor. He tapped the microphone button his headset. "Phoenix Four, repeat your message."

"Phoenix Four here," James responded quickly. "One of the gunners from the Toyota made it inside, back door."

"Team Two, copy that?" McCarter demanded.

The answer came in the form of a short electronic tone,

generated at the push of a button on a headset. A signal that the situation didn't allow a voiced response.

"On my way," McCarter said.

Another short pair of the electronic tones. Two meant no. McCarter stopped.

The Briton experienced a moment of profound doubt. He had to be absolutely sure. "Phoenix One here," he radioed. "Team Two, do you want assistance."

Two low-pitched beeps. *No.*

McCarter stepped into the hall. Every fiber of his being told him to get down there and protect his team. But being a leader sometimes meant trusting the decision making of those he led.

He heard a click from the first floor. Metallic? A footstep?

Agitated and powerless, McCarter stood there feeling as if he were going to jump out of his own skin.

ENCIZO BENT OVER Berel Riskin and yanked plastic cuffs on his wrists, pulling hard on the adjustable end to tighten the cuff on the wounded hand in a makeshift tourniquet. He didn't want the man dying of blood loss before he could answer more questions.

"Rafe!"

Manning was crouching on the opposite side of the glass patio doors, hugging the wall. Encizo made a lightning-quick assessment of cover possibilities and found the kitchen lacking. His niche place behind the refrigerator was in plain view of the patio door. He bolted, jumping through the open space in front of the door and glimpsing the oncoming figure with the Uzi. The gunner was in a hurry, too, and he was trying to watch the entire grounds while he ran, which meant he missed witnessing the spectacle of the airborne Cuban in the kitchen.

When Encizo was at Manning's side, he heard the urgent

warning from James. "One of them got inside—be on the lookout."

"Wonder what happened to the other three?" Encizo wondered.

"Assume they are no more," Manning said. "I don't know if we can put much faith in our friend Riskin."

"We should take this guy alive," Encizo concluded.

The runner from the yard pulled at the door and swept the interior as Encizo and Manning made a retreat through an eating area. The new arrival was fisting an Uzi in each hand, with an air of authority that said he actually could use the guns two at a time. Manning and Encizo found themselves in a formal dining room with seating for eighteen. They were in search of the right place to stage a nonlethal ambush. Nothing presented itself. They heard the gunner closing the sliding glass door, then heard just as clearly the rattle of unsuppressed Uzi fire from upstairs.

The gunner in the kitchen failed to react, waiting out the battle.

The shooting turned to a shout, too muffled to be understood. Then there was a call from McCarter. Manning touched the tiny send button on his headset to tell him he couldn't answer.

McCarter suggested he come join them, Manning gave him a *no* signal to keep him where he was. They needed this guy alive. If McCarter had walked into the scene without knowing what was going down, it could quickly turn into a life-or-death battle.

So what was the two-fisted Uzi-gunner doing all this time?

Manning heard a strange, somehow familiar sound. Liquid, then a guttural wheezing that trailed off. It took him a second to realize it was the sound of somebody getting his throat cut.

So much for Riskin.

Manning was wondering about the savagery of a man who could cut the throat of a bound, unconscious man in cold blood. That took an excessive depth of inhumanity. The kind learned through years of experiencing death as an activity to engage in. There was no human conscience behind his action, because he no longer thought of his victims as humans.

The killer spoke. Two names, harshly whispered. "Come in, dammit!"

He'd just figured out that James had neutralized the pair coming in through the front.

"Fuck," he grated, biting off the word bitterly, and a moment later he was speaking again. Was he saying another name? To Manning it sounded like the name of a brand of coffee. Then, "I'm screwed. I think they've taken our other two men, too. How soon…?" The words faded. Finally, he said, "That will be too late. I'm blowing the whole deal right now."

There was a faint click, then the killer crossed the kitchen with heavy steps. Encizo and Manning moved. So much for taking him alive. Whatever this guy had in mind sounded extreme and immediate.

"Team Two here," Manning radioed as they moved through a media room full of electronic equipment. "He's coming to the stairs—extreme caution."

They emerged in a hallway running from the front door through the middle of the house, spotting the killer with one foot on the stairs. He knew them for what they were and reacted without hesitation, leaping up the stairs a heartbeat ahead of the dual bursts of submachine-gun fire that they sent his way. They raced after him and Encizo arrived first, searching for the target and spotting instead a small cylindrical shadow bouncing on the carpet. As Manning reached his side, Encizo dropped the submachine gun and made a two-fisted grab for the front collar of the big Canadian's

Kevlar vest. Encizo yanked up and pushed back and felt his shoulders wrench in their sockets as Manning's breath left him in a huff and he felt himself become airborne. For a man as big as he was, it was positively odd to be lifted off his feet.

Encizo was stocky, muscular, and he used every ounce of energy to propel Manning's flying body and himself back, away, anywhere but where they were. They landed hard and slid, then Encizo pushed himself to his feet and grabbed at Manning's arm, then the blast came. It was fast-moving freight train of heat and thunder that crashed into Encizo's back and legs and smashed him with a fist of fire, propelling him into his teammate, then hurling him to the hard tile floor.

Encizo shook his head and he tried to get upright. He couldn't do it and he didn't know why. He felt the floor, he felt blood, felt some part of him burning, and over the roar in his ears he heard the chattering of an Uzi that went on and on.

CHAPTER THIRTEEN

Tel Aviv, Israel

While the Jewish people made up eighty percent of the population of the State of Israel, only one in four was actually born there. The rest immigrated from around the world, coming to the Jewish homeland from Europe, America, Africa and even Asia. The mix of races was as varied as that of a busy New York City street.

Rosario Blancanales never felt like a stranger, no matter how strange the land. He had a basic knowledge of the tenets and customs of Judaism and received condensed refresher course in Hebrew phrases and Israeli customs from Yakov Katzenelenbogen via a video link during the flight from the Farm.

More importantly, he was an infiltration specialist, with a rare natural skill for behaving like a native. Wherever he happened to be was his home.

"Do I look Jewish?"

Jack Grimaldi looked him over and shrugged. "Sure, you could be of Mediterranean descent. There are Jews from all over the world in this country, so I think you'll pass muster," Grimaldi said. "How's your Hebrew?"

"I can ask for the men's room and order a beer, and that's about it," Blancanales said with a grin.

"So long as you've got the basics covered."

The thing was, during foreign undercover work, Politician Blancanales relied less on native language and customs and more on an innate ability to interact with anyone, anywhere. He could negotiate anything, which had earned him his nickname, although "the Politician" was too big a mouthful. So his nickname had a nickname: "Pol."

In truth he was a Mexican American. He spent his childhood in East Los Angeles. He was a stocky, powerful figure, with almost black eyes and skin the color of weathered bronze.

Blancanales was considered senior staff at Stony Man Farm. He had extensive Special Forces experience, including time spent with the Black Berets. Later he was recruited into a less well-known organization: it had been called the Death Squad, one of the deadliest vigilante organizations ever to operate within the United States.

That had been a different time. Mack Bolan, the Executioner, was a man hunted by the law, not to mention every crime organization in America and beyond. The American Mafia was the primary target of the squad, and it suffered devastating losses at its hands. In the end, members of the Death Squad were themselves destroyed one by one, until the only original members who survived were Blancanales and Hermann Schwarz—and, of course, Bolan himself.

Blancanales and Schwarz worked side by side under former Los Angeles Police Department detective Carl Lyons. Able Team, under the direction of Stony Man Farm, worked with North America as its primary turf.

But right now Able Team was sitting on the sidelines. Blancanales felt lucky just to have an assignment, even if he had to be away from his teammates. Not that he didn't have other things besides Able Team going on in his life. He and Schwarz co-owned the Able Group security agency, which took a lot of his off time.

But every once in a while a guy had to get out of the office.

"What's the feeling at the Farm?" Grimaldi asked, steering the rental Fiat through airport traffic and heading into the city.

"Kind of grim," Blancanales said. "We're low on leads at the moment. Nobody's sure what to do next."

"How about the rest of the world?"

"They are as stymied as we are, and the politics of the thing are getting out of hand," Blancanales said. "The Arab states are accusing the Israelis of deliberately slowing the investigation. The Israelis claim they're working overtime but say they can't find evidence that the Palestinians were actually attacked in the first place.

"That's what I'm hearing at this end. Only the Israeli media is slanting things even more in favor of the Israelis. They're even hinting that the Palestinians in Khodr killed their own people for evidence of provocation. Tell me this, are the Israelis really stalling?"

"Yes and no," Blancanales said. "Some of them are carrying out the official orders to get this solved as fast as possible—others are slowing things down. From his contacts Katz has learned there are small pockets of support for whoever or whatever it was that did attack Khodr. One thing is definite—Israel won't stand by and let an international task force conduct the investigation."

"I saw on CNN," Grimaldi said. A UN coalition suggested that a cooperative intelligence effort be put in the field, including Arab and Israeli representation, to look into what really happened at Khodr and Shaalvim. The Israeli UN representative had flatly refused to consider the idea. "It doesn't seem like such a bad idea to me," Grimaldi said, then shrugged. "But I'm not an Israeli."

They drove in silence for few minutes, watching Tel Aviv going through the motions of its day. Elsewhere in this same city the almost daily pattern of violence had started. Rock throwing and tear gas. The rubber bullets would be coming soon. They saw an early lunch crowd gathering at a streetside café, young professionals in business attire holding loud, angry conversations. Every person they saw looked mildly outraged. They were both wondering how long this tentative balance between peace and war could continue.

"If the brains back home are low on leads, what are you going to do here, Pol?" Grimaldi said finally.

He shrugged. "Sniff around. Go on hunches and hope they pan out."

"This is the place." Grimaldi pulled the Fiat into a complex of buildings that was clearly industrial, but fronted by upscale brick facades. The English section of the sign told them the complex was made up of high-technology firms, including one called NewMan Electronics.

"Hope you have your story straight," Grimaldi said.

Blancanales grabbed the briefcase and small suitcase from the back of the Fiat and set them at his feet, then tugged his sports jacket to smooth the wrinkles. "I hope I do, too."

GRIMALDI HAD BEEN more than happy to play chauffeur to Blancanales. At least it was something to do in what was looking like another day of inactivity. Playing poker with his copilot had become dull. The young USAF flyer was on temporary assignment at the Farm and had the most expressive game face Grimaldi ever saw. It was an effort not to clean him out of his pocket change too fast and end the game.

They were camped at an airfield outside Tel Aviv. The nearby hangars were home to a contract remanufacturing facility mostly serving cargo jets. Stony Man Farm had purchased a short-term lease there, claiming they needed a place to keep their new Airbus, its pilots and five-member support team before taking delivery of the aircraft. Grimaldi had spent some time checking out the operation, but the foreman found his presence distracting to the mechanics. The pilot knew when he was unwelcome. He waved to some of the crew he had befriended as he drove the Fiat off the tarmac to a spot on the grounds where the Airbus was parked. Phoenix Force's Excursion had returned.

What was left of it.

"Oh, crap."

He was out of the Fiat and up the roll-away stairs in three long leaps, and the first person he met was McCarter, shirt off, chest splattered with angry, plum-colored splotches as big as a fist.

"David, what happened?"

"Rafe got burned."

"Bad?"

McCarter shrugged and the look of pain on his face showed how much he regretted the movement. "He'll live. I don't know how bad he is yet. Cal did what he could for him. Stony had a Navy doc flown in from a destroyer on the Gulf."

"What about to you?" Grimaldi demanded.

McCarter looked down at his chest. "Guy with an Uzi."

"Jesus. Anybody else hurt?"

"Yeah," Hawkins said as he came through the door. "You should see the guy with the Uzi."

MANNING'S ARMS were crossed and his brows knit as he watched the U.S. Navy doctor and male nurse wrap Rafael Encizo's torso. The bandages went from the Cuban's rib cage up to the collarbone. He was staring into space as his body was manipulated, wearing the expression of the heavily drugged.

"He'll be all right," James said, answering the unasked question. "The burns were spread over a wide area of his side and back, but they weren't bad. He'll need to grow some new skin.''

"And new hair," Encizo said with a slow grin.

The doctor got to his feet. "Your friend is correct. He'll be good as gold as long as he has a doctor keep a close watch out for infection. I have done all I can for him."

He was looking from Manning to McCarter.

"Now?" the doctor demanded. "Can I please go take care of those men?"

McCarter nodded.

"Thank God," said the doctor. "Come on!" he said to the nurse. The two of them hurried their wheeled flight cart of medical supplies to the rear of the cabin.

For the first time Grimaldi noticed two figures on the floor of the cabin wrapped in blankets. The doctor sliced off the blankets with quick, controlled movements learned from years of emergency medical experience.

What was underneath the blankets made Jack Grimaldi feel like throwing up.

CHAPTER FOURTEEN

Arnold Fogelman knew physical distress like an old friend. He'd borne up under the anguish of countless wounds. Gunshots. Knife cuts. Shattered bones. Violence and pain were a part of his life. But he never knew agony as he did now; he assumed he was in hell.

Then the veil of smothering darkness was removed and he stared into the face of a man and the inside of a room with a curved ceiling. It was an aircraft interior, Fogelman realized, and the man had a stethoscope.

"Look at this. His pelvis is crushed, and everything below it. There are more broken facial bones and cracked ribs than I can begin to count. Oh, Christ, this man is conscious."

Another man appeared with a hypodermic. Painkillers. Bring it on, Fogelman thought, trying to say it, trying to shout it. Put out the pain.

"No narcotics."

The doctor turned. "He's suffering."

"We need him to answer questions."

There was an argument. Fogelman couldn't follow it. But in the end, like a starving man watching a scrap of bread get tossed to the wind, he saw the hypodermic needle get put away. If he could have uttered a sound, the fierce mercenary commander would have whined like a dog.

IT TOOK SURPRISINGLY little time for the doctor to wrap up his treatment of the pair in the back of the cabin, and the look he gave McCarter would have ignited paper. "He's useless to you now. Thanks to you, that man lived his final moments in excruciating agony."

It was Hawkins who spoke first. "Then he deserved to live longer."

The Navy doctor leaned on the circular table around which they were gathered, putting his reddening face close to Hawkins's. "I don't know who you people think you are, you coldhearted son of a bitch, but I'm damned sure you're not God, and only God has the privilege of making judgments like that. What crime could that man have possibly committed to deserve a lingering, painful death—?"

"I'll show you what he did," Hawkins said, his hand touching the mute button on the remote control. The television news was playing on the wall screen and the sound came up, and the Navy doctor turned to see it.

The Israeli news station had been playing the same clip over and over, and was playing it again now. It was the video from the apartment camera overlooking the street of Shaalvim Settlement. There were the faces of the women and children trapped inside the school. There was the rush of flames that erased those faces, and distant, tiny screams.

The doctor had seen the clip before, of course, but he was stunned. His nurse was staring at the corpse in the corner as if it was something supernatural.

The doctor said finally, "This man—did that?"

Hawkins nodded.

THERE WAS A PYRE of anger burning in the hearts of the Israeli people, and the flames were fanned every time the video played on Israeli TV. And it was played hundreds of times. It was the kind of image that changed the minds of those who had once supported peace efforts and concessions to the Palestinians.

By midafternoon, a sort of general strike had spontaneously occurred in a country too emotionally agitated to continue with the facade of day-to-day life and business. Demonstrations came into being by chance with the extraordinarily heavy ebb and flow of people moving into the streets in every city. The knots of people would form like clots of anger. They would shout and cry and make their voices heard, then the individuals would disperse, more disturbed and energized than before.

Despite calls for peace from the President of the United States, the Russian president, the British prime minister, the Vatican and dozens of other national and religious leaders, the violence escalated throughout that long day.

The unthinkable occurred at four in the afternoon.

THE ARMY HAD BEEN organized via mass e-mail and word of mouth. The call went out for every armed man who called himself an Israeli to come together at an appointed time and place in Jerusalem. One thousand men, boys and even women kept the appointment, most armed with handguns. Some had rifles. Many had police rifles or automatic weapons with the serials numbers of the Israel Defense Forces or the Frontier Guard. The world media was there too.

Israeli police quickly found themselves outnumbered twenty to one, their rubber bullets all but ignored by the massed protesters, and when the police retreated, allowing the makeshift army into Palestinian Jerusalem, it was all recorded. As was the battle that followed. This time twenty Israelis were killed, but the slaughter of the Palestinians was merciless.

"Obviously, the people are ready for us," Kesher Nir said.

"We knew we couldn't coordinate events every step of

the way, but this is still amazing to me," Sandra Honig said, biting her lip and pacing his home office. Nir had been at home more often lately, as if unwilling to venture out in the world he was manipulating, and the day-to-day operations of IsAlliance were being handled by his assistants. Honig herself was energized by the events of the past few hours, but she was also uncharacteristically suspicious. Had Nir engineered the Jerusalem battles without telling her? He didn't do things like that. But he was under a great deal of stress, and his behavior was changing for the worse.

"How can we move up the date for achieving full equipment inventory?" he posed again. They had been returning to this issue for the past hour.

"Kesher," Honig said irritably, "we've gone over this. We have to consider security issues."

"The people are ready and this test proves it! It is the willingness of the people we have to consider!"

Honig heard the word *test,* but she pretended not to notice. As far as she was concerned, he had admitted his culpability in this deed. The implication was that she was losing control of Kesher Nir.

It was time to exert her influence. She leaned close, her mouth sensual and her voice sardonic. "If we get caught," she said softly, "and the people do not support us, the world would lock us away as perpetrators of a holocaust."

She kissed him, pressing herself against him, and he used his hands on her as she murmured in his ear. She used the words he loved to hear, and they played their roles right there on the leather office chair of his Tel Aviv home.

But when it was over, he brought up the subject again. He announced he was going to call his shippers to see if any measures could be taken to accelerate the movement of his purchased goods. Honig was pulling herself back into her bra and blouse. She disapproved, but she said nothing. A lesson she had learned long ago was that, if her most potent tool of persuasion failed to convince him, nothing would.

Stony Man Farm, Virginia

AKIRA TOKAIDO FOUND himself at the front door of the place he wanted to be. It was the internal network for Gold Aeronautic Electronic Systems. The server was a Windows NT. Behind it was the Gold Intranet and access to its PCs and minicomputers. The computer system's security firewall, application-level proxy and network address translation were tough enough to overcome. Military grade. Tokaido nabbed an identity to disguise his entrance and dismantled the applications trying to keep him out, keep him from identifying the IP numbers of user machines on the inside. Once the systems were reduced to pieces, he was able to solve them with small, powerful helper applications built by himself and the others on the Stony Man cybernetics team—well, mostly him. When he had all the pieces of the solution, he went at the security system again, responded with all the answers it required and found himself inside.

Now came the hard part.

Somewhere, on the opposite side of the globe, Phoenix Force was in a tight situation. Tokaido hadn't had the time to absorb the details. They had gone to question the brainiac behind Gold Aeronautic but met a paramilitary response. That meant the house was being monitored by someone, somewhere. Probably Gold himself, watching from a secure spot inside the house, but not necessarily.

Gold almost certainly had a home link into his company's Intranet. Whoever else was in with him on the Palestinian and Israeli villages was probably tied into the home system—an electronic umbilicus tying together players in a very violent game.

There was a way out to Gold's system. It was almost

surely dedicated, so it wouldn't have been shut off. But it was hidden very well.

Or maybe just made to look as if it were turned off.

Tokaido grinned. He'd mapped the system and found dozens of feeds to the outside that indicated no traffic, but the system might be lying. He brought up an external monitoring program, reconfigured it in under a minute, and sat back to watch it trace information flowing through Gold Aeronautic's internal network.

The small application was straightforward, simply looking at the movement of blips over various routes. It didn't interfere or even remember what it had seen. Tokaido was thinking that he would rework the application to make these traces automatically, but for the time being he was looking for anomalies based on the manual search he'd performed himself, and in twenty seconds he found one. An IP address inside the Intranet was claiming to be turned off, but the data flowing into it told a different story. Tokaido followed the data flow. He liked what he found at the end of the line.

He went backward, searching for the source of the data flow, and found himself traveling outside Gold Aeronautic again.

When he landed at the source of the data he slapped the edge of the desk. "Gotcha!"

"Find something?"

Tokaido was grinning. If he was surprised to see Hal Brognola leaning over his shoulder, he didn't show it. He tapped the monitor screen with his fingertip, making tiny hollow sounds on the glass. "I've got more than something. I've got *it*."

"Who is he?" Brognola asked.

The man on the video screen had the slack-jawed look of a corpse.

"This is one of the mercs Cal whacked. Believe it or not,

this is the one who survived, for a while," Barbara Price said.

"Smashed him with chain-link fence," Hal Brognola said again. "Like with a flyswatter?"

"Yes."

Brognola was still trying to form a picture of it in his head. Viewing the ugly results of the act helped make it real.

"ID?"

"Aaron tracked it down," Price said, nodding to Kurtzman.

"Craig Serino. He's a Roman and he's ex-military," Kurtzman said. "The report from Italy is that he got busted as the part of a major bank theft ring. He fled prior to serving jail time—how he got away is not reported—and hasn't been seen in Italy since 1988. He was rumored to have joined up with a mercenary group based in Arizona, run by Arnold Fogelman, a German with U.S. citizenship. The rumor must be true, because this is Fogelman."

The image on the screen switched to a photo of a second body. Like Serino, he had been alive when transported by Phoenix Force back to their operations base on the Airbus. Like Serino, he wasn't alive anymore.

"We can't ID this one yet," Kurtzman said, and a third corpse's photo appeared. "This guy killed Stuart Gold after burning Encizo."

"Yes," Price said. "He planted a grenade on the steps on his way in. Rafe and Gary barely got out of the way. Then he marched into Stuart Gold's bedroom and shot him with three Uzi rounds before turning the Uzi on David."

"What's David's condition?"

"He's bruised but okay," Price reported. "His armor took a few rounds, but he and T.J. took him down pretty quick."

Brognola nodded. "But Gold is dead. We didn't get much out of this action for all the trouble it's brought us."

"Wrong, Hal. At the moment we have more than we could have hoped for. For one thing, we had Craig Serino," Price said. "Serino talked."

"What did he have to say for himself?"

"He's confirmed the mercs were hired by a group of Israelis for the raid on Khodr and Shaalvim Settlement. He doesn't know the names of the people with the money, but he has the name of a company they worked for—IsAlliance Techsystems in Tel Aviv."

"That name sounds familiar," Brognola said.

"It's the same company that served as the originating point for some of the messages coming into the Gold house during Phoenix's raid, according to Akira's trace," Kurtzman said. "Now get this—Bear ran a cross reference on employees at IsAlliance. VP of future development is Sandra Honig. She was buddies with Stuart Gold in college in the mid-1990s, and she's a known radical among the Israeli homeland movement."

"It sounds as if we're getting somewhere," Brognola said. "What are the chances Sandra Honig is the brains behind the recent raids?"

"Could be," Price said. "And we have something else. A name for an organization that is probably behind the whole mess."

Brognola perked up. "Really? What's the name?"

"The Soldiers of Solomon. This was provided by one of Stuart Gold's personal bodyguards during the raid."

"So? Who are the Soldiers of Solomon?"

"That's a problem," Yakov Katzenelenbogen said as he came through the door to join the meeting with his own stack of reports. "There's no record of such an organization."

Brognola tapped his lips with a finger as he mulled over

the new facts. "Israel's home to some of the most effective merc teams on the planet. Why would the Soldiers of Solomon go outside Israel for its hired guns?"

Katzenelenbogen fielded that one, too. "Security, probably. This group has managed to stage extensive operations with very little word of it getting out. They didn't accomplish it except though heavy-handed attention to secrecy, including minimizing the potential for intelligence leaks. Phoenix is sure this Fogelman and his men were the soldiers implementing the land-based military maneuvers against the Palestinian village. That had to be a real logistical challenge. Lots of training time. If it had been Israeli mercs involved, there would have been plenty of opportunity for word to get out."

Brognola sighed and leaned back in his seat, visibly and uncharacteristically relieved. "Well, at least I've got something to report to the President," he said. "You people have made more headway on this than anyone else."

"Including the Israelis," Katzenelenbogen added.

"What's the story there? Have you been able to get an inside perspective?" Brognola asked. "The President is being stonewalled on the issue."

"There's a lot of good people in the Israeli bureaucracy," Katzenelenbogen said. "There are also some people who think we should do to the Arabs what Hitler tried to do us— make them extinct. There's silent conflict going on in virtually every Israeli military and security agency involved in this affair. They're stalling the investigations."

"Are you saying they're cooperating with the Soldiers of Solomon?" Brognola asked.

"Nothing so overt as coordinated treason. Maybe none of them even know who's behind these acts. But I get the feeling there is a work slowdown in effect as they wait to see what the next move will be by whoever is orchestrating events," Katzenelenbogen explained.

Brognola frowned over that, although it was only what he had expected. "So Israel knows the perpetrators are Israelis."

Katzenelenbogen nodded. "Everybody knows that. But there's no evidence, so the Israelis don't have to admit any accountability."

"The closest thing to evidence was the sat pic snapped by Akira," Kurtzman said.

"We use that and we'll expose the Farm," Brognola said, bringing a small roll of antacid tablets out of his pocket. He popped a couple, out of habit more than out of immediate need. "What about Rosario?"

"On the inside at NewMan," Price reported. "Unless Ariel Newman is a good liar, Ariel Newman bought his story. Pol's cover is that he's an ex-Israeli who hasn't been in-country for more than twenty years. He claims to miss his homeland and he wants to share his know-how with the forces working to reestablish the Israel of the Bible."

Brognola asked with raised eyebrows. "What kind of a reaction did that get?"

"Pol is the best," Price said. "He'll wheedle the truth out soon enough. But just because Ariel Newman was close friends with Stuart Gold doesn't mean Newman is also a part of the Soldiers. We may be on the wrong track."

"The technology Pol had to offer sweetened the deal," Kurtzman said. "Newman was quite excited by it, without admitting to any involvement with the group."

Brognola nodded. He was aware of Kurtzman's plan to provide Blancanales with technology with which to buy the trust of Ariel Newman. Newman was a carbon copy of Stuart Gold—a self-made technology millionaire known to have nationalist leanings. He and Gold were known to be buddies, and they had worked on technology development together. It seemed likely he would be in with Gold in the

Soldiers of Solomon—or would at least know something about them.

"So? What did we offer them?"

Kurtzman smiled. "Spy sats. We equipped him with a laptop that breaks into the U.S. National Reconnaissance Office satellite operating system and provides them a short window of undetected satellite access."

The big Fed gaped at him. "Aaron, tell me you're joking."

"He's not," Price said. "I got a demonstration of the laptop from Akira before they put Pol on the plane with it. It does the job."

"I hope there are safeguards...."

Kurtzman smiled and nodded. "Sure, there are. For one thing, the system dials into a secure Farm line before it goes anywhere else. We watch everything that happens. Where Pol goes, we go. My people are monitoring that line twenty-four hours a day."

"So if this computer falls into the wrong hands?" Brognola asked.

"There's no way they can use it without us knowing. We can create diversions and disconnects, and if we need to we can order a self-destruct on the CPU. It's a heating element on the chip, powered by a lithium-ion battery that will last for years or until it is needed. I guarantee you, it will fry if we tell it to, and then nobody will get anything off that chip ever again."

"But will it survive inspection by Newman, or whoever it is Pol eventually ends up dealing with?" Katzenelenbogen asked.

Kurtzman's grin dimmed. "Not a close inspection. If somebody tries to get inside the box they'll figure out something's wrong."

"If they try to read the code?"

"They'll run into a hundred hours' worth of barriers.

They'll never get through those before we can act at this end, I would hope." Kurtzman shifted and there was a rubber squeak from the wheels of his chair on the floor. "Obviously this plan is not foolproof. But it's dramatic. Quite frankly, we need something impressive to catch the attention of the people in control of the Soldiers. They are obviously savvy in the ways of advanced military technology. This'll do the trick." Kurtzman realized he was getting defensive and stopped speaking. The truth was, he felt a tremendous responsibility for Blancanales's safety right then.

Brognola nodded. "It sounds promising."

"I'm not too worried about Pol's cover being blown. My concern is with our target," Katzenelenbogen said. "Newman might not be connected to the Soldiers, which means we are wasting Pol's time and ours." He sat back and rubbed a rubber finger on his prosthetic hand against his temple. "Not that I have any better ideas."

"We'll have to make an assessment soon," Price said.

As Brognola started to stand, he met the gaze of his mission controller and sat back down again.

"There's more?" he asked.

"Akira's trace to IsAlliance turned up a series of outgoing messages," Price said. "Actually, they were the same message. As far as we can tell, they're updating their mailing list on the progress of the Soldiers of Solomon."

"Are you telling me," Brognola said, "that the terrorists have a newsletter?"

"You got it," Price said. "And everybody on the opt-in list is right here in the United States."

CHAPTER FIFTEEN

Clairemont, Louisiana

Hermann Schwarz was in a grumpy mood.

The third member of Able team, Rosario Blancanales, was doing undercover work on the opposite side of the planet. Until a few hours ago there had been no indication that Able Team would be needed to help address the problem in the Middle East, which was why Blancanales had been sent to give Phoenix Force a hand.

Now the team was needed, and here they were in the field without one of their teammates. It screwed up Able Team's group dynamic in a big way. And it reinforced, in Hermann Schwarz's mind, one important and unassailable fact—Carl Lyons could sometimes be a moody son of a bitch.

A strong leader? Yes. A fear-inspiring warrior? Without a doubt.

A perfectionist? Definitely.

A morose, sullen bastard? Without question.

"Gadgets, what the hell are you brooding about?"

"Nothing."

"Well, snap out of it. We're just about there."

Schwarz had been so busy feeling sorry for himself he hadn't registered the fact that they were approaching the road that ran alongside Woodrow Polmar's land.

The old road was empty from the time they turned onto

it until Lyons pulled the rental car into the trees, eight minutes later. It was parish maintained, the vegetation on the shoulder trimmed occasionally, but the undergrowth just off the shoulder was dense. Able Team's rental car became invisible from the pavement. Lyons and Schwarz continued on foot into the woods, using a GPS monitor to put them on a direct route into the Woody Polmar property, which consisted of a few thousand acres that fronted on Lake Pontchartrain. They encountered a few No Trespassing signs and a rusty barbed-wire fence, freshly repaired in spots. Finding a well-positioned tree branch got them over the fence without a problem, pulling themselves hand-over-hand on the branch until they could drop behind it.

After the sodden thud of their feet on the damp earth, the woods were silent. Schwarz and Lyons waited.

If Polmar was what they thought he was, there could be any kind of defense system in place, even this deep in the woods.

THE LIST of those receiving the secure document out of IsAlliance Techsystems had included more than twenty e-mail addresses. The Stony Man cybernetics team had gone to work on it at once, with Schwarz lending a hand to speed up the process.

The first step was to find the destination computers for the e-mail addresses, a tricky task, but not impossible. Next, they nosed around in the e-mail servers, looking for any and all messages from the IsAlliance source, including messages that had been erased. These were downloaded in huge batches and sorted through using a search application that used a profile of coded key words that Stony Man believed could be relevant.

An hour after the search began, the first target presented itself.

A pilot was standing by. As Price called up from the War

Room, Lyons and Schwarz headed topside, where a crew of what looked like farmhands was making quick work of hitching a rusty mobile home to a tractor and towing it off the barren field. The tractor waited as the pair headed into the barn, climbed into the small transport jet, taxied outside and took off.

Then the mobile home was wheeled, groaning and shaking, back into its place.

During the flight more data had been relayed to them on Woody Polmar.

"He's been a fund-raiser for pro-Israeli causes for years and fought hard to open up increasing trade with Israel," Price reported from the profile they were assembling. "He's a shipper. Owns twenty-four oceangoing vessels based in New Orleans, and Israeli firms are some of his biggest customers. Mostly consumer goods, stuff that won't go bad or lose value during a few weeks at sea."

"Weapons?" Lyons asked.

"Not that we can tell. But we found evidence of some sort of clandestine shipments going on between the U.S. and Israel. Whether the receiver is IsAlliance we can't tell."

"What kind of evidence?" Gadgets asked.

"Discrepancies in the shipping logs for a Polmar ship called *Homeland*," Price said. "Nothing you would notice without putting together a lot of files from around the world. We entered logs from harbormaster reporting systems to trace his global traffic and try to find incriminating patterns. Lo and behold, one of his boats has a doppelgänger. It shows up repeatedly in two places at the same time. Right now it is reported to be unloading cargo in Tel Aviv and simultaneously to be docked at New Orleans having mechanical work done."

There was more to it than that. The Farm was having a high degree of success decoding the messages being sent from IsAlliance, only to find that they were full of innuendo and veiled references. Without a frame of reference, the deciphered messages were gibberish.

"They're doing their real communicating over the phone or in person, and we don't have time to tap the lines of everybody on the list and wait for a tell-all phone call," Price said. "Woody Polmar is our best bet. We think."

The message transcript made a reference to "homeland-to-homeland." They were guessing this was an indication of Polmar International making a delivery via one of the twin vessels to Israel. The cargo in question was described as "one thousand modkits."

"What's a modkit?" Lyons had asked.

"Your guess is as good as ours," Price replied.

"It's a lot of something," Lyons said. "If they can't get into the country using legitimate means, then it sounds like weapons or ammunition."

"We're checking on it. Polmar has a lot of high-level contacts, but so far we've found no direct ties to weapons or ordnance suppliers."

"A thousand of something has to leave a paper trail," Lyons said. "If it's there, we'll find it."

THE THREE-MILE HIKE through the woods was easy enough. No black murk seeped out of the soil over their feet unless they strayed into low ground. Soon they came across Polmar's gravel driveway and stayed near enough to it to know there was no traffic in or out during their hike.

"If this is how millionaires live, it's not worth it," Schwarz said when they reached the end of the hike and looked out of the woods on the Polmar house. It was a hundred-year-old relic that had seen little in the way of maintenance during the last half of its life. The roof was intact but sagging like wet cloth. The paint was so long gone they couldn't tell what its color had been. The Greek-style columns had decayed like dead trees into pillars of rotting black-and-brown spots.

Behind it was an old wing that attached to a brick warehouse with claustrophobically low ceilings, with a tin roof sloped down on the river side to channel off rain. None of it looked less than fifty years old, and all had gone years without maintenance. It stank like old, sour garbage.

"I'll bet he brings dinner guests to the apartment in town," Schwarz added after a moment.

"Yeah," Lyons agreed.

"Of course, I've seen your place and it's not much better," Schwarz said.

"Whatever."

Sheesh. The tension was as thick as the hot, thick Louisiana atmosphere. Normally Schwarz and Blancanales would be ganging up to make barbs at Lyons's expense, or at least keeping up some sort of an ongoing conversation, like the two old friends they were. This job was tense enough without adding to it by staying pensive and aloof. The wordplay back and forth helped keep him sharp. He was convinced of that. Of course, Lyons had more than once asked them to please keep their comments to themselves when they were in the field in a hairy situation.

"Able One here, Stony Base," Lyons said into the radio. "Have you got a fix on our man yet?"

"Not yet. We're getting precious little cooperation out of the state and federals in Bayou Country," Price complained. "He could be on the premises, so stay sharp."

"We know what kind of staff is maintained here?" Schwarz asked.

"Could be nobody," Price said. "Hang on, here come updated sat pics."

Price had taken an unusual step in order to procure up-to-the-minute satellite photos of the Polmar house—she bought them. Ever since 1999, with the first successful launch of an Ikonos satellite, Space Imaging Corporation of Thornton, Colorado, had been selling photographs from Earth orbit to environmentalists, cartographers, agricultural concerns, even governments. The optical telescope camera, designed by Eastman Kodak, allowed the satellites to obtain grayscale images of earth with a resolution of one meter.

That image resolution wasn't as detailed as Price was used to getting. When circumstances called for it and access was obtainable, Stony Man Farm could take satellite photos using the U.S. government's National Reconnaissance Office, a high-security government organization with satellites in orbit carrying electro-optical technology to capture photographs using visible or infrared light. NRO also had radar satellites that could pierce cloud cover or be used at night. The NRO sats had another advantage: propulsion systems that enabled maneuverability in orbit, even moving out of their standard altitude into lower Earth orbits to obtain exceptionally detailed photographs and video with resolution of less than ten centimeters.

But the NRO satellites were inaccessible half the time, especially to an organization intent on keeping its existence secret. Buying shots from Space Imaging, even while paying a premium for short-notice tasks, was painless and anonymous.

The shots from the first batch, downloaded three hours ago, had revealed the estate and some of its secrets. Woody Polmar had an old warehouse and a new wharf on-site, with a track-mounted crane for quick and flexible boat loading and unloading. The access way to the lake was long and overgrown enough to hide the loading wharf from lake traffic. Attached to it was a low warehouse.

Woody Polmar wasn't just smuggling a one-time weapons shipment to Israel. It looked more as if he was making himself a career. They theorized he loaded small barges in the facility, which then rendezvoused with the one of two identical boats going under the name *Homeland* for transport to Israel. The illegal shipment, whatever it was, was transferred in darkness, then sent on its way. Customs enforcement was effectively bypassed.

But the first batch of pictures didn't show activity at the facility now.

"We're puzzled by that one," Yakov Katzenelenbogen complained during the conference with Able Team as it was en route to Louisiana. Katzenelenbogen sat with Kurtzman and Price in the War Room at Stony Man while Lyons and Schwarz were being sped across the southeast corner of the country. "If they are sending cargo that's needed for their efforts to start an Israeli war, they should be getting out of there as soon as possible."

"Maybe the repairs in New Orleans are bad enough to delay the next departure," Schwarz suggested.

"We checked it out. It's said to be maintenance work. Overhauls of engine components and some bottom scraping. Nothing that couldn't have waited."

"So chances are good we're going to find nothing when we get to his place," Schwarz said. "No cannabis bales or stolen artwork or Army-surplus M-16s?"

"Maybe, maybe not," Price said. "The repair work on the *Homeland* is wrapping up this afternoon. It could be at the facility in several hours. Maybe there's a shipment staged and ready to go."

"Maybe," Schwarz said. Avoiding the dime-sized lens serving as video feed back to the Farm, he gave Lyons a sour look. Lyons nodded sympathetically. If there was one thing he hated as much as his teammates, it was wasting his time on leads that went nowhere. This one had all the indications that it was going to turn out to be a big waste of everybody's time.

Now that they were on the scene, things weren't looking much better. There was no sign of recent activity.

"Tell me the sat saw something more than an empty parking lot," he said finally.

"Sorry, Able One," Price said. "I don't even have a tired security guard picking his nose. Keep in mind I can't see through the ceilings. Who can say what's inside."

"We can, in about ten minutes."

"Signs of activity?"

"Signs of nothing. We're going in."

"Stay sharp, Able. You never know."

"I ALMOST WISH somebody would start shooting at us," Lyons said.

Schwarz turned his head away from the field glasses and stared at the Able Team leader. It was the most revealing personal statement Lyons has said in days. "Bored, buddy?"

"Something like that."

"I'm about to grant you your wish," Schwarz said, growing a huge grin and placing his eyes behind the lenses of the glasses again.

"You're going to start shooting at me?"

"No, but maybe that guy will if you ask him nice."

Schwarz pointed through the leafy cover to what looked like the office end of the warehouse. A man was emerging with some sort of an automatic rifle draped over one shoulder, its business end pointed at the ground. He shut the door carefully behind him and locked it, depositing a hoop of keys into his pocket.

"I think I'll just call you my fairy godmother."

"I prefer 'Gadgets.'" Schwarz stiffened. "Christ, Ironman, check out that guy's hardware."

Lyons pulled out his own pair of binoculars, training them on the figure outside the door, and tried to put a make on the weapon. It was black, with heavy square lines. It had to be some kind of an automatic rifle, but it looked oversized, with a stock that was narrow, flat, but high and heavy. Lyons could make out two barrels, one slightly recessed above the other, and on top was a heavy optical component. The weapon had a boxy magazine on the stock, another curved magazine toward the front, plus the firing handle and trigger.

"Never seen that configuration before," he said. "You recognize it?"

Schwarz's gaze was locked on the man and his weapon, and at first he didn't appear to have heard the question. Then he nodded, slightly, and turned to look at Lyons with a curious expression.

"I've got a bad feeling about this."

"About what?"

"Ironman, that guy's packing an OICW."

Lyons thought about that for a moment, then shook his head as he put the field glasses back to his eyes, saying, "You're crazy."

"I know what I saw."

"You know what you think you saw." Lyons found his view of the weapon blocked as the man turned and walked purposefully in the direction of the rear of the warehouse, where the satellite images told them they would find the loading dock and the hidden access channel to the lake.

"We have got to check this out," Schwarz insisted.

"We'll check it out," Lyons agreed, and they moved through the undergrowth, keeping themselves parallel with the cleared ground, mostly rock and scrubby grass, around the buildings. The man with the strange gun stopped, examining the short wharf. The crane machinery was silent. He strode to the double doors, set at a thirty-degree angle in the side of the building for crane access, and yanked on the handles, finding them secure. Then he walked to the edge of the dock and aimed the weapon into the water, following the barrel with his head cautiously, but finding nothing. Then he stood there motionless, waiting, listening.

"He's acting kind of paranoid for a security guard," Schwarz whispered. "I bet he knows we're here."

"I think you're right. We must have triggered something coming in."

"We were careful," Schwarz said.

"I know we were. But who knows what kind of alarms they had tucked up in the trees?"

"I guess this confirms that they've got something to hide."

Lyons watched the gunner go back to the rear of the warehouse and unlock the loading doors with a key. The man was still looking around him as if he were waiting for someone or something to appear, and he kept the big gun hugged close to his side. His arm blocked Lyons's view of it. Even if he got a good, clear view he wouldn't be sure he could make a confirmed ID. He hadn't actually seen one outside of a few online pictures. They were still scarce items. The weapons had only entered production a year ago, still on a small scale. As the design was refined, production would ramp up. Lyons knew Stony Man armorer Cowboy Kissinger had somehow acquired some for evaluation, but none had found their way into the hands of the Stony Man field personnel.

So how did this guy get one?

Schwarz had to be seeing things.

"Think we'd be spotted if we made a run for it?"

Lyons shook his head. "Not we. Me. You cover me in case our friend with the hardware shows up again."

"Should be me. I'm better versed in prototype weapons so I can put a positive ID on the OICW, and I think that's relevant information."

The Able Team leader considered that, found no argument with Schwarz's line of thinking. "Okay, it's you. Keep me posted every step of the way."

"You got it," Schwarz said, and eased through the undergrowth at the edge of the woods as Lyons took up a firing position, ready to cover his teammate if the gunner came back.

Schwarz's radio clicked to life and he spoke into it, so softly that Lyons heard it only through his own headset earpiece. "Here I go."

He went, sprinting across open space for a long ten seconds before he reached the side of the building, where he flattened against the wall and waited for a reaction.

The double doors creaked open, just around the corner from where Schwarz was standing, and the dual barrels of the mystery rifle poked out, followed by the head and shoulders of the guard.

"Gadgets, trouble out the rear of the warehouse," Lyons hissed. "Get out!"

Schwarz flew alongside the brick face of the building and came to an abrupt halt at a window where the brick turned to old wooden siding on the office wing. He peered into the glass as Lyons targeted the gunner. At the moment the man spotted Schwarz, Lyons would take him down. The gunner was looking around and taking his time moving away from the door, but he would be in view of Schwarz at any second.

Then Schwarz leaped, landed on the windowsill with one foot and flung his arms onto the roof, getting a handhold and pulling himself up. He rolled away from the edge and disappeared as the gunner rounded the corner and swept his dual barrels across the open ground.

There was nothing for him to see.

He faced the woods, his eyes wrinkling into a squint. Lyons knew the man couldn't see him through the undergrowth, but he seemed to be looking right at him, and he was bringing his weapon up. Lyons had his M-16 targeted on the guy's chest and his finger tightened on the trigger.

Then he released the tightness as the man's vision moved away to another part of the woods.

Lyons got a better view of the weapon. Big, bulky, but it was being carried as if it weighed less than it looked. The optics were definitely high-tech.

But it just couldn't be what Schwarz said it was.

"Able Three here," Schwarz whispered. "That guy didn't just happen to be looking out the window when I made my run. There has to be some sort of an invisible perimeter alarm."

"Able One here. Looks like he convinced himself he scared whoever it was back into the trees. I'll make a retreat just noisy enough to keep him coming."

"No way, Ironman," Schwarz said. "He's got 20 mm high-explosive rounds in that thing."

"Even if he does he won't chance firing them in the trees," Lyons replied. "Here he comes. Get going, Able Three."

Lyons would much rather face his antagonist man-to-man, in the open. He wasn't into the sneaky side of the business, but it was often the best strategy. If they could keep the guy slightly off balance, a little bit confused, they might pull off a clandestine probe that stayed clandestine. As he slipped through the woods, he kept a sharp eye on the gunner, keeping a safe cushion of distance between them.

The man may not have spotted Lyons at all. He was heading slightly away, and the Able Team leader adjusted his direction to keep himself ahead of the man. Maybe he'd never have to make himself known…

His luck ran out then and there. His would-be pursuer came to a stop, listening hard, and decided all at once that he was on a wild-goose chase. As he wheeled on one heel, Lyons rattled the branch of a tree. It was a quick, short sound, the kind that couldn't be attributed to the wind in the leaves. The gunner spun again, pulled the weapon stock into his lower rib cage and triggered it, strafing the woods with automatic fire.

Lyons dropped behind the trunk of a tree and heard the arc of the rounds move by, feeling rather than hearing the thunk of one of the bullets embedding itself into the wood. Then the shooting stopped and he launched himself into a crouched run that carried him a hundred yards before he stopped, listened, heard the footsteps of the gunner in pursuit and ran on. The damp soil made quick, quiet progress easy enough, and occasionally Lyons would veer away from his path to call attention to himself. The tactic kept his pursuer just slightly off his trail. Gunfire peppered through the trees now and again, but the gunner learned not to waste his rounds. The Able Team leader led him farther and farther from Schwarz's probe.

SCHWARZ BENT OVER the greasy skylight. The glass was reinforced with wire, but the window frame was old. Digging in the deteriorating weather seal with a combat knife loosened it and allowed him to pry the window out of its socket, frame and all, and poke his head inside. The interior was dark, damp and silent. He lowered himself onto the top of one of the stacks of crates that filled the space, then stepped to the floor.

Keeping one eye on the pair of double doors at the end of the warehouse, he made use of the combat knife again to jimmy the nails loose around the lid of the box. Under the lid was a thick piece of dense foam packing material, which he pulled off.

He grabbed his tiny digital camera and snapped a few shots of the box's contents, nestled in more molded foam, then snapped in a tiny wire that connected the camera to the radio. This was a small piece he and Kurtzman had worked out together. When the camera was plugged into the radio, Stony Man could go in and download its images, piggybacking the data feed on the voice radio signal, which went to the retransmitter in the rental car and to the Farm—in this case, simply via a trio of secure cellular phone lines.

"Able Three here. Pretty pictures coming your way," he said into the mike.

"ABLE ONE HERE," Lyons radioed as he jogged. "Able Three, how's it going?"

"Able Three here. I'm inside. All by myself as far as I can tell. Where's my man with the hardware?"

"Still hot on my trail," Lyons reported, coming to another pause in the pursuit. "I haven't showed myself. For all he knows, I'm wildlife. But I'm going to have to give him a human target to keep him motivated much longer."

"I'll work fast, Able One," Schwarz radioed in return. "I'm in the warehouse."

"Stony Base here," Price said. "What do you have, Able Three?"

"A whole lot of something, Stony Base. Wooden boxes, maybe four feet square, eighteen inches high. Four-high stacks. Four rows of about fifteen stacks each. Two extra stacks at the back, both with an extra crate on top. Stony Base, I hope this is not what I think it is."

Carl Lyons was concentrating on finding the gunner as he listened to the exchange between Price and Schwarz.

"Stony Base here," Price said. "You sure you're alone in there, Able Three?"

"Far as I can tell," Schwarz responded. "I'm going to pull the nails on one of them. Able One, what's your situation?"

"Unknown," Lyons answered quietly. "My hunter may have given up on his prey. I can't hear him retreating—but be ready to clear out, Able One."

Lyons moved silently, backtracking on the gunner who had been hot on his trail, fully aware that this could all be a waiting game to entice him closer. Becoming motionless and silent was a good way for the hunter to convince gullible prey that he had given up the hunt. If the hunter was patient, the prey might show himself. Lyons couldn't afford to not investigate. If the hunter had turned back for the warehouse, he had to warn Schwarz.

As the seconds moved faster, Lyons glided from tree to tree, pausing at each to search for the man with the gun, and finding nothing.

He moved into a crouch, touched the radio and said, "Able—"

There was a sound like a click, so low it might have been anything. But if Lyons were to make a guess, he would have said it was something small and plastic being switched. It came from hundreds of feet away. He leaned to the side, to look around the tree serving as his cover and saw the gunner, across an open clearing in the woods, lit by acres of sunlight.

The gunner wasn't looking for Lyons, but staring into a handheld unit that dangled from his neck, and his body rotated. Then he raised his head quickly, staring directly at Carl Lyons.

Lyons didn't know how, but he'd just been spotted. Before he could bring his weapon clear of the tree, the gunner had dropped his handheld device and adjusted the big weapon slightly, watching the weapon instead of the target, and the weapon triggered.

Lyons was in midleap when the tree exploded.

CHAPTER SIXTEEN

"Stony Base here. I'm looking at your photos, Able One."

Schwarz recognized the voice of Cowboy Kissinger. Good. Cowboy would know what he was looking at better than anybody.

"At first glance I'm going to say you called it right," Kissinger said. "It does look like an OICW."

Schwarz draped his M-16 on his shoulder and hoisted out one of the weapons with two hands. "It's big but not as heavy as I expected."

"They got the weight down from the early designs," Kissinger said. "They prototyped at better than eight kilograms and had them down to less than 6.4 kilograms last I heard."

Schwarz didn't answer, bringing the weapon close to his face, examining the black surface, the design of the components. Then he knew what it was that bothered him about the design.

"Still with me, Able Three?" Kissinger asked. "I could use some more pictures."

"I'll do you one better," Schwarz said. "I'm going to bring you a sample."

"Not necessary," Price said. "We need you to get out of there."

"Stony Base, we ought to figure this thing out. What I am holding is a copy," Schwarz declared. "This is not an original OICW."

"You sure about that, Gadgets?" Kissinger asked.

"No release handles," Schwarz declared without hesitation. "I've never heard of an iteration of the OICW that was an all-in-one rifle and grenade launcher."

"Neither have I," Kissinger said. "That means somebody took the IsAlliance Techsystems plans and went into the manufacturing business on their own."

"That's what I think. And maybe we can figure out who by examining one of them."

"Okay, Able Three, bring it," Price said. "What else do you see?"

"Three more identical units in this crate. Assuming every crate is identically packed, you've got one thousand units," Schwarz said. "There's also some extra packs with shoulder straps. Ammunition, I'll bet." He took one of the four packs from inside the crate and yanked the heavy-duty Velcro closures, rummaging inside. "Yeah. Ammo. Bayonet. Something else."

Schwarz pulled the device out of the backpack and stared at it in the diffused sunlight from the window above. It was bigger than a remote control for his home theater system, but not by much. Two-inch-by-one-inch LED screen, power switch, couple of extra LED lights. Heavy-duty plastic case. Small electronic attachment port on the bottom of the unit, and there was a plastic-wrapped section of cable taped to the back of the unit.

Hermann Schwarz was called Gadgets for a reason. He'd been an electronics wizard since before the age of pervasive electronics. He'd been helping design new electronic devices for Stony Man use for years. If something electric or electronic was out on the table in front of Gadgets Schwarz, he could figure it out, fix it and probably make a few improvements to the design.

But right now he was stumped.

What was this thing?

Then his eyes fell on the black stock of the weapon lying on the crate and his eyes fell on a stock-mounted socket, which would fit the plug on the other end of the cabling. Whatever it was, the little electronic box was some kind of add-on to the OICW that he had never heard of.

There was something more, underneath the backpack, nestled in the same deep cutout, and he pulled out a curiously heavy, bulky knapsack. It was a rectangle with a squared end and a rounded end, and under a long Velcro flap was a plastic zipper that went from one corner all the way around to the other. Schwarz pulled the zipper a few inches and felt what he guessed was ballistic armor, striated with flat electronic wiring cable. A protective vest with a radio built-in?

"Everything you need for a soldier in a box," he said.

"What's that, Able Three?" Kissinger asked on the radio.

"You're going to call me Santa Claus when you see all the cool toys I'm bringing you, Cowboy," Schwarz said. "Right now I'm getting my butt out of here."

"Good idea, Able Three," Price said.

He and Kissinger would put their heads together over this stuff back at the Farm. They'd figure it out. Schwarz checked the crate again, looking for more surprises. The crate cutouts held three more identical sets of equipment. The gun, the electronic box and the extra knapsack.

Schwarz realized that the knapsack and the ammo pack connected to form a convenient, easy-carrying pack. He nodded appreciatively at the design as he slipped on the joined packs, then burdened himself with the OICW and slipped the nails back into their slots. When he pounded the lid back into place with his fists, it went more or less back into place. In the darkness it wouldn't appear tampered with unless somebody made a close inspection. Schwarz clambered onto the stack and out the skylight with the stolen weapon and the pack secured on his shoulders.

"Able—"

It was Lyons, but he never finished what he was saying. There was a moment of nothing.

"We didn't catch—" Price started to say.

Schwarz heard the explosion and his head snapped up as a brilliance like a fireworks exhibition lit the woods.

He went off the edge of the roof in a sprint and heard the vehicles coming as he hit the ground running. The first one emerging from the trees was a diesel pickup that screeched to a halt when the driver saw him, and Schwarz glimpsed the surprised faces of the pair in the cab and more men standing in the bed. Then a man in the bed slapped the roof of the cab and shouted. "Run him down, dammit!"

There were more trucks and cars in line behind the pickup. Schwarz was almost to the woods, and he slipped away before the pickup got near him. Threading through the trees, he homed in on what he hoped was the source of the explosion, then stopped short when he heard the crash of footsteps approaching from the interior of the woods. The man rushed by Schwarz without ever knowing he was standing there. It was the security guard, shouting to the new arrivals.

"He got away! He's in the woods!"

That was all Schwarz needed to hear.

WOODROW POLMAR GLARED at the man incredulously. "You shot at him with a 20 mm round using full targeting and you missed?"

"It detonated in a tree. I thought it was right on top of him," Reed Cashman said. "When I got there I found blood, but no body."

"Any idea who it was?"

"Some sort of commando. Dressed in camouflage and packing some sort of combat shotgun," Cashman replied. "The one-mile perimeter alarms went off first. The fence alarms never made a sound. I looked around some, then when I was back inside, the proximity alarm went off. I chased the guy into the woods and I never saw him until I got close enough to get a read on the ultra-wideband.''

''Did he look Arab?'' Polmar demanded.

''I just got a glimpse, but he was more of a white-looking guy than an Arab.''

''We have to set up a net,'' said Dirk Brennan, a young, dark-complected lawyer. Polmar knew Brennan had been itching to get his hands on the weapons since the moment they had taken delivery of their first shipment. Now Brennan looked at Polmar sharply, aware of his transgression. Polmar didn't react kindly to being told what steps should be taken under his command.

This time, though, Polmar agreed with the suggestion. ''Whoever it is, we have to keep him from getting his intelligence to the outside world,'' he ordered. ''Break them out.''

The sound that came up from the small crowd was something like a cheer, and Polmar knew it wasn't just that young jerk Brennan who had been itching to make use of the OICWs. The rest of them had to have been lusting after the opportunity. To be honest, he was looking forward to getting his hands on one of the weapons himself, not just in target practice but in a true combat situation.

Cashman, the security guard, had the doors unlocked in seconds, and the crates were pulled out and lined up on the dock in moments. In just minutes the men were going through the process of loading the weapons, as every one of them had in drills a half-dozen times.

Polmar had a total of fourteen men. The commando in the woods didn't stand a chance. He quickly picked a nine-man lineup for Team One. ''You're the bush beaters. Get back to the highway. You know the drop-off points. Move in, stay sharp, and gun down any fucking thing that moves in front of you, got it? Everybody got their phones?''

Everybody did. The portable phones were less than ideal, but the Soldiers of Solomon hadn't seen fit to equip them with a radio communications system. In fact, the Soldiers' commander had forbade them from breaking into the weapons under any account except for the protection of the shipment itself.

"Stay in touch," Polmar urged. "We'll let you know when Team Two starts getting close. Then I want this soldier located and killed. Got it? Remember, we have to have these things reboxed and loaded on the ship two hours from now."

Brennan, the excitement glittering in his eyes, said, "That guy will be long dead in two hours."

"ABLE THREE, Stony Base here. Able One is off-line," Price said. There was urgency in her voice, but she was far more levelheaded at the moment than Schwarz felt.

Of course, she hadn't seen the explosion.

"Able Three here. Stony Base, the security guard shot an explosive at Ironman. I'm trying to get to him now."

"What's the status on the security guard?" she asked.

"He was coming out when I was going in and I was in too much of a hurry to pursue him," Schwarz said. "He's got reinforcements. I saw ten or more guys showing up when I went into the woods."

"Armed?"

"Not yet." Schwarz could feel his breathing getting more labored. The run was hard, but he wasn't giving up the OICW yet. Not until it became a matter of survival.

"Able Three, get to Able One and report. I want you guys to get out of there if you can. If Able One is wounded, get to cover. I'm calling in our pilot for a helicopter extraction."

"Able Three here—do not, repeat, do not send air support of any kind," Schwarz said. "I bet a month's salary those guys are arming themselves out of the boxes in the warehouse. A chopper would be a sitting duck."

Price said nothing for a moment. "Explain that to me, Able Three."

Schwarz came to a halt, staring up into the treetops.

One of the trees had been decapitated, its trunk standing there smoking, a few remaining branches stretching up, black, bare and shrunken. The floor of the woods was a litter of confetti that had once been foliage. There were blankets of green shreds, swatches of black ashes and a splash of red.

"Cowboy, explain it to her," Schwarz said. "I've got to find Ironman."

Stony Man Farm, Virginia

"SIT TIGHT until you get further orders, Jack," Price said reluctantly to her pilot, who was sitting on the tarmac in New Orleans. Kissinger was entering her command center, hoisting a big automatic rifle in two hands. It was a black monster, boxy, with a number of protrusions.

Price was well versed in the state-of-the-art weaponry available to her teams, but it wasn't her passion. Just as she depended on the cybernetics staff to keep her commandos fueled with intelligence, she depended on Cowboy Kissinger, longtime Stony Man Farm armorer, to keep them equipped with the best hardware for the job.

"Okay, Cowboy," she said, one hand still holding a headphone pad to her ear. "Tell me."

Kissinger could have given her a two-hour lecture on the OICW, including its history, its capabilities, its potential impact on the U.S. military. He decided to stick to the basics.

"Objective Individual Combat Weapon," he said. "A dual munitions system developed for the U.S. military, designed for the twenty-first century infantryman. It'll replace the M-16 rifle, M-203 grenade launcher and M-4 carbine, providing firepower superior to all of those weapons. Here's what Gadgets is worried about—the fire-control system uses a laser range finder, pinpoints a target range and gives this information to the fusing system on the 20 mm airbursting round. The laser ranging accuracy at 500 meters is plus or minus half a meter. At a thousand meters it's plus or minus one meter. The damage this round'll do when it explodes within a meter of an unarmored aircraft is almost guaranteed catastrophic. If Gadgets has got ten guys running around with these things when our chopper makes a flyover…'' Kissinger shrugged.

"I'm convinced," Price said. "No chopper." She was picturing a burst like that near a helicopter. Abruptly the mental image changed.

What had it done to Carl Lyons?

Clairemont, Louisiana

"ABLE THREE, talk to me," Price said in his headphones, sounding worried.

"I can't find him," Schwarz said. "He's on the move and he's losing blood, but he's covering his tracks too well."

"We decided on no chopper, Able Three."

"Good plan," Schwarz said, but his thoughts were elsewhere, his eyes flitting around the woods floor as he tried to avoid estimating the full measure of the spilt blood he'd found so far. Lyons was powerful, a berserker, the best there possibly was. But he had to be weakening. Pretty soon Schwarz would catch up and hope to hell Ironman didn't fire until he got a look at the person coming after him.

"Hey, it's my fairy godmother."

Schwarz spun like a top. The last thing he had expected

was for Lyons to sneak up on *him*. But there he was, slumped against a tree, one fist clenched on his weapon.

"I could use a hand," Lyons said through his gritted teeth. "And I don't know if we have a lot of time."

Schwarz spotted the trickle of blood running down the tree, from where Lyons was leaning against the trunk. "You don't know the half of it," he said. "Show me."

Lyons sat down hard and Schwarz leaned over him back, finding his back sodden with blood. Through the rips in the shirt he found a series of long, bloody cuts, but only one of them was major. It started shallow over his vertebrae, but grew deeper as it angled into his left shoulder blade and the protective mantle of muscle.

"Able Three here," he radioed as he worked. "I've found our boy. Actually, he found me."

"What's his status?" Price demanded dispassionately.

"Shrapnel abrasions and cuts up his back. One is bad news," Schwarz reported. "It's a bleeder. I'm taping it up now." From the small first-aid kit in the pack he carried, he found foil packets containing alcohol-soaked linen. He used one to clean around the wound, then used another to probe inside the deep end of the cut for any material that might work its way in deeper before a real doctor could take care of it. Lyons breathed deeply and didn't make a sound.

"His radio out of commission?" Price asked. There was nothing she hated worse than being out of touch. Schwarz reported that Lyons's headset was completely missing.

"I tossed it," Lyons said, forcing himself to sound conversational. "It got sliced in half."

"Barbara says it's coming out of your pay," Schwarz said, making quick work of taping sterile gauze over the wound. He was distressed to see that he hadn't even slowed the bleeding. At this rate, how long would Lyons have the strength to remain mobile? "Listen to me, Carl, we got to move fast. Company's coming."

"Not that asshole with the grenade shooter?" Lyons said, and Schwarz heard a slight slur in his voice.

"Yeah, that asshole and a whole shitload of his asshole friends," he replied, quickly explaining the situation. "We're going to have to move fast."

"No problem," Lyons said, almost cheerfully.

Yeah, right. "Stony Base, we're heading for the car."

"Good luck, Able Three."

TEAM ONE WAS nine men strong, since they had to cover the most ground. Polmar's property was in a conical shape, wide where it bordered the highway and narrowing until it ended at the shore. Team leader Frank Wein staged his men in their predetermined entry points on the highway, saving a center point for himself. He parked and started off into the woods, relishing the weight of the weapon, the solidity and texture of the composite stock.

Wein, a stocky, powerful man in his early forties, had been well-known in the New Orleans Jewish community for his hard-line views on how Israel, and the United States, should deal with the Palestinian problem. Israel belonged to the Israelis. It had been their homeland, as decreed by God, for thousands of years before the Arabs even came up with the Muslim religion. Why didn't everybody see that?

He was an outspoken supporter of all-out war against the Palestinians during the violence in 2000. He complained that any peace process that ceded any land or control of the Israeli homeland to the Palestinians was an affront on God. Barak and Arafat, he had said once while being interviewed on a local news show, should get stuffed into the same barrel and shot. He considered them equally dangerous to the cause of Israel's future.

The interview was picked up by the news wires and shown worldwide as an example of the extreme opinions of a small percentage of Jews around the world regarding the ongoing efforts to forge a Middle Eastern peace.

The clip included details on Wein's war record. He was a decorated Gulf War veteran. As a tank commander, he'd been especially effective at taking out enemy targets, but there were stories from his crew of atrocities against Iraqis. He'd been caught in the act of directing his tank to fire on a group of Iraqi soldiers as they were surrendering. More than once his tank treads were found to lead to the bodies of the Iraqi wounded.

The interview clip was seen on CNN by Kesher Nir himself. Shortly thereafter he had phoned his number-one man in the United States, wealthy Jewish shipper Woodrow Polmar, and asked him to interview this man Frank Wein, find out if his views were sincere, and whether he had the fortitude to back them up with a life of dedicated action for the cause.

Sincerity and fortitude he had. And a skill for business, it turned out. He quickly turned into Kesher Nir's number-two man in the Homeland Loyalists, the Soldiers of Solomon procurement arm in the U.S.

The Homeland Loyalists had two primary reasons for existing. One was to raise funds. Even with the backing of founding partners like Kesher Nir, Stuart Gold, and other wealthy, young Israeli techno-millionaires, funds were insufficient, especially when it came to equipping the armies of the coming war. These soldiers had to be better than state-of-the-art—they had to be cybersoldiers with all the advantages of technology.

Getting access to blueprints for the technology they wanted was the easy part. Reconfiguring the designs to make them better, cheaper and easier to build was second nature. Finding the manufacturers needed to build the weapons to spec had been the difficult part.

That was where Frank Wein had displayed his strongest

skills. He had personally located a U.S. firm to make their knock-off edition of the IsAlliance Techsystems Objective Individual Combat Weapon.

Wein was in love with the weapon. He loved to fire it. He wanted to own one. He dreamed of the idea of fighting in the war for Israel, using this weapon, the way some men lusted for certain kinds of sex. Now here he was, tramping through the woods, wearing the OICW like a medal of honor—like a sword passed down in a family through generations.

He'd fired it a handful of times in training sessions sponsored by Woody Polmar—an expensive exercise. The rounds weren't cheap. But the Homeland Loyalists were insufficiently armed under normal circumstances. Polmar had reasoned that the worst danger would come during the brief periods that they actually had the weapons in their possession, so they'd better know how to use them.

That was weeks ago, when the first shipment had come through Clairemont for shipment to Israel, and Frank Wein had paid out of his own pocket for more cartridges so he could have more time on the weapon. He'd done so again, just yesterday, when this delivery arrived. He had no doubt he was the mostly fully functional gunner using the OICW.

One thing he knew for sure: if it had been his watch shift when this commando showed up poking his nose in the business of the Homeland, Frank Wein would have accomplished a lot more than just defoliating a damned tree. That son of a bitch would be dead.

Which was exactly how it was going to turn out anyway. He'd have a good chance of finding the commando first, being in the prime middle spot on the line. Even if he didn't, those other guys couldn't shoot straight to save their lives. A lot of innocent trees and bushes were going to get shot into salad this afternoon. But after they'd all failed to nab that sucker, it would be Frank Wein who would stitch him across the rib cage with 5.56 mm rounds or plant a 20 mm HE up his ass.

Wein grew somber when he saw the car.

It was a Chrysler Sebring, sitting in the woods with no driver in sight. It was somewhat fancier than he would have expected, but it had to belong to the commando. There could be no other explanation.

"Woody," he said into his phone, "I found the commando's car." He described the scene.

"Have you checked it out, Frank?"

"No way. What if he's waiting in the woods right now, watching the car with that shotgun aimed at whoever steps out into the open?"

Polmar swore softly. Wein heard it and cringed. "Frank, you're two and a half miles away from the storage facility. There's almost no way he could have made it that far. I got reports from my guys at this end that there's a lot of blood. He wouldn't make it that far. Now please check out what's in the car."

Wein was shamed into it. He approached the car carefully, covering the woods in every direction in case the commando appeared. When he stood at the driver's door, he found the interior clean and empty. Not so much as a burger wrapper. And no keys. He was loathe to used the gun on the window and he was lucky enough to find a rock big and sharp enough for the job. He applied the pointed end of the rock to the passenger-side glass and exerted pressure until the window cracked, then crumbled into pellets. Wein unlocked the door and got in, probing under the seats in the glove box, and under the dash. Nothing except a Hertz receipt, not two hours old. The name was undoubtedly fake, but he tucked the paperwork in his back pocket for later investigation as he reported his lack of findings to Polmar.

Then Wein used the latch for the trunk and it popped open. A gym bag sat inside. When he pulled the zipper he found himself staring at something that might be a portable fax machine. It was flat, about the size of a laptop computer, with a cellular phone fitted into a socket on the front. It was definitely powered up, and the color LED display showed three windows displaying almost identical information. He quickly realized what he had in his hands.

"You still with me, Woody?"

"I'm here."

"Listen, I've got a communications uplink back here. It's in the trunk. This thing is feeding his radio signals to wherever his headquarters is."

"Describe it to me!" Polmar said excitedly.

Wein tried, but Polmar cut him off before he got far. "Yes, yes, I think you're right. Listen, I want you to very carefully pick up the phone on the unit. See if you can overhear the back-and-forth."

Woody did so, slowly withdrawing the unit, pressing his hand over the speaker and turning it on. He got nothing, not even a dial tone, although the display told him the phone was ready.

"Nothing, Woody."

"Dammit. It was too much to hope for, though," Polmar replied. "Can you unplug it?"

"No plug. It's running on its own juice. The batteries are big lithium-ion jobs mounted into the bottom."

"Remove them. Power that thing down," Woody ordered.

"They're screwed in. It'll take me a minute."

"Forget it! We can't afford a second of delay," Woody said. "Who knows what he's reporting back. Just smash the thing, Frank. Turn it off permanently."

"You got it."

Frank Wein used his rock again.

CHAPTER SEVENTEEN

Stony Man Farm, Virginia

Yakov Katzenelenbogen was listening to the communication feeds going back and forth between Barbara Price as she issued encouragement to Hermann Schwarz. The Phoenix Force tactical adviser was staring at a map of the Polmar property. The map was an odd conglomeration of green-and-brown geographic features and fluorescent-orange text labeling geographical and man-made features on the landscape. The map was made by combining the best of the digital satellite images with the most detailed survey maps of the area, also digitized and all combined using cartographic software that stripped away superfluous detail and added color accents. The result was a better-than-real representation of the terrain and features. The high-resolution image was printed in high-contrast, so his eyes moved quickly and easily from place to place as he considered the options that Able Team had at this moment.

One man seriously wounded was a bad scenario under any circumstances. While his partner struggled to keep him moving, they were vulnerable to any kind of attack.

If Schwarz and Lyons managed to put some distance between themselves and their pursuit, they could be picked up by helicopter. That would be very difficult. Even if they accomplished it, which was unlikely, how would they know they had enough of a cushion? They would have to be sure they were well over a thousand yards from the nearest of those OICWs before Stony Man could risk sending in a chopper.

They had to get to the car. It was their only hope. But studying the maps, Katzenelenbogen became convinced they would never reach it.

"Look," he said to Price, settling the four-foot-square printout on the table where she could see it. "We think Able is where? About here? That means they're at least a mile and a half from the car. With Carl weakening, he won't make it. If he does, it'll take, what, half an hour at best? That's without running into the enemy."

Price nodded.

"But I'm guessing they've moved some of their gunners out to the highway. It's the logical move. Sandwich Able in the middle. If they haven't thought of it yet they will soon. We know they have the manpower to handle that. Then Able's trapped."

Price nodded again. "I'm open to options, Katz."

"They go this way." He tapped the map. The blue part.

Clairemont, Louisiana

"HOW'S IT FEEL?" Schwarz said.

"Feels painful," Lyons said.

"Oh." Schwarz was getting more worried as he weighed his odds of surviving in the woods, with Lyons, against ten or more heavily armed gunners. They had ended the first leg of their hard hike. They hadn't gone far enough, but that was as far as Lyons could go.

"Gadgets, is that thing really what you thought it was?" Lyons said when they started up again. His flagging energies seemed somewhat revived by the rest. He nodded at the

OICW dangling from Schwarz's shoulder as they started moving again.

"Sort of. Its design is probably based on the Objective Individual Combat Weapon that the U.S. Army has under development. But the design is slightly different. I'm thinking these guys got plans or prototypes for the official IsAlliance Techsystems design. There could be a leak in the system somewhere. IsAlliance is just the top-level integrator. They've got companies like Heckler & Koch doing weaponry, they've got a fire controller from a company called Contraves-Brashear Systems, and so on. The leak could be at or between any of those companies. Now it has been reverse-engineered and redesigned to be a simpler, all-in-one unit that is probably cheaper to build and lighter to carry. This is one of a thousand sitting in the warehouse back there at the wharf."

Lyons nodded slightly as he walked. "Good start to an army."

"Sure is," Schwarz said, falling behind his partner just far enough to see that the red stain over the bandages was growing, clinging to Lyons's back as the material absorbed the blood like a sponge.

"Gadgets, I need you to keep talking," Lyons said, without looking up from the ground. Lyons watched the forest floor carefully for a place to make every footstep. "I need something to concentrate on."

"Okay, you asked for a lecture," Schwarz said. "The OICW is meant to replace the M-16, along with the M-203 grenade launcher and the M-4 carbine. If it's as good as they say it is, it'll be twice as powerful a gun as the M-16/M-203 combo, with twice the range. Everybody is on the list to get them—Army, Navy, Air Force, Marines, Special Operations, even the Coast Guard. But there's a lot more to it than firepower. It's designed to augment the Land

Warrior computerization and communication capabilities scheduled to come online before 2010.''

"Go on," Lyons said. "I don't know much about its optics. Tell me about optics and targeting."

Schwarz took a few steps in silence, wondering if he heard the movement of bodies through the forest behind him. There was nothing.

"There's a laser targeting system for fusing the 20 mm rounds. It'll pick out moving targets, aircraft, buildings, doesn't matter, and deliver a high-explosive grenade accurately up to a thousand meters. It'll fire HEs semiautomatically, as fast as five in thirty seconds. Magazine holds six rounds. The rifle fires 5.56 mm ammo at a rate of 850 per minute. Thirty-round magazine for 5.56 mm rounds."

"Is that all?" Lyons asked.

"Uh, let's see. Housing is composite. You can field-strip the thing in two minutes. That's about sums up all I know," Schwarz said. "How much of that applies to our copy I can't tell you. One obvious difference is the ability of the official OICW to be detached, one for grenade firing and optics and a rifle for firing the 5.56 mm rounds. That's the only difference I saw offhand."

"I think there's other design changes," Lyons said through his labored breathing. "Tell me about the interface."

"What interface?"

"The shooter who used it was tracking me somehow," Lyons said. "He used an interface to help target the grenade on my tree."

Schwarz looked at Lyons, head hanging as he struggled to keep his feet moving, then fumbled in the pack on his left shoulder, pulling out the small electronic device whose purpose he hadn't been able to fathom.

"This?"

Lyons looked at it, nodded. "Yeah. He plugged it into

the gun. It looked to me like he found me with that thing as soon as I started moving around, then he just aimed the gun until the gun told him to stop and he fired. If I hadn't put the tree between us, I'd be dead meat.''

"No shit.''

Lyons looked at him. "You telling me they've improved upon the U.S. military design?''

"Maybe. Maybe it's low-profile technology we already have in the works and they got hold of the plans for it along with the rest of the blueprints.''

"Whatever, we'll need to be damned careful. If their motion detection ranges as far as their grenade launchers, we'll be dead before we can even get to within firing range.''

"Yeah, I was thinking that,'' Schwarz said.

"Stony Base here,'' Price said. "How's he doing, Able Three?''

"Able Three here,'' Schwarz said. "Could be better. Things may have just got more complicated, Stony Base.'' Gadgets briefed Price on the tracking device, and the capabilities Lyons described.

Price listened, then Schwarz heard her conferring briefly with Katzenelenbogen. "We've put together the best plan we could think of, Able Three,'' Price said. "It's still our best bet considering your new intelligence.''

"Give it to me.''

"We want you to backtrack, get to the water. There's at least two boats on the water at the dock. One of them is small enough for you to operate alone long enough to get a mile or so out into Lake Pontchartrain. The chopper is on the way and will be watching for you on the water.''

"We're more than a mile from the water already, Stony Base,'' Schwarz complained, coming to a halt. Lyons stopped and looked at Schwarz. The flesh of his face looked as if it were hanging loosely, and his eyes were half squinted. He looked like a man about to drop from exhaustion.

"Which means you're two miles from the car. Listen, we're convinced Polmar will be putting a bunch of his men out on the highway to come in and put the squeeze on you between the gunners from the warehouse. You'll be trapped. If you can get into hiding long enough to let the gunners from the warehouse get around you, then you might have a clear run to the water."

"Stony Base, that's a big might," Schwarz said. But when he looked at Lyons, he knew that the shortest distance was the only real option. "There's no other exit?"

"Not that you can hope to make, Able Three," said the solemn voice of Yakov Katzenelenbogen.

"Understood," Schwarz said. "We're on our way."

"So is the chopper," Price added.

She probably had more to say, but it was at that moment that the radio stopped functioning.

Somebody had opened the trunk of their rental and busted their retransmitter. Going back to the car was out of the question.

Lyons looked up, his fatigued eyes showing sudden alertness, and then Schwarz heard it, too. The shouts of men, coming up behind them.

Men from the highway. Men from the warehouse. Gadgets Schwarz was feeling like a fox in a gully with hounds converging on both sides.

WOODY POLMAR BENT OVER the map, an aerial reference map custom-made using images from an aerial photographic survey of the property he had commissioned years ago, when he began to see the possibilities the facility offered. He'd been a man without a true purpose back then, without a reason to be alive.

When he was young he led a vicious, unrestrained life,

full of theft, shootings and prison. His father disowned him when he was in jail on his second murder conviction. But then his father died, and Polmar found he hadn't been legally disowned. The inheritance of property and the money was his, but it didn't satisfy him.

He had fallen in with all kinds of organizations, one after another, looking for a truly noble cause, for a reason for his existence.

It had never occurred to look to his own heritage. He hadn't been to temple in years. He didn't really pay attention to the travails of Israel. Then he was approached by an emissary of Kesher Nir.

It had been at a meeting of the True American Army, a ragtag bunch of freedom fighters based in the Houston area. They had emigrated from Kansas because they believed that a second American Revolution was coming, and that the federal government just might bomb the rest of the country to oblivion when it realized its stranglehold on the people was slipping away. They were a strange bunch, the TAA, paranoid and militant without quite being racists. They were ready to fight for the Constitution. They had the weapons for it. They were also ready to get the hell out when they knew the bomb drops were inevitable. Their reason for relocating to Houston was to purchase provisions and vessels that would sustain them on the open sea for years. They now lived on their dilapidated boats, almost a hundred of them with their families, crowded into whatever space wasn't taken up by dehydrated food and water-purification systems.

The TAA didn't exactly win over Woody Polmar, but Mitchell Berman did.

Berman was at one of the group's recruitment meetings as an observer. His employer had instructed him to be on the lookout for groups that could be brought under the wing of his new organization. He had hoped to find a ready-made army of supporters. The trouble was, the U.S. didn't seem to breed extremist pro-Israeli groups, although extremists existed for just about every cause.

So Berman was looking for individuals to help him bring a U.S. group into existence. He would need a man with leadership skills, who could be converted to the cause.

Polmar was converted. He became Berman's leader. When he went to Israel and met Kesher Nir, the young genius recently made president of IsAlliance Techsystems, he wasn't sure what was going to come of the trip and the meeting. He brought his photographic survey of his family's land and unused shipping facility on Lake Pontchartrain for no reason he could really define. By the time he returned home, he was fully under the spell of the exuberant young man and his enthralling vision.

The family's old facility had served the cause well. Polmar thought that maybe his old man, a traditional Jew, would have approved of the cause, if not the methods the Soldiers of Solomon were employing to take back the homeland.

Polmar's maps showed him there was no way out for the commando. The man wasn't going to get away. The soldiers in Team One from the highway would shoot him down or drive him into the guns of Team Two. Polmar's real concern was the extent of the intelligence the man had communicated to the people at his headquarters, whoever they might be.

"Report in, Team Two."

This portable phone system had to go. His message was being broadcast over the phone messaging system as voice e-mail. What a monkey-rigged way of talking to the troops. But Kesher Nir had never suspected there would be trouble on the U.S. end of the operation. He assumed the risk could start only when shipments reached Israel, so a communications system, along with a drilled and permanently well-armed defense force, was deemed unnecessary. Polmar was glad that he had conducted training for the men on communications. Team Two leader called in first. A minute later came the call from Team One leader, Frank Wein.

No sign of the commando. The blood trail had vanished. They were using a leapfrog technique to advance through the woods. Every other man would stay in position, monitoring the area with their ultra-wideband units, or UWBs, while their neighbor moved ahead twenty paces and got into position, and the process repeated. There was no way the commando was going to slip through that net.

Polmar used plastic chits representing his men on the aerial map, positioning them.

He would have guessed that Team Two would have come across the commando by now.

Maybe the guy wasn't as badly wounded as they originally thought.

SCHWARZ WAS BEGINNING to realize that Carl Lyons was in worse shape than he had originally thought.

He welcomed the excuse to stop, but it took him precious minutes to locate cover that might serve their purpose.

They needed to be invisible.

The bole of the tree was good enough. The tree had to have been a looming giant once, but death had come and it rotted. Some kind of insect had set to work on the insides, chewing the wood into smelly junk that crumbled like low-moisture cheese. Schwarz scooped it out with his knife and in thirty seconds cleared out a few square feet of room. Lyons leaned against the tree while he worked. Then Schwarz took him by the shoulders and walked him inside the tree. Schwarz crowded in with him, pulling a few tall weedy plants in front of the opening.

"Snug as bugs," he said in a low voice.

There was no answer. Lyons was out cold.

SCHWARZ RARELY FELT as alone as he did now. No Stony. No Politician. Ironman in god-knows-what state of shock that might kill him at any minute. How long did people survive with that kind of blood loss?

He was thinking about what Lyons had told him about the sensors being used by the gunner with the OICW. He'd said the gunner zeroed in on him when he moved. Not sound, but movement.

So how accurate were these devices? Seems he had heard about technology used to detect the breathing of victims trapped under rubble after an earthquake. If those things were that sensitive, he and Ironman were in a shitload of trouble, because he didn't think they could hold their breath for the entire time it took the line of gunners to walk through their vicinity.

He would know soon enough, because here they came.

First came the voices, calling to one another through the woods, then the sounds of feet tramping on weeds and soft earth. They were pretty sure of themselves, or pretty bad at their job. Skilled or not, they'd be deadly with those weapons from a long way away.

When the footsteps were very close Schwarz spotted the man through the covering of branches over the bole. The man swept the OICW left and right in a practiced rhythm, speaking in a low voice. Schwarz strained to hear what he was saying, then realized the man was counting.

When he reached one hundred, the gunner stopped and pulled something to his face. "Two-Three at stage position," he said.

The man stared at the gun, and Schwarz could see that the small monitor was now mounted to its barrel of the gun, with the tiny cable plugged into the stock. Schwarz tried to be a statue. Tried not to breathe. Tried not to rotate his eyeballs. Any second the gunner could turn and trigger that thing into their tree.

No, Schwarz would take the gunner down if he moved suddenly. But it would only stall their deaths. They'd never outrun and outshoot all the other gunners that would converge on them.

The guy swiveled. Schwarz almost did it. Almost raised the M-16 and blasted him out of existence. Then the gunner spoke. "Not a blip."

"How do we know that thing even works?" someone else asked from a distance.

"I can see you on it," the first gunner said and continued his monitoring as his unseen companion marched into the woods and was gone.

"Two-Four at stage position," said the companion a minute later through the gunner's phone. The gunner answered with a grunt and started forward, disappearing into the trees.

Schwarz didn't move a muscle. He didn't know how sensitive those motion detectors were. He wasn't about to take any chances.

They weren't, he thought, acknowledging the pun with a grim smirk, out of the woods yet.

CHAPTER EIGHTEEN

Woody Polmar became more agitated as the rows of chits drew closer together on the map.

"Maybe he's dead," Frank Wein said. "Or just unconscious."

"Yeah, maybe," Polmar answered. He'd considered that. They could do a more thorough visual search when the rest of the men arrived from New Orleans. The *Homeland* was on Lake Pontchartrain, less than an hour away. It would be top priority to get the shuttle boats loaded for the rendezvous and take the chance of a daylight transfer.

If that commando had alerted some sort of authority agency, they'd have to abandon the warehouse and find another way of staging their shipments for transfer to Kesher Nir and his army. They could deal with that later. Right now they had to worry about getting this shipment safely away.

What if the guy wasn't dead or unconscious, but hiding?

He would hide if he knew he was trapped. Wouldn't a commando have the training to get past a bunch of amateur gunners in the woods, clearly unskilled in the fine points of paramilitary maneuvers? And if he somehow knew that even stealthy action was out of the question—if he had knowledge of the capabilities of the UWB. He would turn the things against them, take advantage of the enemy's reliance on the electronic devices. He'd hide, stay quiet, let them walk right past him....

"Team Two leader, this is Polmar!"

"Go ahead."

"Turn your team around—he's behind you! He'll head back in this direction, probably try to get to the water."

"You sure about that?"

"Pretty sure. Get your men turned around and keep them organized. He'll be moving fast now, so increase your pace."

"Understood."

"Wein here, Woody. You want Team One to close in for backup?"

"Not yet, Team One," Polmar said. "Keep your men coming the way they are. Keep them on pace and on track. Just in case I'm wrong."

"What are you going to do, Woody?"

Polmar had already considered that. "I'm going to be ready to meet the bastard myself."

"COMPANY COMING."

"What?" Schwarz stopped and stared at Lyons. He'd thought Ironman was only partially conscious—just enough to keep his legs partially supporting his weight as they hiked back the way they'd come.

"I hear them."

"How you feeling?"

"The nap did me good. I think the bleeding has stopped," Lyons said.

Schwarz didn't think that was likely but he wasn't going to argue it now. He could hear the calls of the men as they came through the woods after them.

"We've got to get into hiding. Those motion detectors can spot us. We need to stay perfectly still."

"What we need to do is take those guys out," Lyons declared. "I'm up for it."

"Yeah, right."

"I'm not kidding, Gadgets. Let's make a stand."

Schwarz knew he could press the point and maybe— maybe—Lyons would do what he said. But they could only hike so fast, and the gunners were coming faster.

"All right," Schwarz said.

"Good. First thing we do is fuck with their heads."

TEAM TWO leader Martin Horn had never had so much fun. Like most of the men in the Homeland Loyalists, he'd been a street hood. He'd done his share of skull cracking. He'd been recruited in prison, as most of the others had. He was offered a chance to redeem himself in the eyes of his people. And maybe, just maybe, he would get the chance to be a big shot, when the war came and Israel was reborn as the Israeli homeland, dominating the Middle East.

Something about it appealed to him, and he'd thrown in his lot with the Loyalists. There had been shakedowns, and several times the Loyalists had been called upon to exert pressure on their outside business partners. Or silence potential leaks. Good work, but infrequent and subdued. Now Martin Horn was really going to enjoy splitting somebody's skull.

"Come on, move your butts," he called to his left, where one of his men was lagging.

His man jogged several paces to bring him up to the line, then hustled to keep pace with Horn.

"What's that?" the man asked, peering into the distance.

The shot rocked through the trees and the slow man exploded in midstride, his leg still making the step as his torso blew into fiery pieces that blew back into the forest.

Horn was yelling wordlessly when he hit the ground. He'd thrown himself before he even knew what was happening, and he was saved from decapitation by the chance that he landed in a shallow depression that had once been a mud puddle. It took him precious seconds to overcome his shock, then he jumped onto his hands and knees, his mind unable to process the red stain that was all that was left of the man he'd been barking orders at.

"That was one of ours!" shouted Alvin Kushnir, next man down in the line as he approached in a hurry. "Who fired that round—holy shit!"

Kushnir had just come upon the stain that had been one of their comrades until a few seconds ago.

"Kushnir, you stupid shit, get down on the ground."

The man dropped flat. "Who did it? Who killed him?"

"I don't know yet," Horn shot back, then cupped a hand to his mouth and shouted. "Hey! Hey goddammit! You're firing at friendlies."

The response was a burst of fire, the staccato voice he knew well from their practice sessions. The machine-fired 5.56 mm rounds ripped through the trees, shredding foliage.

"He's crazy," Kushnir said.

There was another burst. They were so far away Horn couldn't even see the gunner. That was the problem with a weapon with a range of a thousand yards.

"Hey, you stupid asshole, it's us!" Kushnir bellowed indignantly. "It's Kushnir and Horn!"

In answer there came a third burst, closer and more controlled. The gunner had finally got a feel for the weapon, because this time he didn't miss. Kushnir took a machine-fired pair of 5.56 mm shockers in the forehead, and his skull cracked open explosively.

Horn was starting to get the truth. That wasn't one of theirs. It was the commando. And he'd got his hands on one of the OICWs. Horn jumped to his feet and took a step and heard the sudden retort of the grenade launcher. He'd done just what they wanted him to do. Showed himself just like

Kushnir showed himself. A 20 mm high-explosive round ripped through the atmosphere and exploded a foot from the back of his head. His spine was cut to pieces and his tattered corpse collapsed.

"SHEESH," Schwarz muttered. He'd watched the man die through the optics of the weapon, so far away it felt as if it were impossible that he could have caused it.

"That's a handy piece of work," Lyons muttered. "Let's go."

"Can you walk?"

"I'll do my best."

The woods grew sparser nearer the water, and the first of Team Two was moving in at a quick pace, shouting to one another from right and left. Could they use their motion detectors while moving that fast? Schwarz doubted it. Without discussion he and Lyons crouched in a low stand of dense, ground-hugging ferns, the only cover evident.

"Where are you, you son of a bitch!" cried the red-faced gunner who came storming through the woods. "Who is it! Who fucked up! Cashman, is that you? I'll kill you!"

He was a wiry, olive-skinned, black-haired man in a faded flannel shirt and oil-stiffened jeans. He was waving his OICW from one point to the next, as if seeing glimpses of an enemy behind every tree.

"Here I am," Lyons said, pushing to his feet before Schwarz could stop him.

The gunner's lower jaw dropped when he cranked his head around and saw the stranger, standing thigh high in the ferns. In his hands the stranger carried some sort of combat shotgun, the likes of which Red Face had never seen before. Red Face moved fast to bring the OICW around to target the stranger, but he'd blown it. Walked right past the guy. He couldn't make the turn and he knew it. He started to say something. The sound never left his mouth before the customized Atchisson spoke, firing a burst of steel shot that chopped into the gunner's left shoulder, arm and torso, flailing the skin off in an eye blink. He slammed into the dirt, still conscious, but died so fast his last second was spent in awe of the curious sensation of the blood rushing out of his body all at once.

Another gunner emerged at the crucial moment and watched his companion die. He tried to turn and run, tried to aim his earth-pointed weapon at Lyons. He should have concentrated on one or the other. Lyons pivoted, erect as a puppet twirling on a stick, and fired the Atchisson again, slamming down the gunner.

"This way," Schwarz said, starting off to the left. "We gotta take out the rest of these guys to make passage to the lake."

It was clear that the gunners' time for slow, safe leap-frogging through the woods with their motion detectors was over, and Schwarz and Lyons didn't restrict their movements as they hunted for the remainders of Team One. They encountered a burst of autofire and stepped into the cover of the nearest trees.

Lyons was breathing hard, but his eyes were wild. Despite his injuries, despite the weakness, the Able Team leader was in berserker mode. "Gadgets, let them push you back. Make it visible."

"You're just going to stand around and let them walk up to you?"

"Yeah. I can't run fast enough to take your role, but I can shoot."

Schwarz tried to come up with a better option. He didn't care what Lyons said, the guy seemed capable of passing out again any second. Schwarz did as ordered, racing into the open, triggering a long autoburst of 5.56 mm rounds from his OICW, emptying the magazine in a flash. He hoped that wasn't long enough for those optical targeting devices to get a lock. Then he was retreating noisily.

He found the cover of a tree, listening to pursuit coming. Three of them. Maybe more. What had he done? Ironman, weak and slow, against three soldiers? Where's the sense in that? It was too late to rectify the error.

"Ironman, you better come through for me on this one."

LYONS KNELT behind the tree like a man in prayer, breathing deeply, thankful for the pain that was keeping his senses sharp. The tightness was beginning across the wound, and the moist seepage had turned to a hard crust. No more bleeding. But he knew he was feeble. Slowed.

He heard them coming. at least three gunners.

The Atchisson was an old friend. The assault shotgun was originally customized for him by Andrzej Konzaki, Stony Man Farm armorer from the days before Cowboy Kissinger.

Konzaki was buried on the Farm, one of the dead who had been haunting Lyons over the past few days. But his handiwork lived on in the Atchisson, a selective-fire weapon with single shot, triburst and full automatic fire. It had a twenty-inch rifle barrel and a 7-round magazine. During the years, Lyons had learned the function of the weapon intimately, and it had done immense good in his hands. He could change a magazine with no more concentration than others required to snap their fingers.

There was a round in the chamber. There was an extra magazine on his belt. His equipment was ready for war. But was he? He blinked, shook his head, fighting against the depletion that threatened to suck him into darkness. With gritted teeth he raised his arms to shoulder level and shoved his elbows forward. The skin pulled tight on his back and the fresh scab ripped, sending electric pain through the fog in Lyons's mind. Exhaling through his teeth, almost dropping onto all fours from the agony, he heard the approaching footstep of the remaining gunners in Team One. Close enough.

The time was now or maybe never.

Lyons got to his feet and stepped into the open. He faced five gunmen.

The shooting started.

"OH, NO."

Schwarz heard the shooting start with a sense of dread. The sound of the Atchisson mixed it up with the now-familiar chatter of the automatic fire of the OICW. Lyons had made his attack too early. The gunners weren't near enough for him to have the advantage. Schwarz was still trying to draw them into Lyons's best range.

Schwarz swore and bolted back the way he'd come.

The shooting never seemed to end.

THE FLICK of the nearest gunner's head proved he was alert and quick to react, and Lyons judged he had to go down first or it was all over. He triggered a 3-round burst that launched four hundred steel projectiles in less than two seconds. The gunner's body was hit with three explosive blasts, each flaying a deeper layer of flesh from his body, so that the man disintegrated into an airborne cloud of blood that rained onto the forest floor. Lyons turned hard, fired again, and another triburst slammed like a wrecking ball into a pair of side-by-side gunners as the first of them was getting a finger on the trigger of his weapon. They were swept down together, and Lyons ignored the whizzing of rounds that cut through the air and slammed into his tree. The remaining two gunners triggered wildly and tracked away from each other, seeking cover.

When Lyons fired the Atchisson at the first man, it was a fraction after the gunner dived, driven by an instinct that gave him a few extra seconds of life. The buzzing mist of steel pellets ripped the bark off the tree where he would have been running.

Lyons removed the magazine, snapped in the new one and was firing again before there was even a pause to tell the other gunners his ammunition was depleted. The barrel of the Atchisson turned on a short bank of dark undergrowth a hundred feet away, spotted a shiver of movement and triggered an explosive 3-round burst that ripped the vegetation away and slammed the gunner onto his back, knocking the breath out through the countless perforations that had suddenly been created in his lungs, and tiny spurts of blood jetted from the wounds.

Only the one with the good instincts was left alive. Lyons twisted and fired into the woods, homing in on an eruption of automatic fire, but the man was still on the move in a way that was beyond Lyons's power. He couldn't give chase and he couldn't dodge.

The gunner ended up behind a tree that absorbed the flurry of steel shot, exposing the white, fleshlike wood under the peeled-off bark.

He emerged again, triggering his weapon as he aimed, cutting a half moon of damage through the forest. He was hoping he would luck out and deposit a single dollop of steel into the intruder. Lyons wanted the same thing, but he had just one round left and couldn't afford to be wasteful. As the OICW's vicious 5.56 mm fire ripped across the forest to where he stood, Lyons lined up the slug sights and squeezed the trigger on the Atchisson. The blast of the last remaining round erupted from the gun a microsecond after the 5.56 mm round crashed into Lyons at gut level. It slammed into his Kevlar with a terrific blow, like a two-by-four swung hard into his stomach, and he bent double and fell flat on his face, knowing as he suffered and fought for control that the last round had been diverted from its target. The gunner was still alive.

Ignoring the absence of air in his lungs, the searing pain in his gut and the screaming of the freshly opened wound slicing through his back, he grunted, pushed himself erect and swept the .357 Magnum Colt Python revolver from the holster on his back. The gunner saw the revolver, triggered his OICW and brought it to bear on Lyons as the Able Team leader triggered his gun, stepped into the stream of 5.56 mm rounds as they swept toward him and triggered it again.

The chatter of autofire stopped abruptly. The barrel of the OICW hit the ground, dangling loosely from one limp hand as the gunner stared at bloody holes gaping in his ribs and stomach.

Lyons's neck and arms were quaking from exertion when he took his last step at the gut-shot gunner, his energy level so low he could scarcely maintain consciousness. He raised the big Python level with the gunner's face, and it was like lifting a concrete block. Something crashed through the woods behind him. He heard the chatter of the OICW automatic rifle from somewhere back there.

If that was Gadgets he was saved. If it was one of Woody Polmar's soldiers, he was dead. He reserves were gone. He couldn't react. He couldn't even turn to see who it was. The gut-shot man raised his OICW, as well, prepared to take Lyons to hell with him.

That was the moment Lyons recognized the man. It was Cashman, the security guard who had wounded him.

Lyons grinned grotesquely as he triggered the revolver, and the gunner's face disappeared in a mask of blood.

Then Lyons fell to the ground like a dead man himself.

CHAPTER NINETEEN

The homeland was in jeopardy.

Jeopardy's cause could not be allowed to continue.

Woody Polmar felt dark, grim inside. Never had he believed so fervently in the cause of the Soldiers of Solomon until this moment, the moment when the danger was greatest.

He didn't understand what was happening out there, in the woods that had been his home since he was a boy. Team One was getting slaughtered. None of them responded.

This was clearly not a case of a single commando in those woods. More like an army. Team Two was on the run now, double-timing it on foot through the woods, trying to get to Team One to provide assistance, if that was possible. If Team One was a loss, they were to get to the warehouse immediately. The number-one priority had to be getting the shipment out of there. This was now an unsafe place, and the shipment, and what it meant to the cause, was far too valuable to be allowed to be confiscated. Its dollar value was in the millions, of course, but because of the limitations in manufacturing and the timetable faced in the Middle East, it was quite simply irreplaceable.

The weapons were more important than Team One. They were more important than the lives of all the men present.

Polmar stood at the doors to the warehouse, watching the growing late-afternoon shadows. He had a full cartridge in the grenade launcher and a pair of extras in his pack. At the first sign of the commandos, he was going to start firing. He'd light up the skies. He'd mow down every tree within a mile. He wouldn't stop firing until his ammunition was exhausted. No matter how good they were, they wouldn't survive that kind of barrage.

As he paced before the doors, his eyes flitted to the trees. He heard the final clatter of 5.56 mm autofire die down. There had been other gunshots. Handguns. Some sort of blasts that came in lightning-quick succession, like some sort of rapid-fire shotgun, of all things.

Who the hell were these guys? How had they tracked him down?

He looked at his watch. Team Two was three or four minutes away at best. His team wasn't trained for an armed march through the woods, and it might take them twice as long as his estimates.

The shadows of the trees were creeping inexorably in his direction.

Where in hell was Team Two?

Woody Polmar froze, horrified, his scalp growing cold as the blood drained from his head.

The man that had materialized in front of him was some sort of madman, insanity and hatred scrawled on his face. Darkness fell in the shallows of his skull, but Polmar saw that the whites of his eyes were red like blood, the brown was glinting with a lust for vengeance. His camouflage clothing was ripped and bloodied, his face scratched and clawed by the forest, and darkened by the shadows of the lengthening afternoon.

The thing draped on his shoulder could only be a human corpse.

"Woody Polmar."

When the madman spoke his name, Polmar's horror intensified, taking scant comfort from the OICW that separated them.

"You're the one who killed my men," Polmar said, swallowing the words. He tried to sound accusatory, but the words came out in a whine.

"No. This is the man who wiped out your team of killers."

The figure with the wild, shadowed eyes moved his head to indicate the corpse. The madman had a fearlessness about him—it was the fearlessness of insanity. Why else would he have walked out of the woods without a weapon?

Polmar considered that the man, even burdened with the body of his companion, had managed to sneak up on him somehow. He jabbed the business end of the OICW at the chest of the madman and told him, "I can't let you leave."

"I can't let you live."

"Huh." It was a kind of a laugh, and Polmar felt a grin come to his face. The commando's sudden appearance had spooked him, as if he were a teenage girl in the haunted house at a carnival. What was his problem? Whatever—he was over it. "My friend," Polmar said with a sneer, "you don't have much say in the matter."

The eyes hidden in the shadows opened farther. Blood seeped along his eyebrow and down his face as he said in a slow, level voice. "I am not your friend."

"Neither am I," said the corpse.

Polmar's fear flooded his body again, and for a fraction of a second he thought he was actually seeing the dead come back to life. The man had to be dead. He was soaked with blood. He looked gaunt, as if his life essence had been drained away and left only a hollow shell, incapable of sustaining life.

But the living dead didn't use handguns. A revolver had materialized in the dangling hands of this corpse, and it fired with a roar. The .357 round struck Polmar in his rib cage, deformed, and took out his heart.

His legs went out, his body was falling, and before his backbone cracked on the hard earth Woodrow Polmar was dead.

Tel Aviv

IF THE DEAR, departed Mrs. Blancanales happened to walk into the meeting room at NewMan Electronics, all she would have seen was a pair of Jewish businessmen sitting in front of a laptop with an auxiliary display positioned on a low desk. Even she would have been hard to convince her son Rosario was one of the businessmen.

But there he was, fiddling with the laptop he brought from the U.S. He was calling himself David Ragen, and he was on the verge of a breakthrough—or exposure as a fraud, and probably death.

"All right, Ragen, I've got our head man on the line," said Ariel Newman, chief director and founder of NewMan Electronics. "Hello, sir."

"Good day, Ariel," a man's voice said from the speaker on the low-profile telephone. That, Blancanales assumed, would be Kesher Nir. "I have my assistant with me."

"Good morning," said a woman's voice. She would be Ms. Sandra Honig, if Stony Man Farm intelligence was accurate. It usually was.

The two of them didn't bother identifying themselves for Blancanales's benefit.

"Hello, sir. I'm very glad to be given this opportunity," Blancanales said, smiling, looking enthusiastic. "You can't imagine how excited I was when I realized what was about to happen here, in Israel I mean. I really hope you'll find what I have to offer is acceptable—I want to be a part of this. It's going to be more than historic."

Blancanales felt pretty good about the performance. Gushing, eager, not too simpering. The personality he was trying to get across was that of a man not here to take advantage or to get rich, but to be a part of a milestone event in world history.

"Mr. Ragen, if you have what you claim to have," said Nir, "well, let's just proceed with the demonstration. We'll talk when it's done."

"All right," Blancanales said. So far so good. They appeared to have bought into his cover story. Israeli native, taken to the U.S. by his parents as a child. Never returned to Israel to live but came back for a few brief visits. But, he told Newman, he had developed a strong loyalty and attachment to his homeland. He came to believe in the biblical-ordained destiny of Israel. That superseded all national loyalties. It absolved all crimes of national espionage. He had a career in satellite-security technology, with a position with the one of the aeronautics conglomerates that served as a primary supplier to NASA. As a navigation-protocol specialist, he had inside access to the control systems used for the satellites put up by the National Reconnaissance Office.

"I was actually called in on several occasions to go through diagnostic maneuvers on satellites that are in-station," he was explaining again for the benefit of Nir and Honig. "I was able to learn the access procedures that enabled us to get in and upload software updates."

"But surely they changed the security procedures after every such update," Honig challenged.

"Of course they did. I know the current system," Blancanales explained, allowing the nonsense Tokaido and Kurtzman had written out for him to flow forth as if he actually understood satellite-security issues. He went into the details of the NRO system to be accessed, including a high-level firewall that included stateful packet inspection and a packet-analysis system that would likely dynamically analyze allowed information to any of hundreds of variables for real-time verification. Even if a user entered the system, he would likely be booted if he didn't continually justify his presence to the system's satisfaction. That was the lower-level system that provided entrance to a higher-level satellite access subsystem. Security there was tougher. "First there's a security password that tells the satellite it is getting a legitimate transmission—"

"A password?" Honig demanded.

"Well, yes. It's fourteen thousand characters long and comes from results of an algebraic formula, variable dependent on the date, time and other factors provided by the system dynamically. That's just to get the CPU on the satellite to pay attention."

There was a silence as Blancanales waited for this explanation to be accepted or rejected. Kesher Nir said, "Please continue, Mr. Ragen."

"So, I knew there was no way to replicate that password, so what I did was search out other holes in the security behind the password. If I could get into the system at the National Reconnaissance Office itself and make it think I was a legitimate operator, then I could bypass all the problems of gaining control of the sats via remote uplink."

Honig made a sound that was a sort of derisive laugh. "Are you telling me that you can provide us with access to an NRO satellite operating system, from Tel Aviv, undetected?"

"That's correct," Blancanales said. "The opening they left was small, but I made it bigger."

"Explain that for me," Nir said.

"The agency has a sort of expanded firewall that is designed to keep out everything," Blancanales said, allowing his voice to grow more excited. "No electronic signals can go through it without security authorizations, which I tried but failed to duplicate. So when I was developing software diagnostic tools, I built in a small, free-ranging application that would passively absorb information about procedures for selectively sending coded information outside the satellite control system. It took me two years of sporadic visits to get enough information for a workable duplicate procedure. I built a test procedure. After a few tries, the test procedure functioned as I had hoped. It took down the security wall from the inside. Just for a microsecond. And just long enough for my test blip to get inside. But it worked. Finally, I built an application that would install a small, hidden pipe. My own little way in and out. Nobody can see it except me.''

"You're kidding me," Honig said. "You expect me to believe that?"

"Of course not," Blancanales said, sounding friendly. "It's outlandish. But I can prove it's there. I'll do it right now."

SANDRA HONIG TOUCHED the mute button and shook her head, looking sour. She glared at the monitor with Newman and his new recruit, the bizarre Mr. Ragen. "This guy is full of shit," she said, tapping the screen.

Kesher Nir was thinking hard.

"You can't possibly believe this crap," she continued.

"I believe it's possible," Nir said slowly. "I believe it could be done. Has this man done it? I won't believe him until I see it. I see no reason not to go through with the test. Then we won't have any doubt, will we?"

Honig stewed for a moment, considering her response.

"What's your problem with going through with the test?" Nir said. "It won't take but a few minutes. If the test fails, we proceed in one way. If the test succeeds, we consider Mr. Ragen's offer."

"It just seems too good to be true," Honig said. "First

him tracking us down, then putting this in our laps. There's something wrong here."

"On the contrary," Nir said, voice dropping low, becoming solemn. "I have faith in the inevitability of the Israeli people to see the truth of their destiny. He didn't, by the way, track us down. He tracked down Newman. He does not know who we are, and he has no evidence against any of us. Why not put our faith in those of our kind who have come to this realization ahead of the masses?"

Honig had a hard time digesting the spiritualist crap Nir liked to spoon out. The truth was her conviction in the inevitable domination of the Middle East by Israel had more to do with nationalism than it did the Bible. She hated the Arabs more than she loved the Jews. But in her position she didn't dare contradict the theological aspect of the argument. There was an unspoken understanding between them. Nir didn't question her faith in the Jewish God. But that didn't stop him from using it to put a stop to an argument he saw as fruitless.

Nir was sitting back in a leather chair behind the desk in his office, staring at a blank computer screen, feeling the gentle rush of air from the vents as the building's environmental-control system adjusted to accommodate the heat lingering inside the building from an especially hot afternoon.

They'd been off the line for a half minute or more. On the monitor, Ragen and Newman were waiting expectantly, looking at the walls. Nir touched the mute button and spoke.

"Still with me, Mr. Ragen?"

"I'm here, sir."

"I think we are ready to see what you have to show us."

"Right. You online with us?"

Honig and Nir exchanged glances. They hadn't told him that as soon as he plugged his laptop in they would be monitoring his activity via a remote display, not just replicating the image on his computer but recording every keystroke. "Yes. Please go ahead, Mr. Ragen."

There was a moment of nothing, then the screen started up.

He was dialing out on a modem.

That somehow symbolized the absurdity of the whole thing to Honig. She hadn't used a modem since she was in college. And yet it had been Newman who insisted on this method of interfacing with his U.S.-based server. A deliberately miswired telephone line into the NewMan offices would mislead a trace, just in case there was one. If this guy was for real, and he did get into the U.S. NRO satellite control systems, and his Internet access was traced back to an IP on the NewMan corporate intranet, well, the result could be disaster.

Ragen had agreed at once. Using a simple interface with his NT server in Virginia, he said, he could access his application, run the break-in and feed the photos piecemeal through his pipe into the NRO system.

All Nir had to do was name a set of GPS coordinates.

Honig cackled suddenly, and her finger tapped the zoom key on the screen monitoring the over-the-shoulder video feed from NewMan. The camera moved in hard on the laptop. The icon on the front of the computer was a familiar recessed design showing an apple with a bite taken out of it.

Sandra Honig made a derisive snort. "And you want me to take this guy seriously?"

Stony Man Farm, Virginia

THE QUIET in Huntington Wethers's corner of the Computer Room was broken by a strident alarm. He turned from the station he was working on to the unit that was making all the noise and turned it off with the touch of a key.

"Pol's on the line from Israel," he reported over his shoulder. Needlessly, as it turned out, because Aaron Kurtzman was already speeding across the room. He came to halt beside Wethers and grabbed the phone. He rang it, said a single word and Akira Tokaido was slipping through the door almost before the receiver was set down again. He was still chewing a bite of dinner.

"We recording?" Kurtzman asked.

"We are," Wethers said.

"We tracing?"

"Yes, sir," Tokaido replied.

"Okay," Kurtzman said in an exhale. "I sure hope this goes okay."

What he didn't say was that the safety of Rosario Blancanales might depend on it.

"It'll go okay," Tokaido said without a shred of hesitation, but he said it with the determination of the hopeful rather than the assurance of the confident.

"He's into the server," Wethers said in a slow rumble. He was watching the progress the remote-access software was making, establishing a low-security-level link with an NT server. The server was one of the boxes sitting in the vast computer hardware section of the Annex. It was filled with data copied from a PC belonging to an actual programmer for one of the aerospace subcontractors. The man never even knew his hard drive had been raided. Kurtzman was sure Blancanales's story would be checked through a clandestine, remote search of his hard drive later. These people certainly would have a hacker capable of breaking into even a highly secure home system. There had to be corroborating evidence there to be perused.

Blancanales, sitting on his laptop somewhere in Israel, typed in a password, all consonants that were meaningless, except that if he changed the last character to a vowel it would have changed his description of his situation. *A* meant he was being tortured for information, *B* meant he was sure his cover was blown and so on.

Kurtzman's relief was audible in his sigh when the password told them Blancanales was okay.

Blancanales entered the NT server, found and launched the application he was claiming to have written personally and waited for it to get to work.

The software wiggled through the Internet and found its way to a stateful packet inspection and authentication access protocol that constituted one of the most devious security firewalls on the planet.

Tokaido's fingers were poised over the keyboard like some concert pianist poised to attempt a speed record for "Für Eliese."

"We've got a stall tactic," Wethers stated.

Tokaido's fingers launched into the keys, bringing up applications designed to get past the authentication steps the systems designers had put in to distract users attempting to get into their system. If the users fell for the stall, they'd be targeted as unauthorized and asked to satisfy extra entrance requirements. All this was presumably handled by whatever software a typical high-security user was given to access this part of the system—a handful of people at most. But Tokaido had to handle the responses manually, bringing up the appropriate applications as required. He launched six independent applications in under twenty seconds. Some took a series of numbers provided by the security software, performed a specific set of calculation to them based on the security software's dictum of the moment and provided an answer. Others provided alphabetic answers to questions asked in a code buried inside pages of binary code. Others were straightforward.

Then the access came.

Tel Aviv

"I'M IN," said the strange newcomer, gesturing at the screen. "It looked easier than it actually was. I promise you it took months to get everything in place to enable what you just saw."

Sandra Honig was trying to read the sincerity of the man on her screen. He looked confident. If he was trying to yank the chain of the Soldiers of Solomon, he was as cool as a cucumber about it. But the story he was giving them just had to be bullshit.

Honig knew a thing or two about hacking. She'd broken into a dozen high-level corporate systems herself during her college years, and she was probably the third or fourth most highly skilled machine-language developer in Israel, which meant the entire Middle East. This guy would have to be some sort of a wacko genius to do what he said he could do.

But for the life of her, she couldn't think how he could possibly fake the evidence that he was about to provide them. If the evidence came, she would have to believe he was doing what he said he was doing. It would, in fact, be a stupendous windfall for the Soldiers of Solomon.

"Okay," said the man sitting in the office over at NewMan Electronics. "I've told you where we can expect the NRO sats to be now. You give me the coordinates, I'll tell the sat to snap a picture at maximum resolution. If your marker is big enough, we'll see it."

The man called Ragen waited. Newman shifted in his seat.

"One moment," Nir said. He muted the phone, staring at the video monitor, then at the computer screen duplicating the screen in Newman's office. The display was stupidly simple. It was like the interface to somebody's private e-mail account.

Could it really give him access to one of the most powerful intelligence tools devised by man?

He picked up the phone and dialed. A moment later a voice said, "Berman."

"Do not tell me where you are, understand? Are you ready?"

"Sure."

"This is what I want you to do—there's a bar in New York City. We planned a part of a venture there a year ago. You drank Scotch. I drank beer. You remember this?"

"Of course."

"Give me your GPS."

Mitchell Berman read off the coordinates. Nir wrote them on a pad of paper and pointed at the screen. Honig immediately got on the line to Newman's office and read the coordinates to Newman and the American, Ragen. She watched Ragen punch in the coordinates in the simple entry form provided.

Now, he had explained to them, if the coordinates were within the purview of one of the most powerful spy satellites in existence, and if the satellite wasn't currently allocated for a priority mission, such as a CIA emergency mission, then the satellite would change focus to the coordinates, take the shots, then go back to its previous mission. The priority code that caused this override of standard operation was a NASA test code.

If the temporary mission was brief, it simply wouldn't be debated by NRO operators. If it did anger somebody, they might report it to the security staff. The security staff might check it out, but unless they did a full system scan to trace the input of the command they'd believe it was a legitimate. It would be too much trouble to track down the user personally and make him justify his mission.

That's what Ragen claimed.

Stony Man Farm, Virginia

"UH-OH." It was Wethers. "Looks like there's a priority override already in place on that bird."

Tokaido said something graphic and crude, and Kurtzman wheeled to Wethers's workstation.

"Who is it?"

Wethers shook his head slightly. "They didn't exactly log in, Aaron."

"Stupid question. Can we override?"

"We can't override an override priority," Wethers said patiently. "Priorities are set by the director of the National Reconnaissance Office. He answers to his constituents, so to speak. CIA, Justice, whoever. If Hal went to the director and bargained for access…"

Wethers shrugged. He was telling Kurtzman what Kurtzman already knew. And there was certainly no time for going through channels.

"Can we kick them off?"

"Hal, that's somebody pretty important. Military intelligence, CIA, who knows?"

"Pol's life may hinge on our success right here. Right now. Can we kick them off? We'll deal with the consequences later."

"Yeah. Shut down the application at the NRO end," Tokaido said.

"You can shut it down?" Even Kurtzman, who was never amazed at what the young prodigy could accomplish, couldn't imagine how he could force a highly secure remote system to crash and restart.

"Kind of. You put a shitload of commands through the CPU, over and above its capacity," Tokaido said, talking fast. "Any processor will balk when it gets overwhelmed. This system has a contingency plan in place to deal with it. They'll purge the excess commands or cache them or something, and while it's gagging we force through our own set of instructions.''

"That's not quite a shutdown, but I see where you're going with it," Kurtzman said. "I still don't understand how this gives us a window of opportunity to take control."

Tokaido nodded, thinking it through at the same time he was explaining it. "I've been rummaging around in this system for the past few days. It's made to be crash-proof. It's made to not go off-line, not ever, and to protect itself it will dump commands it can't handle into RAM, then to hard drive. I'm talking gigaflops of command lines here. Way more than the CPU can handle no matter how powerful. This is a simplification of what actually occurs but you get the drift.''

Tokaido brought up a page of command lines he had staged for the NRO system, all benign and quick, designed to go through the system unnoticed. He highlighted a command line: "new maintenance user; time?''

"Dirt simple, right, but what if you did this?'' Tokaido rattled as he copied the line and pasted it, holding the command keys down and filling the page with the command line repeatedly. The command line field at the bottom of the page said "133.'' Then Tokaido selected the entire document of command lines and began pasting it into the document again and again. Kurtzman and Wethers watched the display of command lines expand faster than they could read. Tokaido paused. The command line field read "45220.'' He repeated the procedure, and in a moment, and when he stopped the command line field read "30659160.''

"Thirty million command lines. We parallel the inputs to shove them all in at once,'' Tokaido declared, moving to the top of the column and typing in: "parallel process:.'' Then he moved to the bottom of the column and typed in, "end parallel process, process command 'Directive Express'.''

"It'll not only have to handle all those commands—it will

have to allocate resources prioritizing a sudden growth in total users. Even if we don't have top priority, it'll bog its brain, I guarantee it.''

"Why won't the top-priority commands take precedence?" Kurtzman asked. "If your code is ignored, it does us no good.''

"The CPU won't let anybody have exclusive rights, not the CIA, not Justice, not anybody," Tokaido said, talking faster, his explanation rambling into overdrive and his impatience growing. "Our ingress is under the auspices of a maintenance and event-planning channel, always the last to be allocated CPU time but guaranteed to be allocated some CPU time—Aaron, we're wasting time! They're waiting for this, and we need to do it now if we're going to do it!''

Kurtzman was rarely indecisive. Right now he was. His mind was boiling over with questions and contradictions to everything Tokaido had said. There were a dozen reasons the computer might be safeguarded against just such an event.

But why would the NRO even think to safeguard against an event like this? It would never happen, would it?

Because somebody might force it to happen, and it might succeed.

This was the kind of drastic act that he and his cybernetics staff tried to plan ahead for. They would discuss all the possible outcomes, secretly evaluating the system in question from every possible angle before making a decision as to how to proceed. Now he had not weeks, but seconds to decide.

The most important factor in the decision making was that the man making the recommendation was one of the world's most skilled computer systems trespassers ever. If Tokaido said it would probably work, then it would—probably—work.

"Okay.''

"Yeah!" Tokaido said, and his fingers furiously worked

to shove the commands into the satellite-control and function-maintenance system at the National Reconnaissance Office.

Somewhere in the Eastern United States

EVEN AKIRA TOKAIDO didn't know where the NRO hardware, a mixture of old mainframes and newer, more compact supercomputers, was actually located. It was a well-protected place, accessible electronically from anywhere in the world, to the people who knew how, but accessible physically to only a handful of operators.

The document from Stony Man Farm came through the data pipe in one meaty chunk.

The computers had been programmed to allow those who input the commands to establish their level of importance. When it saw the ''New Maintenance User'' command, it automatically gave the request priority level three. But it also set a guaranteed-action flag. No matter what happened, the command would be performed when its place in line was reached. This contingency was a way of making sure no important maintenance function would get ignored to the detriment of system operation.

It performed its other navigation functions—churning through more than ten thousand data lines in under an eye blink—before it found time to take care of the first command line.

Because the maintenance user was a new maintenance user, output space needed to be created on the hard drive.

Since no output user identification was specified, the command results—''What time is it?''—couldn't be written. The computer erased the small results segment it had created on its hard drive and generated an error message. When it looked for an input source to follow back with the error messenger, there was none.

In the interest of efficiency, the computer simply forgot about the error message and moved on to its next line.

The system hadn't been designed to handle standard, old-fashioned parallel processing. But when the software demanded it, the programmer could specify it, and the system would allocate its resources to carrying out a specified set of parallel commands.

It went through the process again, building space for the new user, realizing there was no way to identify the new user, trying to send an error message, realizing it couldn't send an error message.

It wasn't a loop. The system would have recognized and halted a loop.

Higher-priority commands were demanding attention, but more and more CPUs were dedicated to the parallel-processing task. The computer would do its best to get it done and out of the way fast so it could get back to its other jobs.

In under one second there became no system processing power available.

It wasn't a crash. No warning lights went off. No failures were reported. But in-process missions had to fend without mainframe support for the time it took to churn through thirty million requests.

When the last request was processed and promptly forgotten, it began to handle every higher priority command in cache. The directive express command, rattled off by Akira Tokaido in seconds, went unchallenged by higher-priority directives.

The National Reconnaissance Office's North American Survey Satellite Number One stopped what it was doing, and started doing what the Israeli terrorists asked it to do.

Stony Man Farm, Virginia

TOKAIDO WAS grinning like a fool as he saw the scheme begin to work.

He loved this. *Loved* it. This was the kind of loophole he usually warned government agencies about, but it sure was fun to worm your way through of one occasionally.

Huntington Wethers watched it happen and bit his lower lip as his head turned and his eyebrows raised.

"It worked, Aaron."

"I see that, Hunt."

"I wonder which agency we just kicked off a U.S.A. spy satellite?" Wethers asked rhetorically.

"I wonder that myself," Kurtzman replied. But he didn't really want to know.

"Whoever it is," said Akira Tokaido, the corners of his mouth almost touching his ears, "they are gonna be *pissed!*"

He was the only one smiling.

Tel Aviv, Israel

SANDRA HONIG WAS watching the small display in the operator's window, holding her breath. She wanted this to work. She wanted Ragen to be what he said he was. She wanted to have this power under her control.

She already knew what she would do with it.

"Nasat staged."

"Tell him to start taking pictures," Nir ordered. Then into the phone he said, "Okay, do not say it—show me the name of the woman in the bar that night."

Berman sounded like he was grinning. "Sure thing."

Edina, Minnesota

MITCHELL BERMAN was standing in the control booth high in the stands over a vacant football field. The Edina Technical College Bobcats played there, and the man standing at the controls ran the board for all the games. The board technician was wondering what he was going to do with the easiest five hundred bucks he'd ever made.

"Listen close," Berman said to him. And he spelled the name.

The board technician for ETC typed it in and the letters appeared one at a time, spelled out in brilliant lights on the huge screen.

Three letters. That was nothing. The display was top-of-line, just a year old. The board technician could make all kinds of colorful animated images, including fireworks, birthday cakes with flickering candles, wedding bells and, of course, the roaring bobcat head that raised a paw and slashed the screen. He loved that one. Everybody loved that one. You could even use a scanner to digitize an image and put up any picture you wanted up there. There was always some freshmen who was trying to bribe him to use a digital nudie shot of an ex-girlfriend during a big home game.

Berman could almost feel the heat from the lights on his face. The letters were the maximum size allowed by the screen—eleven feet tall, the technician said.

"I'll be damned," Nir said delightedly on the other end of the line. "You spelled out 'Sam.'"

Berman laughed. "That's what we called her. I assumed you didn't want the full 'Samantha.'"

"Now tell me where you are," Nir said. "Is that a stadium?"

"I'm right outside Minneapolis on a college football field. That's one of those big game displays."

"Shit. This is fantastic. I think we just got handed a secret weapon."

"Do we need another one?" Berman asked, infected by Nir's good spirits. Nir wasn't usually an expressive man.

"This is *more* than a secret weapon," Nir said. "This is the weapon that will help us learn secrets."

BERMAN GAVE the technician at the stadium an extra hundred for his trouble and walked away a happy man.

He wasn't destined to stay happy for long. His cell phone beeped as he was getting into his car.

"Berman," he said. He was already worried about it. The phone display IDed the caller as Frank Wein. Wein was Polmar's number two or number three down in Clairemont. Why would Wein be calling him?

He listened for just a few seconds before he responded.

"Oh, shit!" he said.

And the news just kept getting worse.

CHAPTER TWENTY

The Middle East was moving into a meltdown.

In Egypt, the people were in the streets. There were calls for suspending the peace accord with Israel until the killers of the Palestinians at Khodr were convicted. The demonstrations grew in their ferocity as the night progressed, until the leaders went public with calls for immediate military action against Israel. These were the extremists, but the furious mob took up their call and soon Cairo and Alexandria, Port Said and Menia rocked with the chants, "Bomb Israel! Bomb Israel! Bomb Israel!"

In Lebanon's Tripoli, Muslim demonstrators collided with pro-Israeli Christian demonstrators and street fighting turned into a brawl that left hundreds wounded and twelve dead. The dead and wounded were left where they had fallen as the battles continued throughout the night.

In Jordan, government officials who had decried the overtures of peace with Israel went on public television and into the streets demanding the government apologize for its role in the failed attempt at a summit with Israel and the PLO, and that it rescind its 1994 agreement with Israel that ended the state of war that had officially existed between them since the Six-Day War of 1967. The government at Amman responded by condemning these officials, only to find themselves suffering a stormy public backlash, while the agitators were suddenly elevated to the status of unofficial spokesmen for the masses of Jordan. Sensing a growing political instability, the government at Amman acceded and apologized on state television and radio for even considering playing a role in the summit. It would not, it said, consider further negotiations of any kind with Israel until the Israelis responsible for the murders at Khodr were convicted.

In Iraq, the government was more direct in its approach. It announced that it would consider any nation that attacked an Israeli Jew to be an ally and a friend. Baghdad residents received a free meal for their participation in an anti-Israeli rally.

In Libya, a government declaration called the dead of Khodr martyrs. The Khodr men and boys who marched on the Israeli settlement to avenge those deaths were "the new champions of Islam."

The violence continued in East Jerusalem throughout the evening and into the dark of a long night. Soon the mobs of rock-throwing Palestinians and riot-equipped police squads had given way to small bands of freedom fighters and quartets of police. The strategy was the same. Whichever group saw the other first, struck first.

New stocks of weapons, trucked in secretly that day from Iran and distributed in the name of freedom, had managed to bypass Israeli roadblocks and arrive in Jerusalem. It was after three in the morning when the violence accelerated again. Sixteen Israeli police and military died in the space of twenty minutes, cut down by automatic-weapons fire.

The military moved in. Any Palestinian found on the streets was gunned down. A new battle broke out when an army of Palestinians surged through guards and into the Old City Jewish Quarter, chanting that the quarter should be razed anew. Homes were set ablaze with Jewish families inside. The contest raged until Palestinian ammunition supplies dried up and the gunners fled back to East Jerusalem, many gunned down before reaching safety.

The streets became still in the last hours before dawn, but it was an expectant stillness.

New Orleans, Garden District

As THE CORPSES were being removed from the streets of Jerusalem, a fat man in a scarlet silk robe was having a drink on his patio in New Orleans.

He lived in the Garden District, an old neighborhood by American standards. The mansions had stood for a hundred, some for 150 years. They were grand and graceful. The fat man wasn't thinking about Middle Eastern troubles. There were always Middle Eastern troubles. He didn't care about five-thousand-year-old cities, or the legacies of history, or the fanaticism of religious idealism. What Sam Marino cared about was making some cash and keeping up the appearance of legitimacy. He had numerous business ventures to handle, a lifestyle to maintain.

That included this house, and it cost a fortune for upkeep on a piece of history. Everything had to be done by specialists. You couldn't just go putting a coat of paint on the walls; you had to hire some guy who knew which paints would be safe and which wouldn't eat through the 150-year-old wallboard. He had high-end Scotch whiskey he needed to buy and a couple of cars to keep in good repair and a pretty regular turnover of mistresses to keep happy and horny. And diamonds always kept them horny.

Marino lay way back in an iron chair watching the stars through the branches of the two-century-old oak tree, a portable phone tucked to his ear. His overstuffed head made the phone look like a toy. He was smiling, a bemused wrinkle crossing his broad face.

"Let me get this straight. You want me to export hot merchandise, by air, no planning, and you want it done in like the next forty-five minutes. Do I have it straight?" Marino couldn't quite believe what he was hearing.

"That's what I need, Sam," said Mitchell Berman. Marino had helped Berman arrange a few export flights in the past. It had been a few years now since the last job. Berman always paid well, but he also gave Marino plenty of advance warning.

"I can't do it, Mitch. It's too dangerous. The risk is too much."

"Don't shit me, Sam. You're the one guy in the entire South that could pull this off."

"Maybe. Probably," Marino agreed, nodding and smiling and chomping on the cold cigar stub he'd discovered in the robe pocket. He'd taken the call out on the patio of his ancient mansion to avoid waking up Sheila. Sheila needed her sleep. She'd been very energetic that evening and had to be tired. "But you know I like to cover my bases in advance, Mitch. How could I know all the possible complications? I couldn't. Sorry."

"Listen to me, Sammy. I know you can do this job. Name the price."

Marino chuckled, crooked a hand over the stub and pulled it out. "Tell you what, for a million dollars, I'll take the job." He chuckled again.

To his surprise, Berman wasn't phased.

"Let me get the official okay. I'll call you back in five."

With a click, Berman was gone, and Marino stared at the phone, smiling with amusement. Well, if the guy actually came up with a million bucks, the risk would be worth it.

Minneapolis

BERMAN WAS PULLING onto Interstate 35 when Kesher Nir came back on the line. Berman had been in touch with him already, quickly relating the events as he understood them from the confused account of Frank Wein. Two commandos had raided the warehouse, led the men all over the property, slaughtered a third of their number, including Woody Polmar. The pair was spotted in the water in one of Polmar's boats, where they launched a flare and were picked up by unmarked helicopter a mile offshore. One of them had been dragged up limp, maybe unconscious, maybe dead.

Berman explained the terms of Marino's deal.

"A million dollars? It's extortion."

"A million dollars?" cried a voice in the background. It was that plump bitch, Honig. She was always around Nir these days. Like they were lovers or something. "Who does he think he is? Tell Berman and his Mafia buddies to go to hell."

The sound became muffled, and Berman could hear Nir chewing out Honig with his hand over the phone. He ought to get rid of her. He came back on the line.

"There has to be a less costly way," he said.

"If we had the time, I could come up with something," Berman said. "I guarantee we don't have the time, Kesher. That was some sort of a commando team that struck the warehouse, and they have to be tied some government agency. There will be Feds searching the entire state in an hour or less. We have got to get this shipment out of Louisiana right now, or we take a very serious risk of having it found and confiscated. Then you've lost a lot more than one million dollars. You lose the seven million that went into manufacturing that shipment of units."

"Get them into hiding!" Nir shot back in frustration.

"We've got no place to hide them," Berman said. "Not that I know of. I'm a couple thousand miles away, anyway. You want to coordinate some sort of strategy for storing the units, you need to talk to the new guy in charge. Frank Wein."

"Wein," he said, as if the name were profanity.

Berman knew what he was thinking. Wein was an excellent business strategist, who had found their weapons manufacturer, but outside of a corporate office he was a buffoon. Nir would never trust him to handle their safekeeping.

"You do have the new Stuart Gold assets to offset the loss," Berman reminded him. Nir had convinced Stuart Gold to make him his sole beneficiary. All the Gold cash, patent rights and corporate ownership were his—a far larger sum than the contributions Gold had been making out of his petty cash. The reminder was enough to tip in Nir's decision.

"Fine. Fine! Do the deal," Nir said. "I'll authorize transfer of funds into Marino's account in the next fifteen minutes. Hell, I'll take it out of Gold's Cayman account."

"I'll get back to you with the number."

Berman clicked off, redialed Marino's number.

"It's a deal, Sam."

"No shit?"

"Our trucks are already on the road to New Orleans. I'm routing them to your hangar. They'll be there in—" he glanced at the car clock "—twenty minutes."

"Whoa, butch, we need to talk payment."

"I'm arranging that now, Sam. Give me an account and the money will be there before you start transferring cargo."

Berman waited. "Still with me, Sam?"

"You guys are desperate, huh?"

Berman heard the hesitation. "You wouldn't back out on a deal, Sam."

Another pause. "Don't sweat it, Mitch. I'll get your cargo where you want to go. Give me a destination so my pilot can file a flight plan."

"We'll say Mexico City. I'll phone you in a couple of hours with an alternate destination."

"Okay, Mitch." They exchanged numbers. Berman got

an account number for the payment deposit. Marino got the number to Berman's cell phone.

Marino clicked off and looked up into the stars, peeking through the green, dark foliage of the ancient oak. It was one of those dignified and ancient trees that was as much an edifice as the house. Together they had witnessed decade after decade of American history. More than one U.S. President had been a guest in these walls, but no more ruthless a man than Sam Marino had ever lived here.

He had his doubts. But a million was a million. It took his organization three weeks to net that kind of cash.

He began alerting the troops.

"HOLY CRAP!"

That sounded like Francis Leek, and Leek wasn't shocked by anything. Andy Downing went to the rear of the old panel truck to see what the problem was.

Leek and Bob Adata were walking a crate to the rear of the truck, faces tight, and they put it down in a hurry.

"What the problem?"

"Andy," Leek said, "there's like ten dead guys back there!"

Downing stepped into the panel truck and walked to the front, where the last row of crates was being unstacked. Behind it was open space. Piled on the floor was a miserable orgy of corpses, fresh and bloody.

Downing didn't know who these guys were. Surely not a part of any of the regular Families Marino's organization dealt with on a regular basis. He'd thought this group was a bunch of amateurs. Business guys with a bright idea for making a fast buck.

"Did you kill those guys?" he demanded as he stepped off the rear of the truck and landed on the gravelly asphalt of the airport.

Frank Wein shook his head, his face drooping from slack facial muscles. "No. Those are our people."

"Whoa. Who got you?"

Wein just glared at him and turned away.

Downing was on the line with Marino seconds later.

"I didn't like this job from the start," he told Marino after describing the makeshift abattoir. "Whoever these losers are, they got whacked good."

"Nobody told me 'bout that," Marino said.

"I hate these impulse jobs, Sam," Downing shot back. "They're never worth the risk. This one's a disaster in the making, and we'll be pretty damned lucky not to get caught up in it." Even as he was speaking, Downing was scanning the dark reaches of the airport, expecting the blue lights of law enforcement to appear any second.

"Yeah, well, let everybody know I'm giving a bonus for tonight. A grand a head. Danger pay. Five grand for you, Andy."

"I appreciate it, Sam," Downing said in a sigh, "but in the future, it would be just the same with me if we avoided this kind of danger completely."

THE GARDEN DISTRICT was like London, with a ghost story for every house. Including the great old 1854 mansion that was home to Sam Marino. He told these stories to his guests, as entertainment, but he didn't believe any of them.

When he saw the black thing come out of the shadows of his den, he almost changed his mind. His tumbler bounced on the carpet and his feet became very wet and cold. The air filled with the smell of Finnish vodka.

Marino realized the ghost had a suppressed subgun, and at least three friends were standing in the shadows like pitch phantoms.

"Who the fuck are you?"

The man with the MP-5 SD-3 was in the light of the small desk lamp Marino had flipped on, and the look on his face made Marino wish he'd asked in a nicer tone of voice.

"My friend," the man said in near whisper, "almost died."

"Sorry to hear that," Marino responded carefully. "Do I know him?"

"The people responsible were in contact with you tonight. We know this. We know they've been adding cash to your offshore accounts."

Marino laughed lightly. "You've got the wrong man. I don't even have offshore accounts."

"Then it won't concern you to learn that a million-dollar deposit made an hour ago was diverted from the account. By us."

"What?" Marino stared, then shook his head. "You didn't do that. It can't be done."

"We did it. That's just the beginning."

There was a scream from upstairs, quickly muffled. Sheila entered the room a minute later as a blanket-wrapped bundle over the shoulder of one of the figures in head-to-toe black.

"We're taking you apart, Marino. We've already downloaded every file from your personal hard drive, and the locals are opening your offices as we speak."

"You have nothing on me! This is against the law!"

"I don't represent the law," said Hermann Schwarz. "Complain to the authorities when they come to arrest you, if you can still talk. Now I want to know what your connection is to the people who almost killed my friend."

Marino saw the corpse in the corner, its mouth wide open in an eternal scream. It was Joe Jardin, the guy who was supposed to be on watch at the front door of the house.

Marino started to talk.

THEY WERE LEAVING the Garden District minutes later, turning onto St. Charles Avenue and heading away from the historic hub of New Orleans.

The first of the trio of olive-green Hummers hit the steel-pipe gate at fifty miles per hour. The chain that was looped and padlocked into the gate never gave way, but the concrete base of the support pipe on one side failed to keep its grip in the earth. It was extracted like a tooth on a string, and the support pipe was flung to one side with a crash.

Before they reached the two-level building and attached hangar they saw the Lincoln Towncar and boxy Cadillac Seville emerge from behind it, lights off, then accelerate through hard U-turns that took them in opposite directions across the airstrip.

Schwarz hit the accelerator and bore down mercilessly on the Towncar as the blacksuits in the other Hummers pursued the Cadillac. The Hummers had been flown in for the occasion. They were Stony Man Farm equipment, engineered for extra speed. When the armored front end of the seven-ton vehicle slammed into the rear quarter panel of the Lincoln, it twisted the frame, burst the tire and wrenched the wheel ten degrees out of alignment. A cloud of dust filled the night as the Towncar twisted through a donut and a half.

The doors flew open and a man emerged on either side, planting himself in the crook between the door and the body and launching a volley of handgun fire. The rounds scored the paint and bounced off the glass, and Schwarz ignored them as he plowed forward again, aiming at the front driver's-side corner of the long hood.

The gunners had the choice to dive away or into the Lincoln. One chose poorly, launched himself away from the Lincoln and hit the ground in the path of the Hummer. It rolled into him, slamming him to the ground and leaving him there, crushed. The other gunner dived into the Lincoln and rode out the crash, finding himself bouncing off the dashboard and rebounding into the back seat. Then the door near his head came open and hands extracted him by the collar.

Andy Downing, small-time hood and occasional murderer, found himself dangling like a cat toy, only his heels digging into the earth. He didn't know who or what had him.

He wasn't going to stand for it. The Browning had flown away at some point, but there was the little Smith & Wesson he kept around for emergencies. He grabbed at his back pocket, where it was holstered behind his right hip, under the shirt. The S&W was in his hand—and then it was gone.

Downing looked up. The man who was now holding on to the Smith & Wesson looked angry.

He rapped the gun across Downing's nose, flattening it in a spray of blood, and starlight knives shot through his head. He sputtered helplessly for the eternity it took him to be carried across the tarmac, where he was tossed on top of somebody else.

He was getting angry. He knew his rights. He knew what the cops could and couldn't do.

"You miserable fuck," he wailed through a mouthful of blood, trying to focus on the man who hit him. It was a big guy, brown haired, not too dangerous looking except for the very angry look in his eyes. The rest of the men were virtually invisible in their head-to-toe blacksuits. He managed to push himself off whatever he had landed on. It was the crushed remains of Francis Leek. "I'm going to sue your ass!"

"You can do what you want, after you give me the answers I need," Schwarz said.

"Fuck you! Fuck you!" Downing was enraged like never before. "I want my attorney, I want my phone call and I want some fucking humane treatment!"

Schwarz took a step at the screamer, thrust the MP-5 at the ground and triggered a single shot. The cough of the suppressed round was only as loud as the crunch of the shattering knee joint. And not nearly as loud as the screams that followed.

"Humane enough for you?"

Downing finally got the picture. This guy and his black-suits weren't the police, or even the Feds, and they didn't give two shits about the rights of the guilty.

Downing, through his gasps, told them everything he knew.

"WE TRACKED the plane. It's in Mexican airspace already," Barbara Price reported as Schwarz and his convoy of black-suits left the private airfield.

"There's nothing we can do?" Schwarz demanded.

"It's a Boeing. A long-range cargo configuration."

"That's not going to get them all the way to the Middle East—won't they stop to refuel?" Schwarz demanded.

"We can watch close. We'll have a satellite photo of every mile they fly," Price promised. "Even if they land to get gassed up, they'll be gone again before we could swoop down on them."

"It doesn't sound promising."

"Look at it this way," she said, "we have a cushion of maybe fifteen hours for Phoenix to break open the Israeli end of this venture. Once the organization is exposed, we'll have full justification for forcing the aircraft down before it reaches Israel. Or the President can shame the Israelis into doing it themselves."

"I vote we handle it and do it decisively," Schwarz protested. "The Israelis will insist on arresting and trying the passengers. They'll seize the cargo, and the next thing you know there'll one thousand OICWs that have vanished mysteriously, only to show up in the hands of the Soldiers of Solomon or somebody just as bad."

Price didn't respond to that. She knew he was correct.

"How's Ironman?" Schwarz asked.

"He's stitched up and getting a fill-up," she said. "The Clairemont, Louisiana, police are eagerly awaiting his return to wakefulness so he can identify himself and explain how he got the way he is. I'm going to have a Justice Department team there to extract him before that happens, but I want to wait a few hours, until he's got some of his strength back."

That was good news. If Price was planning on moving the Ironman, his wounds were not life threatening. "And Pol?"

"No news," she said. "No news since the satellite demo. That was hours ago."

"Barbara, what do you think's going on over there?"

"Gadgets," she said pensively, "I sure wish I knew."

CHAPTER TWENTY-ONE

Tel Aviv, Israel

Rosario Blancanales raised an eyebrow when a contingent of Israeli customs agents showed up at the dock.

His new best friend, Ariel Newman, founder and chief operating officer of NewMan Electronics, was the man taking official delivery of the shipment on the docked vessel, the *Homeland.* He'd be the one signing off on the shipment and taking responsibility for the cargo, including illegal items. If those illegal items were found and if the customs officials cared.

But they didn't care, as Blancanales learned soon enough. What they did care about was having a drink with Ariel Newman in a well-appointed limousine parked at the dock. There was limited-edition single-malt Scotch, and envelopes for all the officials. There was some pleasant chatter before the officials needed to be on their way.

"Looks like you've got things pretty well under control here," Blancanales said.

"Oh, yeah," Newman replied with a grimace. "We have a long-standing business arrangement. It's expensive only on the surface—those guys get paid a fortune, but the costs and headaches we save long-term makes it very advantageous."

"Could you even hope get this shipment into the country legally?"

Blancanales was clearly asking the man to tell him what was in the crates, and Newman responded with a thin-lipped look that said he might be pushing the man too far. Buddies or not, he knew Newman couldn't trust him implicitly. "Probably not," Newman answered coolly, then he shrugged. "What the hell. Who're you going to tell? Come on."

They walked across the dock. It was barely dawn, and there was a dank chill clinging to the air. The workers were in heavy gloves and worked in a peculiar silence, without discussion except for the shouts to the crane operator and the foreman's barking occasional orders.

The *Homeland* was a ninety-six-meter dry-cargo vessel with 4,800 square meters of cargo space in two holds, which was far more than she needed for this load. She was well-maintained to judge by the gleam of the deck equipment. She unloaded her cargo on tethered pallets rather than big shipping containers. When a pallet set down on the dock, its binds were released and the pallet was attacked by forklifts, removing smaller pallets from the shipping platform. The smaller pallets held crates.

Newman spoke quickly to one of the workers in Hebrew, and the man withdrew one of the wooden crates from the pallet he was about to load into one of a small fleet of panel trucks. Newman took a crowbar from one of the workers and attacked the lid with a sparkle in his eyes, grinning like a kid. When he pulled the top up, he batted away the protective foam covering and waved grandly at the contents, although he held the lid in place to block the contents from being seen outside the immediate area.

Blancanales thought he knew what he was seeing inside the foam cutouts of the box, but just as quickly convinced himself he had to be wrong. The OICW was still very much in the prototype phase. There weren't supposed to be enough of these weapons in existence to fill a single pallet, let alone the entire shipment.

In the interest of his role as David Ragen, security programmer for U.S. defense contractor, he played dumb. "Is it a machine gun?"

"Machine gun?" Newman asked in disbelief. "Well, yeah, kind of, but it's a lot more than that. It's an OICW. They call it the Objective Individual Combat Weapon. The U.S. Defense Department has been working on them for years. They haven't got far yet, you know, with all that bureaucracy they've got to go through."

Blancanales had a hard time believing it and just as hard a time asking the wrong questions. "You stole them from the DoD?"

Newman grinned. "Kind of. We stole the plans. Actually, it was our main man's girlfriend who did it. The one we were talking to last night? She's an annoying bag of wind, but she's sharp as a razor's edge. She figured out how to find the CAD drawings for this son of a bitch, and she downloaded them."

"So you guys are making them yourselves," Blancanales finished.

"Yeah. See this thing is one of those multinational, co-operative ventures," Newman went on. "They've got electronics firms, gun makers, optics companies, lots of other companies involved. She knew there would be files going back and forth between those companies as they all made refinements on certain systems. She put together a sort of electronic watchdog. It kind of sat there, watching unsecure computer traffic. She guessed that sooner or later there would be a slipup and somebody would accidentally send something over an unsecure channel. The watchdog would simply copy it before sending it on its way. We got the files in bits and pieces, but it only took eighty-three days before we had a complete CAD schematic for this baby.''

"But, I mean, why go to the trouble? Why not just buy a bunch of Uzis and AK-47s? Can this thing do anything that a regular automatic weapon can't do?''

"Oh, yeah, a lot." Newman launched into a detailed description of the capabilities of the OICW system. Blancanales knew most of it from what he had read through the years about the development of the weapon system. Last he had heard it wasn't scheduled to be delivered into grunts' hands until 2007. "The grenade targeting is a blast. I've used it myself. One guy could wipe out a village with one of these things and a box of 20 mms. And he would never have to get within range of the villagers' rifles to do it.''

Blancanales made appreciative noises, then tapped the pack in its own cutout. "What's this?''

Newman grinned fiercely as he pulled out the pack and withdrew an electronic device, small and made of dense black plastic. "This is a rat-catcher. It's one of the improvements we made to the U.S. weapon system. I designed it myself.''

Blancanales took the bait. "Okay. So what does it do?''

Newman leaned in close and said slowly, "It hunts down rats. Or Arabs. Whichever. It uses technology called ultra-wideband.''

"I've heard of it," Blancanales said. "I thought it was for communications and wireless LANs, that kind of thing.''

"True, it is, but it's also good for detecting motion, in a way you've never seen before. Look, if you're a soldier you put this thing into your pack or on your vest or something, or you can mount it right on the gun stock. Plug this end into the gun. Now, you point the UWB detector in front of you when you're in combat with hidden enemies. Like an Arab city, see? There's some Arab slimeball creeping around behind the walls. You use this to look for him. You can see him behind the walls. You can see him even if he's just creeping along quietly, just so long as he's moving. Then you aim it, and the UWB interfaces with the targeting system. It aims for you and kills that piece of slime dead, right through the damned wall!''

Blancanales tried to look impressed, but his mind was racing. He'd have to get this information back to Stony Man Farm, and he was going to need a way to do it. The trouble was, Newman had been insistent that Blancanales lodge at his penthouse the night before. He hadn't dared disagree. That morning they had been together every minute, along with the Newman's silent, armed retinue of bodyguards.

''What's that?'' Blancanales asked, spying the second pack in the foam cutout. ''Ammo pack?''

Newman grinned again and looked up and down the dock. The workers were ignoring them. There was no one around who wasn't involved in the transfer of the shipment. But Newman demurred. ''I can't show you that right now. It's body armor.''

''Like a bulletproof vest?''

''Yeah, like that but more,'' Newman said. ''More stolen plans. We actually had the plans for this a year ago. It's Land Warrior stuff.''

Blancanales almost swore out loud and he exerted himself to keep his face neutral. ''Even I've heard of Land Warrior,'' he said. ''It's computerized soldier gear, right?''

''Yeah, and since it is not all weapons-based, the plans were less secure, I guess. They were easier to appropriate,'' Newman said. ''Our version is better than U.S. military versions I've seen. It's got GPS, communications, a collapsible helmet with a sensor array for thermal and night vision, you name it. It all works together, run by a central CPU in the backpack. And it all is framed in the best new body armor, which is real lightweight material, better than anything else out there, so it's like wearing natural clothing. You know, it moves the way you move."

"But how in the world did you make all this stuff?" Blancanales asked, genuinely amazed at the level of sophistication he was seeing here. This was all prototype-level stuff by the U.S. Department of Defense standards. Stony Man had been using Land Warrior technology in various forms for the past few years, but the Farm had access to black budget funds and Justice Department technology feeds. How could a bunch of foreign-terrorist wanna-bes procure the technology and find a way to build the units?

"A lot of it we just bought," Newman said with a grin. "The radio in the Land Warrior set-up? It's a Motorola. They sell them commercially. We bought a few thousand and dismantled the cases on our assembly line, and put the electronic into the suit in the modkit. It's exactly the same electronics the U.S. is using."

Newman was extremely pleased with himself.

"Modkit?"

"This whole package," Newman explained. The OICW, the modular armor with Land Warrior computerization, sensor, and communications electronics, and the ammo pack. You put it all together and it's everything a soldier needs to walk into the field of combat and put up one hell of a fight. I did the interface, and I'm telling you it is so user-friendly any eight-year-old who's ever used a computer would know how to make everything work."

"It must cost a fortune just to make one kit," Blancanales said.

"Well, yeah, it does cost a hell of a lot. But the Americans based the Land Warrior design on commercial technology so it would cost them less, and it costs us less, too. What we can't get, I can make," Newman declared proudly. "We make some of the electronics here at my plant, ship them to the U.S. as a part of our regular supply chain to some defense and mining contractors, and get them back all put together as a part of this.''

"You've got a thousand units here. You guys are putting together an army of cyber-soldiers to drive the Palestinians right out of Israel." Blancanales sounded astonished, and he truly was.

Newman took it for admiration. "Or wipe them out," he added with a smirk. "Kind of our own final solution to the Palestinian problem."

CHAPTER TWENTY-TWO

The Middle East came awake with a growl.

It was less than forty-eight hours since the killing began at Khodr, but the anger had spread with the rapidity of a brush fire in a drought. Jordan, Syria and nearly every other Middle Eastern nation had issued threats, veiled thinly or not at all, warning of dire consequences for Israel if the violence was allowed to continue. The Israeli government issued statement after statement decrying the violence and accusing the Palestinians of Khodr of sparking it.

The PLO, along with the U.S., Russia and much of the rest of the world, had been decrying Israel's refusal to allow Palestinians to join in the investigations at Khodr and Shaal-vim Settlement. This violation of Palestinian authority went unexcused by the Israelis, but finally they agreed that, the next morning, Palestinian investigators would be allowed to "tour" the massacre sites. Palestinians were quick to point out that this still wasn't giving them the access guaranteed in agreements signed with the Israelis on West Bank policy, and that the leader of the Israeli team at the investigation, Elihu Tsaig, was well-known for his anti-Arab leanings and his public statements that concessions of any kind to the Palestinians were tantamount to treason.

When the Palestinian investigators were allowed on their "tour," they found a city full of bodies—and evidence of a sort of "civil war" that had occurred there. "As it stands, we find no evidence of an attack by outside forces,'' Investigator Tsaig was quoted as saying. ''These people fought each other, using weapons brought into Palestine illegally. Probably some sort of a turf battle.''

Within an hour of the ''tour,'' the Palestinians newspapers were publishing photos of the village of Khodr and its street full of dead. One of the Palestinian investigators had tucked a digital video camera up his sleeve and recorded the tour, words and images. Already there were holes developing in the civil-war explanation being touted by Tsaig. A corpse of one woman, her head smashed, was leaning against a wall with a gunshot wound to the chest. Forensic specialists around the world agreed she had been staged in that position. A close-up digital image showed her head was caved in by a massive blow, which bled profusely, while the bullet wound showed no blood. She had died when her skull was hit, and was shot hours later.

This news—and the growing tally of dead on both sides from violence begun in response to Khodr and Shaalvim— spread throughout the West Bank, Israel and the world, and by 1:00 p.m., Tsaig was pulled off the investigation in a storm of negative publicity. It was too little and far too late a response to appease Palestinian critics, and served to infuriate some Israelis, and street fighting erupted in the heat of the afternoon in cities throughout Israel and the occupied territories.

In the eastern U.S. the clock said it was seven hours earlier. Stony Man Farm was cool and quiet, the mountains tranquil. In the Annex, an impromptu task force was evaluating the equipment transported home by Hermann Schwarz.

Schwarz had insisted on being a part of the team of Justice Department bureaucrats sent in to extricate Carl Lyons from the Clairemont Parish Hospital. There had been a small scene when the doctor on call became possessive and refused to allow the "unauthorized" removal of an unconscious patient. A local law-enforcement official was on the scene, as well, and was unimpressed by Justice Department badges and authorizing paperwork. At one point he stood in the doorway, refusing to allow Lyons to be wheeled out of his room until he had an adequate explanation as to the circumstances of his wounds.

Schwarz was bone weary and he'd been pushed around enough for one day, starting with Lyons himself during the trip down to Louisiana. The small-town sheriff, or police chief or whatever, may have been a good man and effective at his job, but this night he had chosen to push the wrong button.

Schwarz arrested him.

He snatched the sheriff's wrist in the middle of a condescending air poke and twisted it behind his back, spinning the man and slamming his chest into the doorjamb while he deftly extracted his revolver and jangling metal handcuffs. A moment later, the shouting, irate sheriff was being walked out of the building with a face as red as boiled crayfish.

"Which of you is this man's second in command?" Schwarz asked as they reached the hall and a bevy of deputies in uniforms nervously tried to determine a course of action.

"I am," said a deputy, tall and slim except for a huge beer belly, with a scraggly head of hair and a sad, drooping face. "Deputy Jette."

"Deputy Jette, I imagine you are in command for the foreseeable future. This man is being transported with us to Washington, D.C."

"What? Now?" Jette said, startled.

"Immediately."

"But—"

"Jette," barked the handcuffed sheriff, "don't just stand

there, you moron. Arrest these men and get me the hell out of these bracelets!''

"Deputy Jette," Schwarz said, "your sheriff will stand charges in Washington for interfering with a federal investigation. That's a felony. I hope you will make more intelligent decisions in your role as new commander of the local law enforcement."

Jette nodded thoughtfully. "I hope so, too."

"But," Schwarz added, "we do have room for more bodies if you'd like to come along."

The extra room wasn't needed. Jette ignored the barking of the sheriff, who became redder every minute until he saw that his deputies wouldn't fight the Feds on his behalf and he was indeed going into the big helicopter in the parking lot.

The sheriff became humble for all of five minutes, then got his nerve up and began lambasting Schwarz, the Justice Department, the federal government and the President of the United States. Schwarz borrowed some gauze from the Army doctor who was accompanying them to watch over Lyons and put a fist-sized wad of it in the sheriff's mouth.

The ride was peaceful then, but the trio of Justice Department officials was getting nervous. Halfway over Lake Pontchartrain one of them whispered, "Sir, you know we can't take that man out of the state. I'm not even certain your arrest is legal."

"You're right," Schwarz agreed. "And think of the paperwork it would take to run him through channels."

"I'm not worried about the paperwork," the official started to say.

"I am." Schwarz went into the cockpit briefly, then dozed in his seat until he felt the helicopter descending.

They were at the west shore of Lake Pontchartrain. The lights of Metarie and the airport could be seen a few miles away, but at their landing point there was nothing visible for miles except a dark and untraveled parish road, badly in need of resurfacing.

"This is where you get out," Schwarz said, and hustled the sheriff to the door as the helicopter descended on the road, its lights illuminating a forlorn, empty corner of Louisiana back country. "They tell me I can't take you out of the state."

The sheriff's eyes were wide, and he was making an attempt to shout through the gauze. It came out as a groan.

Schwarz lowered him by the collar of his shirt, and the sheriff stood there, staring at him pleadingly.

"Next time maybe you'll think twice before insisting on being the big shot," Schwarz said. "There's nothing wrong with going with the flow every once in a while."

The sheriff nodded vigorously, as sincere as a man in his predicament could be, hoping against hope that the helicopter wouldn't take off and leave him stranded.

The helicopter took off.

They transferred to the jet at Metarie, losing the Justice Department officials but retaining the doctor, who kept Lyons sedated. The rest of the blacksuits came on board, as well. They transferred aircraft again at D.C., and this time a Stony Man Farm doctor was on hand to take over monitoring Lyons. When they reached the Farm, the doctor put the unconscious Able Team leader safely away for the night—Lyons hadn't opened his eyes once.

Schwarz had himself spent most of the trip from Metarie in a state of unconsciousness that wasn't really sleep, but it was going to have to be good enough for the time being. It was midday in the Middle East, where the two sides were barreling heedlessly into escalating conflict. It seemed destined to turn into war.

War was exactly what the leader of the Soldiers of Solomon wanted.

Now, they had evidence that the Soldiers would be ready for the war when it came.

Schwarz, Kissinger, Kurtzman, Price and Katzenelenbogen were all on hand, gathered around a young Ranger who was a member of the Farm's blacksuit team. A year before he had been a part of a Fort Benning, Georgia, outfit that ran training-testing exercises on the current iteration of the Land Warrior gear. The Ranger had been a part of the Louisiana mission and had just sacked out when Kissinger roused him, but he was happy to get the chance to be on the inside of a Farm strategy session.

"I could tell at once that it was based on the Land Warrior technology," Kissinger was explaining to the gathering. "We've made use of this technology ourselves, as you know—even as far back as the early Soldier Integrated Protective Ensemble, demonstrated in 1992. Some SIPE design elements were adopted for our own use. SIPE more or less launched the Land Warrior program. Phoenix uses Land Warrior components in their field equipment today."

"You said 'based on,'" Price said.

"Yes. This equipment is designed to be lighter. The body armor is from a different source and is more modular than Land Warrior design as we've seen it. The armor pieces also have the ability to expand and seal, even sealing with the foldable armor helmet and gas mask for covering the entire head. This creates an environment that is almost a dry suit. There's very little circulation when the system is locked up."

"For withstanding gas attacks," Kurtzman guessed. "Chemical and biological attacks."

"Yes," Kissinger agreed. "Also simply for withstanding cold temperatures outside. When the modular armor pieces aren't expanded for this level of protection, the suit is lighter overall than Land Warrior armor and hardware. Designed specifically for arid climates, if I were to guess."

"I would never have guessed I was carrying around a full Land Warrior equipment inventory in that pack," Schwarz said.

"Compared to the radio backpack I tested last year, it's less than half the weight and maybe two-thirds the size," the Ranger observed.

"Not surprising," Kurtzman said. "Land Warrior was based on commercially available components, and all commercial electronics reduce in size, weight and cost continually. Add to that the fact that we're talking about world-class electronics and computerization engineers putting this thing together. Based on Land Warrior designs, yes, but they must have seen plenty of room for improvement."

"The optics are way better, too," the Ranger said. "This is the video camera for mounting on an automatic rifle, but it also plugs into the armor system. This pickup mounted on the armor is less bulky than the Land Warrior digital imaging I used last year, but the picture quality is unbelievable."

"Now check this out," Kissinger said, nodding at a wall screen. "Bear tapped us in to the feed."

The screen showed themselves as seen through the tiny digital pickup. The image resolution was crisp, better than the Farm achieved using its own field video pickups. The image was digitally smoothed for further improving image quality. The mouthpiece microphone for the soldiers was augmented by an omnidirectional microphone to pick up ambient sound.

"One role of a Land Warrior for the Soldiers of Solomon is getting news footage, along with ambient audio," Price said with a joyless smirk.

"Yeah, that's what I think," Kissinger said. "It all gets transmitted back in real time to a base computer system where a director can choose the most flattering shots to release to the media."

"Does it achieve good long-distance viewing?" Schwarz asked.

"See for yourself," the Ranger said, and with a click removed the blackened mantle that went over the eyes, trailing a flexible, light cable attached to his back modules . Schwarz put it on and saw a small screen under his left eye showing the video camera image.

"I'll increase it," the Ranger said. He adjusted something on his wrist and the image filled Schwarz's left eye vision. It was crystal clear. Schwarz couldn't even guess at the perceived resolution. Then the image began to zoom, until the screen was filled top to bottom with a gold letter *P*. It was a part of the word *Parker* on the barrel of a ballpoint pen on the conference table, about a millimeter high.

"It's got night vision, autodarkening for bright-sunlight operations, and an autoblock that can be used to mask bright light sources. You can go out on a summer afternoon and stare at the sun," Kissinger explained. "The sun will be digitally blackened, so you can see that fly ball or hand grenade that's coming down on top of you. It does an audio zoom, too. Very handy for picking up the nasty things the enemy says about you. Other components are integral to the mission computer. Compass-GPS, for example. It has an automatic signal for identifying the soldier and for tracking him later if he's lost. Essentially the same electronics as the Combat Survivor-Evader Locator user segment. CSEL is a system developed by U.S. for locating and rescuing downed pilots, and the segment the user carries is over a pound and a half and forty cubic inches big."

"Too big for a soldier to carry on top of everything else, so they figured out how to build it into the computer system," Kurtzman commented.

"But CSEL requires a unique U.S. military system to track it," Kissinger said. "So why did they bother?"

Nobody answered. Kurtzman hazarded a guess. "Because

they have figured out a way to track it themselves. Maybe they wanted the technology battlefield tested. These are defense contractors, after all. Hell, the U.S. happens to track down one of these suits and sees how much smaller this CSEL segment is compared to the bulky unit they have now, they'd look into acquiring that technology.''

"There's more," Kissinger went on. "The computer has the day-night target sensor feedback and handles radio operation. Get this—the CPU is redundant. In the arm piece there is a duplicate of the primary CPU, mounted in the backpack. The system mirrors the backpack CPU in the arm-mounted CPU in real-time. If the one in back gets trashed, the one in the arm piece takes over without missing a beat.''

"Sounds expensive," Price said.

"Chips are cheap," Kurtzman shrugged. "Especially compared to some of the other technology at use here.''

"Other functions incorporated into the suit and run by the computer include an ion mobility sensor for detecting chemical agents," Kissinger stated. "A good example of some of the advantages this configuration has of the Land Warrior, which doesn't have any such detector. The U.S. military uses equipment like that, of course, but they have to carry around four-pound handheld units and sometimes a laptop to accomplish it. Batteries are secondary silver-zinc cells from Eagle-Picher Technologies' Federal System. Silver-zinc chemistry is expensive but provides a high ratio of energy to weight, reliability, shock and vibration resistance, everything you need. All smart battery functions—remaining-charge time and fast—recharge control—are managed by the CPU. Batteries are scattered throughout suit modules, unlike the U.S. Land Warrior design. Because this is the heaviest single component in the suit, the design helps balance the weight throughout the user's body. Most of the cells are still in the backpack, but if the backpack is damaged severely, there will be enough juice pouring in from other cells to keep the CPU going, along with GPS and radio maybe. Now get this—there's a lithium-oxyhalide reserve battery in the backpack. This is rocket science, literally. They put this kind of what they call reserve batteries into missiles that they think might be sitting around for fifteen years before they get used.''

''Explain your definition of 'reserve battery'?'' Price asked.

Kissinger pointed to a small pack with two lengthwise bulges in the backpack frame. ''The active components are separate. They'll get mixed if and when emergency power is needed. It's a one-time-use system and you had better have good explanation for using it because it ain't cheap.''

''Any way to put a use time on the secondary silver-zinc cells and the reserve battery?'' Schwarz asked.

''Depends on use,'' Kissinger said. ''In a heavy combat situation with extensive use of system functions, two or three hours. In a CPU sleep mode, a guy could walk around in his Land Warrior outfit for a few days.''

''The armor isn't DoD standard?'' Schwarz asked.

''No, but it could be some day,'' Kissinger said, pointing to a neat cut he had made in the shell material, exposing the stiff insulation in one of the flexible chest modules. ''This is the newest of Verseidag-Indutex's Ultrax composite materials for ballistic protection. I've tested older versions of Ultrax and found them to very good for stopping bullets and fragments. But this is a new composite, only hit the market a few months ago. It's chemical resistant, water resistant, and the stuff won't burn if you spray it down with gasoline. It's good.''

''Ballistic protection?'' Schwarz asked.

''Ranks with the best available, if what I hear is true.''

''Can we assume that any of these companies are complicit with the Soldiers of Solomon, based on the use of their products in the outfits or the weapons?" Schwarz asked.

"No. I think we would assume just the opposite. None of these companies knew what they were selling their products for," Price said. "Keep in mind that the companies that purchased the materials may well have been regular customers already. We are talking about defense contractors. Naturally they would be buying materials from defense subcontractors."

"So the guilty parties are as we have guessed," Katzenelenbogen stated. "Members of a few small Israeli defense companies. Small but financially successful, fiercely nationalist but willing to sell technology to the Chinese, the U.S., anybody who'll pay for it. They're run by technomillionaires of a unique Israeli subclass—rich, bored, young compared to your average corporate CEO, and egotistical."

"If this is true, it confuses things in my mind," Schwarz said. "Why come to the U.S. for the manufacturing?"

"Why not? Kurtzman said. "The Israeli companies we're talking about are usually dedicated to making small electronic components. They don't have metalworking expertise for making weapons, or the experience marrying together complicated components into working end-products. If they went to one of the big contractors in Israel, such as Israel Military Industries or Israel Aircraft Industries, and tried to convince them to take on the job, word would have spread. The Soldiers have avoided exposure almost fanatically."

"So they chose a manufacturer in the United States, with the expertise to take this on," Price said. "That firm should not be too hard to track down once we start tracing the serial numbers off the components in that suit. That's a step that can wait until after the crisis has ended in Israel."

There was a moment of silence, then one by one every face in the room turned to the mission controller.

Schwarz was the one who finally articulated it. "So what is the next step?"

Price weighed the question heavily. She had no contact from Rosario Blancanales. She had no real targets for Phoenix Force to investigate without risk of forcing the hand of the Soldiers of Solomon.

She said, hating the words, "We wait."

CHAPTER TWENTY-THREE

Tel Aviv, Israel

Rosario Blancanales took a huge chance when he nonchalantly grabbed a pay phone and dialed the United States.

Not that he had any choice. If he did nothing, the Soldiers of Solomon were going to call for recruits and place the most powerful all-in-one soldier kit imaginable in the hands of Israel's most enraged citizens. People would die. Maybe by the hundreds and maybe a lot more. But the real danger lay in the international reaction to those attacks. It was conceivable that the Middle East would erupt into war immediately.

If Blancanales didn't stop the distribution of those weapons, the Middle East would sink into chaos and warfare. It was simple as that.

Using his dedicated number set off priority alerts in the Stony Man Annex. He didn't hear the phone ring a second time.

"Yes, Pol," Barbara Price said.

Blancanales knew his time was limited, since at any second Newman might reappear and demand to know what the hell he was doing. He had planned the call and he wasn't going to waste a word. "I may get cut off at any second so listen sharp, Barbara," he stated quickly. "The Soldiers of

Solomon are importing massive numbers of crates containing high-technology weapons, combat equip—''

''We know this, Pol,'' she interjected. She recognized his predicament and wanted him to get out as much good intelligence as was possible in what time he had.

Thank God, he thought. ''Do you know the insertion points?''

''One only. A ship called *Homeland* docked now in Tel Aviv.''

''I was there this morning and the cargo is moved. I can give you the locations of two of three sites warehousing the cargo from this morning and four previous shipments.'' Blancanales rattled off the addresses, his eyes roaming the lobby casually for Newman or one of his stick-like-glued bodyguards. ''The last address is the big one. Two thousand of their modkits. It's somewhere in Jerusalem. They're going to use it to take the city for the Israelis. I'll report it if and when I learn it.''

''Got it,'' Price said. ''Positive ID on other principals beside Newman?''

''Negative. They're as vigilant as hell, although I can tell you they fit the profiles we developed. They're all part of Israeli defense and electronics industries, all rich, mostly thirtysomething or fortysomething, fed up with providing their technology to China and other countries they're ambivalent about while their own cause goes unsupported. I'm convinced on the circumstantial evidence that the names you have are correct. Whoever it is has more support hardware than I would have imagined.''

''Is Israeli military providing any of it?''

''Not that I can tell. Not yet. But if they're on the same wavelength as the citizens, then a significant number of them are sympathetic to the cause of the Soldiers. Some of them will throw in with the Soldiers when the time comes. But right now I would say they don't even need the military

The first big strikes are planned with the equipment and firepower they've already got. They acquired a gunship there, troop transport vehicle there, and so on. Ten or more techie firms bought the equipment over the past twelve month, and all have documented commercial reasons for needing the units to test their product. But all of it can be converted to combat readiness when the Soldiers want to make use of it.''

''Which will be when and where?'' Price asked.

''Unknown,'' Blancanales said, hearing the bitterness in his own voice. ''These people are close-lipped, and I'm surprised I got as far as I did into the organization as fast as I did. One thing I know for sure—Newman's not at the top of the heap. He's strictly second tier, and I get the distinct impression he's expendable. Only he hasn't figured it out yet.''

''That means you are, too, even with your cover intact,'' Price said. ''What's your situation now?''

''I'm Ariel Newman's new best buddy. I don't know if that means he trusts me, but for now he's got me tagging along from place to place as the Soldiers stage their matériel for the coming war.''

''Where are you now?''

''Private club. It's a place called Shehori in Tel Aviv. We're having a nice lunch. If I didn't know it, I'd say I was in a damned country club on Long Island talking big business.''

''Tell me about this place,'' Price asked.

''I think I know what you're asking,'' Blancanales said. ''Is this where the Soldiers of Solomon recruits its wealthiest partners? I think it might be. Members aren't the traditional upper crust of Tel Aviv, from what I've seen in my half hour here. These are the techie millionaires everybody has been talking about. I haven't seen anybody over forty, unless you count the Russian bartender. There are nationalist slogans spelled out in ceramic tile in the foyer. The joke of the day mounted over the urinals has something to do with ninety-eight dead Arabs.''

''Pretty circumstantial,'' Price said. ''Still, worth checking it out. If it turns out to be the Soldiers of Solomon Social Club, then a membership list would be very helpful.''

''I hope you're planning on dedicating Phoenix to going after the modkits,'' Blancanales said.

''I am. Believe me, that's my top priority, Pol,'' Price said. ''And we'll be standing by to act on any more information you can send our way.''

''I'll do that, Morty,'' Blancanales replied with a new tenor to his voice.

''Got company?'' Price asked.

The Able Team warrior smiled and chuckled. ''You got it. More women than I can count and they're all in bikinis.'' He gave a smile to Ariel Newman, who had emerged from the bar. Newman's expression was puzzled. Suspicious? Blancanales couldn't tell. Maybe he was about to be accused of being a spy. Maybe not.

''Don't get yourself in trouble, Pol,'' Price said.

''Trouble? How can I enjoy my vacation without raising a little hell, Morty! Anyway, I'll see you next Monday.''

Blancanales hung up the phone. ''My supervisor,'' he said casually. ''He thinks I'm in Belize.''

''Belize?'' Newman asked.

''Yeah. I told them I was taking a vacation and got a great last-minute deal to one of those primitive resorts in Belize. In exchange for granting me a last-minute vacation request they made me promise to call in regularly in case there was a system screwup that nobody else could handle.''

''Think they believe you?''

Blancanales shrugged. ''Why shouldn't they? I'm not on anybody's lists of suspicious personnel. I know because I've been sneaking into my own security files for months.''

"You're a cool son of a bitch," Newman said, a truncated version of his previous playboy grin coming back.

"And you're just a plain son of a bitch," Blancanales replied with a smug grin. It was the kind of insult he knew the other man would appreciate. Newman laughed at the ceiling like a barking dog.

"You slay me!" Newman shouted.

Blancanales couldn't wait to get the chance to lay this coldhearted bastard on his keister.

RAFAEL ENCIZO SAT UP on the bunk, eyes glazed. He shook his head and regretted it, the throbbing pain emerging from the veneer of numbness maintained by the drugs. The pain was bad enough, but the dizziness that came with it was worse, and he closed his eyes.

"That's what I thought," McCarter said.

"You can't do this without me," Encizo protested, blinking through the blurs. "This stuff will wear off in an hour."

"I can't put you in the field in your condition, Rafe."

"You can't do it without me."

McCarter looked grim. "You had better believe I don't want to do it without you, buddy. The whole thing will be wrong without you there to make the team work right. But if you think there is any way I am letting you get into range of the enemy in the state you're in right now—well, just forget it, Rafe."

Encizo slumped on the bunk and stared at the interior of the aircraft. After just one night he was already sick of being held prisoner by his burns in the Airbus. Everything in his being told him it was wrong for him to be on his back while Phoenix Force went into the field on a hard probe.

On the other hand, it was pretty hard to argue with McCarter's simple logic. He was in no shape to put one foot after another, let alone enter a combat situation. While he was thinking it over, trying to rationalize it, another numb interval swelled over him, and when he opened his eyes again McCarter had left the room. Instead there sat the Stony Man copilot going over some sort of paperwork on the far end of the empty cabin.

"Where's McCarter?" he demanded.

Looking up, the young USAF pilot looked confused for a moment. "Sir," he said, "they left more than a half hour ago."

Israel

SINCE ACQUIRING another armored vehicle would have been risky, Jack Grimaldi spent the night returning the rental Excursion to driving condition. The damage to the vehicle was mostly superficial, and he had confidence the big beast of an SUV was up to the job. Of course, it all depended on the job.

Phoenix Force, and Stony Man Farm, had little in the way of working intel. Their list of facts included just two items: a street address and an inventory. It was the inventory that was unnerving. Modular kits containing armor and firepower enough to turn one thousand angry and impassioned human beings into a dangerous military force.

Grimaldi had observed that the Soldiers of Solomon recruits couldn't possibly be skilled in the use of body armor and OICW weapons. Price had explained that it was a reality all the components of the modkits were designed to accommodate. OICW laser sites made an unskilled shooter into a long-range marksman.

"Maybe we'll get the chance to snag a few of those OICW for ourselves," he suggested as he steered the big Ford into the Israeli city of Netanya.

McCarter shook his head. "I don't know if I'd trust one of those things. Who knows who designed it or even built it?"

"That's right," Calvin James said. "Chances are it wasn't manufactured to the highest quality standard, you know?"

Grimaldi nodded.

"On the other hand," James added thoughtfully, "it would be foolish not to take advantage of the hardware if and when we have access to it. At least level the playing field if we go up against the Soldiers."

"Yeah," McCarter agreed grudgingly. "Maybe. I just don't like the idea."

"I do," Manning said. "Use their own guns against them? That's ironic justice."

"And maybe it'll keep us from getting hit like Ironman," added T. J. Hawkins. The youngest Phoenix Force commando had always been a little in awe of Carl Lyons. He had heard the stories of what the man was capable of in extreme situations. Hawkins would be the last to admit it, but it had shaken the foundation of some of his beliefs to think that a berserker like Carl Lyons had been brought down, if only temporarily, by one of those weapons with the unspeakable names.

Lyons and Encizo, both down. It wasn't often that the Sensitive Operations Group got hit this hard. The others in the car were silent and Grimaldi sensed grim determination. There was no sound, but it was as if every one of the commandos were gritting his teeth and the grinding noise was filling the inside of the vehicle.

Conveyed in it was seething anger, and intense conviction.

These so-called Soldiers would go down. For what they had done to the people of Israel, for what they had done to the people of Palestine. And for what they had done to the people of Stony Man Farm.

CHAPTER TWENTY-FOUR

Netanya, Israel

The sign said it was the finest health club in Netanya, with a landscaped indoor pool, sauna, Turkish bath, fitness equipment and "authentic American-style yoga classes." It was the size of a couple of merged department stores, with parking for four hundred cars. Three of the spaces were taken.

"Hi!" said the young woman at the counter when Jack Grimaldi greeted her in English. "Would you like to sign up?"

"Maybe," Grimaldi said, trying to keep from staring. The woman was twenty, tops, outfitted in a white glimmering body suit that adhered to every curve and dimple. And she had the body for it, tall and trim with firm, high breasts and a derriere sculpted by exercise. She smiled with her entire face, somehow putting a glint in her eye and a hint of sex in her lips. Her dark, shining hair, long and full of curls, bounced on her shoulders and caressed her neck like it was right out of a shampoo commercial. The Stony Man pilot struggled for a moment, trying to remember who he was and why he was there. Oh, yeah. "I'm a lawyer from Chicago and I'm going to be moving here for six months on business," he explained. "I'll need a place to work out. Can you tell me about the place?"

"Oh, sure, it's going to be fabulous. Olympic-sized pool

if you like to swim. I think they're about ready to start putting water in it! We'll have a jogging track and a workout room, too, of course. We're getting in sixty machines. StairMasters, treadmills, rowers, and all kinds of aerobics machines plus lots of LifeFitness weight stuff and Universal and Nautilus machines.''

Although he enjoyed watching her mouth make the words, Grimaldi managed to tear his eyes away and look around the big atrium-like reception area, nodding with interest. The floor was still bare concrete and the sections of the walls were sanded but not yet painted. When he turned back he had moved enough to her right to see into the open spaces behind her. The rear doors, beyond the passageway dividing the building, led to the pool deck, and it was opening swiftly to allow in a pair of figures in combat cosmetics.

''What about classes?'' Grimaldi asked, raising his voice a little. ''I'm into kickboxing aerobics. You know, the ones where they mix up step-aerobics and kung fu and all that.'' He froze in a stance he had seen on the infomercial, bounding in rhythm from foot to foot, and suddenly delivered a one-two-three punch to a nonexistent foe. ''I get a pretty good workout, too.''

''Well,'' the woman said doubtfully, drawing the word out. ''That's not really popular anymore.''

Grimaldi's arms dropped to his side. ''It's not?''

''Well, no, but there's a lot newer fitness classes now. There's Afro-Brazilian Cardio. There's Sunrise Tai Chi. Grind Aerobics. Walk-Away Workout—''

''How about a tour?'' Grimaldi asked.

''A tour?''

''Sure. Last time I joined a new health club in New York they let me tour the whole place so I could see what it was like.''

''Yes, but there's nothing to see here. We're still under

construction,'' the woman pointed out, trying not to sound impolite. ''We don't have any equipment yet or anything.''

Grimaldi glanced at his watch. Time was up. ''Then why don't you just show me that room?'' he asked, pointing to the locked door behind her half-moon desk.

She looked at the door. She looked at Grimaldi. ''You want to see the supply closet?''

''How DID YOU DO with the receptionist?'' Hawkins asked as he joined them in a passage leading to the future activity centers.

''She took me to her supply closet,'' Grimaldi said with a shrug.

''You lucky SOB.''

''Not so lucky for her. She's still locked inside.''

The drop ceiling panels and overhead lights had yet to be installed, leaving only the glowing emergency signs and illumination from the glass doors around the corner. Hawkins and Manning stepped through the first entrance, covering the interior with their weapons, and found themselves inside a gymnasium. Skylights revealed a large, empty space, with white dust littering the floor from ongoing construction.

Across the passage they found three smaller rooms with lower ceilings, looking out on the swimming pool. No furniture, fixtures, or floor coverings. More importantly, no place to store a thousand crates of Objective Individual Combat Weapons and sophisticated Land Warrior battlefield cybernetics-armor systems.

''Sure hope this is the place,'' Manning said as they headed for the other wing.

''For Pol's sake,'' Hawkins added. ''If they fed him some line of bullshit, it means they were on to him.''

''Yeah,'' Manning said, then his hand went up and the trio came to a halt. Manning pointed and they took cover around a corner.

They heard the pair of guards emerge into the passage, their footsteps swishing on the dust-covered floors. One of them began complaining to the other in Hebrew, accompanied by the sound of a hand tapping something. Manning chanced a look around the corner and found himself watching two men in security guard uniforms, coming down the unlit passage with their mini-Uzis in hand. One of them was also trying to keep an eye on a small display strapped on the underside of his forearm.

They argued again in brief whisper, then one of them called out, "Sarah?"

Manning didn't reply.

The guard exclaimed something in frustration and stalked around the corner, coming nose-to-chest with Gary Manning. He made a grunt of surprise and another grunt when the big Canadian planted a fist in his abdomen. The guard staggered into the passage, bent double before collapsing, and his companion shouted in alarm. By then Manning had emerged and covered with the business end of the Heckler & Koch MP-5 SD-3 targeted at him.

The well-engineered submachine gun was considered one of the best in the world, it was adopted as standard equipment by special forces units around the world, including the U.S. Navy SEALs, and came with factory-installed sound suppressors. Add to that a collapsible metal stock, and the submachine gun was about as quiet and small as could be manufactured.

The man in the security guard outfit apparently wasn't up to speed on just how effective the MP-5 SD-3 could be. He twisted the Uzi at Manning as if he were flipping a tennis racket to return a spiked ball, but Manning fired first. A quick burst of 9 mm rounds cut into his stomach and took him down like a heavy tackle. The rounds sounded like overlapping coughs through the suppresser.

Grimaldi grabbed the discarded mini-Uzis while Hawkins

covered the passage. After cuffing the live one, Manning took the dead man's hand and removed the device on his forearm. It strapped into place and curved to conform to the shape of the arm. The display was semiflexible and offered high resolution for a device so small. A clear plastic overlay was printed with what appeared to be the layout of the health club. On the display, the passage they were standing in showed three tiny red stars, flashing in the vicinity of a steady blue *O* and a flashing yellow *X*.

"Some sort of motion detector," Grimaldi said, glancing at it. "We're the red stars. The dead guy is the yellow *X* for malfunction, and the other one is the *O*."

"I haven't seen a display like this before," Manning said. "And I haven't spotted a single sensor in this place."

He turned to his prisoner. "What's the story with this item?"

"BC," the prisoner hacked, still trying to get his breath back. "Ballistocardiac sensor display."

Hawkins grunted in surprise. "That thing tracks us by our heartbeats?"

"That's just the display. The sensors are behind ceiling panels. Only three sensors to cover the entire place."

"I've never heard of sound-sensing technology sensitive enough to do something like that, at least not outside of a laboratory," Manning said.

"It doesn't have to be as sensitive as you think," Hawkins said. "The mechanical motion of your heartbeat is what they call the ballistocardiac effect, and it's strong enough to perturb the walls and floors of vehicles. The harmonic peaks are unique so they can be identified with analysis software. I've heard of devices being tested to scan trucks for illegal immigrants at the Mexican border. Never saw anything like this, though."

Hawkins bent to the prisoner. "Tell me how it differentiates us from you?"

The prisoner had his lungs back and decided he would stop being cooperative. When he spoke it was in Hebrew but the meaning was crystal.

"You just got told to go to hell," Manning said.

Hawkins grabbed the dead man's wrist, finding a watch with black plastic straps. A tiny red error message showed beneath the time-of-day display. Hawkins found the same device on the cuffed prisoner.

"Your receptionist have one of these?" Hawkins asked Grimaldi.

"Yeah, I remember thinking it didn't match her outfit."

"This is cool and clever, I have to admit," Hawkins said. "I think these watches have heart-rate monitors, just like the kind used by fitness buffs, but they're feeding their signals to the ballistocardiac sensor system. It runs real-time comparisons to signals coming through the ballistocardiac sensors. If you have one of the heart-rate monitors, it can keep track of you. Otherwise it assumes you are an intruder and you get labeled as such."

"Now we have them." Grimaldi grinned.

Hawkins grinned, too. "Yeah."

Manning was a step behind them and frowned. "So."

"It's like the old movie cliché," Grimaldi said. "Instead of knocking out the guard and putting on his uniform, all we have to do is put on his wristwatch."

Manning got it. "It's a free pass."

"But will it work at the other Soldier of Solomon facilities?" Hawkins asked.

"We're not exactly finished here yet," Manning said. "Jack, would you put this slime in the closet with your lady friend?"

"Uh-oh," Hawkins said, still staring at the dead man's wrist display, where he could now see two new flashing red stars appear at the edge of the display, moving closer to a side building entrance. A red warning light outside the display panel began flickering in alarm. Two more solid blue *O*s began moving to intercept.

"If I read this right, I'm seeing David and Cal about to make their entrance and there's another pair of these dudes coming after them," Hawkins said.

"Let's go give them a hand," Manning suggested.

THE SMALL side entrance was intended to be an emergency exit, but the emergency alarm wasn't installed and the lock on the door was a temporary one. McCarter's lock pick managed to throw the bolt in under a minute, but at the cost of loud metal-on-metal scratching. James covered the interior when the Phoenix Force leader swung the door open, and they stepped out covering themselves each step of the way.

It had taken little time to find that the new health club in Netanya was a tax shelter for IsAlliance Techsystems, the company whose name came up again and again as the organizational force behind the Soldiers of Solomon. The intelligence from Rosario Blancanales that had identified this as one of the staging sites for the modular soldier kits had also verified that Kesher Nir, the IsAlliance CEO, was becoming the most likely candidate to be the idea man and commander of the Soldiers. His name also emerged as the finance man behind the health club.

A quick scout to the left showed James he was in a future shower room, with an adjoining sauna and a long bank of orange lockers. With McCarter guarding his back, he crossed the passage and found a mirror-image shower room, sauna and locker room. No signs of guards or construction crew. One for the women and one for the men, although they had yet to be designated.

"This place is half-finished," James said. "Shouldn't there be a construction crew?"

"Lucky blokes got the day off so their boss could start a war," McCarter said.

Next were a few small offices, a maintenance room and to the right a long, open space that would eventually be divided into smaller rooms. Most of the space was obscured from their view by a wall that had been framed in steel brackets but only half-filled with wallboard.

McCarter and James moved stealthily to the wall and listened, hearing nothing but both feeling uneasy about the layout. Anything could be behind the wallboard. They'd be exposed if they looked around the corner, and then they'd be sitting ducks. If there was an ambush waiting for them, the enemy could fire through the wallboard without compromising the killing effect of their rounds at that proximity.

McCarter noiselessly withdrew a lightweight extendible aluminum rod with an angled mirror on the end, like a dentist tool. He pulled it to its full twelve-inch length and moved it carefully to the corner of the wall.

The firing started before he even had the mirror in view of the enemy. First came a snick and the sudden chatter of machine-gun fire, and James witnessed the appearance of wallboard perforations, traveling lightning fast to the point where they would intersect his chest. He tossed himself to the floor, hearing another machine gun join the racket, and then the coughing of more suppressed machine-gun fire.

How many gunners were behind that wall? He landed flat on his chest and legs with his own MP-5 SD-3 pushed out in front of him. He was now looking into the room beyond, and one of the gunners was exposed. James triggered the submachine gun from the floor and cut the gunner's shins out from under him, then fired another burst into the body when it had collapsed to ground level. The Phoenix Force warrior crawled on his elbows to the opening to see more targets in the room and spotted a gunner with a mini-Uzi firing in the wrong direction. He was triggering the submachine gun away from the wall. James didn't stop to think about it. He triggered a swift burst of 9 mm shockers that took the gunner by surprise. The look of wonder locked on his face as he jittered on the floor and became still. McCarter ran in a crouch around the corner as James jumped to his feet and both of them took cover in the gunner's room behind a big, movable steel toolbox.

"Hey, now, strangers," said the voice of T. J. Hawkins from the far end of the room. "No need to hide. We won't shoot ya."

IF THE WRIST DISPLAYS were to be believed, there were no more guards on duty at Kesher Nir's health club. McCarter wasn't ready to put his faith in the devices, even though the gunners had used them to target him and James through the wall, with nearly fatal effectiveness. He ordered the teams to stay sharp during the search of the construction site.

But there wasn't much left to search. Between the two pairs, they had covered every room and began wondering if there were hidden storage areas they weren't meant to discover.

When they returned to the utility closet, the receptionist was crying wildly. It became apparent that she was a hireling and mostly clueless. The surviving gunner insisted that they were guarding the building site, nothing more, and when McCarter brought up the subject of modkits he shut up altogether.

Grimaldi took the girl out into the reception area, knowing that just being free of the cramped, airless room would improve her spirits, and he turned on his best barroom smile. It did him little good.

"I swear I don't know anything," she sniffed.

"What about any hard-to-find rooms or storage areas?" he pressed. "Do you remember there being any large spaces

n the original framing that were covered up later on during
he construction?''

She thought about it, face serious, then shook her head.

''I just don't remember anything like that.''

''Any strange activity?''

The girl absently twisted in her seat, wriggling her wrists
n the cuffs behind her back. ''Well, I always thought that
ust having all those guards here all the time was strange
enough,'' she said. ''There was one night when they had
more than four guards here. I didn't see them, but there were
footprints in the dust when I got to work the next day.
There's no way the regular four guards could have left that
many footprints in one night.''

''Describe the footprints,'' Grimaldi ordered. ''Where,
now many and so on.''

The girl described them.

Grimaldi moved her into a locked office and chuckled as
he rejoined the restless commandos. ''At least one of us
should have thought of this in the first place,'' he said, and
ed them back through the passage and into one of the locker
rooms. The lockers were new and shiny under their covering
of construction dust. Grimaldi opened one, whistled and extracted a black automatic weapon with twin barrels and big
optics.

''It's big,'' he said. ''This what we're looking for?''

McCarter grinned. ''That's it.''

''Looks like they've got everything ready to go,'' Hawkins said, opening another locker and finding an identical
setup. ''They've got an OICW, modular battle armor and
pack and all the electronics. It's put together in the locker
so their new recruits can just come in, get dressed and depart
battle ready.''

''Five hundred lockers,'' James said. ''I thought that was
a lot. Another five hundred across the hall, and we've got
a full thousand-unit shipment accounted for.''

McCarter examined one of the OICW units for himself It was a heavy piece of work, but when he powered up the electronics he found himself staring at a simple, icon-based touch screen on a half-inch-wide LCD strip on the optical base. It was easy to see the controls had been designed to require no instruction. It would have to be, if the Soldiers of Solomon expected to bring in any Israeli off the street to fight in their war.

"Let do a quick audit. I want to be sure we have all one thousand units. Then let's hustle out of here," he directed "We've got another target to hit."

Lod, Israel

WATCHING THE NEWS made Greer Hurwitz feel strangely alive. It seemed hyper-real, the violence in the streets. The dozens of dead Israelis and Palestinians in Jerusalem were evidence that the battles were finally started. The war had begun and he had helped begin it. When it was done he would be a hero of the new Israel, the restored holy land.

Which made sitting in his security cubicle all the worse It was at the bottom of a set of stairs in the hotel, which had been built resort-style and far exceeded the tourist needs of the region. Business had been slow since the day the hotel opened, and now it was barely staying in business.

During its first few weeks of business, the hotel made use of the locker rooms, showers, cafeteria and other basement level amenities put in to support a large around-the-clock staff. When reality hit, most of the personnel were let go and management closed off the basement-level facilities They were too expensive to keep up for a handful of personnel.

Now the basement level was rented out. It was a unique arrangement. It was money the hotel was glad to get. Man agement had no clue what was going on beneath their feet, and they didn't want to know.

Hurwitz had a small portable television that he plugged into the hotel antenna wiring, giving him access to CNN Europe and BBC World, both with a lot of coverage of the violence in the Middle East. This day's first indicator of increasing tensions was that the fighting started in the morning, erupting well before the heat of the afternoon that had spawned the street fighting of previous days.

What were the commanders of the Soldiers waiting for? Hurwitz asked himself time and again. Why not take the final steps now?

If he had to sit in this damned office for one more day watching it happen on television, he just might go in there, grab one of those modular soldier kits and put himself in the field as a one-man army. Drive the Arabs out on his own.

With an alert tone the display showed four Blues coming in the entranceway, which was a set of doors to the employee parking lot. The alarm gave him one sound for the arrival of Blues—so-called because they made a blue *O* on the sensor displays and on Hurwitz's monitor—and another alarm for a non-Blue. This group wasn't expected company, but they had people coming and going often enough.

When the four Blues were halfway down the corridor there was another beep, this one more insistent, and a flashing red dot at the door.

Dammit. It was off-line. Did those guys bust it when they came in? Maybe they just didn't close it all the way. Assholes. He shook his head.

They were coming down the passageway, which took them right past his cubicle so he could check them out. He was supposed to make them sign in. Nobody ever checked his sign-in sheet, so it wasn't a rule Hurwitz exactly enforced.

When these guys came through, he'd tell them to go back and make sure the door was closed and latched.

There was a BBC guy in Jerusalem looking out from a fourth-story balcony onto street fighting. It was a cool shot. He could see the little Arab brats tossing rocks, and there was a gang of Israeli teenagers trying to muscle past the Israeli police. "Go on, let them through," he urged the cop.

He looked up when the Blues arrived at his window. They weren't dressed in the security guard uniforms most of them wore when on duty here.

"Hey, did you guys forget how to close a door?" he demanded. "One of you is going to have to go back and do it again."

They stared at him as if he were speaking Martian instead of Hebrew. Then he noticed there were just three of them. Hadn't he seen four on the display? When he glanced back at the display, he saw that there were indeed just three blue *O* symbols standing in front of the window to the enclosure, but there was a fourth *O* moving around to come through a side door to the small concrete-brick cubicle.

When the fourth *O* came through the entrance, it was a black guy, of all things. He had the business end of a compact submachine gun leveled at Hurwitz, who stared at it, stunned.

"Speak English?"

Hurwitz finally got the picture. Who these guys were didn't matter, but what they were trying to prevent would be a disaster for the cause of the Soldiers and for the future history of Israel. In a second he had made the decision to die rather than let them get into the Soldiers' territory unnoticed.

Hurwitz leaped for the alarm button, fully expecting to feel submachine-gun rounds lacing his torso.

He never expected the black man to react with a traditional tae kwon do *hyung* routine. The submachine gun went unfired, but a fist crashed into his forearm before he could touch the alarm switch and another hand slammed across his cheekbone like a crowbar. Hurwitz's world went black so fast he didn't have time to know he had failed.

Phoenix Force was inside, and nobody who was conscious knew about it.

EIGHT MORE MEN were on the premises, being monitored by the ballistocardiac sensor system. Manning and Hawkins found three of them sleeping on cots in a darkened rear room. One of them woke up while the other two were being placed in cuffs. The butt of Manning's 92-F put him back to sleep.

James and McCarter found two more guarding the entrance corridor that led up into the hotel. Their weapons were hidden in niches in the wall. So far the guards had never needed to remove their suppressed Uzis from their wall niches. Only one time had anyone even entered the corridor, a befuddled woman in her late eighties. The doorman came and led her back to the lobby.

When the time came that the guards could have actually made use of the weapons, they didn't get the chance. They looked up curiously as the two Blues came around the corner. One of the guards was leaning back on his stool. The other was holding a paperback against his chest. It took them seconds to see the danger. It was too late anyway. Going for the Uzis at that point would have been suicide, with the silenced ends of the H&K submachine guns nudging their bellies.

The last pair was stationed to apprehend anyone who tried to get off the utility elevator in the basement, the only other way in or out of the basement labyrinth. Having stationed guards there was overkill. Management had changed the settings so that the elevator wouldn't even stop at the basement unless it was with one of the override keys or by a fire department key. There was always a chance that one of the management staff, for some unknown reason, would accidentally end up in the basement.

One of the guards was dozing when the other noticed the extra blue *O* symbols on his display. Somebody was touring the site. Maybe it was one of the leaders of the Soldiers, the as yet faceless commanders of their army. It wouldn't do to be seen sleeping on the job, so the man woke his companion and told him to be ready for important visitors. They tried to appear eager and alert without looking as if they knew they were about to get a VIP visit.

If they had been truly alert, they would have noticed when the men first appeared, two from one end of the corridor, two from the other, that this wasn't a team of Soldiers. It wasn't even a part of the mercenary team that had been helping to train the Soldiers. When they finally noticed something wrong, they grabbed for their weapons and started firing.

It was a strange mix of rapid-fire suppressed noise when the coughing of the quartet of MP-5 SD-3s and the chatter of the Uzis filled the concrete-block utility corridor like a rumble of thunder, quick, then gone.

The pair gave their lives to guard that elevator. At the moment their hearts ceased to function, the displays in the hands of Hawkins and James began to beep out a malfunction alarm.

McCarter grinned. The probe had worked the way it was supposed to. Their success had contingent on subduing—without killing—any of the first sets of guards so as not to alert remaining guards. It had gone as well as he could have hoped.

"Let's check the inventory, mates," he said.

CHAPTER TWENTY-FIVE

It was Kesher Nir's custom to have his lunch brought into the penthouse suite that was his office at IsAlliance Tech-systems. The lunch came, as always, with a cooler containing an eight-pack of bottled iced tea under ice, whatever his favorite brand and fruit flavor was this month. He ate at his desk, but he ate sparingly. Stress was playing havoc with his appetite.

Sandra Honig ate at an aluminum tray table, which was set up for her each day and removed when she was finished. There were several other tables in the room that would be more comfortable, but Nir liked her there. It satisfied his sense of order.

Honig, he noticed, wasn't having a problem with her appetite. But she was always a healthy eater.

He twisted the top off an icy bottle of tea and sipped it, considering the problem of the multinational commando team. He disliked this unknown factor. They were messing with his plans and might screw up his timetable.

On the other hand, their coming brought with it hidden benefits. Stuart Gold's death, the more he thought about it, was a blessing in disguise. Now Nir had unfettered access to Gold's cash and resources. Maybe not useful today, but he could well be starved for electronics-manufacturing capability as the war progressed and his supply of modular soldier kits became depleted. By then Israeli popular opinion would be fully behind him. He could come out into the open as the leader of the Soldiers of Solomon, the army of the people, and by then he would need tens of thousands of modular soldier kits. The public would be clamoring to go into battle....

He also had to consider the unexpected pluses that had materialized, like the arrival of Mr. David Ragen. Ragen was playing his cards close to the chest, but his enthusiasm for the Soldiers' cause was evident.

Nir had seen this phenomenon before. Intelligent, successful individuals whose lives lacked fulfillment. That description applied to every partner who helped the Soldiers. They were techno-geeks who had made their millions, formed and sold and re-formed their companies and ceased to be intrigued by the trappings of this success. Some buried themselves in their work and sought increasingly to expand their portfolio of corporate involvement. That was where Nir had been a few short years ago, struggling to be the wealthiest and most powerful techno-millionaire Israel had ever produced.

But he was bothered by the way his money was being earned. His companies sold millions of dollars of goods to nearly every nation in the world. China was his biggest customer. Trouble was, he didn't care about China.

What he cared about was his homeland, Israel. And Israel, despite its emerging weapons-technology capabilities, refused to use these resources to solve its biggest problem. The Palestinian problem.

He decided to do something about it, forming a small distribution system, funded from corporate profits, to get the best weaponry into the hands of the Israeli militias, the only people doing what needed to be done.

But they weren't the sharpest bunch. They misused his technology—or failed to use it at all. They didn't have the understanding, and they didn't have the patience for making technology work.

Another problem was that the hardware he had access to was largely componentry, of no use without the weapons systems they went into. Nir played on his friendship with Stuart Gold, a man whose expertise included more basic weapons electronics. Gold, it turned out, was also dissatisfied, in search of a cause. Kesher Nir gave him that cause and realized there had to be many, many more out there like Gold and himself among the expanding subclass of Tel Aviv and Haifa high-tech entrepreneurs, rich, intelligent and aimless.

Nir abandoned the militias and began gathering a flock of high-tech entrepreneurs around him, with a goal far more ambitious than a few half-baked attacks on Palestinian school buses.

He would build the trappings of an army, then deliver a message to the people of Israel, seeking those who would see the Palestinian issue resolved, finally and resolutely. He knew these potential soldiers were there, filling every niche of Israeli society. When they answered his call, Nir would have his army.

The people of Israel would become the soldiers behind the Soldiers of Solomon. Enough of them just didn't know it yet.

They would know it soon. Their emotions were still being tuned. His video production in Shaalvim Settlement had started the process. The anger was ripening. Soon he would need to add a little more sugar to keep the process going, and then the time would be right.

Another forty-eight hours. A little more public-relations effort. Then his hard-bought final shipment of modkits would be on-site, and the people would rush to take them up.

With that shipment winging toward Israel, his problems

in the United States were over with for the time being. Now all they had to do was avoid those commandos.

Again, almost obsessively, he fell into thinking about the commando team. He had come to the conclusion that this had to be an extralegal enforcement arm of NATO maybe, or the UN Security Council, probably funded and supported by the U.S. and other power wielders in the UN. Nir had some definite opinions about the usefulness of the United Nations, which actually had a division dedicated to the so-called inalienable rights of the Palestinian people.

Would Israel be one of the countries that helped fund this secret paramilitary group? Did the Israeli government know the commandos were here?

Whoever they were, they were striking at the heart of the matter more effectively than the Israelis were. Or anyone else. But they hadn't come close enough. They had struck down a key player in Stuart Gold, and whittled away nearly a third of Nir's costly mercenaries. But if they had any real intelligence, they would have done real damage to the Soldiers of Solomon. Nir wouldn't let that happen.

One of the array of notebook computers on his desk began to shrill urgently, and Kesher Nir sat forward, reading the message.

It was the worst possible news.

SANDRA HONIG FOLDED the computer closed with a slap. "Listen to me, Kesher, this is a reactionary strategy. You need to think this through."

"I have done nothing but think my plans through," he retorted. "I have been thinking and scheming and preparing for months! I have been gathering my people around me and hiring my consultants and planning how to best wield my finances for this undertaking. I have brought together joint-venture partnerships throughout Israel and companies in Europe and the United States and equipped the best army on the planet, only to have half of it taken away from me in a single hour!''

"Which means you still have half!'' she shot back. "That is enough to equip an elite army. There will be more then enough backup troops supplying their own hardware. But we can't waste them by tossing them out on an unscheduled release. We haven't weighed our options.''

"Two days—what's the difference?'' he shouted.

"Yes, what's the difference?'' she demanded. "Why not just wait for the time we chose to make our move, the time when the people are fully primed and ready to join us?''

"If we lost half the modkits in just one morning, think what will happen in the next two days,'' Nir complained. "We may have nothing by then. Someone among the Soldiers of Solomon is a traitor, and we can't guess how much information they've released to the outside world,'' Nir said.

"We can move the Jerusalem inventory,'' Honig said, trying to sound reasonable. "We can take the final shipment wherever we want.''

"We would have to keep moving them from place to place to keep these men from tracking us down!''

"We'll keep moving them, then,'' she said. "We'll leave them in the trucks and keep them in motion up until the moment we need them—''

"Every minute they're in transport they'll be more at risk than if they were hidden,'' Nir retorted. "I've made my decision, and I'm finished discussing it. I'll start my recruitment now. Today.''

Honig's entire body spun into the backhand that struck Nir's face and sent him staggering back, his knees hitting the cheap, tattered chair that she normally sat in. He landed in it with a thump and sat looking up at her. For a moment she was smug and silent, then she inhaled and spoke as if making a declaration. "I've fought for this cause for years and years, Kesher, long before I brought you on board. No person has put more hours and more sacrifice into making it a reality. I have nurtured you from a spoiled brat with his own company to possibly one of the most important figures in the history of the Israeli people. I will not let you throw all of it away on one shortsighted decision.''

There was a moment of silence, and Honig knew the tables were turned. She was done with being the secondary she had always been. No longer was she the fat friend of all the pretty girls in college. She was finished with being the intelligent but unpersuasive propagandist for the pro-Israeli movements. She was done whoring herself to Kesher Nir's lunatic need for a dominant yet controllable matron and lover.

''Get up, Kesher.''

Nir got up. He brought the aluminum tray table with him. With a pull he removed one of the foldable metal legs and wordlessly began to beat her with it while she screamed.

Her hands received the worst of it—she held them up to protect her head and body, until she had fingers broken on both hands, and then she toppled. He clubbed her face, breaking her nose, then beat her chest and stomach. By then she was merely grunting when the blows hit.

In the other hand he still had her tray table, amazingly enough, and when the beating was done he dumped the contents on her. It was fettuccine and antipasto. Sandra loved Italian.

''Finish your lunch.''

Her eyes rolled up at him, already black and starting to swell closed on one side of her face, her breath heaving.

''I said finish your lunch!'' He screamed it, a raw, throat-scorching sound full of malice. Honig pawed at the food with puffy, twisted fingers and began stuffing tiny bits into her mouth.

''Good. While you eat, I have a lot to arrange.''

Kesher Nir went back to his desk.

CHAPTER TWENTY-SIX

Israeli television was providing ongoing coverage of vehement anti-Israeli protests proceeding throughout the West Bank and other occupied territories, throughout the Middle East and indeed throughout the Muslim world. Footage of enraged Arabs, juxtaposed with the days-old video of the slaughter at Shaalvim, played neatly into the newest footage.

It was the first really fresh video the news had had in days. The industry knew one shot of Palestinian boys throwing rocks at police in riot gear looked pretty much like another, no matter how soon it was aired.

The new footage was different, graphically arresting and designed to be inflammatory. The elite staff of one of the biggest television advertising firms in Tel Aviv had put their filmmaking expertise and computer-generated-graphics technology behind it.

Several miles north of Jerusalem, in the Muslim town of Al-Birah in the West Bank, was the army the Israelis had been fearing. The Palestinians were consolidating their numbers, gathering in secret.

"This is footage taken by a Christian Arab using a hidden camera, according to our sources," the news anchor reported. "This was taken less than three hours ago, and plainly shows an unknown number of Palestinians unpacking weapons. Our sources say this fighting force numbers in excess of forty thousand fighting men. I repeat, forty thousand Palestinian soldiers. They plan to march on Jerusalem and seize the city tonight.''

The footage was excellent. Wildly swinging views got just enough of the stamped Arabic on the crates for the Israelis to translate their source: Iraq and Jordan. The boxes contained Kalashnikov-style automatic weapons and tripod-mounted grenade launchers made from the Soviet AGS-17 design. Some weaponry looked ancient, including a stack of U.S.-sourced LAW units, disposable light antitank weapons, their fiberglass tubes scuffed and worn. Other equipment was obviously new; crates of Kalashnikov AK-74 autorifles were being pried open, the gleaming weapons still in foam cutouts, and on a forty-foot-long table were lined up more than a hundred tagged new Galil assault rifles—Israeli-made weapons to be used against Israelis.

There were shots of Palestinians cursing the hated Israelis, denouncing them and their god and their claims to Arab land. ''We will kill their men and use their women and raise their children to be our vassals,'' one of the commanding Palestinians exhorted, to the cheers of his comrades.

It was all fiction, but it all looked very, very real to a nation that was ready to believe.

Tel Aviv, Israel

JUST WHEN Rosario Blancanales was itching for something to happen, it did. As he and his new best friend, Ariel Newman, were whiling away the hours watching the news in Newman's Tel Aviv apartment, there was a phone call, clearly from the commander of the Soldiers of Solomon. After hanging up, Newman had reported there had been some ''troubles.'' As a result, the schedule was changing.

Newman didn't go into details, and Blancanales didn't probe. Were the ''troubles'' the Netanya and Lod probes by

Phoenix Force? What was the outcome? "We'll see how it all works out soon enough," Newman said. He brought out the whiskey.

By midafternoon Newman was thoroughly soused, while Blancanales was just pretending to drink. He couldn't have swallowed the stuff if he tried. What Newman was celebrating was fake news footage released to Israeli media. It purported to show a Palestinian army preparing to march on Jerusalem.

There *was* no Palestinian army. The Israel Defense Forces knew it was a hoax, but when their hastily assembled evidence was aired an hour after the army footage, it was ignored or lambasted as a government cover-up. Still, the government had no intention of putting the Israeli army in place to fight imaginary Palestinians.

But Blancanales knew there *would* be an army marching on Jerusalem, made up of hundreds or thousands of Palestinians going to great lengths to get Jerusalem, to be a part of the liberation of their holy city. There *would* be an Israeli army of two thousand of the most inexperienced and most effectively equipped soldiers in history.

The fake footage was a self-fulfilling prophecy.

With the OICW firepower at their fingertips, fighting against Palestinians with rocks and knives and maybe a scattering of automatic weapons, the Israelis would probably wipe out the Palestinians, even if greatly outnumbered.

Unless Phoenix Force accomplished its mission in Netanya and Lod, armies would be suiting up in each of those towns, as well, one thousand cyber-warriors piling onto transports to take them into the occupied territories to confront two more fictitious armies preparing to attack Israel. The conjured-up Israeli fighting force would end up murdering bystanders in nonaggressive villages.

By morning it wouldn't matter what had been truth and

what had been a figment of Kesher Nir's imagination, because the only reality would be war.

ARIEL NEWMAN was slumped on a cane-backed chair, his lead crystal tumbler threatening to ease out of his hands and crash on the Italian ceramic tile floor, when the phone rang and he bolted to alertness.

"Newman," he answered. He listened, then blanched and murmured monosyllables in Hebrew before clicking off.

"We're going to be putting your plan in action earlier than expected," he said. "Let's go."

"Where to?" Blancanales asked as they slid into Newman's Jaguar XK8 convertible.

"To see a friend of mine named Kesher."

Blancanales suggested he be the one to drive. Newman smirked and ignored the comment as if it were an unfunny joke, starting the 4.0-liter V8 engine and tearing out of his parking space with a drunk's abandon.

"Who is Kesher and why are we going to see him?" Blancanales asked. He was happy to be going in the Jag instead of the limo because it meant Newman's muscle wasn't coming along. On the other hand, Newman was plastered, and he still had an inch of amber liquid in the tumbler on the dash.

"You know Kesher," Newman said in the slobber of the very intoxicated.

"He the big guy with the good tennis game that we met at the Shehori Club yesterday?" Blancanales asked.

Newman squinted at him. "No. That was Paul Asher. Kesher is Kesher's first name. Last name Nir. Kesher Nir is the man who started the Soldiers."

"Oh," Blancanales looked suitably impressed, as Newman's dramatics indicated he should. "By all means, let's go meet Kesher Nir."

They drove across the city with the horns of other drivers

blaring at them. Blancanales weighed his options. Finally, he had confirmed the commander's identity. Now there were choices. One, Stony Man Farm could use that information to file a report, through Hal Brognola, with the U.S. government, at which point it could be made public knowledge and Israel would have no choice but to arrest the man. Two, and a much better option, would be to send in Phoenix Force and rid the world of this problem definitively. When a group run by an egotist lost its leader, it was a wheel without a spoke.

Newman was looking ill at ease. "Kesher's really going to do it. It starts tonight."

"But I don't see how he'll do it," Blancanales asked. "Convince the people, I mean. Why will the common folk of Israel respond the way Kesher Nir wants?"

Newman glanced at him oddly as he worked to keep the Jaguar on Ben Yahuda, a main thoroughfare of Tel Aviv that carried them along the shore, although they only spotted the glistening Mediterranean between gaps in close-set apartment buildings. "Why wouldn't they, Ragen?" he demanded.

"I guess I don't know the people of Israel, Newman," Blancanales said. "I'm just wondering if they are really angry enough to do what Kesher Nir is asking them to do."

"Angry enough?" Ariel Newman repeated as he drove by the marina, then pulled into a cloistered subdivision of large homes near the water. "Oh, yeah, they're angry enough."

The house was sprawling and its interior was generically Chinese. The expensively lacquered cabinets had no flavor to their lines. The paintings on the screens were muted as if seen through a beige lens. The house was devoid of life and interest but pretended not to be. The woman on an antique lace daybed in the large front parlor, with her broken, crippled hands held over her like paws and her blackened face swelled until one eye squeezed shut involuntarily, was in keeping with the interior ambience, if not the motif. Empty bottles of injectable painkillers were strewed on the table next to the daybed, along with a used syringe. Blancanales and Newman exchanged a glance. Newman was tense, and the sight of the woman made it worse. Blancanales wondered if it was Sandra Honig.

The man who let them in knew Newman, and Blancanales counted nine other men in their thirties and early forties wandering about the house, full of energy but without real purpose. They spoke in energized but quiet conversations and nodded to Newman, ignoring Blancanales.

As they entered a dining area, Blancanales realized that he was standing in the war room of the Soldiers of Solomon. Under an Israeli flag tacked into the ceiling, the six men and women, the oldest in their early thirties, worked on multiple workstations, wired into hubs and more auxiliary portable computers than Blancanales could count. These were the people who had operated the electronic functions during the raids in the West Bank. They remote controlled the robot vehicles that detonated on the bunker in Khodr, killing women and children. They had flown the rotor-driven Unmanned Aerial Vehicle as it took video footage of the conflagration that burned the school.

If these were the operators, it had to mean that all the men standing around with nothing to do, watching events unfold, talking in low voices, were the partners. The financiers. The Soldiers of Solomon themselves.

Blancanales was in the lions' den now, but the lions weren't intimidating once you got behind the mask of devices protecting their identities.

Kesher Nir barked when he saw them. "Come on, let's move. You, Ragen, we need to get online at NRO. The sooner the better."

FOR THE SECOND TIME Blancanales found himself going through the charade of dialing into the National Reconnaissance Office and logging on to an eye in the sky. This time it wasn't a test.

"I have several coordinates to investigate," Nir told him.

Blancanales could see the man was in a frenetic state, his hands shaking with excitement. "Prioritize them. Once I get on the sat we have no idea how long the link will last."

"I need to view all these coordinates!" Nir stated.

"Mr. Nir," Blancanales said, playing it prim but cool, "I am here because I want to help you. I told you during the demo that I don't have authority to access the sat and once I'm identified as an intruder they'll kick me off. I'll try to show you everything, but I make no—"

"Shove the disclaimers. We'll start with the vital targets." Nir gave him a set of GPS coordinates.

Stony Man got him into the NRO sat without delay this time, and Blancanales breathed a sigh of relief when he received an okay response to his link. The satellite began to adjust its focus. The landscape that came into view was a swath of gray, marbled with darker blots of color. As the view zoomed in, pinpricks of white appeared and became larger.

"It's them. It's their fires and lights," Nir said. "I called them up and they came." It wasn't gloating, but more like self-affirmation, another aspect of egocentric behavior from a man Blancanales had already decided was narcissistic on an immense scale, perhaps a symptom of subtle derangement. Were Newman and the others blinded to this?

"But you didn't call them. Not yet," Newman protested.

"Not the Israelis, Ariel," Nir explained, grinning foolishly at his own accomplishment. "That's the Palestinians. They're coming together in the West Bank and lighting fires as they wait for the Muslim army marching south from Al-Birah. They believe it, too. When the army fails to materialize, they'll attack Jerusalem anyway. It will take them a while to get up the nerve, but I guarantee you—they won't come all that way, from all across the West Bank, and fail to fight. My army will be ready to fight back.

"Out of nothing," Nir added with immense self-satisfaction, "I will have conjured a war."

Newman was looking startled and gave Blancanales a question glance. So Nir's behavior came across as unusual even to his friend of many years. Had Nir snapped? Or had he been building up to this level of sensible delirium for a long, long time. Blancanales wondered what the beaten, broken woman in the living room had to do with it. If that was Honig, her level of authority in the group was...diminished.

"Let's move quickly, sir," Blancanales said to Nir, trying to sound urgent. "We don't know how long we have."

"Right," Nir said, his focus returning. "Let's look at the school."

"What school?"

"That's where the OICWs are," Newman admitted. "You might as well know. It'll be public knowledge soon anyway."

"I thought they were in Netanya and Lod, at the sites you drove me by this morning," Blancanales said.

Newman flinched. Nir appeared not to have heard. "Those sites became public knowledge prematurely," Newman admitted in a low voice. "The Israeli government is guarding them. They're inaccessible."

Good work, Phoenix, Blancanales thought.

"The only units accessible to us now are at an abandoned high school, in Jerusalem," Newman said.

"All two thousand units are in one place?" Blancanales asked. "That's risky."

"Which explains why we're moving quickly," Nir rattled off suddenly. "Once the OICWs are in the hands of the people, the risk is abated."

This guy, Blancanales thought, had a pretty curious definition of the word *risk*. "Okay, give me the GPS and we'll take a look at this high school."

Nir read out the coordinates. Blancanales typed them in, and added a few extra coded keystrokes to the input, sending a message to Stony Man Farm.

CHAPTER TWENTY-SEVEN

Stony Man Farm, Virginia

Barbara Price stared at the screen, reading the translation of the message from Blancanales, and felt relief wash through her like physical sensation.

"Good work, Rosario," she said quietly to herself.

"It's a school," Carmen Delahunt burst out. Even as Kurtzman and Tokaido were baby-sitting Blancanales's satellite uplink to the NRO, Delahunt had been identifying the landmark at the coordinates.

"Hanoch Technical High School in Jerusalem," Yakov Katzenelenbogen read from the results scrolling in from a Hebrew database. "It's closed down. Has been for months. City arguing over what to do with it until it was purchased by a Haifa-based high-tech firm, ostensibly for a possible new research facility. It's Lipkin Electronics."

"They're on our list of firms suspected of providing resources to the Soldiers," Price confirmed quickly from memory. "I'm sending in Phoenix."

Jerusalem, Israel

PHOENIX FORCE and Stony Man Farm had decided on a new base of operations in Jerusalem. Without knowing where exactly, there was a strong belief that the final conflict would come in Jerusalem, the coveted prize of Israelis and Palestinians both. Sitting in rented landing space beyond the west end of the city, their impatience had been compounding by the hour as they watched developments on the television and received reports from the Farm without actually getting anything to do. That all changed when Stony Base reported Blancanales's dial-in.

"We're five minutes away by air," Jack Grimaldi declared as the coordinates of the abandoned school came.

"We may have just minutes," David McCarter replied.

"What's that supposed to mean?" Gary Manning demanded as they jumped on board the transport.

"Pol's sending a coded ASAP-response message," McCarter reported. "Stony thinks this is all coming to a head."

"Even I can see that!" Manning snorted.

"They think Kesher Nir is about to offer his supply of hardware to any pissed-off Israeli who wants it," McCarter clarified. "They think he's been driven to accelerate his schedule."

"By us," Calvin James added.

The Dauphin AS 365 N2 helicopter was a loaner, borrowed from an American oil company that used it for security patrols of Saudi Arabian oil sites, and discreetly delivered to Israel.

The twin Turbomeca Arriel 1 C2 engines gave the Dauphin a listed top speed of 277 kilometers per hour, or about 172 miles per hour. Grimaldi was about to see how conservative the published specs actually were. He didn't know what the airspeed limits over Israeli metropolitan areas were, but he knew they were about to be exceeded.

The helicopter rose, sat at forty feet as if awaiting a starting gun, then tilted forward in an abrupt headlong rush over the tops of the ancient city, rising to five hundred feet and banking in across the mile-wide patch of no-man's land laid out by the 1949 Armistice Line. Below they could see the makeshift torches, campfires and flashlights of the gathering throngs of Palestinians, eager to join the soldiers in an army that didn't exist. A blockade of Israeli military was hemming in the crowds, and military and police vehicles were arriving from all directions.

"Stony Base here. It's happening," Barbara Price said on their headsets. "Kesher Nir's taped statement is on the air in Israel."

ERIC SNELL HAD seamlessly assumed control of the mercenary operation of the late Arnold Fogelman. He had worked as Fogelman's second in command for more years and more operations than he could remember, and he had no doubts that he had the skills needed to lead this team. But he was having his doubts about the readiness of the army that his employers assured him would materialize, as if out of the ether. But Snell really didn't care about the outcome.

Just prior to taking their leave of Israel, Nir had asked Snell and his shrunken mercenary team to perform one last job—an easy job for a big wad of danger money. Guard this site, with two thousand modkits prepped for immediate use, until ten minutes prior to the release of the Nir's videotaped announcement. Nir confided in Snell that he no longer trusted the capability of his own militiamen. With good reason—every one of them, in Snell's opinion, was a few screws short.

The merc team had been through hell in Israel. Snell did the democratic thing. He put it to a vote. The lure of more cash had convinced them to stay.

Problem was, Nir was on television sooner than Snell expected.

"Why's he doing this now?" Snell growled. The plan

called for him and his men to be gone from the facility when the announcement was made.

The television showed them a Nir they hadn't seen before, dressed in yarmulke and cassock, trying to look very Jewish. With the flag of Israel as a backdrop, he began describing the horrors about to be perpetrated on the city of Jerusalem by the Palestinian army that was even now massing on the West Bank within sight of the ancient holy city.

"He's about to announce our position!" one of Snell's mercs exclaimed. "We going to just sit here until the Israel Defense Force comes to get us?"

Snell spit. "No way in hell."

They jogged through the musty, littered halls of the condemned high school, from the upper-floor administration offices to the small parking lot beside the building, and as Snell pushed through the doors the stab of white brilliance and rotor blast hit him. He raised his hand in front of his eyes as he retreated through the door, pushing against his men.

"We're too late!" Snell announced.

"They got here in forty-five damned seconds?" a merc asked in disbelief.

Snell ignored him as he silently evaluated a series of quick plots, then chose the one with the best odds.

"Our transportation is out there—we need those vehicles to get out," he announced. "I saw one chopper. We go out fast, we cut those fuckers out of the sky with everything we've got, we get in our vehicles and go home."

There was no time for discussion before Eric Snell shouldered through the door and triggered his Steyr Army Universal Gun, putting a burst of 5.56 mm tumblers into the source of the spotlight. The crash of glass came at the same moment a barrage of return fire slammed into Snell from two directions.

THE GUNNER with the AUG collapsed in a bloody pile along with the man who had been directly behind him, and the others retreated inside in a hurry.

"Jack, you okay up there?" McCarter demanded as he rushed to the door alongside Manning.

"We're okay, but we just lost the security deposit on the chopper," Grimaldi answered.

"Jack, stay close!" McCarter reminded him.

"We're not going anywhere."

James and Hawkins reached the bodies first. The young Texan rolled the corpse of the gunner with the AUG. He wasn't gentle about it.

"That's one of the soldiers from the settlement," he declared accusingly. "We should have shot this son of a bitch in the gut and led him suffer awhile."

"Enough!" McCarter declared. This was no time to make it a vendetta. "Inside!"

McCarter took point as they pulled the door and met with a burst of gunfire from the shadowy end of a hall that stretched into murky blackness. He returned a brief burst and heard a shout of pain, then stepped inside. Beside him Manning yanked a flare out of his combat webbing.

"Careful where you put that thing," McCarter said.

"I'm always careful," Manning replied as he lit the flare and tossed it into the blackness.

The light stick revealed a jittering corpse. Up and down the long hall they found foot-wide niches built against the concrete walls, tagged with faded numbered plates. The paint that had highlighted the digits was long gone.

There had to have been a degree of trust among the students of the school. The open bins were in place of lockers. But the books and notebooks and sack lunches were long gone. Instead, inside each niche was an OICW, butt end to the ground, nestled in with a pack containing ammunition and electronics, and a second pack containing battlefield cybernetics and armor.

James had his flashlight out, and he moved it up the wall. It was a rare event when the Phoenix Force commando used profanity. "Holy shit."

There was a poster on the wall. No text. Just diagrams. A cartoon, foot-tall human figure was shown going through the paces of getting into the Land Warrior gear and powering up his OICW hardware. They were looking at the instruction manual.

"Guess you don't even have to be able to read to be in Kesher Nir's Soldiers of Solomon," James muttered, appalled.

"G-Force here, Phoenix," said Grimaldi over the headsets. "You're about to have company. The people are taking to the streets of Jerusalem, and they're headed your way."

Tel Aviv, Israel

BLANCANALES WAS going to take down Kesher Nir. The man was a lunatic and a mass murderer. Never mind that they were in a house surrounded by the lunatic's followers. Blancanales would do the deed and worry about the consequences later.

What he needed was a weapon.

He found one.

Nir had a small studio in one of his unused bedrooms, set up for shooting the video to air on Israeli television. The video feed was displayed on monitors in every one of the sitting rooms and parlors that filled the sprawling house. Sitting at Nir's side were all the implements of the Soldiers' modkits.

"What's that doing here?" Blancanales asked Newman.

"Watch and learn," Newman said with a finger in his mouth. He had begun biting his nails while they were watching the news footage—actual, real news footage—of the growing mass of Palestinians in the West Bank. The military was having a hard time keeping control. Every minute more troops were arriving to control the mob, but the mob grew faster. This was unlike the street fights Jerusalem had witnessed uncounted times. This was thousands of people; this was revolt. Newman was getting more nervous by the minute.

His agitation increased when Nir went on the air and delivered his message. The message included a video demonstration to the Israeli people on harnessing themselves in the Land Warrior outfit and firing the OICW. "Once you are suited up, you will be in communications with my command center. We will guide you and all our warriors to a decisive victory against the Arab...."

Blancanales asked, "Are those live rounds in that thing? He's gonna shoot up his own house if he's not careful."

Newman wasn't interested. "He's careful," Newman said, then his voice descended to a whisper. "Ragen, my friend, I am getting the hell out of here."

Blancanales stared at him. "Why?"

"You been listening to him?" Newman asked. "I think he's lost it. Did you see what he did to that stupid bitch Honig? I mean, he beat the hell out of her. I think he's going to expose us. I don't trust him. When that tape airs, all hell is gonna break loose."

"When will that be?"

Newman shrugged. "In like one minute."

"Oh."

Newman ripped a shred of skin of his finger with his teeth and spit it out. "I'm out of here."

Blancanales glared at him. "You're abandoning the cause?"

"I'm abandoning the maniac who's running the show," Newman hissed. "Nir's out of his head. I mean, he's never acted like this before. He's over the edge. Who knows what he's capable of!''

That was an ironic statement to make about a man who had used genocide as advertising, Blancanales thought.

''You coming?'' Newman said.

''I'm staying.''

''Have it your way. Just don't rat me out until I'm gone.''

''I won't,'' Blancanales said. Of course not. There was honor among homicidal madmen.

As Newman departed, Blancanales was observing the other partners spread throughout the house. They were all agitated. These Soldiers were getting more than they had bargained for. Nir was acting strangely. Maybe he was unhinged. Maybe they were all in personal danger.

When the taping of the video ended, Blancanales was there. Nir emerged amid a small throng of assistants and supporters, and a pair of his militia gunners. He looked triumphant, a glimmer in his eyes, but it faded when he saw Blancanales.

''What?'' Nir demanded.

''I don't know if I should be telling you this...'' Blancanales muttered, playing his Milquetoast role to the hilt.

''Just say it!''

''It's Newman. He bolted. He's giving it up.''

Kesher Nir's forehead rolled down over his eyes. ''I thought it might happen,'' he said. ''It is a shame. He was useful.''

''Now he's your enemy. He said you've gone crazy,'' Blancanales declared. ''He'd going to the police. Said he'd bargain for immunity in exchange for intelligence about the Soldiers.''

Nir's eyes flashed, as if reflecting his pale hair. ''How long ago did he leave?''

''Ninety seconds. No more.''

Nir gave quick orders in Hebrew, marching his retinue into his control center.

Blancanales moved into the studio and found a single man packing the OICW in the foam cutouts of a handled carrying case. The man said something in Hebrew, but Blancanales ignored him as he bent by the big commercial video camera and unplugged the cable from the camera with the snap of his wrist. The man got to his feet making a noise of protest, until Blancanales kneed him heavily in the groin. The man's face blanked and he doubled over. The cord looped around his neck and went taut until he dropped.

There were voices nearby. Coming closer? Blancanales hefted the OICW in two hands and checked the magazines.

He had a full load of both 5.56 mm assault rifle rounds and 20 mm high-explosive grenades. He pocketed extra magazines just in case. He powered up the weapon, tossing away the motion detector.

Rosario Blancanales went hunting.

NIR HEARD the sudden retort of the OICW, followed by the heavy sound of a body tumbling against a wall before collapsing. Then someone bolted out of a short passage from the back wing of the home, arching his back when the brief burst of rifle fire came again, louder and closer.

The man at his feet was already dead and Nir started when he realized it was Ohad Lipkin. The man was a millionaire. He was an engineering genius. He had contributed $1.2 million to the Soldiers.

As people all around him pushed and shoved to clear out of the house, the American, David Ragen, emerged with the Objective Individual Combat Weapon gripped in his hands as if he actually knew what to do with it.

"You're not a programmer at all, are you?" Nir demanded.

Rosario Blancanales smiled, and his finger tightened on the trigger.

"I want to tell you something!" Nir said in a panic. A horrible reality had just struck home. Ragen wasn't going to arrest him—this man was going to execute him. "I want you to know—"

"No last words," Blancanales interrupted. "You don't deserve to be heard."

"Wait!"

Blancanales didn't wait. He autofired 5.56 mm burst after burst from the weapon with a sound like the overhead cracks of thunder, and the Able Team warrior swept the streams from side to side in a figure-eight that cut across Kesher Nir, then cut across him again. Other Soldiers of Solomon trying to escape Nir's presence died under the onslaught and they deserved no better, but they weren't vital in Blancanales eyes. What he wanted was Nir, the mastermind, the brains behind the madness. And he got him good.

When all that was left was a bloody mass of a cassock, the magazine ran dry.

Then the Israeli militiamen stormed in, anguished and wild. Blancanales snapped in the fresh magazine and triggered another brief burst, then another, taking them in the chest.

He heard laughing. It was the woman he had seen sprawled in the daybed, now on her feet and standing in the archway leading to the front room.

"Sandra Honig?" Blancanales asked.

"That's me," she said. "You going to shoot me, too?"

She was a wreck, her clothes disheveled and ripped and coated in filth, her broken fingers curled like a scarecrow's, her flesh splotched purple and black. She seemed lucid enough, although a fresh injection wound bled on her inner arm.

"I think I'll let you take care of it yourself."

"You son of a bitch," she said, spitting out the words. "You killed Kesher. I wanted to kill Kesher. Now I'll have to make you kill me."

She pulled the handgun from behind her back, fumbling to get a grip on it with broken fingers until she found one to operate the trigger. The Jericho 941FB shot a .40 S&W round. This one was equipped with a luminous combat sight, which she lined up, using her one good eye, on Rosario Blancanales.

Blancanales wasn't seeing her at that moment. He was seeing her handiwork as the video images of the burning teacher in Shaalvim came unbidden into his head. It made it easy to do as Honig had requested. The OICW chugged again, and Kesher Nir's mansion fell into dead silence.

Jerusalem

THERE WAS a burst of fire, then the sound of footsteps retreating. James waited for them to fade, then poked his head through the entrance again, found himself in a hallway configured like the one below and scanned for signs of an enemy. He saw nothing and no one—and the clock was ticking fast.

"Cover me," he said to Hawkins, who braced the door with his foot as James bolted down the hall. His didn't even pause as he dropped off the packages, one, two, three, every ten paces or so. Each package landed inside one of the student bins that had served this school as lockers. They landed among the neatly placed modular packs of battle armor and ammunition.

"Down, Cal," came the urgent order from Hawkins, and James landed flat as he spotted the emerging figure in the archway ahead of him. The gunner targeted James on the floor. Hawkins was on one knee at the other end, lining up the M-16 A-2 like a sniper's weapon and aiming high. It would be too easy to send a round astray, and James was just a few feet outside the line of fire....

The first round slammed into the mercenary at the temple, cutting a half-inch gash through the flesh and the skull plate. The second round cracked into his collar and put him down.

James gave Hawkins the thumbs-up and quickly tossed his last pack in a niche at the end of the hall.

The packs were the creation of Gary Manning, who had come up with packs containing two explosive compounds. Tetracene, readily reactive to open flame, served as the initiating explosive. Its detonation would in turn detonate the C-4, a cyclonite-based plastic high explosive. The addition of tetracene made detonating electronics unnecessary.

All that was required was flame.

James backed his way down the hall in a hurry, but it wasn't until he nearly reached Hawkins again that another figure emerged from the administrative wing, triggering a blind blast into the hall to clear the way. James pulled back for a heartbeat, then moved into the open and triggered a sustained burst from the M-16 A-2, filling the center of the hall with 5.56 mm rounds. His top priority was to avoid hitting an explosive pack.

The mercenary caught the stream and did the dance. When James released the trigger, the merc stood there, as if he didn't know he was dead yet. By the time he was collapsing, James and Hawkins were hurrying away.

"G-Force here," said Grimaldi in their headsets. "If you're gonna do the deed, you better do it soon!"

"Understood," McCarter replied. "Phoenix Four and Five, what the hell is taking you—?"

"Right here," James replied as they emerged on the bottom floor. "The second level is ready to blow."

"We're coming, Jack," McCarter said.

"I'm ready and you've got a hell of an audience."

As they ran from the building, they were met with wild

cries from the security fences. The three-yard chain-link fence was rattling like paper in the wind. The Israelis were shaking it, demanding entry. They had been told this was where they enlisted for the holy war, and nothing would keep them out.

"Get back," Hawkins shouted, waving for them to retreat. "This place is going to blow!"

His voice was drowned by the rotor thunder and the cries of the crowd itself. Then he heard the rattle of automatic gunfire and in the shifting lights of the Dauphin spotted chips of old concrete flying around his feet. As he bolted from the gunfire, he spun and targeted the upper floor of the building, source of the muzzle-flash. It was a large window, the glass long gone and the protective plastic sheeting ripped away. Hawkins aimed into the muzzle-flash and squeezed out a long burst that disappeared into the darkness. The gunfire came to a halt, but he had no idea if it was his doing.

He was the last of Phoenix Force on the ground and he bolted for the Dauphin, feeling as much as hearing the return of the automatic gunfire, chasing on his heels, and he made a headlong dive into the side hatchway of the helicopter. Powerful hands instantly gripped his arms, his body armor, the collar of his shirt, and someone was yelling, "Jack, go now!"

Hawkins torso was inside but his legs dangled in space as the floor of the Dauphin pressed against his chest and the world fell away beneath him, and distinctly over the rotor roar he heard the pursuing rattle of the automatic-weapons fire from the condemned school.

The chopper reached six hundred feet before Grimaldi brought the beast to an anxious hover. Hawkins was hauled inside and the side hatch was rolled shut.

"Okay, we're secure," McCarter said. "Let's finish it."

The Dauphin moved again underneath them. Grimaldi

steered her back down toward the school as James patted him down.

"Talk to me, T.J. You hit?"

"No," Hawkins said. "I'm okay."

Then, over James's shoulder, he saw the image of the school swing into view out the front windows of the helicopter. He crowded at the front of the cabin with his partners as Manning pushed the side door open and leveled the OICW at the school.

There had to a thousand angry men clustering at the school already. They were going to flatten the fence like a rolling tank.

Manning fired. The 20 mm round impacted on the front of the building and burst like fireworks, taking out a bite of masonry and metal roofing.

"Damn!"

Hawkins knew the problem. "Gary, it's fusing too accurately for what you're trying to do," he said. "You want it to go off inside the building. Give it a few extra yards of flying time by getting a target through the windows. You can't see inside, but it can."

Manning nodded and did it. The next round triggered with a thump and the upper-story window lit up. The explosion was brief and bright, and started to fade, then one of the tetracene initiating explosive pieces came in contact with the flame. The C-4 blew in a sudden bolt of sound and pressure, followed instantly by the answering thump of the rest of Manning's packages and the thousands of OICW 20 mm rounds bursting, too, going off in such rapid succession it sounded like a single sustained and endless explosion. The school turned white, then went supernova. The sky above Jerusalem glowed, like the augur of a miracle.

For a long minute the Dauphin hung in space, watching the brilliance fade into fire.

"Only one mess left to mop up," Manning stated.

McCarter grinned over his shoulder at them. "Not so, mates. Stony Base has just been in touch with our able friend Politician Blancanales. Seems he's been at Kesher Nir's uptown house shooting up the place. Nir and Sandra Honig are no more."

"All right Rosario!" Manning shouted.

"Needless to say, he didn't stick around for the local authorities to make an appearance," Grimaldi added. "He's wandering down by the seaside, and we're supposed to go pick him up."

As the Dauphin banked away from the chaos below, Hawkins could see the masses of Israelis on the streets. Their anger wasn't gone. The vengeance they had come to perpetrate had been snatched away like a prize.

Hawkins considered himself to be an ethical man, capable of understanding basic tenets of justice. When he looked a last time at the conflagration that consumed the school, he wondered if justice even existed for this part of the world. Every party to this madness had suffered. The death toll continued to climb. The fires of Jerusalem, sparked long before the coming of Kesher Nir and Sandra Honig, burned out of control. It was as if no one truly wished to extinguish them.

He was amazed at the intensity of the school fire. The building was brick—what was fueling it? But that was a good thing. Because on one side of the fire stormed the fury of Israel. On another side seethed the rage of Palestine. If those two sides came together before this passion died, what then?

To Hawkins, the only conceivable outcome was war.

James Axler
Outlanders®

DRAGONEYE

Deep inside the moon two ancient beings live on—the sole
survivors of two mighty races whose battle to rule earth and
mankind is poised to end after millennia of struggle and subterfuge.
Now, in a final conflict, they are prepared to unleash a blood
sacrifice of truly monstrous proportions, a heaven-shaking
Armageddon that will obliterate earth and its solar system. At last
Kane, Grant and Brigid Baptiste will confront the true architects
of mankind: their creators…and now, ultimately, their destroyers.

In the Outlands, the shocking truth is humanity's last hope.

**brings you a brand-new
look in June 2002!
Different look...
same exciting adventures!**

Salvation Road

Beneath the brutal sun of the nuke-ravaged southwest, the Texas desert burns red-hot and merciless, commanding agony and untold riches to those greedy and mad enough to mine the slick black crude that lies beneath the scorched earth. When a Gateway jump puts Ryan and the others deep in the hell of Texas, they have no choice but to work for a rogue baron in order to win their freedom. If they fail...they face death.

In Deathlands, the unimaginable is a way of life.